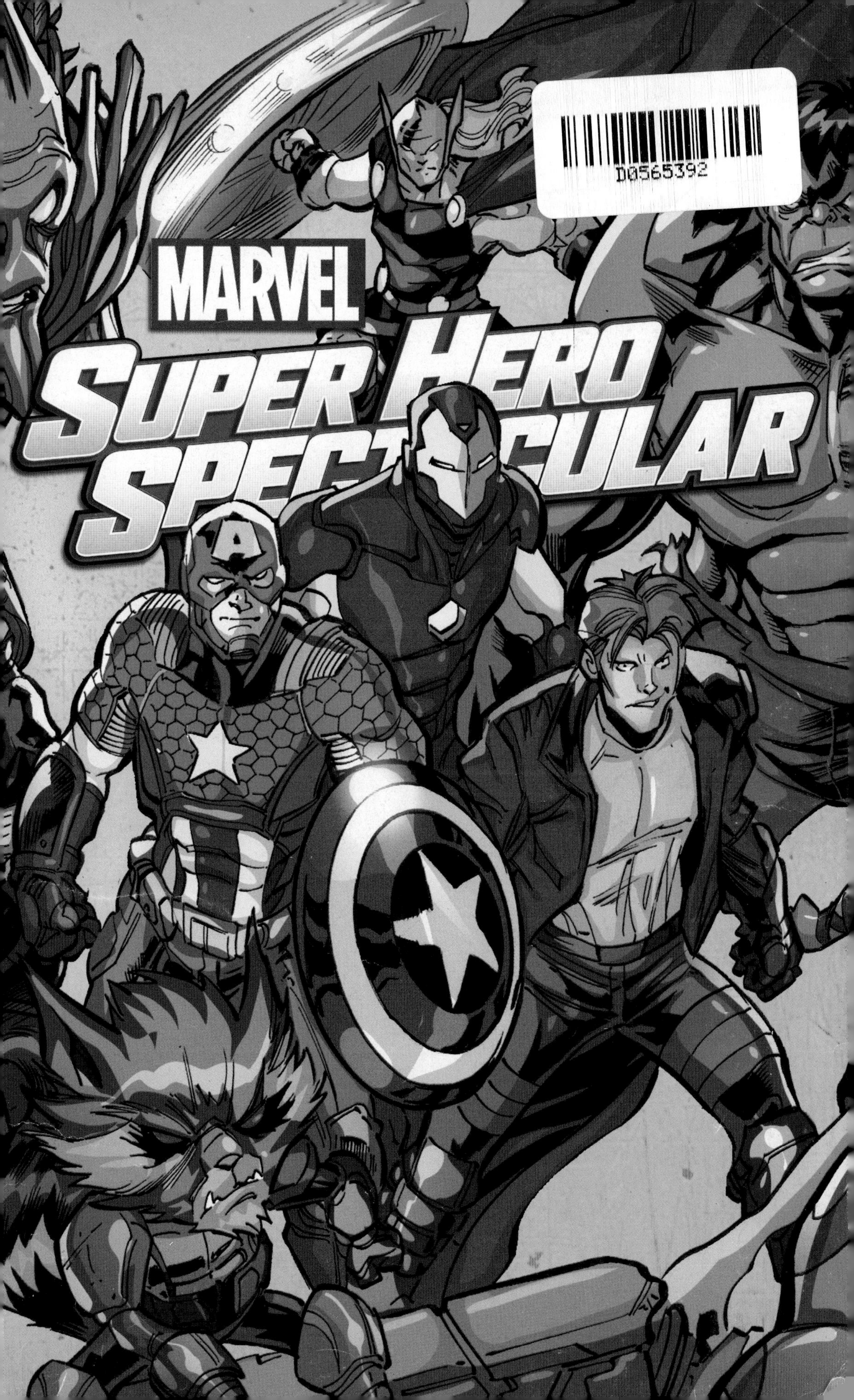
MARVEL
SUPER HERO
SPECTACULAR

MARVEL SUPER HERO SPECTACULAR. Contains material originally published in magazine form as MARVEL SUPER HERO SPECTACULAR #1 AVENGERS VS #1 and AVENGERS VS INFINITY #1. First printing 2016. ISBN# 978-1-302-90242-1. Published by MARVEL WORLDWIDE, INC., a subsidiary of MARVEL ENTERTAINMENT, LLC. OFFICE OF PUBLICATION: 135 West 50th Street, New York, NY 10020. Copyright © 2016 MARVEL No similarity between any of the names, characters, persons, and/or institutions in this magazine with those of any living or dead person or institution is intended, and any such similarity which may exist is purely coincidental. **Printed in the U.S.A.** ALAN FINE, President, Marvel Entertainment; DAN BUCKLEY, President, TV, Publishing & Brand Management; JOE QUESADA, Chief Creative Officer; TOM BREVOORT, SVP of Publishing; DAVID BOGART, SVP of Business Affairs & Operations, Publishing & Partnership; C.B. CEBULSKI, VP of Brand Management & Development, Asia; DAVID GABRIEL, SVP of Sales & Marketing, Publishing; JEFF YOUNGQUIST, VP of Production & Special Projects; DAN CARR, Executive Director of Publishing Technology; ALEX MORALES, Director of Publishing Operations; SUSAN CRESPI, Production Manager; STAN LEE, Chairman Emeritus. For information regarding advertising in Marvel Comics or on Marvel.com, please contact Vit DeBellis, Integrated Sales Manager, at vdebellis@marvel.com. For Marvel subscription inquiries, please call 888-511-5480. **Manufactured between 7/15/2016 and 8/22/2016 by R.R. DONNELLEY, INC., SALEM, VA, USA.**

10 9 8 7 6 5 4 3 2 1

MARVEL SUPER HERO SPECTACULAR

writers	**Karl Kesel & Joe Caramagna**
artists	**David Baldeon, Andrea Di Vito, Ron Lim, Dario Brizuela & Wellinton Alves**
inkers	**Scott Hanna & Anderson Silva**
colorists	**Andres Mossa, Laura Villari & Carlos Lopez**
letterer	**VC's Joe Caramagna**
cover artists	**Todd Nauck & Rachelle Rosenberg; Tom Raney & Tamra Bonvillain; Michael Ryan & Javier Mena; Ron Lim, Scott Hanna & Wil Quintana; and Kalman Andrasofszky**
editors	**Bill Rosemann & Mark Basso** with **Emily Shaw**

WITHDRAWN

collection editor	Sarah Brunstad	vp, production & special projects	Jeff Youngquist
senior editor, special projects	Jennifer Grünwald	svp print, sales & marketing	David Gabriel
editor, special projects	Mark D. Beazley	book designer	Adam Del Re
editor in chief	Axel Alonso	publisher	Dan Buckley
chief creative officer	Joe Quesada	executive producer	Alan Fine

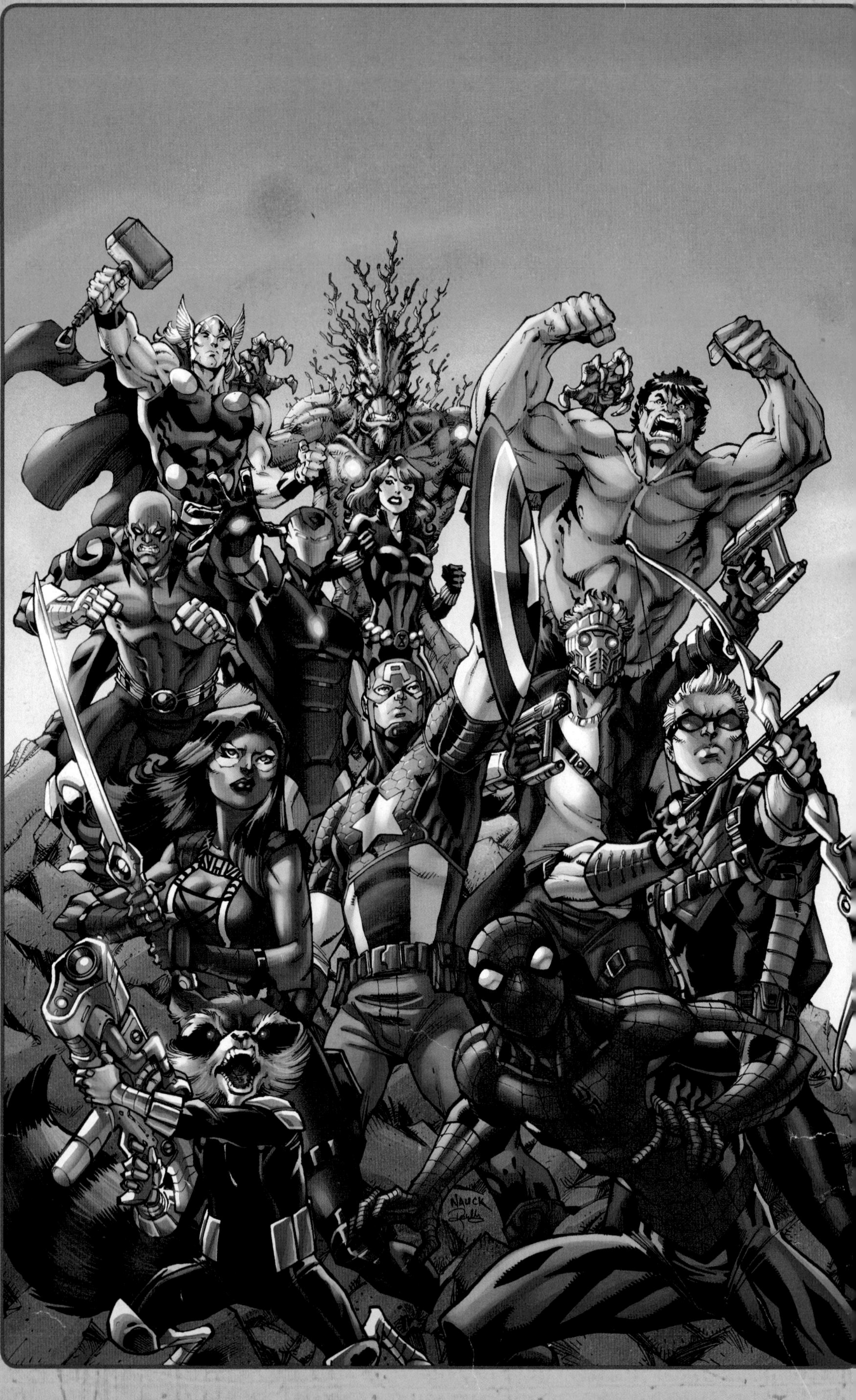
NAUCK

MARVEL SUPER HERO SPECTACULAR #1

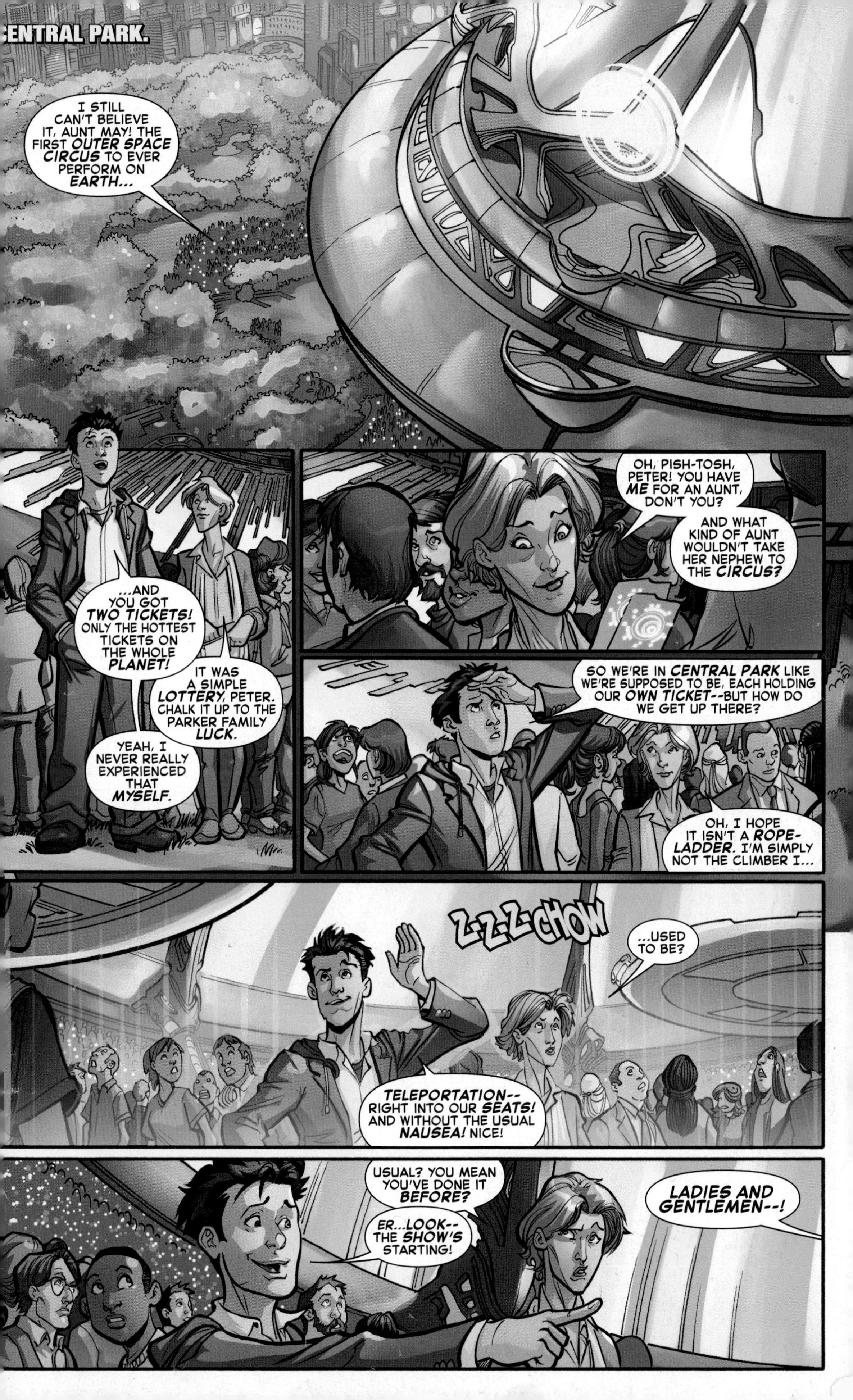
ENTRAL PARK.
I STILL CAN'T BELIEVE IT, AUNT MAY! THE FIRST OUTER SPACE CIRCUS TO EVER PERFORM ON EARTH...
...AND YOU GOT TWO TICKETS! ONLY THE HOTTEST TICKETS ON THE WHOLE PLANET!
IT WAS A SIMPLE LOTTERY, PETER. CHALK IT UP TO THE PARKER FAMILY LUCK.
YEAH, I NEVER REALLY EXPERIENCED THAT MYSELF.
OH, PISH-TOSH, PETER! YOU HAVE ME FOR AN AUNT, DON'T YOU?
AND WHAT KIND OF AUNT WOULDN'T TAKE HER NEPHEW TO THE CIRCUS?
SO WE'RE IN CENTRAL PARK LIKE WE'RE SUPPOSED TO BE, EACH HOLDING OUR OWN TICKET--BUT HOW DO WE GET UP THERE?
OH, I HOPE IT ISN'T A ROPE-LADDER. I'M SIMPLY NOT THE CLIMBER I...
Z-Z-Z-CHOW
...USED TO BE?
TELEPORTATION-- RIGHT INTO OUR SEATS! AND WITHOUT THE USUAL NAUSEA! NICE!
USUAL? YOU MEAN YOU'VE DONE IT BEFORE?
ER...LOOK-- THE SHOW'S STARTING!
LADIES AND GENTLEMEN--!

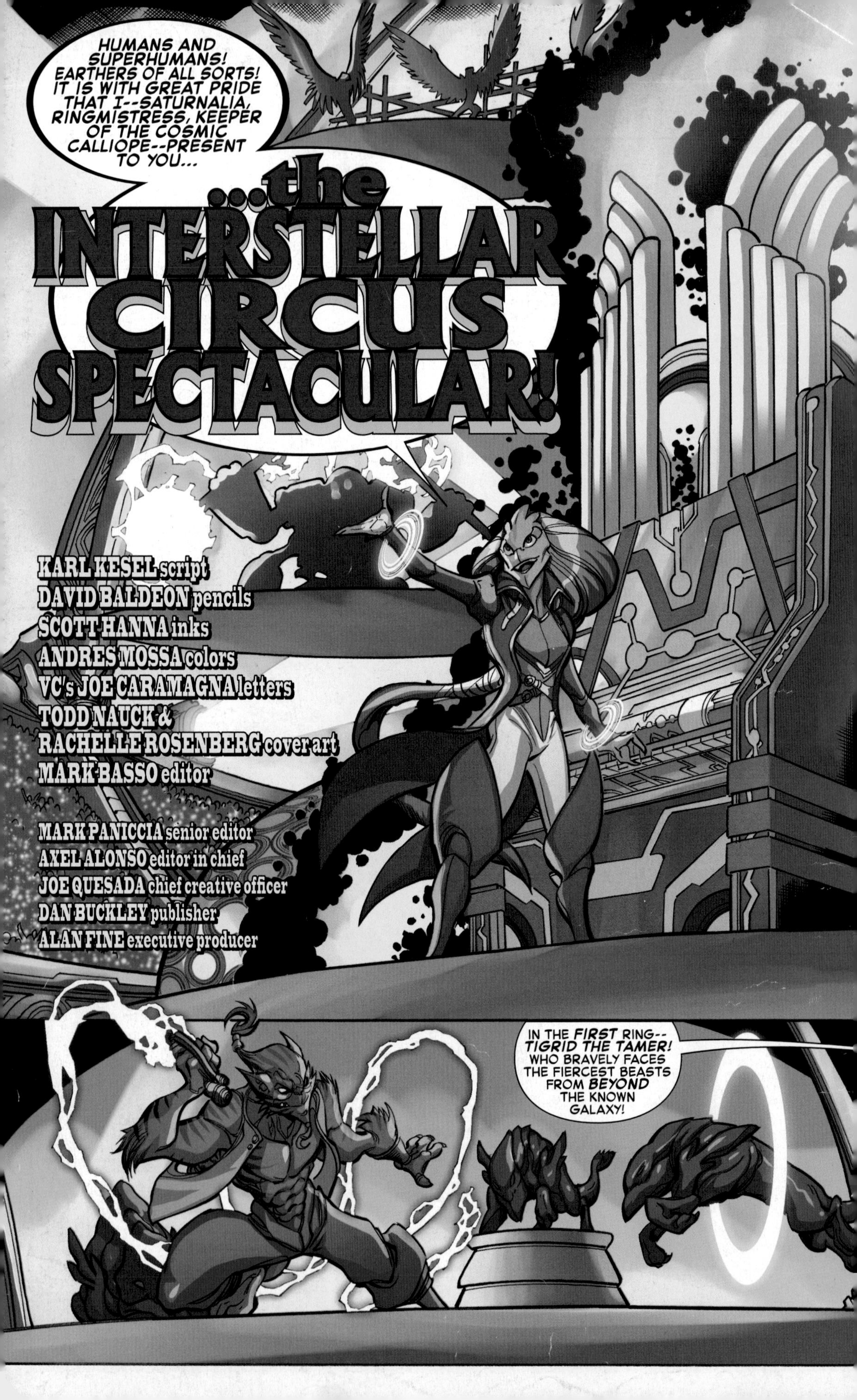
HUMANS AND SUPERHUMANS! EARTHERS OF ALL SORTS! IT IS WITH GREAT PRIDE THAT I--SATURNALIA, RINGMISTRESS, KEEPER OF THE COSMIC CALLIOPE--PRESENT TO YOU...
...the INTERSTELLAR CIRCUS SPECTACULAR!
KARL KESEL script
DAVID BALDEON pencils
SCOTT HANNA inks
ANDRES MOSSA colors
VC's JOE CARAMAGNA letters
TODD NAUCK & RACHELLE ROSENBERG cover art
MARK BASSO editor
MARK PANICCIA senior editor
AXEL ALONSO editor in chief
JOE QUESADA chief creative officer
DAN BUCKLEY publisher
ALAN FINE executive producer
IN THE FIRST RING-- TIGRID THE TAMER! WHO BRAVELY FACES THE FIERCEST BEASTS FROM BEYOND THE KNOWN GALAXY!

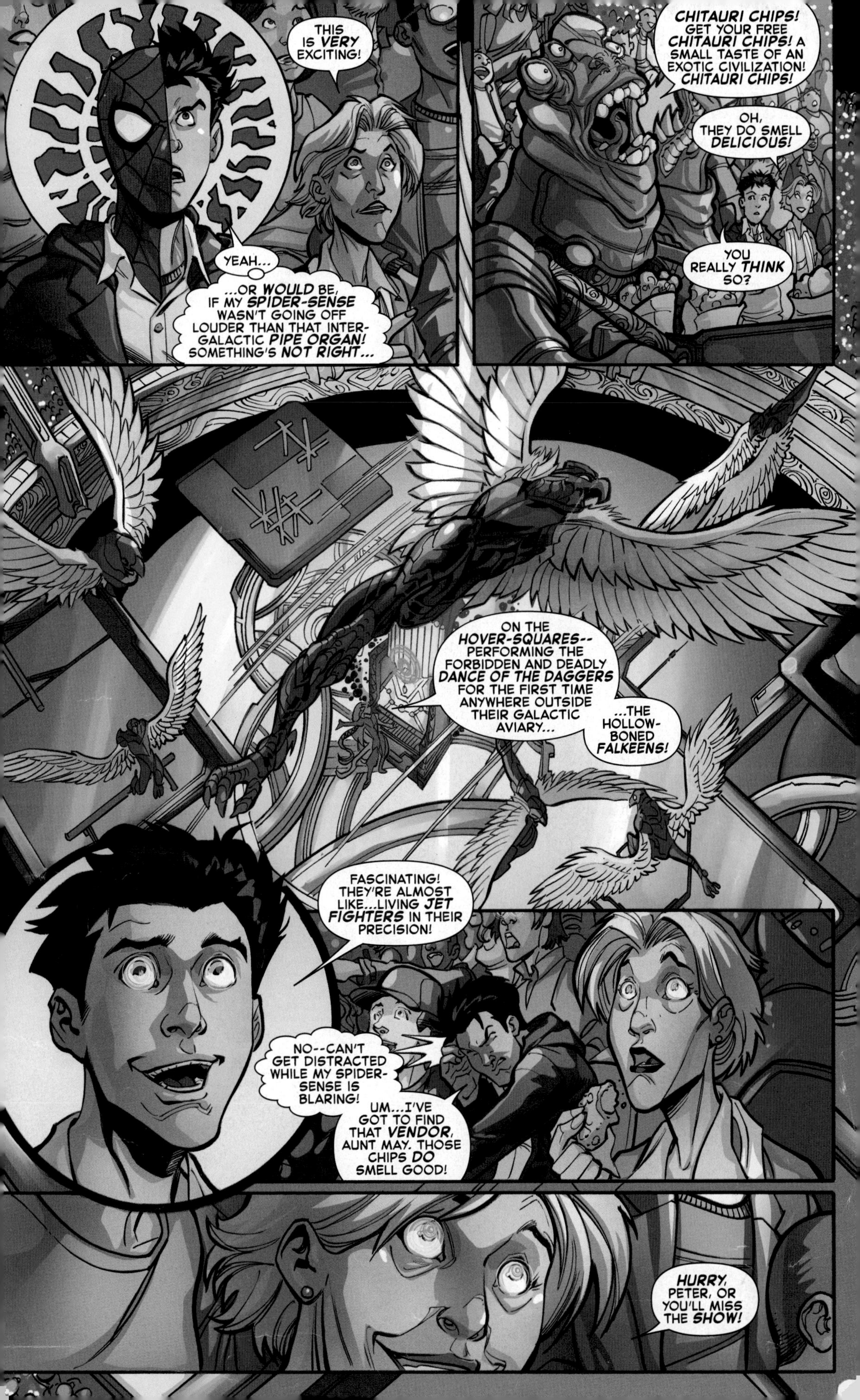
THIS IS VERY EXCITING!
YEAH...
...OR WOULD BE, IF MY SPIDER-SENSE WASN'T GOING OFF LOUDER THAN THAT INTER-GALACTIC PIPE ORGAN! SOMETHING'S NOT RIGHT...
CHITAURI CHIPS! GET YOUR FREE CHITAURI CHIPS! A SMALL TASTE OF AN EXOTIC CIVILIZATION! CHITAURI CHIPS!
OH, THEY DO SMELL DELICIOUS!
YOU REALLY THINK SO?
ON THE HOVER-SQUARES-- PERFORMING THE FORBIDDEN AND DEADLY DANCE OF THE DAGGERS FOR THE FIRST TIME ANYWHERE OUTSIDE THEIR GALACTIC AVIARY...
...THE HOLLOW-BONED FALKEENS!
FASCINATING! THEY'RE ALMOST LIKE...LIVING JET FIGHTERS IN THEIR PRECISION!
NO--CAN'T GET DISTRACTED WHILE MY SPIDER-SENSE IS BLARING!
UM...I'VE GOT TO FIND THAT VENDOR, AUNT MAY. THOSE CHIPS DO SMELL GOOD!
HURRY, PETER, OR YOU'LL MISS THE SHOW!

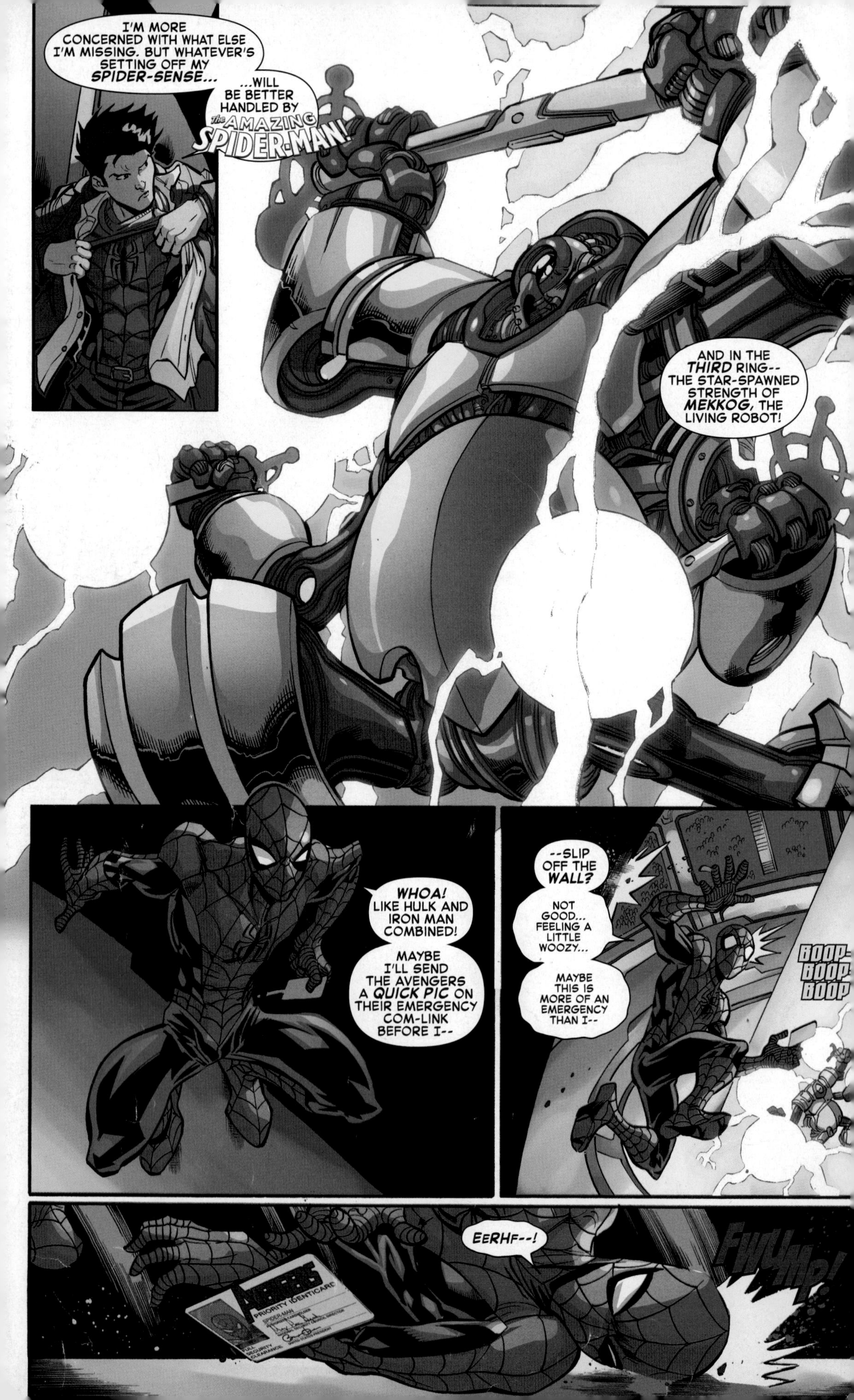
I'M MORE CONCERNED WITH WHAT ELSE I'M MISSING. BUT WHATEVER'S SETTING OFF MY SPIDER-SENSE...
...WILL BE BETTER HANDLED BY The AMAZING SPIDER-MAN!
AND IN THE THIRD RING-- THE STAR-SPAWNED STRENGTH OF MEKKOG, THE LIVING ROBOT!
WHOA! LIKE HULK AND IRON MAN COMBINED!
MAYBE I'LL SEND THE AVENGERS A QUICK PIC ON THEIR EMERGENCY COM-LINK BEFORE I--
--SLIP OFF THE WALL?
NOT GOOD... FEELING A LITTLE WOOZY...
MAYBE THIS IS MORE OF AN EMERGENCY THAN I--
BOOP-BOOP-BOOP
EERHF--!
FWUMP!
PRIORITY IDENTICARD

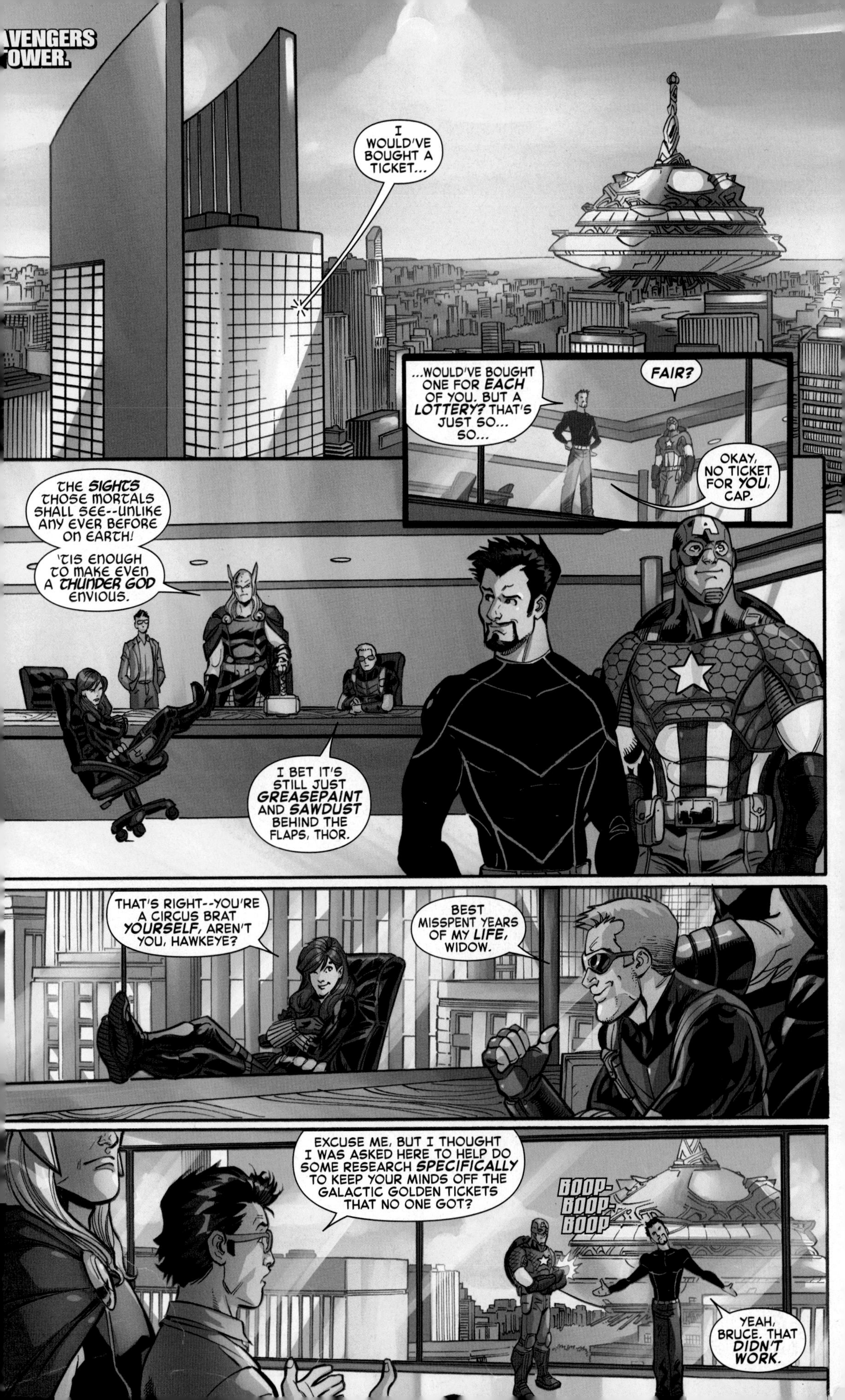
AVENGERS TOWER.
I WOULD'VE BOUGHT A TICKET...
...WOULD'VE BOUGHT ONE FOR EACH OF YOU. BUT A LOTTERY? THAT'S JUST SO... SO...
FAIR?
OKAY, NO TICKET FOR YOU, CAP.
THE SIGHTS THOSE MORTALS SHALL SEE--UNLIKE ANY EVER BEFORE ON EARTH!
'TIS ENOUGH TO MAKE EVEN A THUNDER GOD ENVIOUS.
I BET IT'S STILL JUST GREASEPAINT AND SAWDUST BEHIND THE FLAPS, THOR.
THAT'S RIGHT--YOU'RE A CIRCUS BRAT YOURSELF, AREN'T YOU, HAWKEYE?
BEST MISSPENT YEARS OF MY LIFE, WIDOW.
EXCUSE ME, BUT I THOUGHT I WAS ASKED HERE TO HELP DO SOME RESEARCH SPECIFICALLY TO KEEP YOUR MINDS OFF THE GALACTIC GOLDEN TICKETS THAT NO ONE GOT?
BOOP-BOOP-BOOP
YEAH, BRUCE. THAT DIDN'T WORK.

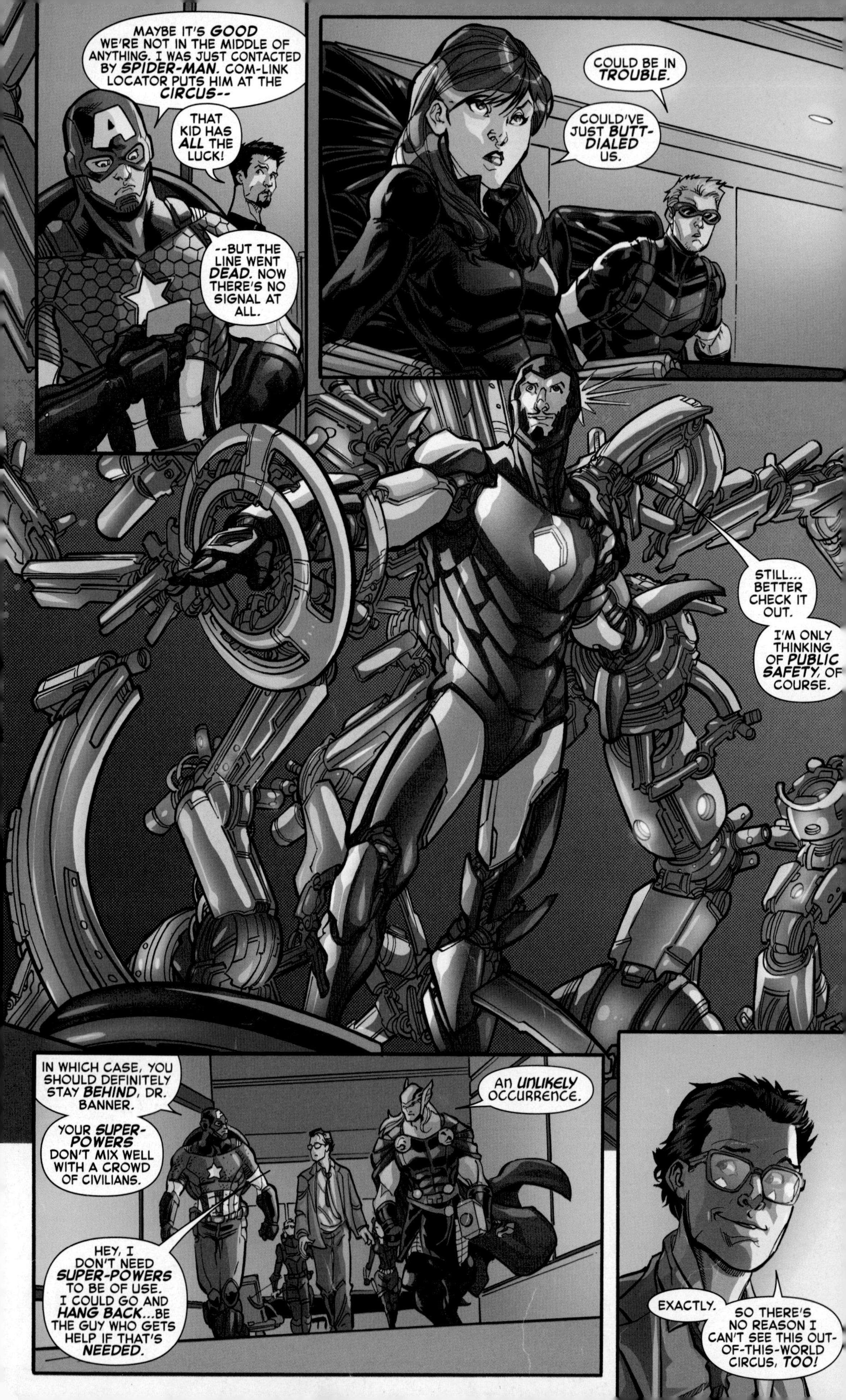
MAYBE IT'S GOOD WE'RE NOT IN THE MIDDLE OF ANYTHING. I WAS JUST CONTACTED BY SPIDER-MAN. COM-LINK LOCATOR PUTS HIM AT THE CIRCUS--
THAT KID HAS ALL THE LUCK!
--BUT THE LINE WENT DEAD. NOW THERE'S NO SIGNAL AT ALL.
COULD BE IN TROUBLE.
COULD'VE JUST BUTT-DIALED US.
STILL... BETTER CHECK IT OUT.
I'M ONLY THINKING OF PUBLIC SAFETY, OF COURSE.
IN WHICH CASE, YOU SHOULD DEFINITELY STAY BEHIND, DR. BANNER.
YOUR SUPER-POWERS DON'T MIX WELL WITH A CROWD OF CIVILIANS.
An UNLIKELY OCCURRENCE.
HEY, I DON'T NEED SUPER-POWERS TO BE OF USE. I COULD GO AND HANG BACK...BE THE GUY WHO GETS HELP IF THAT'S NEEDED.
EXACTLY.
SO THERE'S NO REASON I CAN'T SEE THIS OUT-OF-THIS-WORLD CIRCUS, TOO!

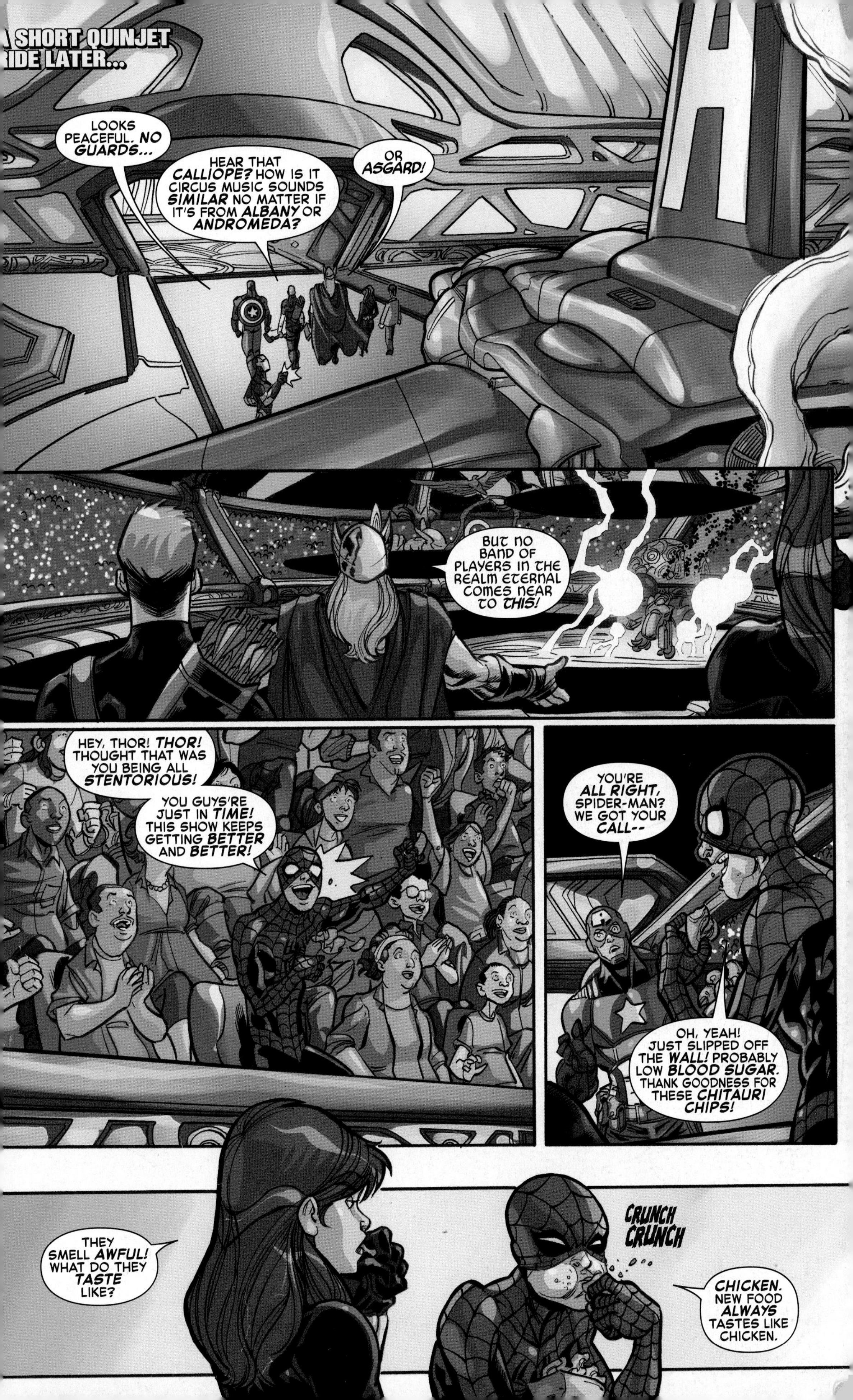
A SHORT QUINJET RIDE LATER...
LOOKS PEACEFUL. NO GUARDS...
HEAR THAT CALLIOPE? HOW IS IT CIRCUS MUSIC SOUNDS SIMILAR NO MATTER IF IT'S FROM ALBANY OR ANDROMEDA?
OR ASGARD!
BUT NO BAND OF PLAYERS IN THE REALM ETERNAL COMES NEAR TO THIS!
HEY, THOR! THOR! THOUGHT THAT WAS YOU BEING ALL STENTORIOUS!
YOU GUYS'RE JUST IN TIME! THIS SHOW KEEPS GETTING BETTER AND BETTER!
YOU'RE ALL RIGHT, SPIDER-MAN? WE GOT YOUR CALL--
OH, YEAH! JUST SLIPPED OFF THE WALL! PROBABLY LOW BLOOD SUGAR. THANK GOODNESS FOR THESE CHITAURI CHIPS!
THEY SMELL AWFUL! WHAT DO THEY TASTE LIKE?
CRUNCH CRUNCH
CHICKEN. NEW FOOD ALWAYS TASTES LIKE CHICKEN.

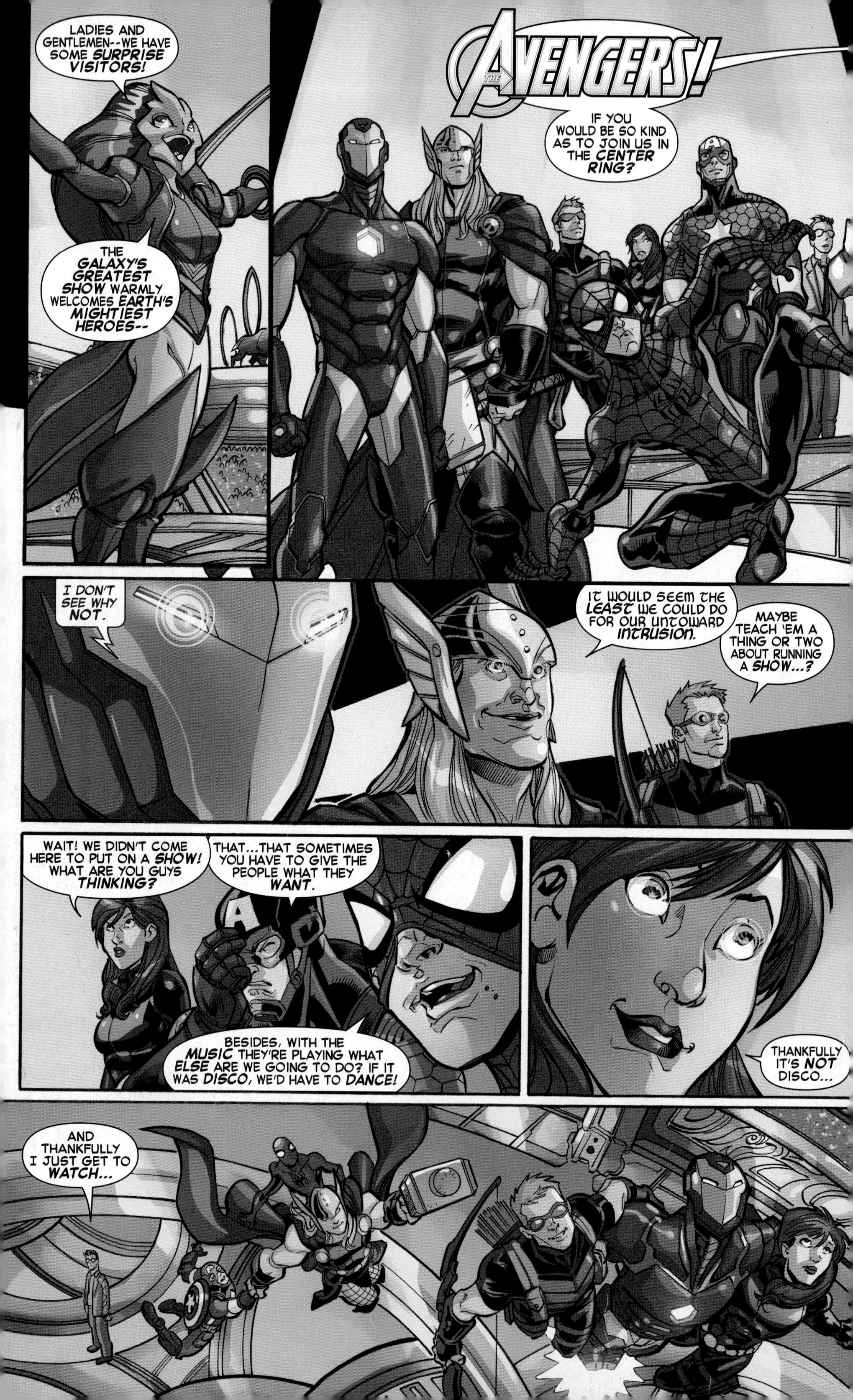
LADIES AND GENTLEMEN--WE HAVE SOME SURPRISE VISITORS!
THE GALAXY'S GREATEST SHOW WARMLY WELCOMES EARTH'S MIGHTIEST HEROES--
THE AVENGERS!
IF YOU WOULD BE SO KIND AS TO JOIN US IN THE CENTER RING?
I DON'T SEE WHY NOT.
IT WOULD SEEM THE LEAST WE COULD DO FOR OUR UNTOWARD INTRUSION.
MAYBE TEACH 'EM A THING OR TWO ABOUT RUNNING A SHOW...?
WAIT! WE DIDN'T COME HERE TO PUT ON A SHOW! WHAT ARE YOU GUYS THINKING?
THAT...THAT SOMETIMES YOU HAVE TO GIVE THE PEOPLE WHAT THEY WANT.
BESIDES, WITH THE MUSIC THEY'RE PLAYING WHAT ELSE ARE WE GOING TO DO? IF IT WAS DISCO, WE'D HAVE TO DANCE!
THANKFULLY IT'S NOT DISCO...
AND THANKFULLY I JUST GET TO WATCH...

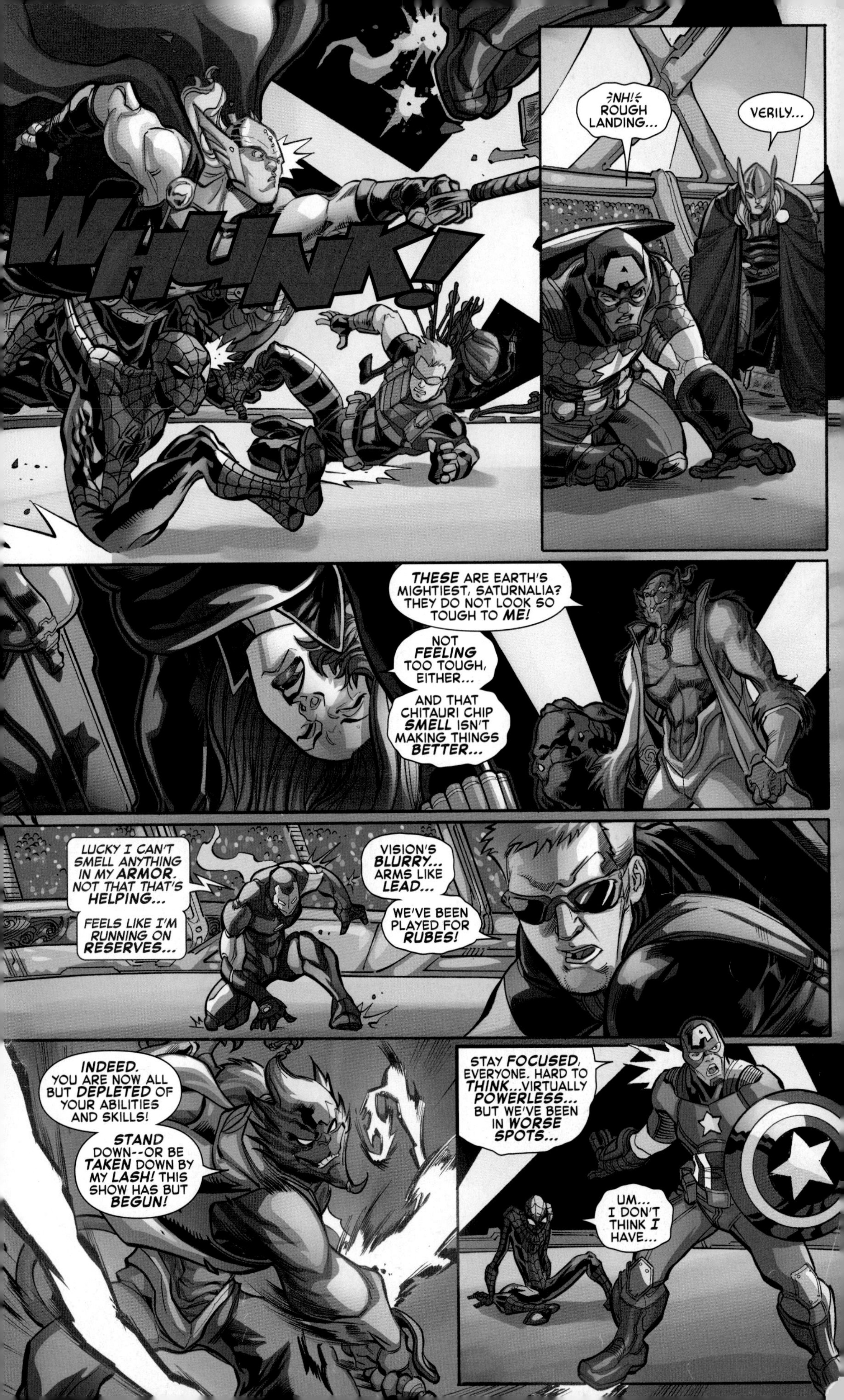
WHUNK!
ʒNH!ʒ ROUGH LANDING...
VERILY...
THESE ARE EARTH'S MIGHTIEST, SATURNALIA? THEY DO NOT LOOK SO TOUGH TO ME!
NOT FEELING TOO TOUGH, EITHER...
AND THAT CHITAURI CHIP SMELL ISN'T MAKING THINGS BETTER...
LUCKY I CAN'T SMELL ANYTHING IN MY ARMOR. NOT THAT THAT'S HELPING...
FEELS LIKE I'M RUNNING ON RESERVES...
VISION'S BLURRY... ARMS LIKE LEAD...
WE'VE BEEN PLAYED FOR RUBES!
INDEED. YOU ARE NOW ALL BUT DEPLETED OF YOUR ABILITIES AND SKILLS!
STAND DOWN--OR BE TAKEN DOWN BY MY LASH! THIS SHOW HAS BUT BEGUN!
STAY FOCUSED, EVERYONE. HARD TO THINK...VIRTUALLY POWERLESS... BUT WE'VE BEEN IN WORSE SPOTS...
UM... I DON'T THINK I HAVE...

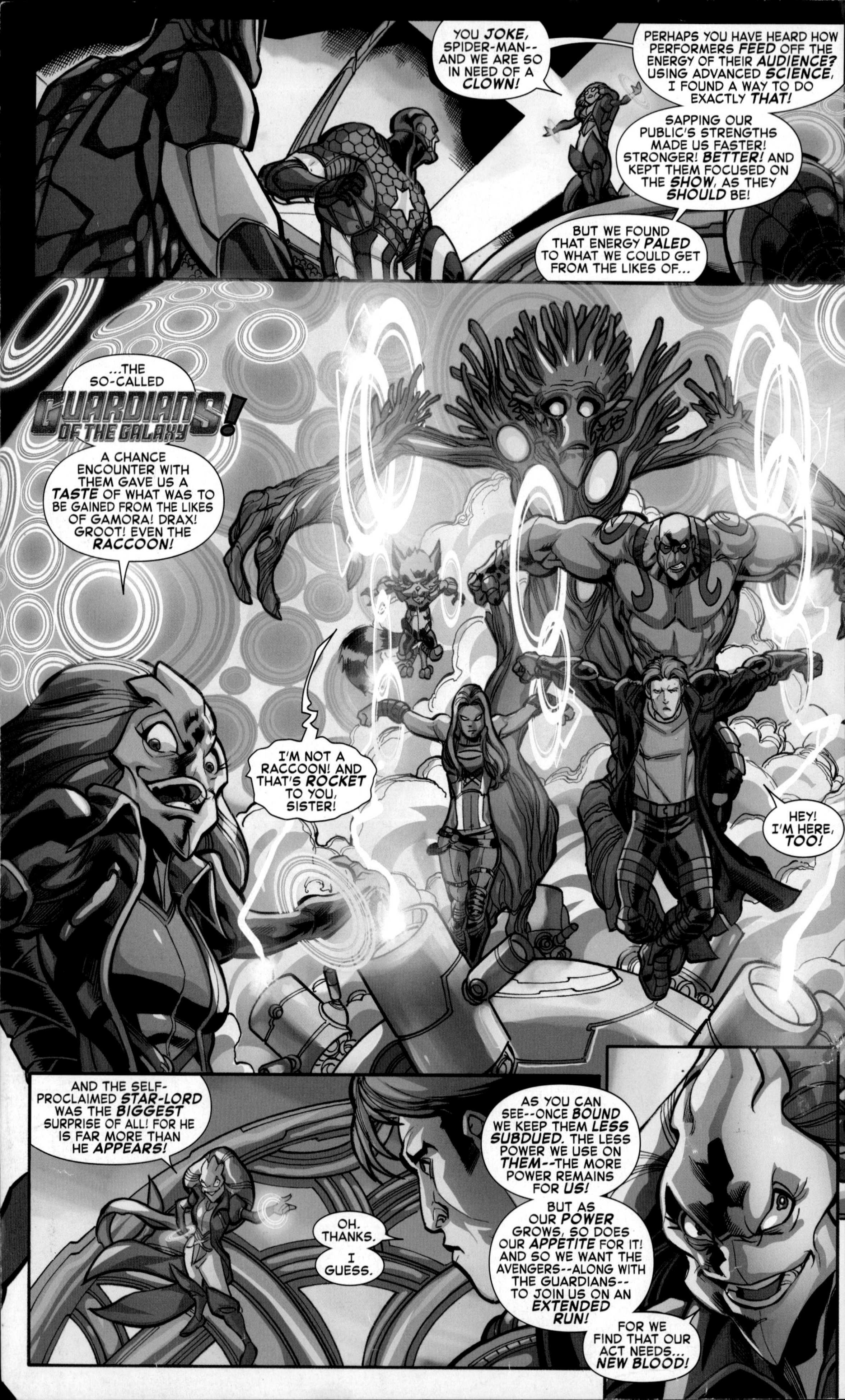
YOU JOKE, SPIDER-MAN-- AND WE ARE SO IN NEED OF A CLOWN!
PERHAPS YOU HAVE HEARD HOW PERFORMERS FEED OFF THE ENERGY OF THEIR AUDIENCE? USING ADVANCED SCIENCE, I FOUND A WAY TO DO EXACTLY THAT!
SAPPING OUR PUBLIC'S STRENGTHS MADE US FASTER! STRONGER! BETTER! AND KEPT THEM FOCUSED ON THE SHOW, AS THEY SHOULD BE!
BUT WE FOUND THAT ENERGY PALED TO WHAT WE COULD GET FROM THE LIKES OF...
...THE SO-CALLED
GUARDIANS OF THE GALAXY!
A CHANCE ENCOUNTER WITH THEM GAVE US A TASTE OF WHAT WAS TO BE GAINED FROM THE LIKES OF GAMORA! DRAX! GROOT! EVEN THE RACCOON!
I'M NOT A RACCOON! AND THAT'S ROCKET TO YOU, SISTER!
HEY! I'M HERE, TOO!
AND THE SELF-PROCLAIMED STAR-LORD WAS THE BIGGEST SURPRISE OF ALL! FOR HE IS FAR MORE THAN HE APPEARS!
OH. THANKS. I GUESS.
AS YOU CAN SEE--ONCE BOUND WE KEEP THEM LESS SUBDUED. THE LESS POWER WE USE ON THEM--THE MORE POWER REMAINS FOR US!
BUT AS OUR POWER GROWS, SO DOES OUR APPETITE FOR IT! AND SO WE WANT THE AVENGERS--ALONG WITH THE GUARDIANS-- TO JOIN US ON AN EXTENDED RUN!
FOR WE FIND THAT OUR ACT NEEDS... NEW BLOOD!

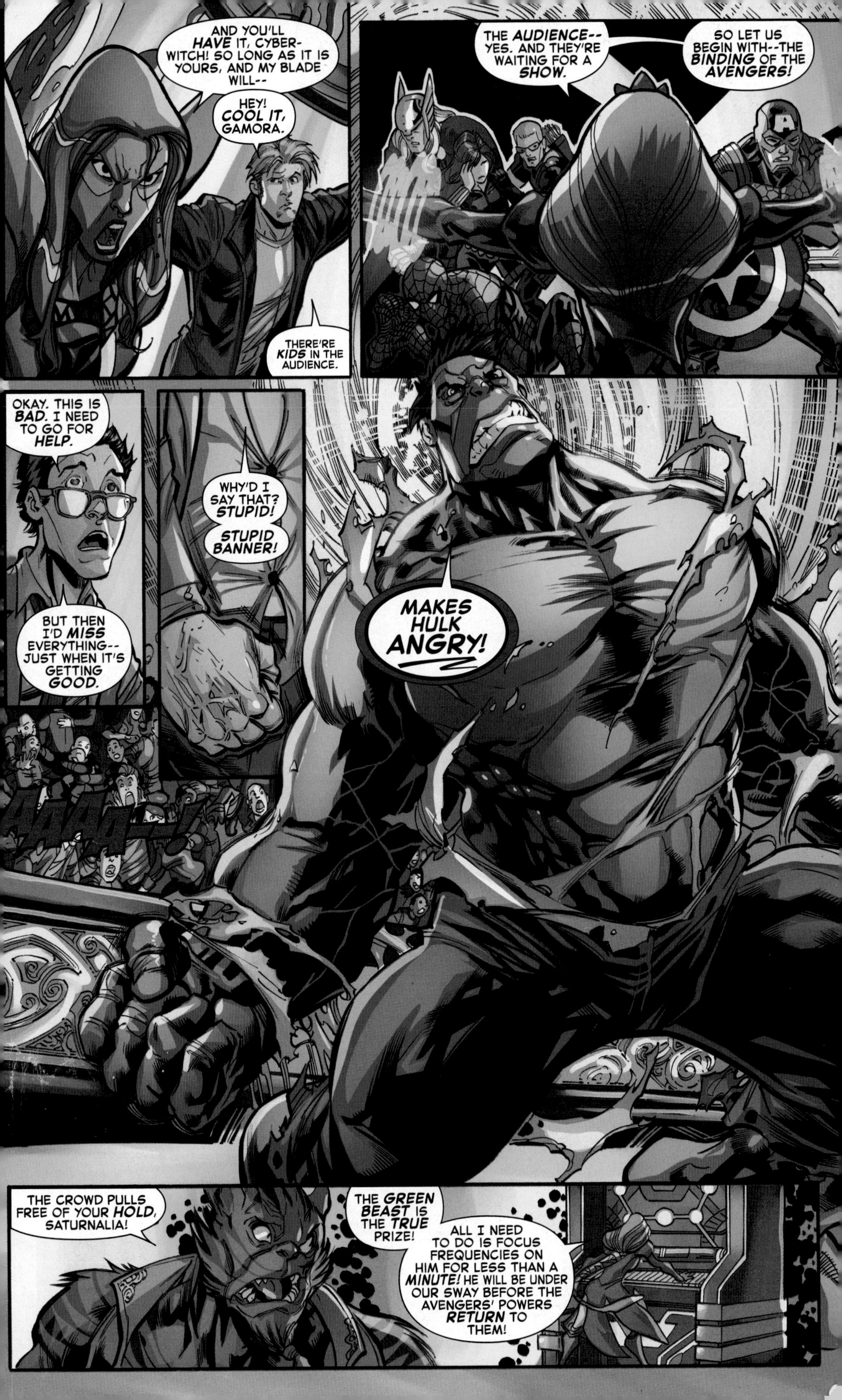

AND YOU'LL HAVE IT, CYBER-WITCH! SO LONG AS IT IS YOURS, AND MY BLADE WILL--
HEY! COOL IT, GAMORA.
THERE'RE KIDS IN THE AUDIENCE.
THE AUDIENCE--YES. AND THEY'RE WAITING FOR A SHOW.
SO LET US BEGIN WITH--THE BINDING OF THE AVENGERS!
OKAY. THIS IS BAD. I NEED TO GO FOR HELP.
BUT THEN I'D MISS EVERYTHING--JUST WHEN IT'S GETTING GOOD.
WHY'D I SAY THAT? STUPID!
STUPID BANNER!
MAKES HULK ANGRY!
AAAA--!
THE CROWD PULLS FREE OF YOUR HOLD, SATURNALIA!
THE GREEN BEAST IS THE TRUE PRIZE!
ALL I NEED TO DO IS FOCUS FREQUENCIES ON HIM FOR LESS THAN A MINUTE! HE WILL BE UNDER OUR SWAY BEFORE THE AVENGERS' POWERS RETURN TO THEM!

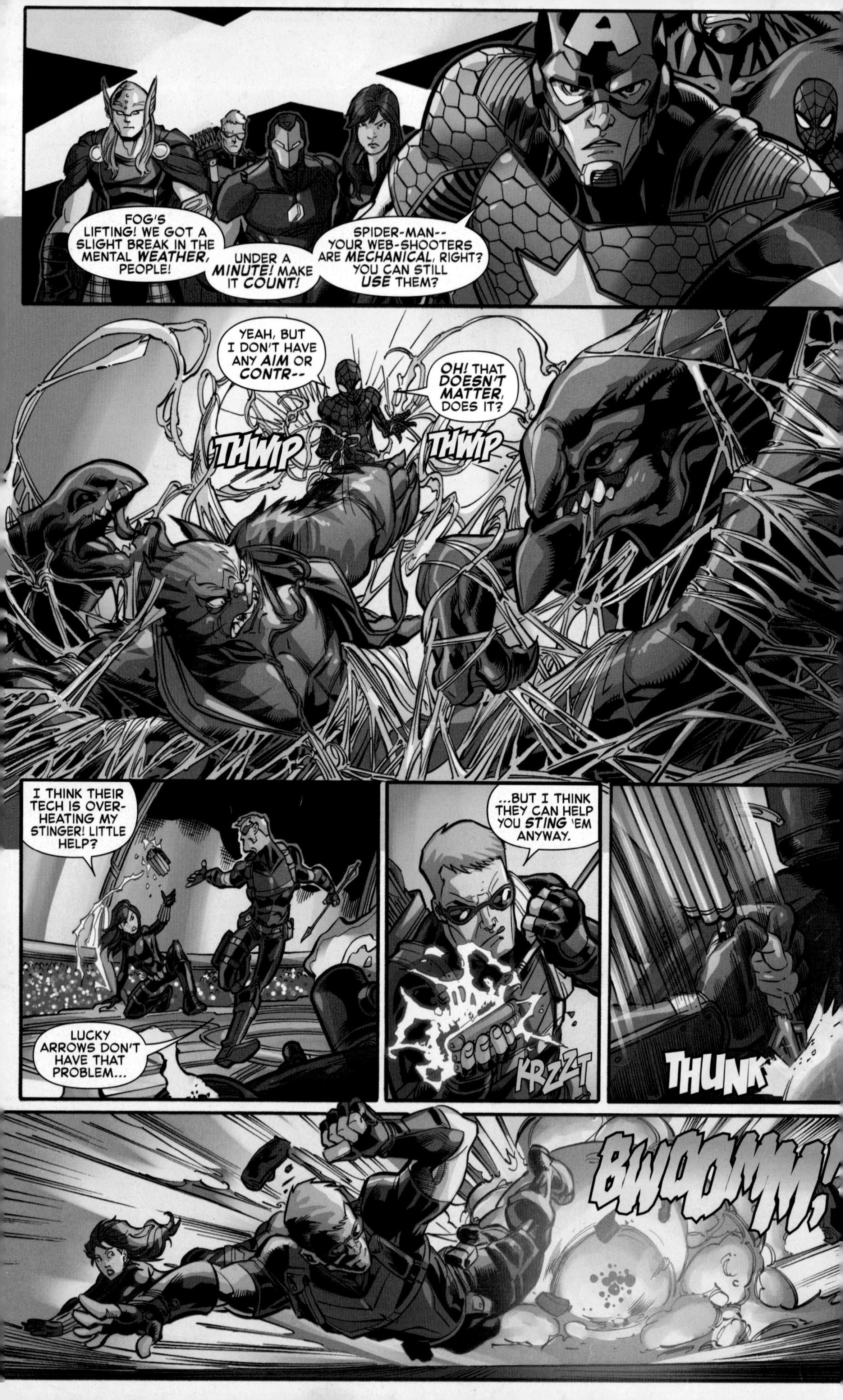
FOG'S LIFTING! WE GOT A SLIGHT BREAK IN THE MENTAL WEATHER, PEOPLE!
UNDER A MINUTE! MAKE IT COUNT!
SPIDER-MAN-- YOUR WEB-SHOOTERS ARE MECHANICAL, RIGHT? YOU CAN STILL USE THEM?
YEAH, BUT I DON'T HAVE ANY AIM OR CONTR--
OH! THAT DOESN'T MATTER, DOES IT?
THWIP
THWIP
I THINK THEIR TECH IS OVER-HEATING MY STINGER! LITTLE HELP?
LUCKY ARROWS DON'T HAVE THAT PROBLEM...
...BUT I THINK THEY CAN HELP YOU STING 'EM ANYWAY.
KRZZT
THUNK
BWOOMM!

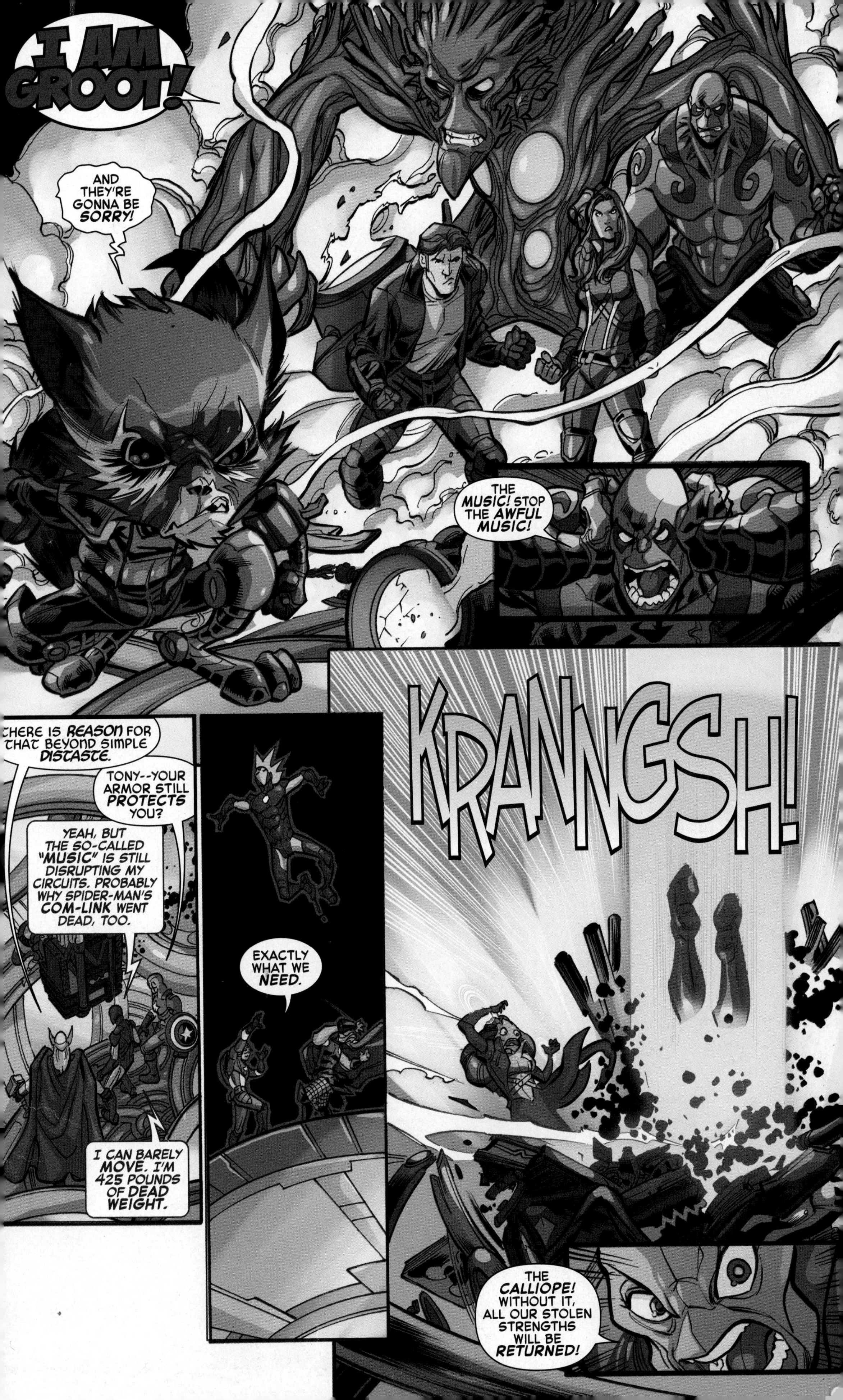
I AM GROOT!
AND THEY'RE GONNA BE SORRY!
THE MUSIC! STOP THE AWFUL MUSIC!
THERE IS REASON FOR THAT BEYOND SIMPLE DISTASTE.
TONY--YOUR ARMOR STILL PROTECTS YOU?
YEAH, BUT THE SO-CALLED "MUSIC" IS STILL DISRUPTING MY CIRCUITS. PROBABLY WHY SPIDER-MAN'S COM-LINK WENT DEAD, TOO.
I CAN BARELY MOVE. I'M 425 POUNDS OF DEAD WEIGHT.
EXACTLY WHAT WE NEED.
KRANNGSH!
THE CALLIOPE! WITHOUT IT, ALL OUR STOLEN STRENGTHS WILL BE RETURNED!

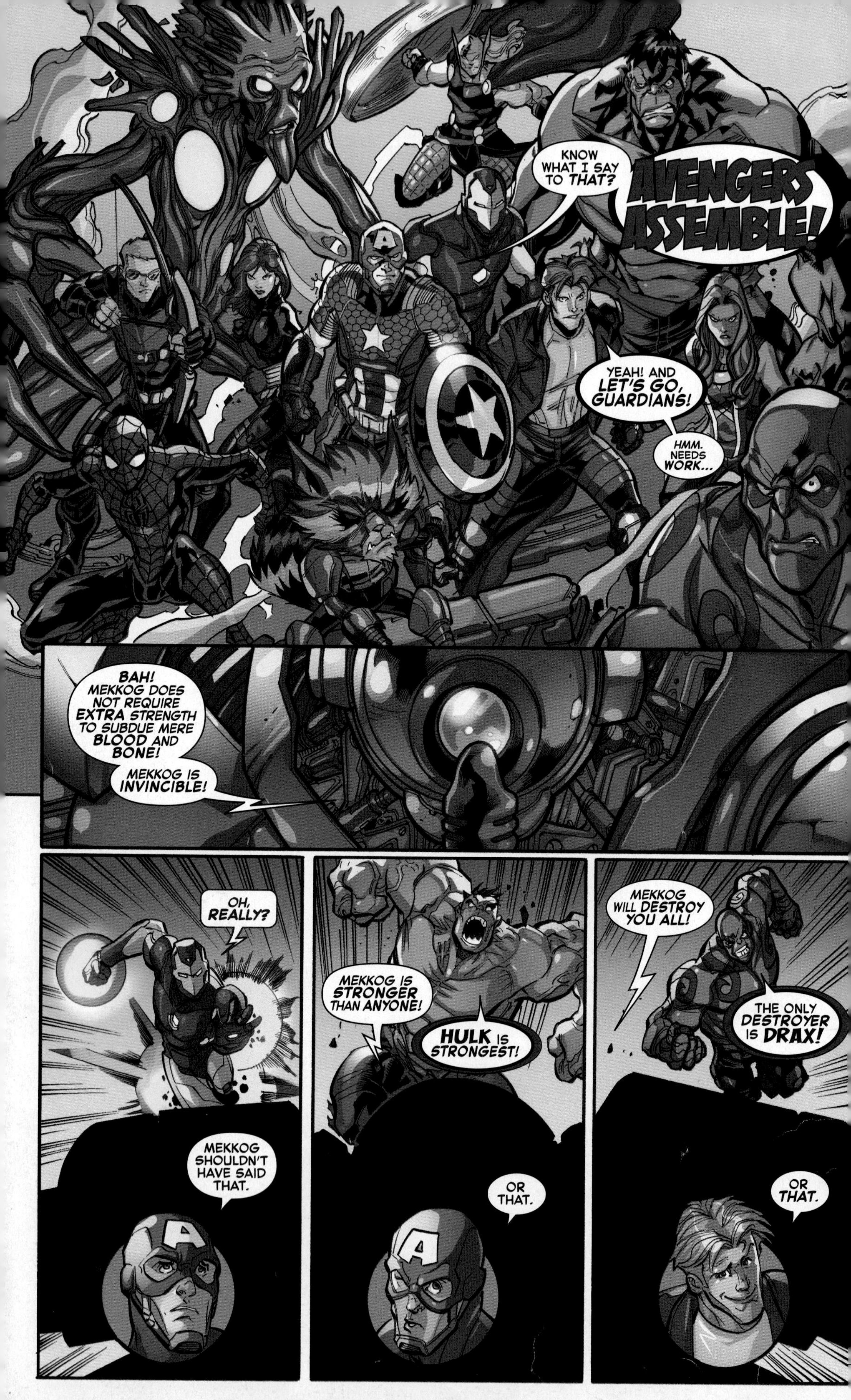
KNOW WHAT I SAY TO THAT?
AVENGERS ASSEMBLE!
YEAH! AND LET'S GO, GUARDIANS!
HMM. NEEDS WORK...
BAH! MEKKOG DOES NOT REQUIRE EXTRA STRENGTH TO SUBDUE MERE BLOOD AND BONE!
MEKKOG IS INVINCIBLE!
OH, REALLY?
MEKKOG SHOULDN'T HAVE SAID THAT.
MEKKOG IS STRONGER THAN ANYONE!
HULK IS STRONGEST!
OR THAT.
MEKKOG WILL DESTROY YOU ALL!
THE ONLY DESTROYER IS DRAX!
OR THAT.

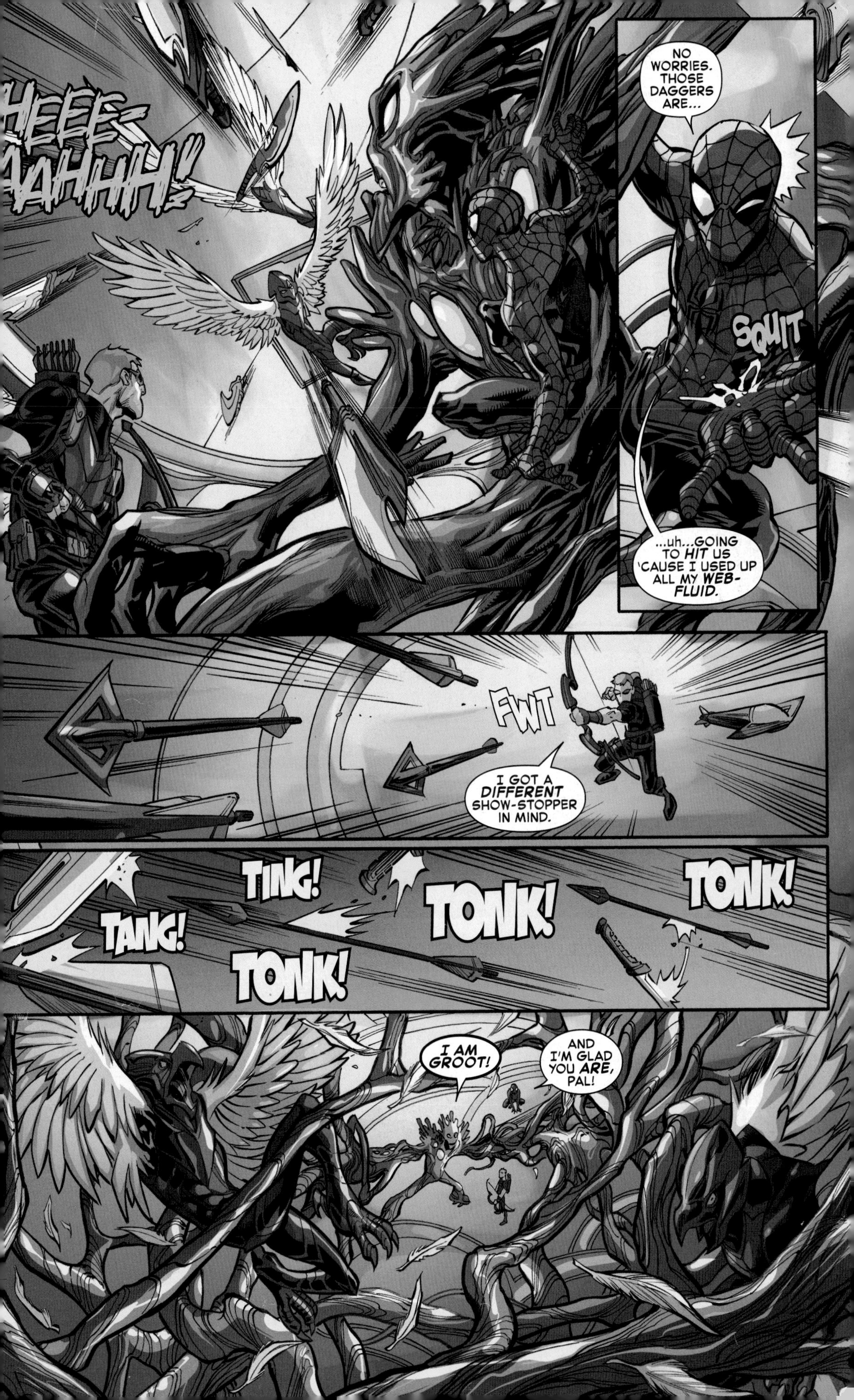
HEEE-AAHHH!
NO WORRIES. THOSE DAGGERS ARE...
SQUIT
...uh...GOING TO HIT US 'CAUSE I USED UP ALL MY WEB-FLUID.
FWT
I GOT A DIFFERENT SHOW-STOPPER IN MIND.
TING!
TANG!
TONK!
TONK!
TONK!
I AM GROOT!
AND I'M GLAD YOU ARE, PAL!

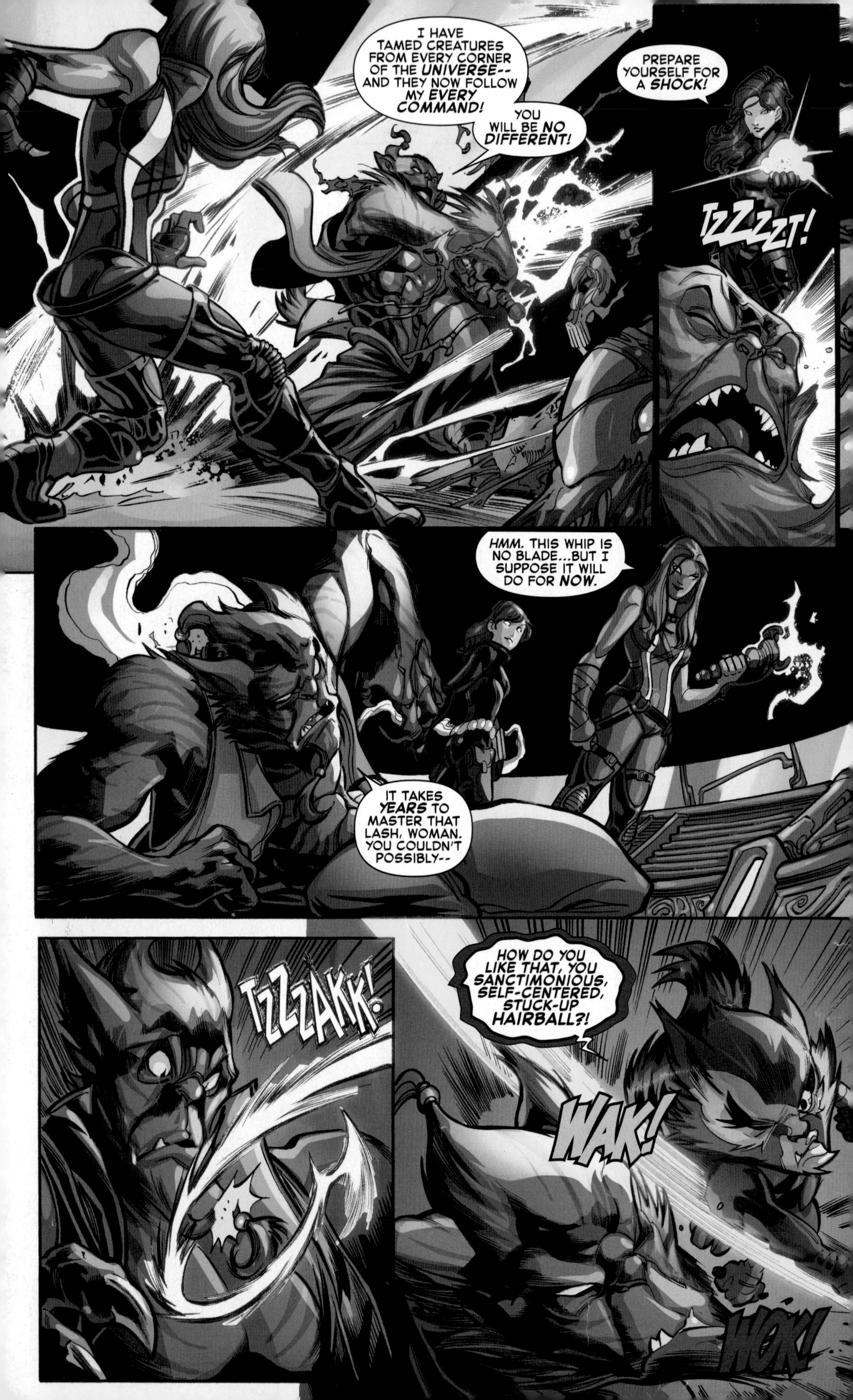
I HAVE TAMED CREATURES FROM EVERY CORNER OF THE UNIVERSE-- AND THEY NOW FOLLOW MY EVERY COMMAND!
YOU WILL BE NO DIFFERENT!
PREPARE YOURSELF FOR A SHOCK!
TZZZZT!
HMM. THIS WHIP IS NO BLADE...BUT I SUPPOSE IT WILL DO FOR NOW.
IT TAKES YEARS TO MASTER THAT LASH, WOMAN. YOU COULDN'T POSSIBLY--
TZZZAKK!
HOW DO YOU LIKE THAT, YOU SANCTIMONIOUS, SELF-CENTERED, STUCK-UP HAIRBALL?!
WAK!
WOK!

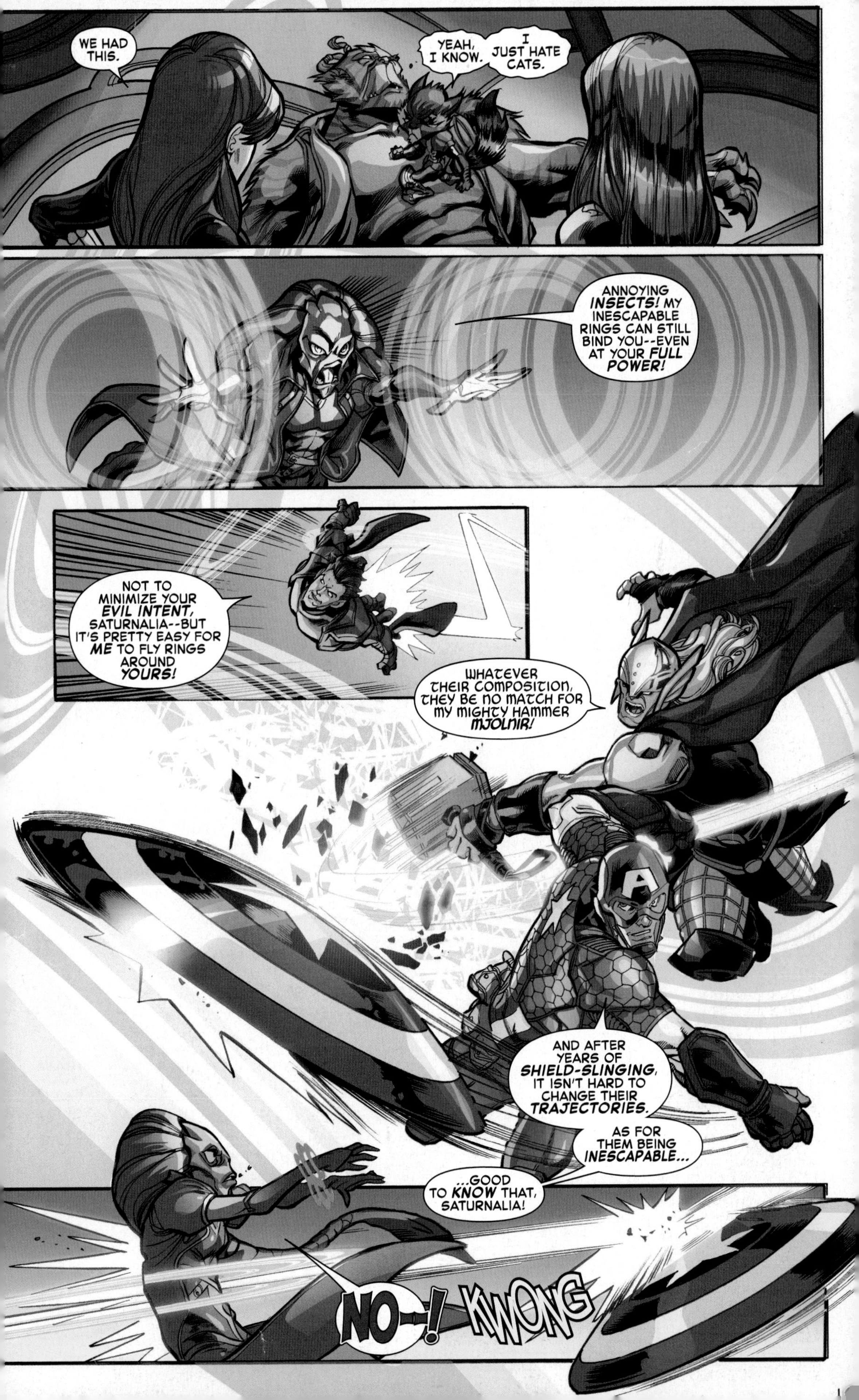
WE HAD THIS.
YEAH, I KNOW.
I JUST HATE CATS.
ANNOYING INSECTS! MY INESCAPABLE RINGS CAN STILL BIND YOU--EVEN AT YOUR FULL POWER!
NOT TO MINIMIZE YOUR EVIL INTENT, SATURNALIA--BUT IT'S PRETTY EASY FOR ME TO FLY RINGS AROUND YOURS!
WHATEVER THEIR COMPOSITION, THEY BE NO MATCH FOR MY MIGHTY HAMMER MJOLNIR!
AND AFTER YEARS OF SHIELD-SLINGING, IT ISN'T HARD TO CHANGE THEIR TRAJECTORIES.
AS FOR THEM BEING INESCAPABLE...
...GOOD TO KNOW THAT, SATURNALIA!
NO--!
KWONG

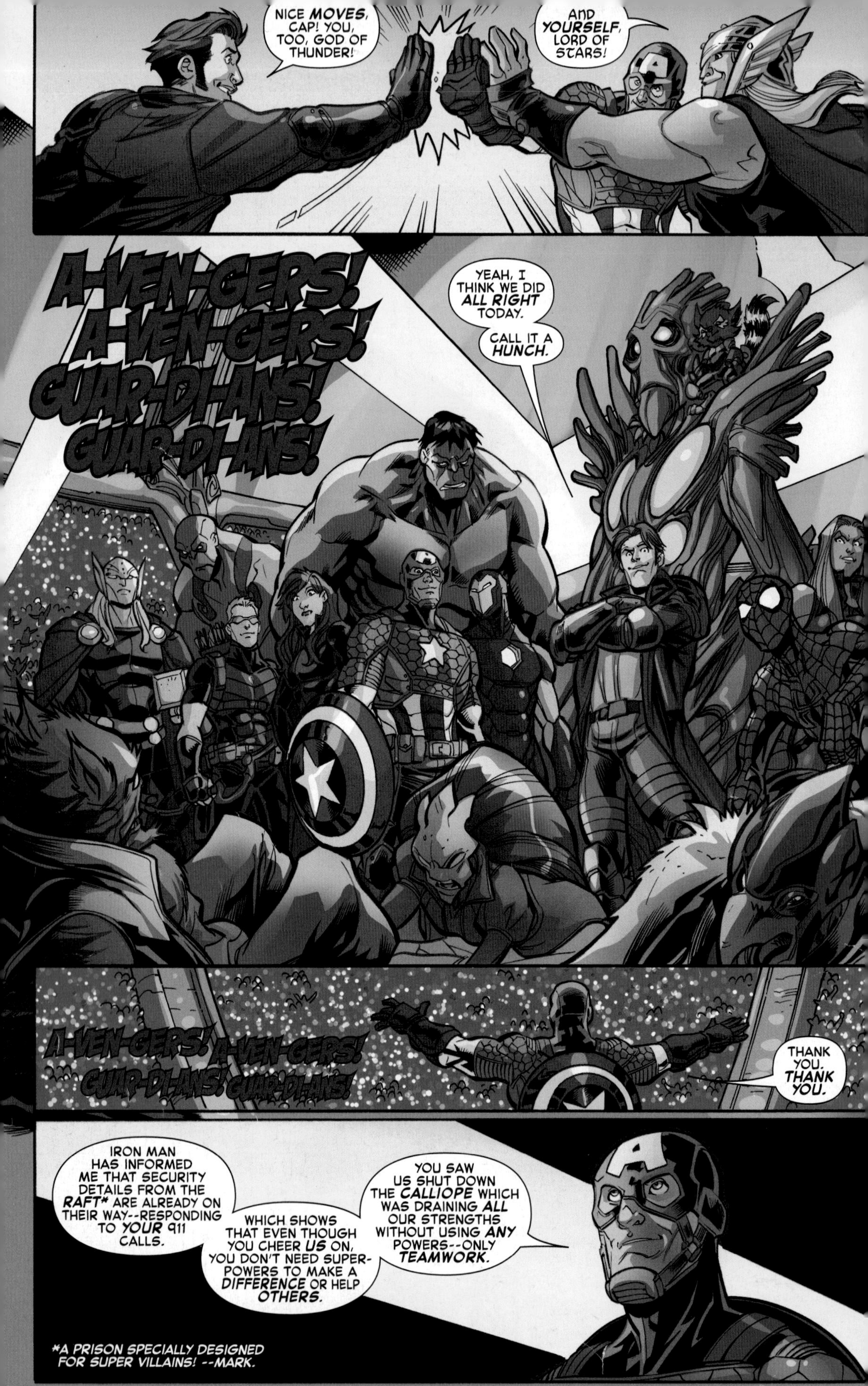
NICE MOVES, CAP! YOU, TOO, GOD OF THUNDER!
AND YOURSELF, LORD OF STARS!
A-VEN-GERS! A-VEN-GERS! GUAR-DI-ANS! GUAR-DI-ANS!
YEAH, I THINK WE DID ALL RIGHT TODAY.
CALL IT A HUNCH.
A-VEN-GERS! A-VEN-GERS! GUAR-DI-ANS! GUAR-DI-ANS!
THANK YOU. THANK YOU.
IRON MAN HAS INFORMED ME THAT SECURITY DETAILS FROM THE RAFT* ARE ALREADY ON THEIR WAY--RESPONDING TO YOUR 911 CALLS.
WHICH SHOWS THAT EVEN THOUGH YOU CHEER US ON, YOU DON'T NEED SUPER-POWERS TO MAKE A DIFFERENCE OR HELP OTHERS.
YOU SAW US SHUT DOWN THE CALLIOPE WHICH WAS DRAINING ALL OUR STRENGTHS WITHOUT USING ANY POWERS--ONLY TEAMWORK.
*A PRISON SPECIALLY DESIGNED FOR SUPER VILLAINS! --MARK.

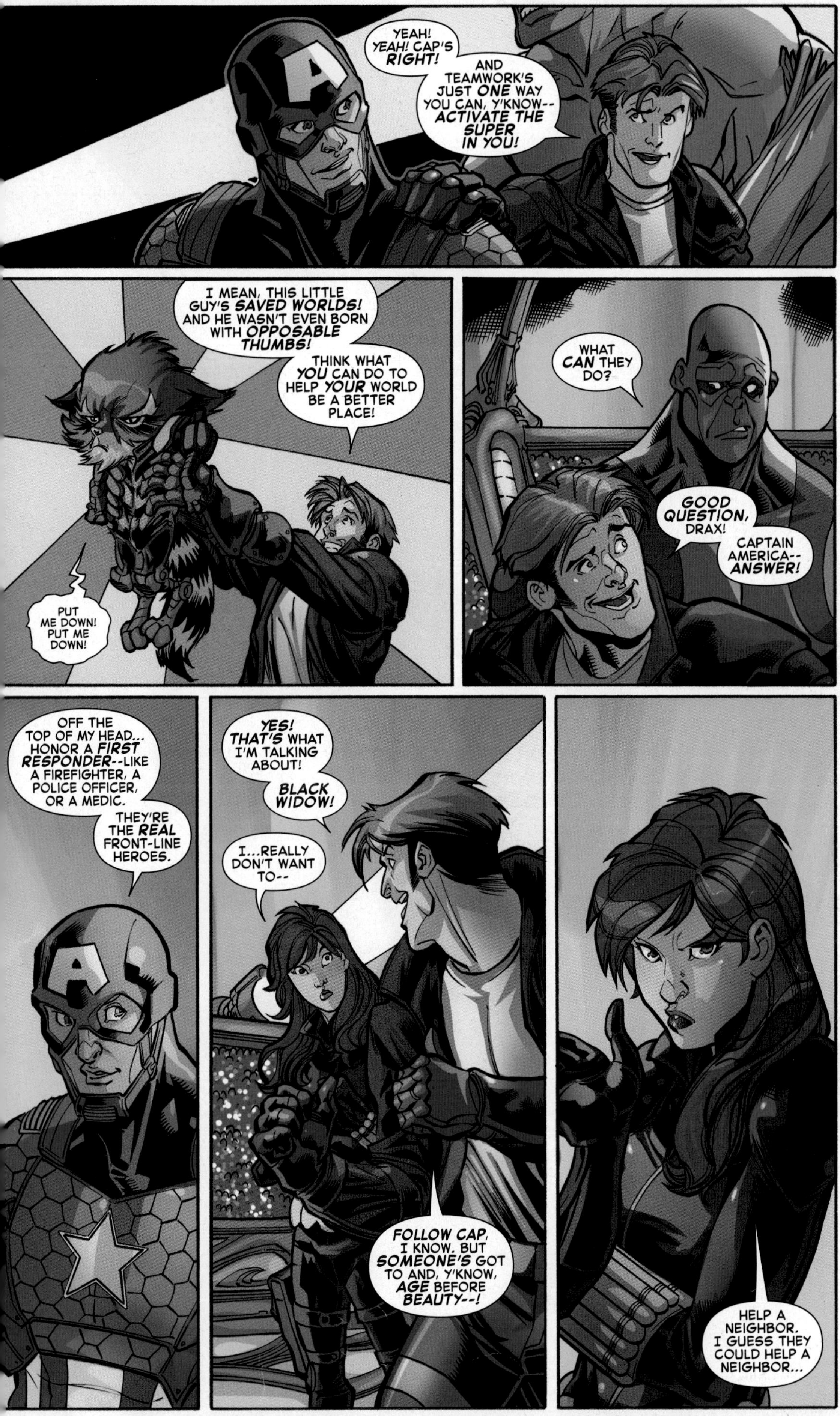

YEAH! YEAH! CAP'S RIGHT!
AND TEAMWORK'S JUST ONE WAY YOU CAN, Y'KNOW-- ACTIVATE THE SUPER IN YOU!
I MEAN, THIS LITTLE GUY'S SAVED WORLDS! AND HE WASN'T EVEN BORN WITH OPPOSABLE THUMBS!
THINK WHAT YOU CAN DO TO HELP YOUR WORLD BE A BETTER PLACE!
PUT ME DOWN! PUT ME DOWN!
WHAT CAN THEY DO?
GOOD QUESTION, DRAX!
CAPTAIN AMERICA-- ANSWER!
OFF THE TOP OF MY HEAD... HONOR A FIRST RESPONDER--LIKE A FIREFIGHTER, A POLICE OFFICER, OR A MEDIC.
THEY'RE THE REAL FRONT-LINE HEROES.
YES! THAT'S WHAT I'M TALKING ABOUT!
BLACK WIDOW!
I...REALLY DON'T WANT TO--
FOLLOW CAP, I KNOW. BUT SOMEONE'S GOT TO AND, Y'KNOW, AGE BEFORE BEAUTY--!
HELP A NEIGHBOR. I GUESS THEY COULD HELP A NEIGHBOR...

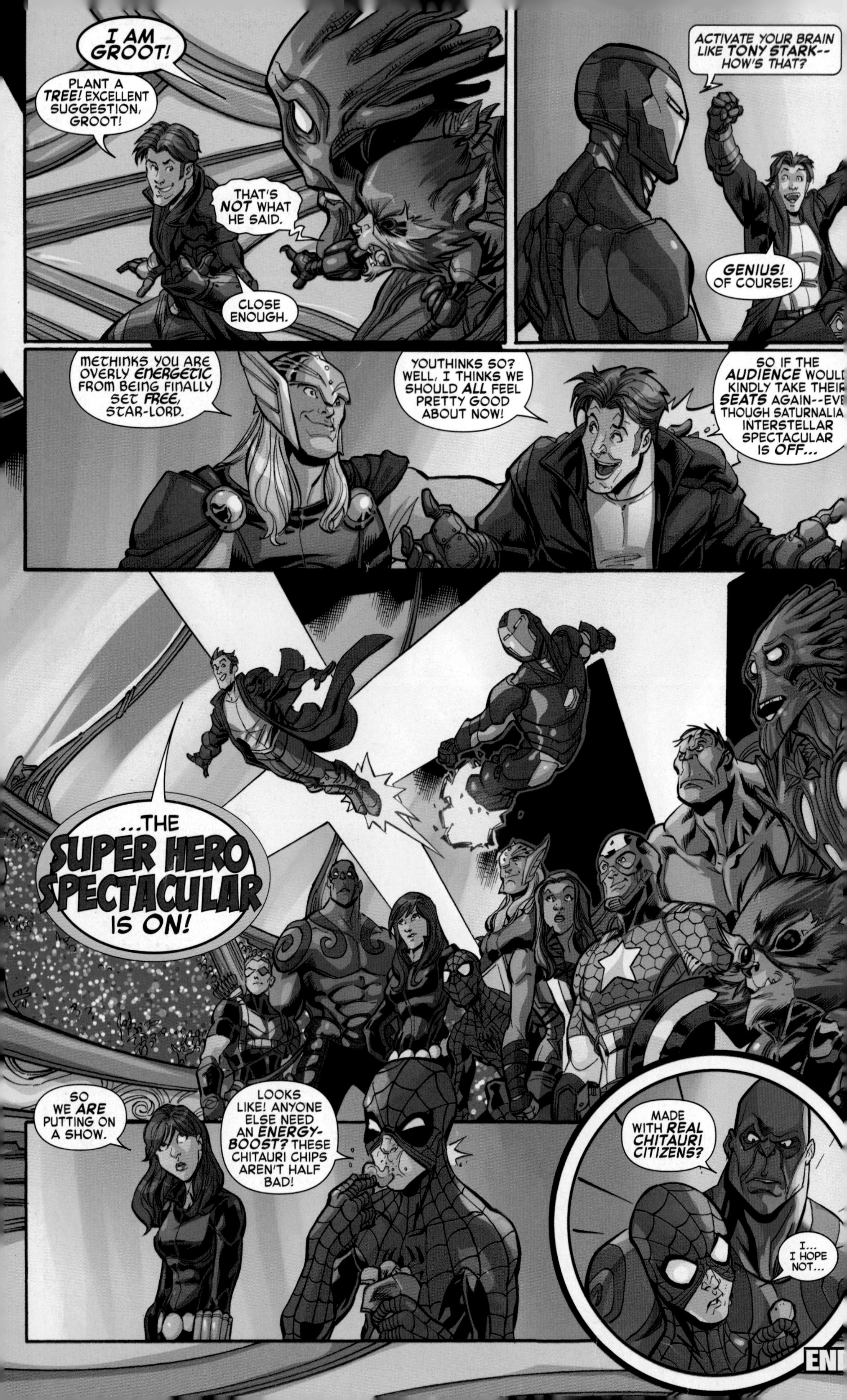
I AM GROOT!
PLANT A TREE! EXCELLENT SUGGESTION, GROOT!
THAT'S NOT WHAT HE SAID.
CLOSE ENOUGH.
ACTIVATE YOUR BRAIN LIKE TONY STARK-- HOW'S THAT?
GENIUS! OF COURSE!
METHINKS YOU ARE OVERLY ENERGETIC FROM BEING FINALLY SET FREE, STAR-LORD.
YOUTHINKS SO? WELL, I THINKS WE SHOULD ALL FEEL PRETTY GOOD ABOUT NOW!
SO IF THE AUDIENCE WOUL KINDLY TAKE THEIR SEATS AGAIN--EVE THOUGH SATURNALIA INTERSTELLAR SPECTACULAR IS OFF...
...THE SUPER HERO SPECTACULAR IS ON!
SO WE ARE PUTTING ON A SHOW.
LOOKS LIKE! ANYONE ELSE NEED AN ENERGY-BOOST? THESE CHITAURI CHIPS AREN'T HALF BAD!
MADE WITH REAL CHITAURI CITIZENS?
I... I HOPE NOT...
ENI

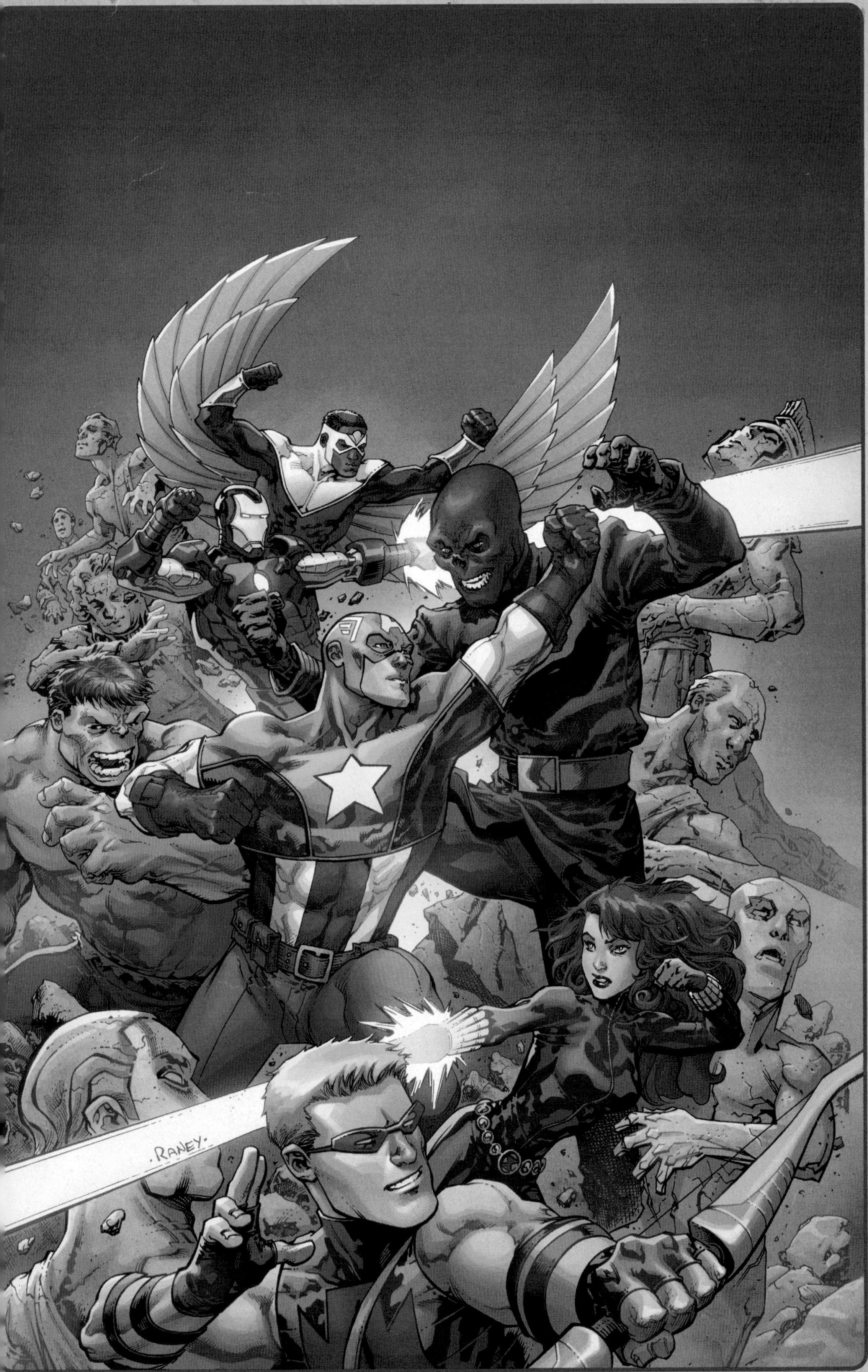
RANEY

AVENGERS VS #1: THE ART OF WAR

COVER ART BY TOM RANEY & TAMRA BONVILLAIN

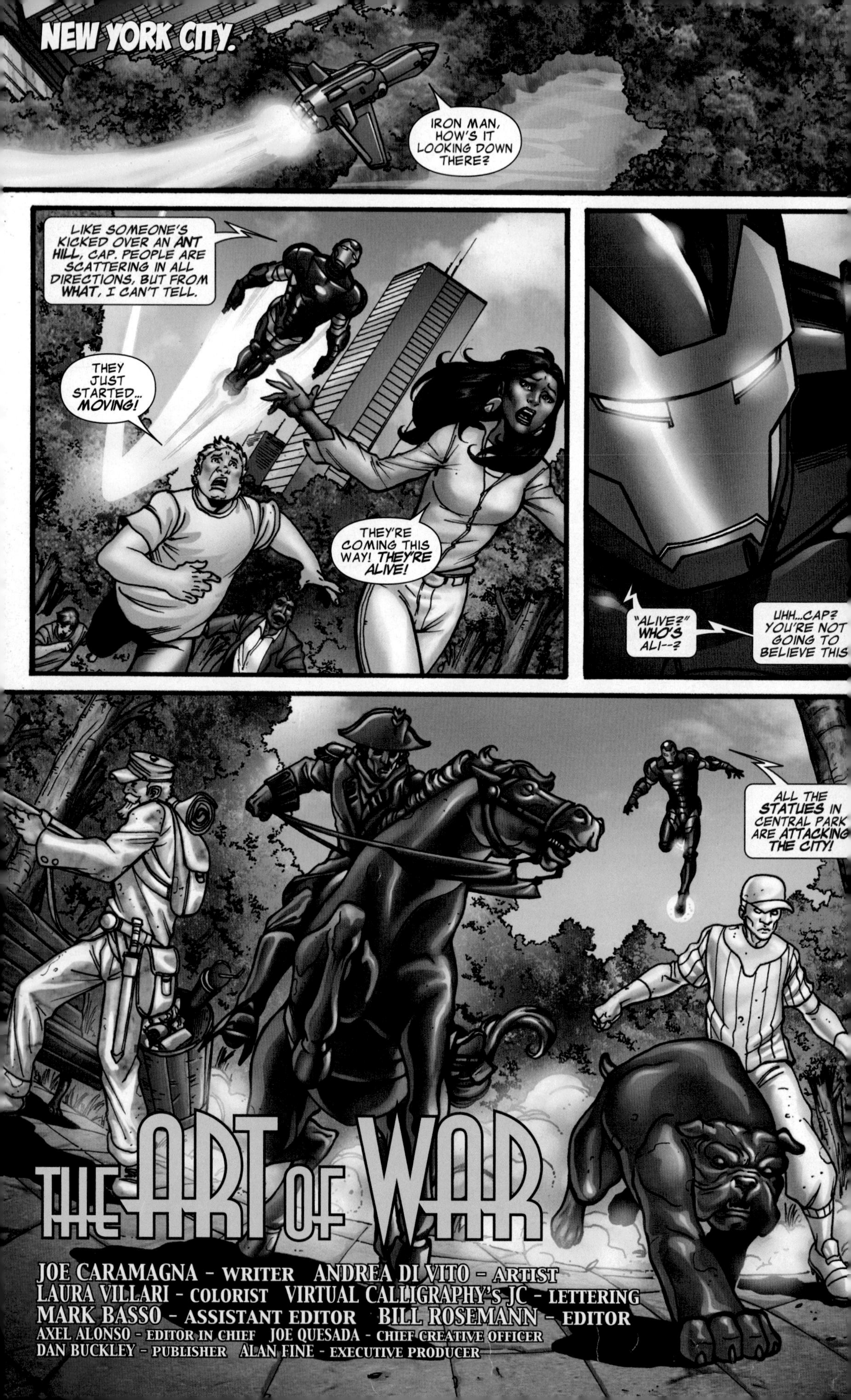
NEW YORK CITY.
IRON MAN, HOW'S IT LOOKING DOWN THERE?
LIKE SOMEONE'S KICKED OVER AN ANT HILL, CAP. PEOPLE ARE SCATTERING IN ALL DIRECTIONS, BUT FROM WHAT, I CAN'T TELL.
THEY JUST STARTED... MOVING!
THEY'RE COMING THIS WAY! THEY'RE ALIVE!
"ALIVE?" WHO'S ALI--?
UHH...CAP? YOU'RE NOT GOING TO BELIEVE THIS
ALL THE STATUES IN CENTRAL PARK ARE ATTACKING THE CITY!
THE ART OF WAR
JOE CARAMAGNA - WRITER ANDREA DI VITO - ARTIST
LAURA VILLARI - COLORIST VIRTUAL CALLIGRAPHY's JC - LETTERING
MARK BASSO - ASSISTANT EDITOR BILL ROSEMANN - EDITOR
AXEL ALONSO - EDITOR IN CHIEF JOE QUESADA - CHIEF CREATIVE OFFICER
DAN BUCKLEY - PUBLISHER ALAN FINE - EXECUTIVE PRODUCER

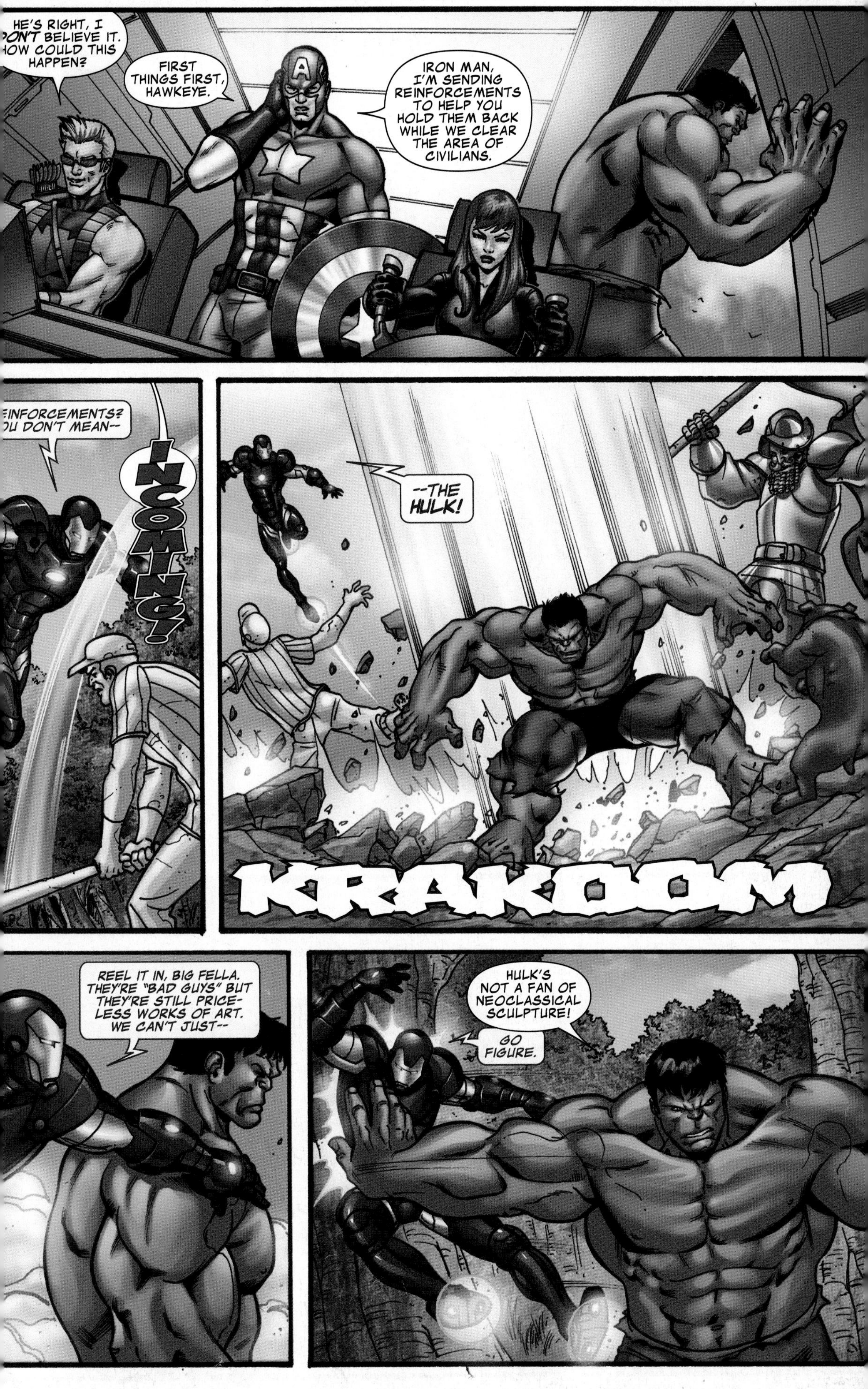
HE'S RIGHT, I DON'T BELIEVE IT. HOW COULD THIS HAPPEN?
FIRST THINGS FIRST, HAWKEYE.
IRON MAN, I'M SENDING REINFORCEMENTS TO HELP YOU HOLD THEM BACK WHILE WE CLEAR THE AREA OF CIVILIANS.
REINFORCEMENTS? YOU DON'T MEAN--
INCOMING!
--THE HULK!
KRAKOOM
REEL IT IN, BIG FELLA. THEY'RE "BAD GUYS" BUT THEY'RE STILL PRICELESS WORKS OF ART. WE CAN'T JUST--
HULK'S NOT A FAN OF NEOCLASSICAL SCULPTURE!
GO FIGURE.

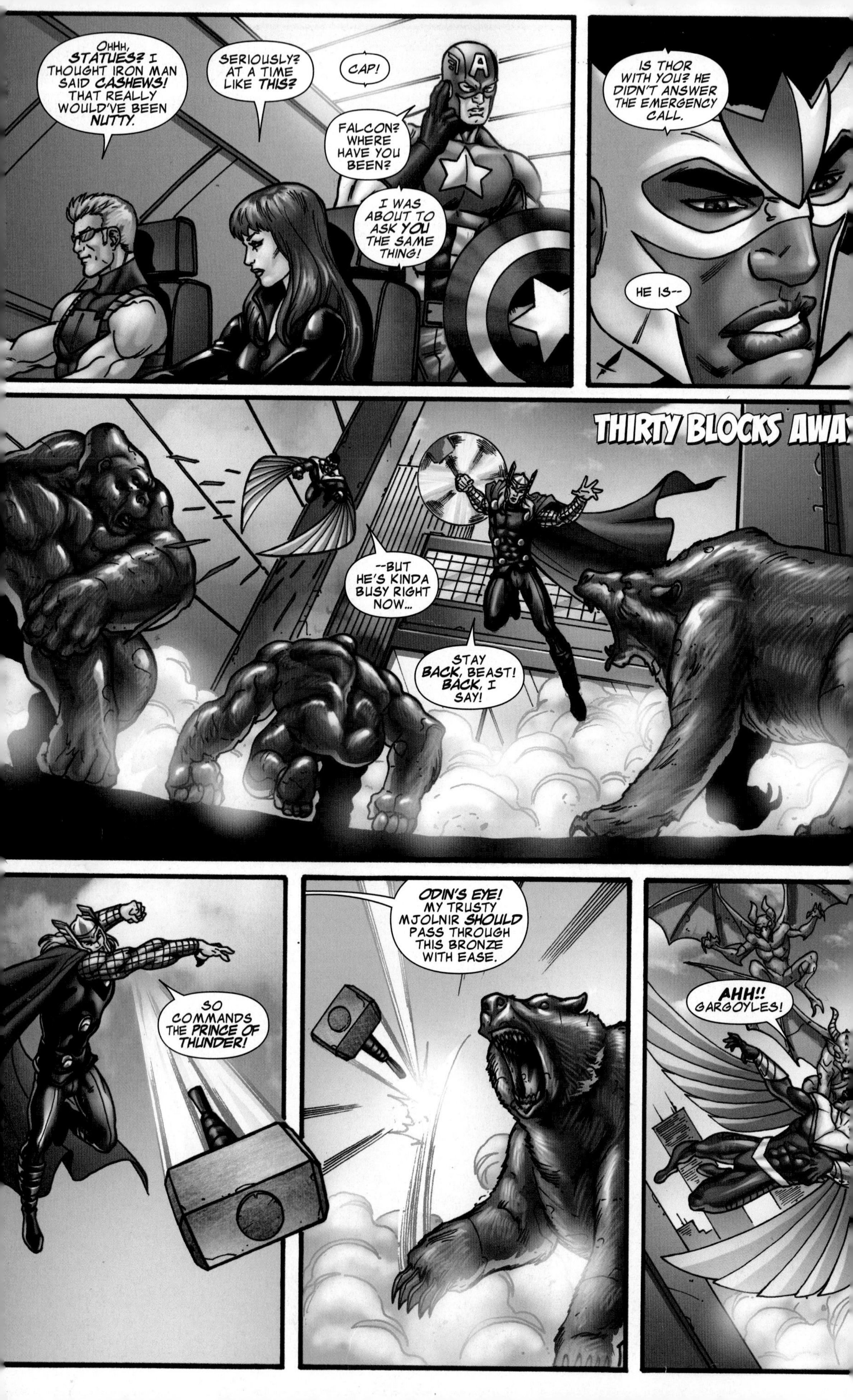
OHHH, STATUES? I THOUGHT IRON MAN SAID CASHEWS! THAT REALLY WOULD'VE BEEN NUTTY.
SERIOUSLY? AT A TIME LIKE THIS?
CAP!
FALCON? WHERE HAVE YOU BEEN?
I WAS ABOUT TO ASK YOU THE SAME THING!
IS THOR WITH YOU? HE DIDN'T ANSWER THE EMERGENCY CALL.
HE IS--
THIRTY BLOCKS AWA
--BUT HE'S KINDA BUSY RIGHT NOW...
STAY BACK, BEAST! BACK, I SAY!
SO COMMANDS THE PRINCE OF THUNDER!
ODIN'S EYE! MY TRUSTY MJOLNIR SHOULD PASS THROUGH THIS BRONZE WITH EASE.
AHH!! GARGOYLES!

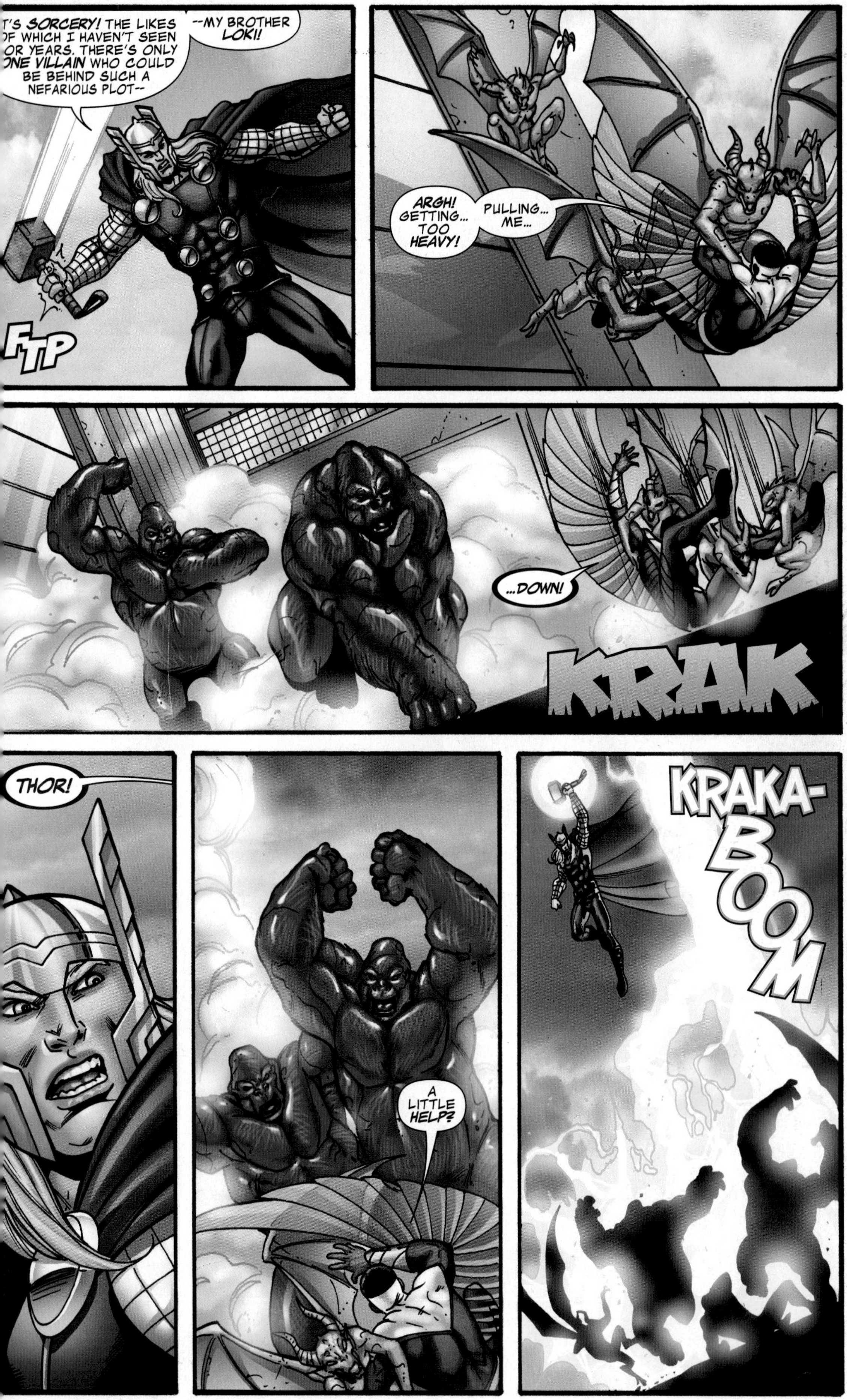

T'S SORCERY! THE LIKES OF WHICH I HAVEN'T SEEN OR YEARS. THERE'S ONLY ONE VILLAIN WHO COULD BE BEHIND SUCH A NEFARIOUS PLOT--
--MY BROTHER LOKI!
FTP
ARGH! GETTING... TOO HEAVY!
PULLING... ME...
...DOWN!
KRAK
THOR!
A LITTLE HELP?
KRAKA-BOOM

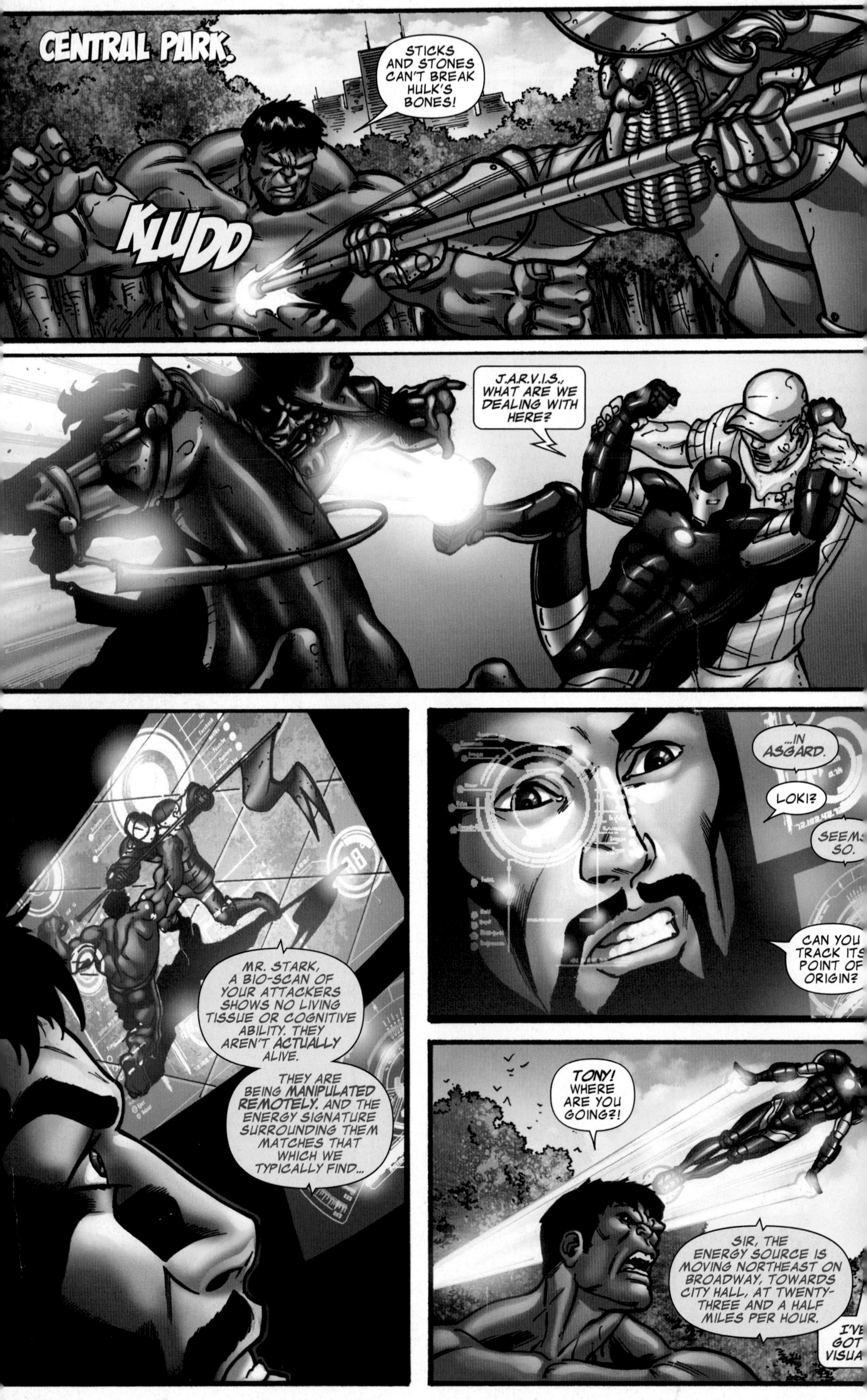
CENTRAL PARK.
STICKS AND STONES CAN'T BREAK HULK'S BONES!
KLUDD
J.A.R.V.I.S., WHAT ARE WE DEALING WITH HERE?
MR. STARK, A BIO-SCAN OF YOUR ATTACKERS SHOWS NO LIVING TISSUE OR COGNITIVE ABILITY. THEY AREN'T ACTUALLY ALIVE.
THEY ARE BEING MANIPULATED REMOTELY. AND THE ENERGY SIGNATURE SURROUNDING THEM MATCHES THAT WHICH WE TYPICALLY FIND...
...IN ASGARD.
LOKI?
SEEMS SO.
CAN YOU TRACK ITS POINT OF ORIGIN?
TONY! WHERE ARE YOU GOING?!
SIR, THE ENERGY SOURCE IS MOVING NORTHEAST ON BROADWAY, TOWARDS CITY HALL, AT TWENTY-THREE AND A HALF MILES PER HOUR.
I'VE GOT VISUA

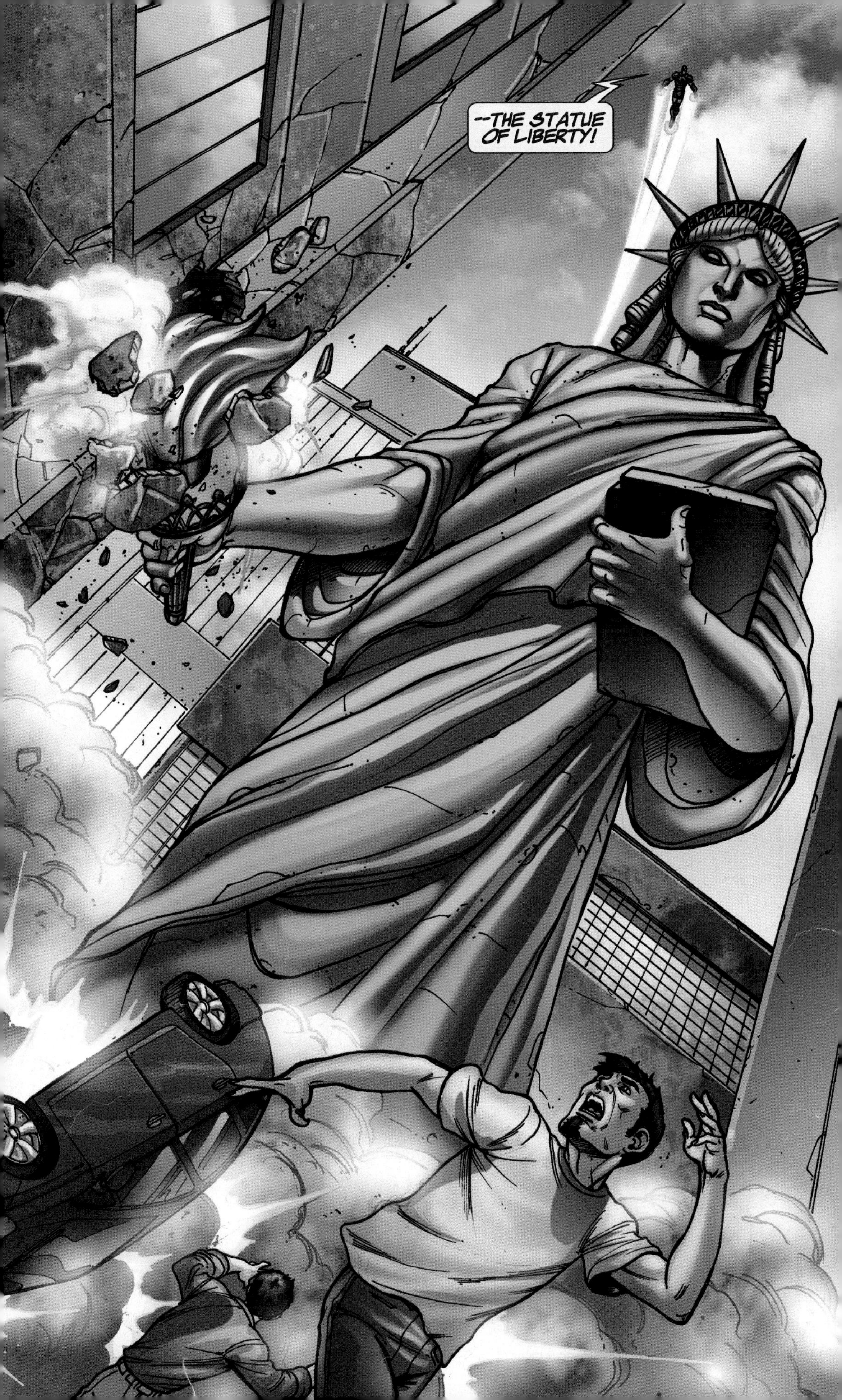
--THE STATUE OF LIBERTY!

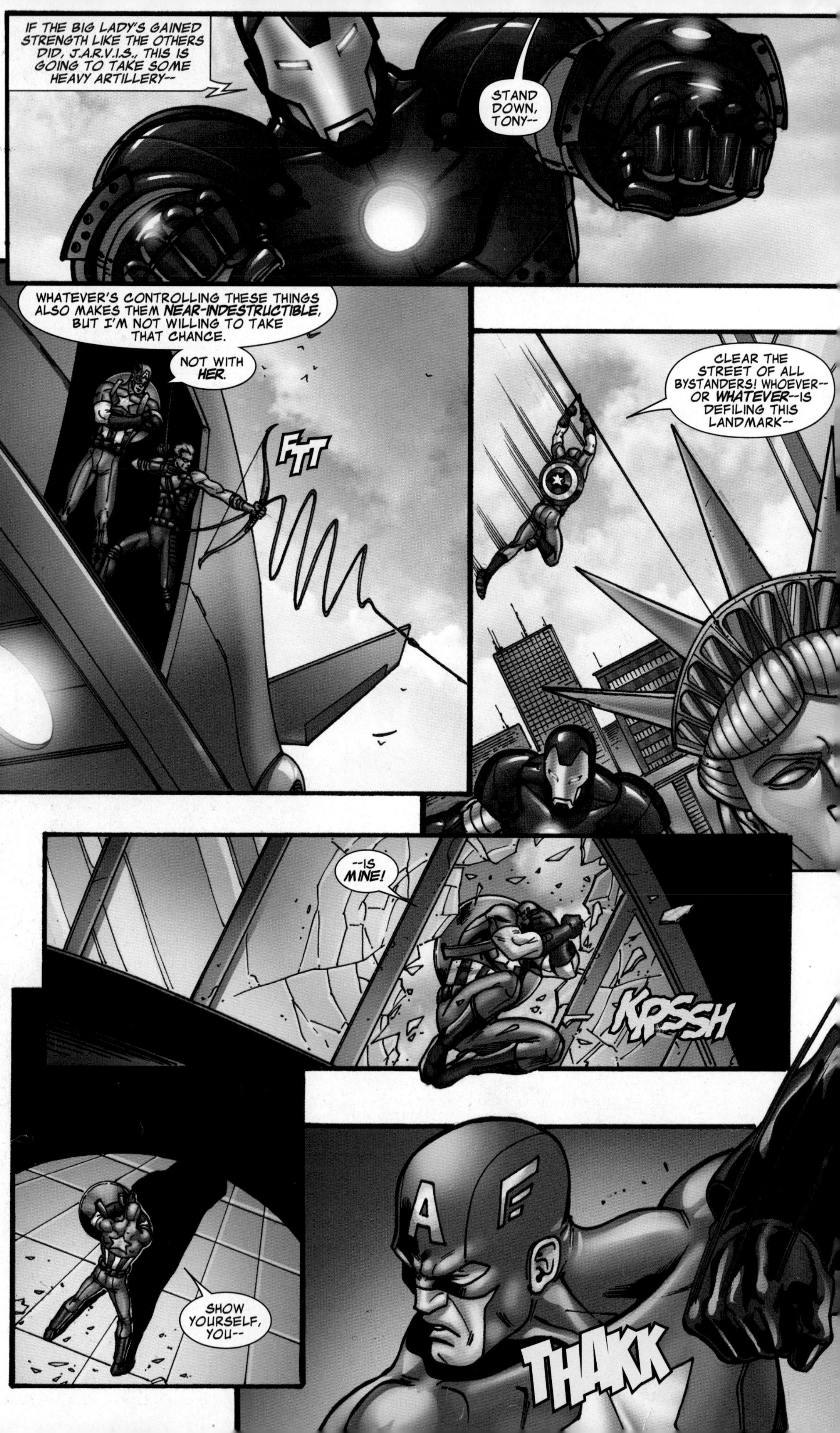

IF THE BIG LADY'S GAINED STRENGTH LIKE THE OTHERS DID, J.A.R.V.I.S., THIS IS GOING TO TAKE SOME HEAVY ARTILLERY--
STAND DOWN, TONY--
WHATEVER'S CONTROLLING THESE THINGS ALSO MAKES THEM NEAR-INDESTRUCTIBLE, BUT I'M NOT WILLING TO TAKE THAT CHANCE.
NOT WITH HER.
FTT
CLEAR THE STREET OF ALL BYSTANDERS! WHOEVER--OR WHATEVER--IS DEFILING THIS LANDMARK--
--IS MINE!
KRSSH
SHOW YOURSELF, YOU--
THAKK

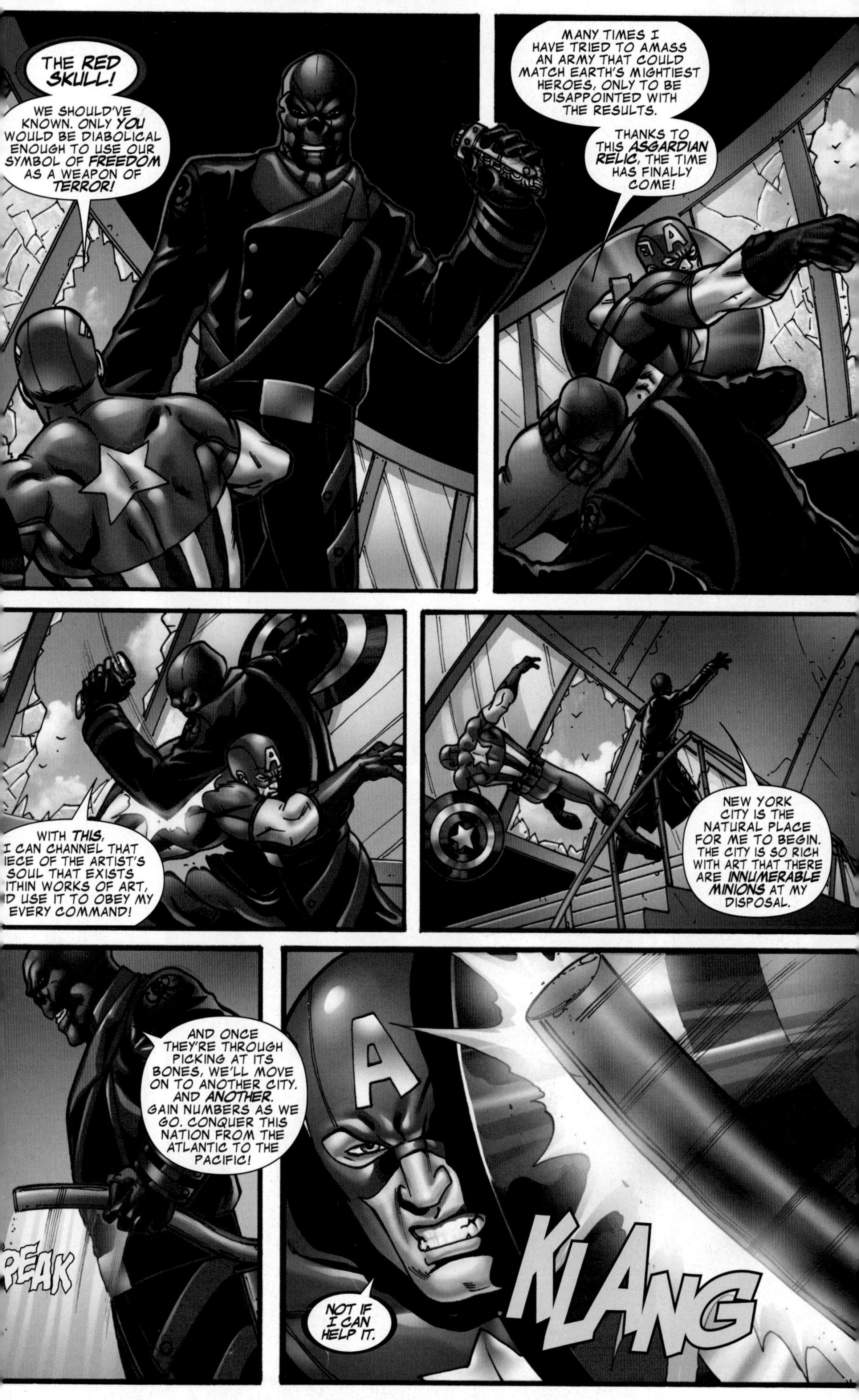
THE RED SKULL!
WE SHOULD'VE KNOWN. ONLY YOU WOULD BE DIABOLICAL ENOUGH TO USE OUR SYMBOL OF FREEDOM AS A WEAPON OF TERROR!
MANY TIMES I HAVE TRIED TO AMASS AN ARMY THAT COULD MATCH EARTH'S MIGHTIEST HEROES, ONLY TO BE DISAPPOINTED WITH THE RESULTS.
THANKS TO THIS ASGARDIAN RELIC, THE TIME HAS FINALLY COME!
WITH THIS, I CAN CHANNEL THAT IECE OF THE ARTIST'S SOUL THAT EXISTS ITHIN WORKS OF ART, D USE IT TO OBEY MY EVERY COMMAND!
NEW YORK CITY IS THE NATURAL PLACE FOR ME TO BEGIN. THE CITY IS SO RICH WITH ART THAT THERE ARE INNUMERABLE MINIONS AT MY DISPOSAL.
AND ONCE THEY'RE THROUGH PICKING AT ITS BONES, WE'LL MOVE ON TO ANOTHER CITY. AND ANOTHER. GAIN NUMBERS AS WE GO. CONQUER THIS NATION FROM THE ATLANTIC TO THE PACIFIC!
PEAK
NOT IF I CAN HELP IT.
KLANG

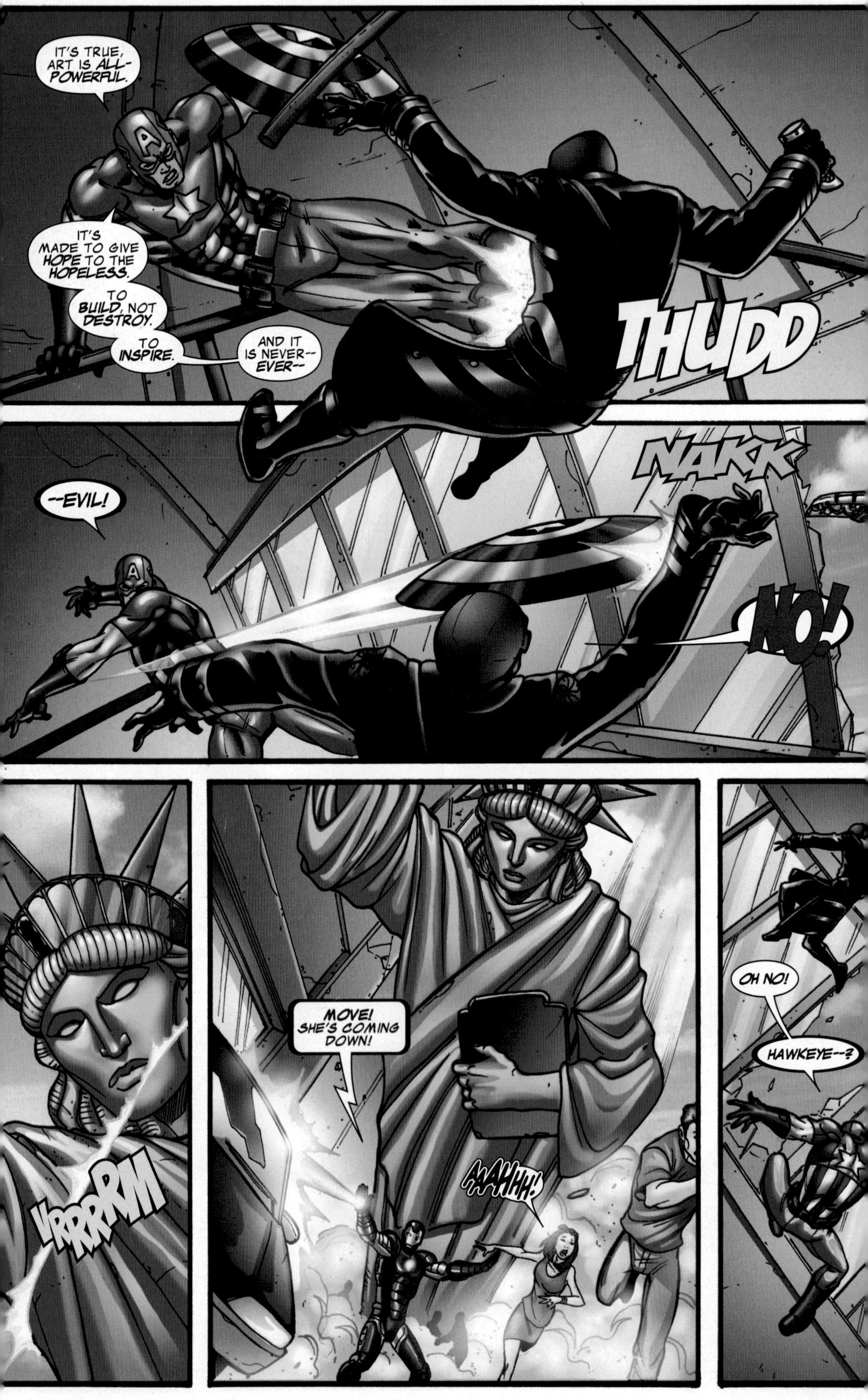
IT'S TRUE, ART IS ALL-POWERFUL.
IT'S MADE TO GIVE HOPE TO THE HOPELESS.
TO BUILD, NOT DESTROY.
TO INSPIRE.
AND IT IS NEVER-- EVER--
THUDD
NAKK
--EVIL!
NO!
VRRRRRM
MOVE! SHE'S COMING DOWN!
AAAHHH!
OH NO!
HAWKEYE--?

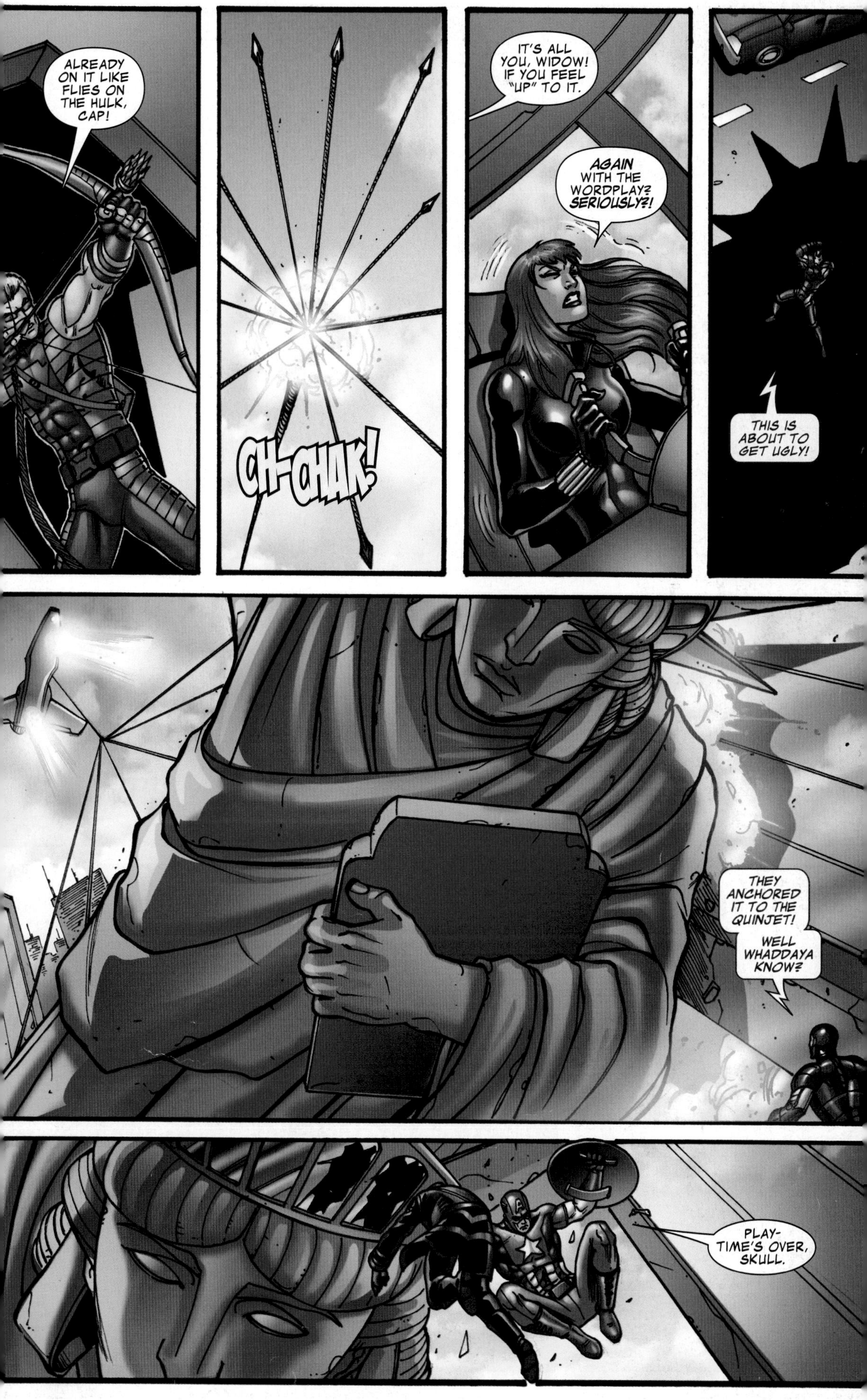
ALREADY ON IT LIKE FLIES ON THE HULK, CAP!
CH-CHAK!
IT'S ALL YOU, WIDOW! IF YOU FEEL "UP" TO IT.
AGAIN WITH THE WORDPLAY? SERIOUSLY?!
THIS IS ABOUT TO GET UGLY!
THEY ANCHORED IT TO THE QUINJET!
WELL WHADDAYA KNOW?
PLAY-TIME'S OVER, SKULL.

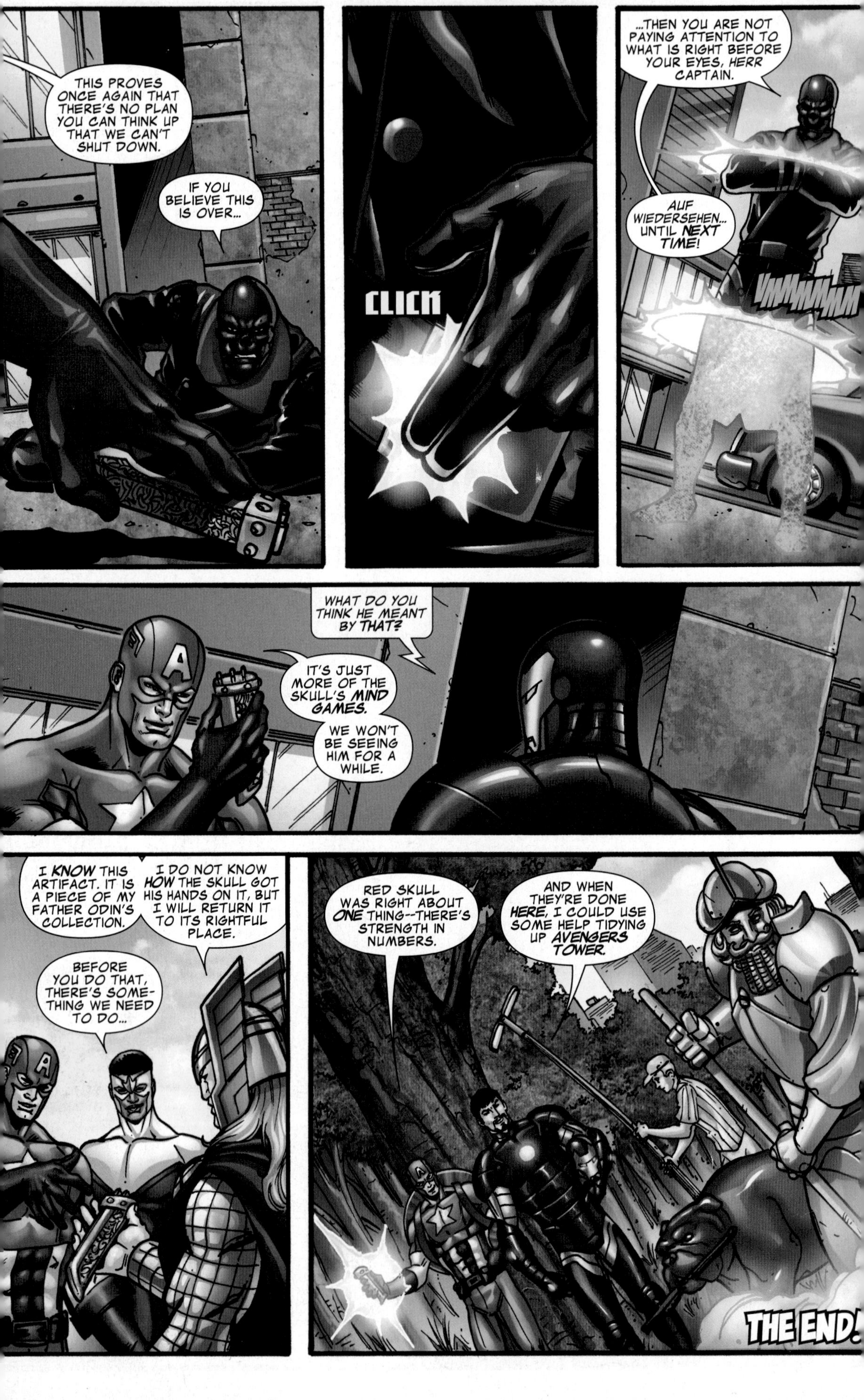
THIS PROVES ONCE AGAIN THAT THERE'S NO PLAN YOU CAN THINK UP THAT WE CAN'T SHUT DOWN.
IF YOU BELIEVE THIS IS OVER...
CLICK
...THEN YOU ARE NOT PAYING ATTENTION TO WHAT IS RIGHT BEFORE YOUR EYES, HERR CAPTAIN.
AUF WIEDERSEHEN... UNTIL NEXT TIME!
VMMMMMMM
WHAT DO YOU THINK HE MEANT BY THAT?
IT'S JUST MORE OF THE SKULL'S MIND GAMES.
WE WON'T BE SEEING HIM FOR A WHILE.
I KNOW THIS ARTIFACT. IT IS A PIECE OF MY FATHER ODIN'S COLLECTION.
I DO NOT KNOW HOW THE SKULL GOT HIS HANDS ON IT, BUT I WILL RETURN IT TO ITS RIGHTFUL PLACE.
BEFORE YOU DO THAT, THERE'S SOMETHING WE NEED TO DO...
RED SKULL WAS RIGHT ABOUT ONE THING--THERE'S STRENGTH IN NUMBERS.
AND WHEN THEY'RE DONE HERE, I COULD USE SOME HELP TIDYING UP AVENGERS TOWER.
THE END!

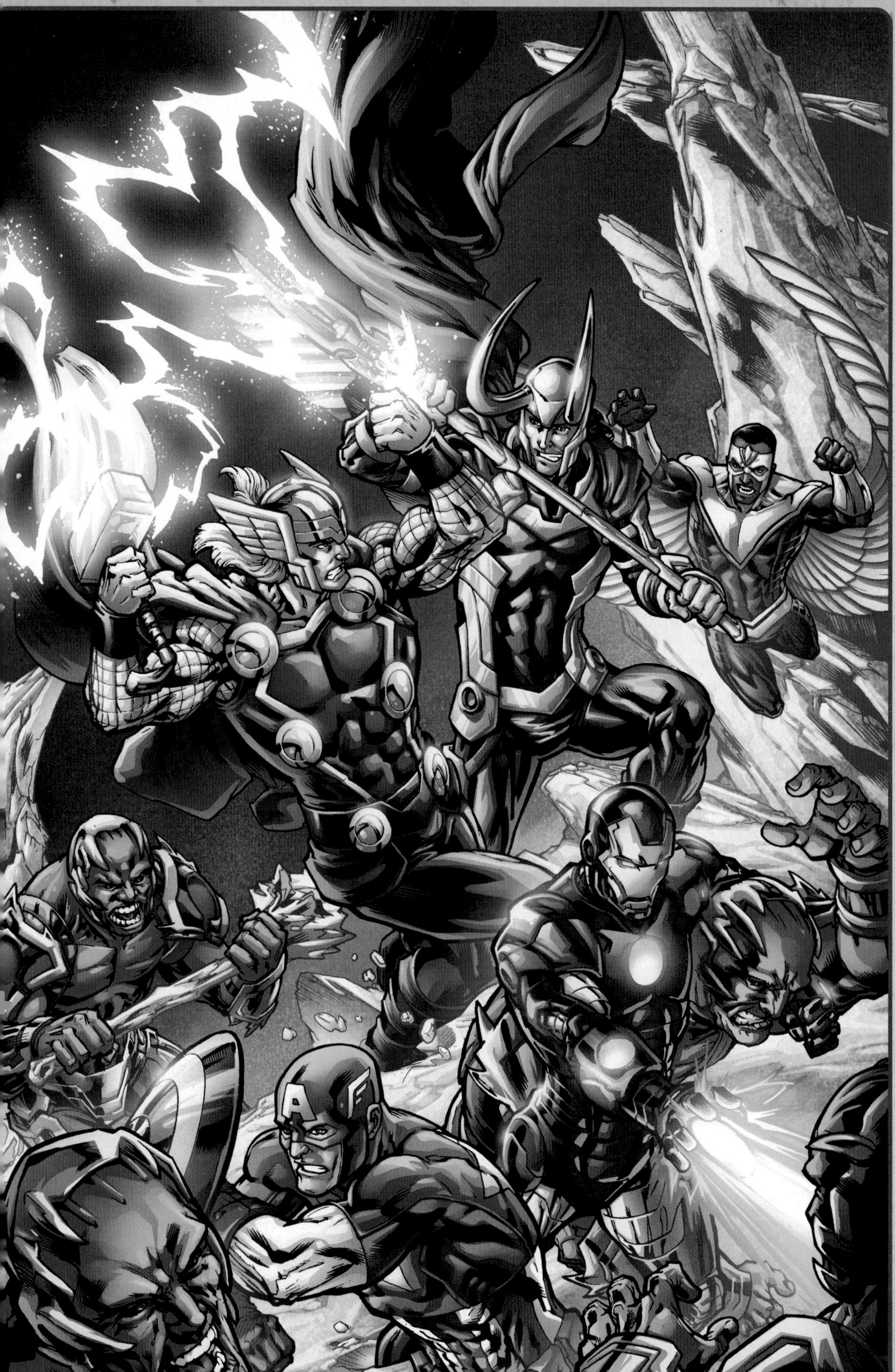

AVENGERS VS #1: ASGARD ON ICE

COVER ART BY MICHAEL RYAN & JAVIER MENA

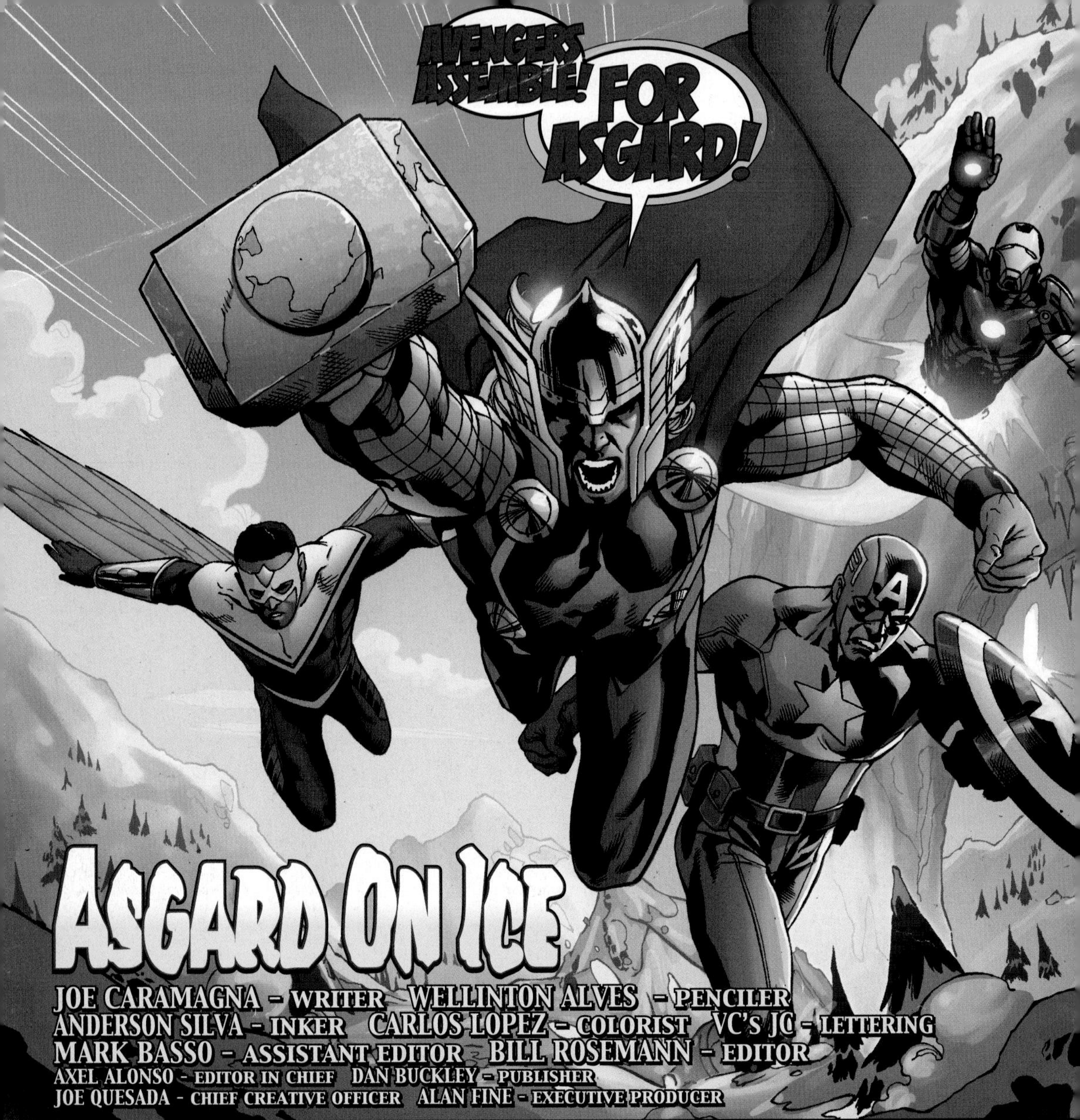
AVENGERS ASSEMBLE!
FOR ASGARD!
ASGARD ON ICE
JOE CARAMAGNA - WRITER WELLINTON ALVES - PENCILER
ANDERSON SILVA - INKER CARLOS LOPEZ - COLORIST VC's JC - LETTERING
MARK BASSO - ASSISTANT EDITOR BILL ROSEMANN - EDITOR
AXEL ALONSO - EDITOR IN CHIEF DAN BUCKLEY - PUBLISHER
JOE QUESADA - CHIEF CREATIVE OFFICER ALAN FINE - EXECUTIVE PRODUCER

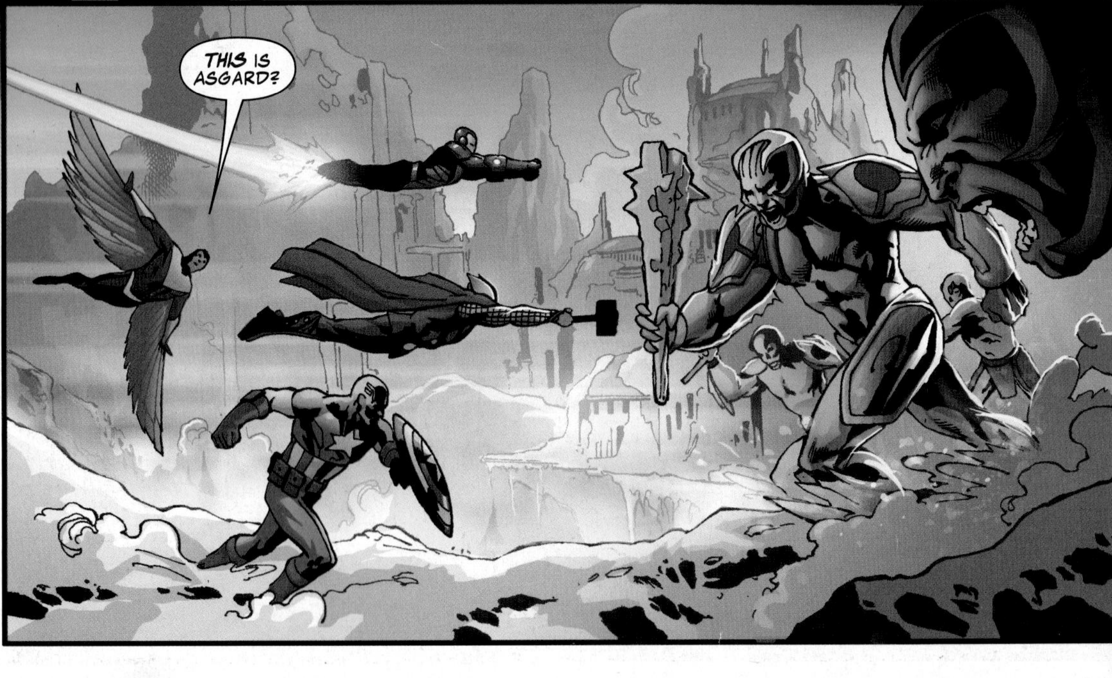
THIS IS ASGARD?

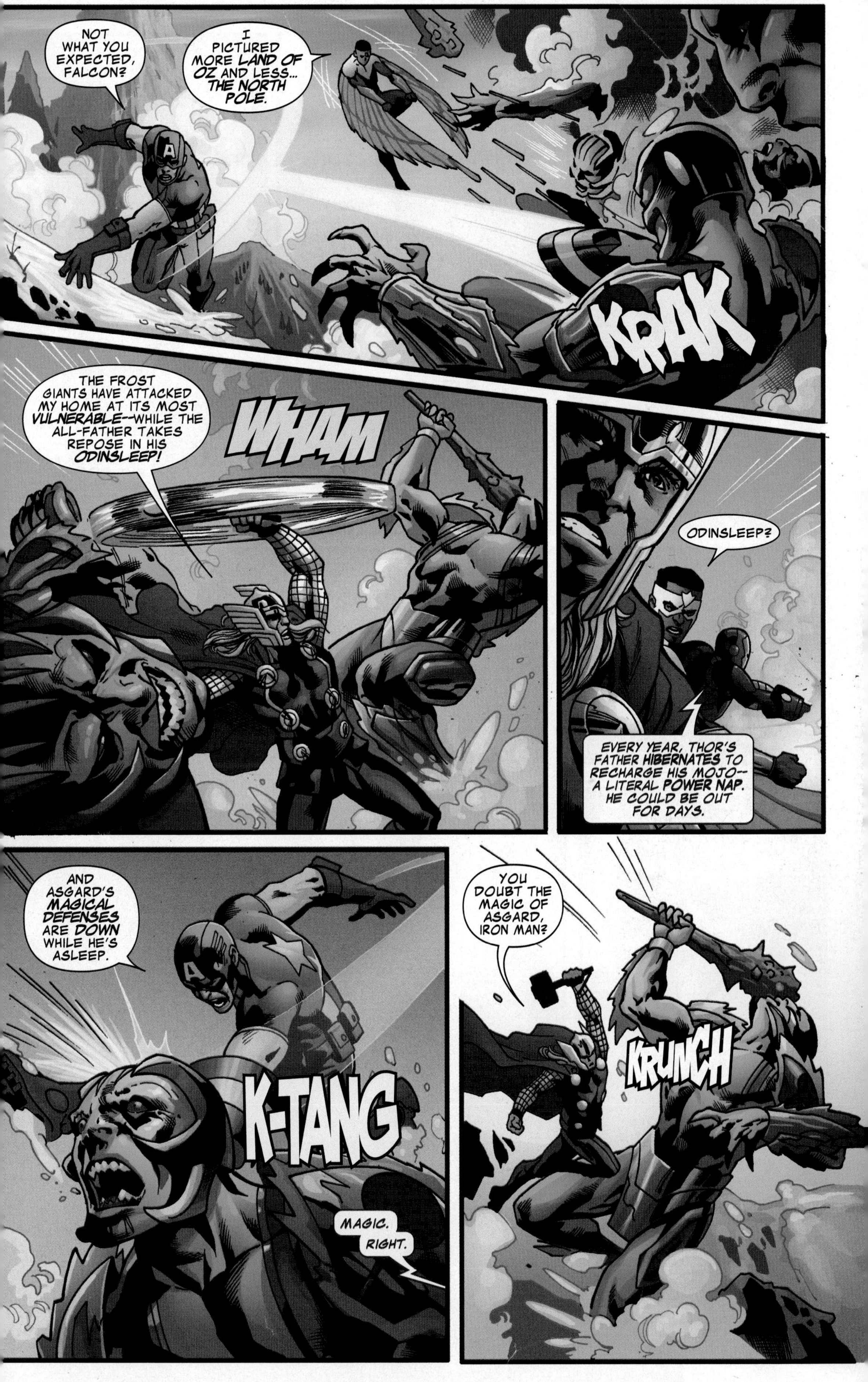
NOT WHAT YOU EXPECTED, FALCON?
I PICTURED MORE LAND OF OZ AND LESS... THE NORTH POLE.
KRAK
THE FROST GIANTS HAVE ATTACKED MY HOME AT ITS MOST VULNERABLE--WHILE THE ALL-FATHER TAKES REPOSE IN HIS ODINSLEEP!
WHAM
ODINSLEEP?
EVERY YEAR, THOR'S FATHER HIBERNATES TO RECHARGE HIS MOJO-- A LITERAL POWER NAP. HE COULD BE OUT FOR DAYS.
AND ASGARD'S MAGICAL DEFENSES ARE DOWN WHILE HE'S ASLEEP.
K-TANG
MAGIC.
RIGHT.
YOU DOUBT THE MAGIC OF ASGARD, IRON MAN?
KRUNCH

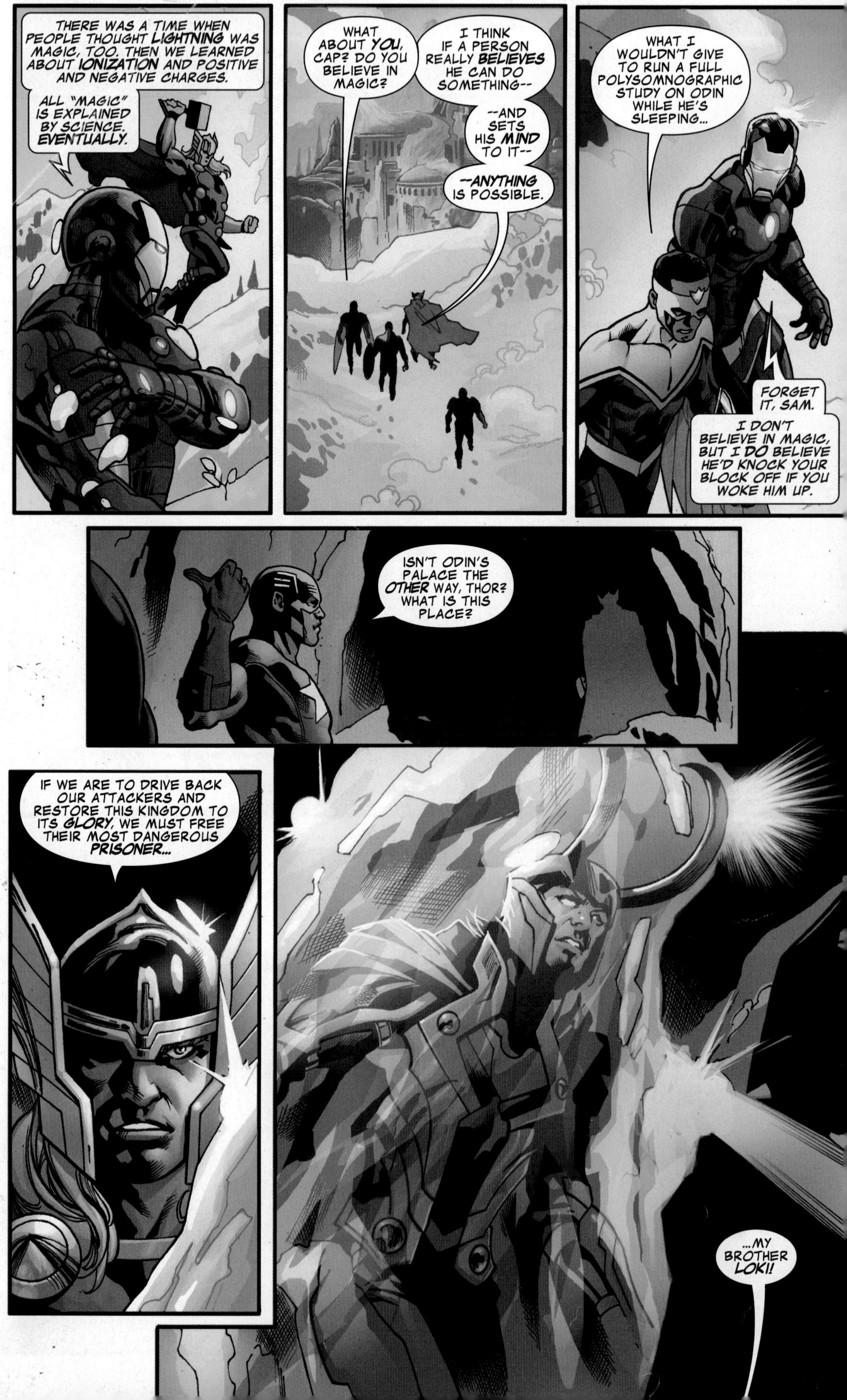
THERE WAS A TIME WHEN PEOPLE THOUGHT LIGHTNING WAS MAGIC, TOO. THEN WE LEARNED ABOUT IONIZATION AND POSITIVE AND NEGATIVE CHARGES.
ALL "MAGIC" IS EXPLAINED BY SCIENCE. EVENTUALLY.
WHAT ABOUT YOU, CAP? DO YOU BELIEVE IN MAGIC?
I THINK IF A PERSON REALLY BELIEVES HE CAN DO SOMETHING--
--AND SETS HIS MIND TO IT--
--ANYTHING IS POSSIBLE.
WHAT I WOULDN'T GIVE TO RUN A FULL POLYSOMNOGRAPHIC STUDY ON ODIN WHILE HE'S SLEEPING...
FORGET IT, SAM.
I DON'T BELIEVE IN MAGIC, BUT I DO BELIEVE HE'D KNOCK YOUR BLOCK OFF IF YOU WOKE HIM UP.
ISN'T ODIN'S PALACE THE OTHER WAY, THOR? WHAT IS THIS PLACE?
IF WE ARE TO DRIVE BACK OUR ATTACKERS AND RESTORE THIS KINGDOM TO ITS GLORY, WE MUST FREE THEIR MOST DANGEROUS PRISONER...
...MY BROTHER LOKI!

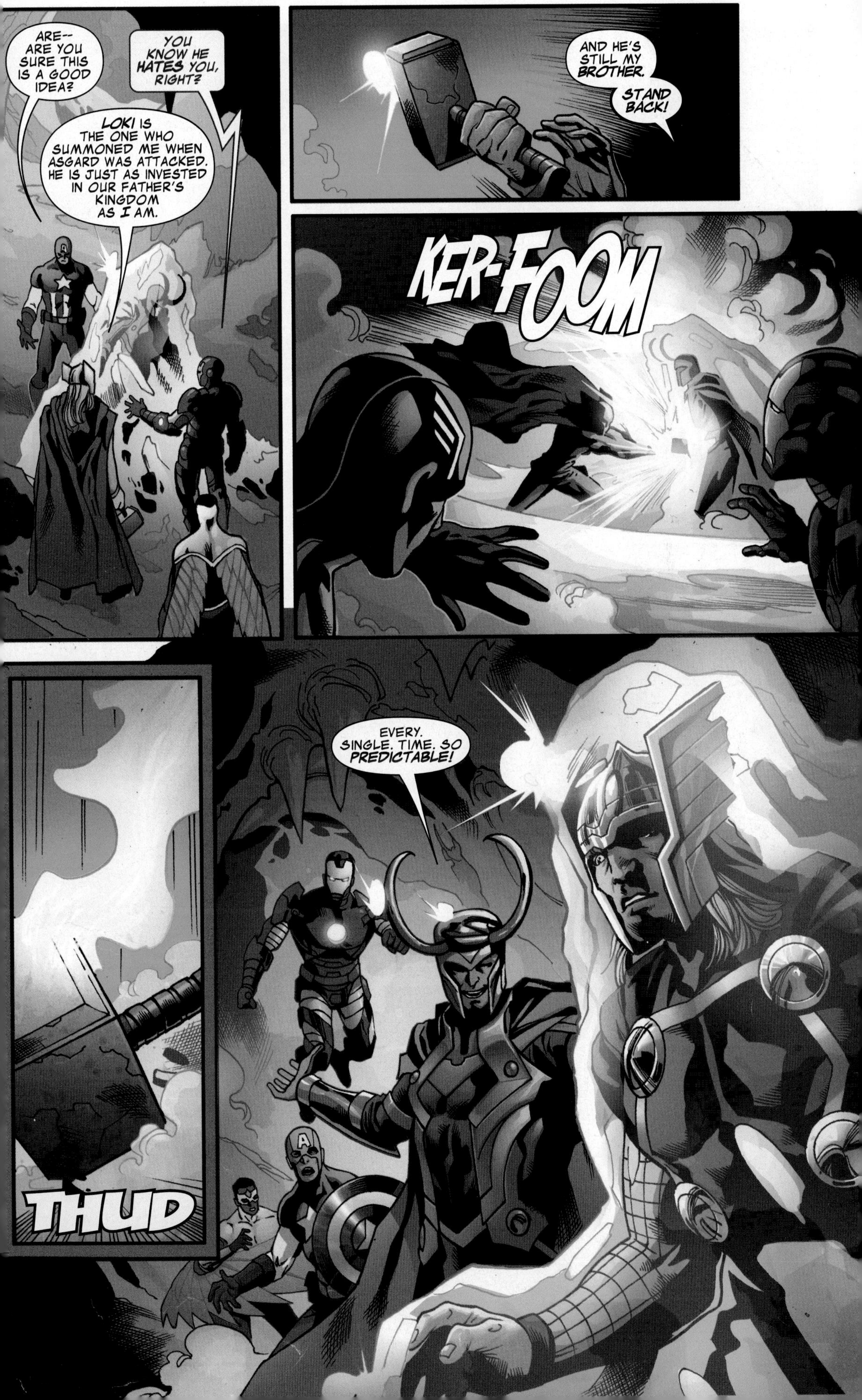
ARE-- ARE YOU SURE THIS IS A GOOD IDEA?
YOU KNOW HE HATES YOU, RIGHT?
LOKI IS THE ONE WHO SUMMONED ME WHEN ASGARD WAS ATTACKED. HE IS JUST AS INVESTED IN OUR FATHER'S KINGDOM AS I AM.
AND HE'S STILL MY BROTHER.
STAND BACK!
KER-FOOM
THUD
EVERY. SINGLE. TIME. SO PREDICTABLE!

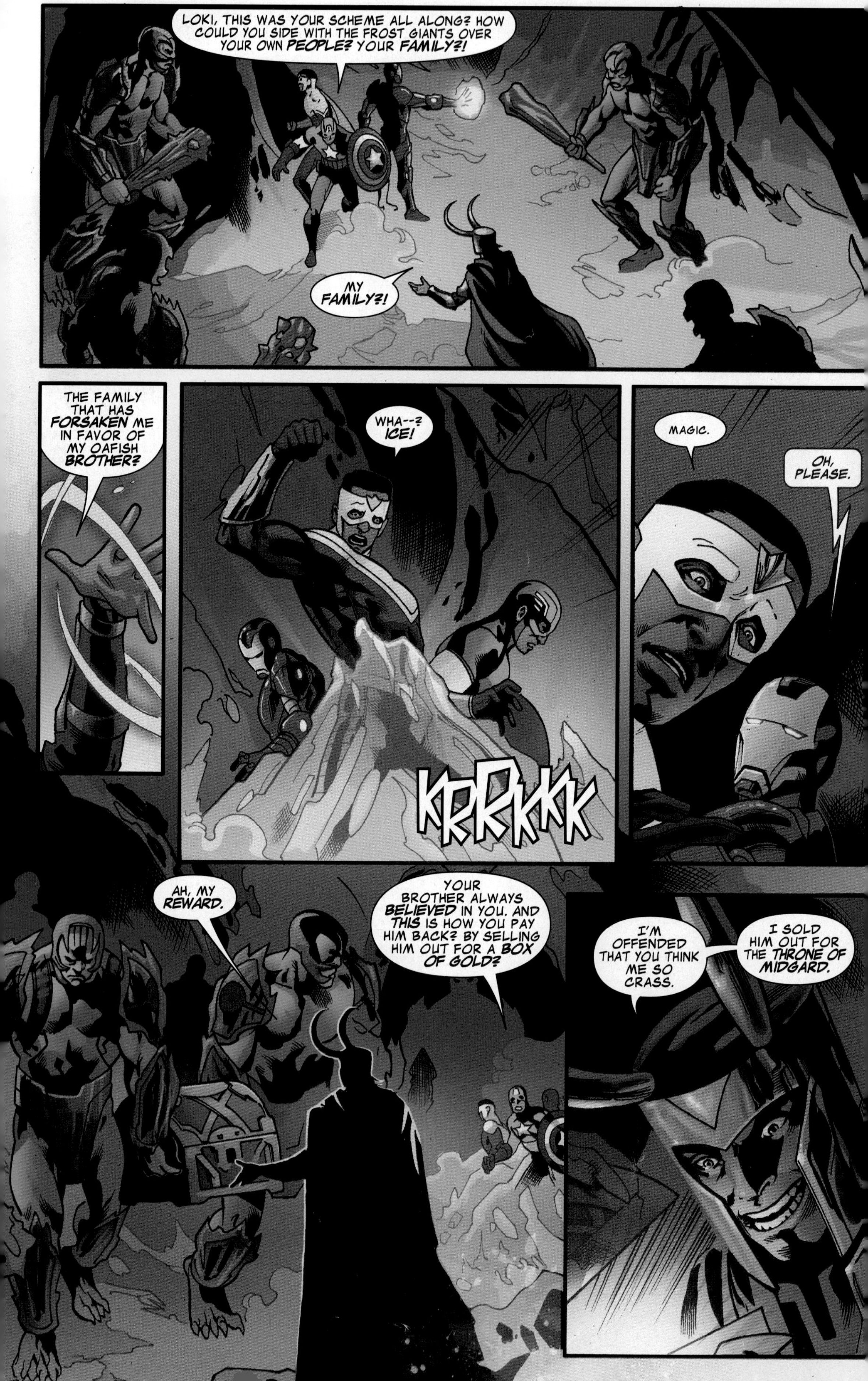
LOKI, THIS WAS YOUR SCHEME ALL ALONG? HOW COULD YOU SIDE WITH THE FROST GIANTS OVER YOUR OWN PEOPLE? YOUR FAMILY?!
MY FAMILY?!
THE FAMILY THAT HAS FORSAKEN ME IN FAVOR OF MY OAFISH BROTHER?
WHA--? ICE!
KRRKKK
MAGIC.
OH, PLEASE.
AH, MY REWARD.
YOUR BROTHER ALWAYS BELIEVED IN YOU. AND THIS IS HOW YOU PAY HIM BACK? BY SELLING HIM OUT FOR A BOX OF GOLD?
I'M OFFENDED THAT YOU THINK ME SO CRASS.
I SOLD HIM OUT FOR THE THRONE OF MIDGARD.

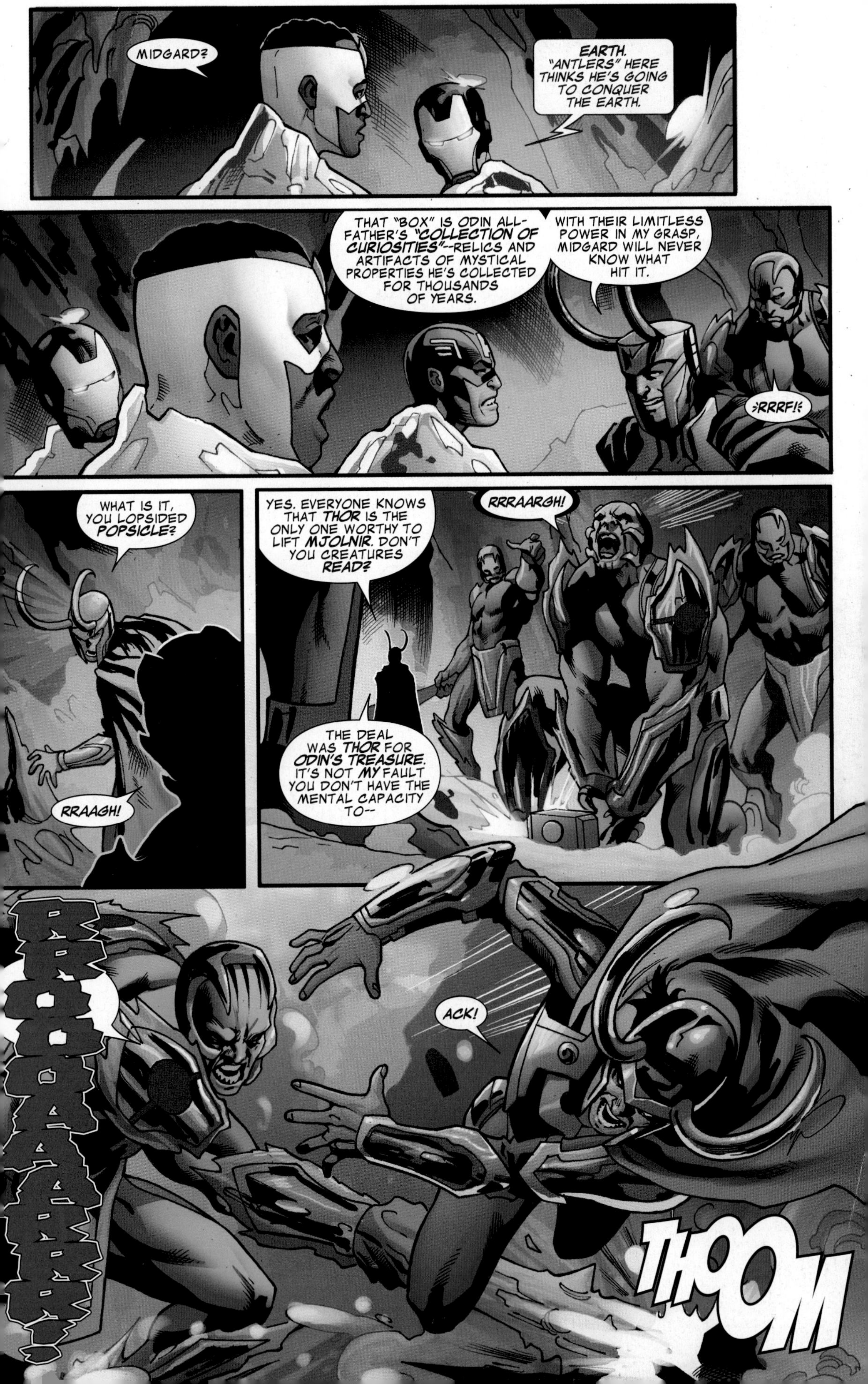
MIDGARD?
EARTH. "ANTLERS" HERE THINKS HE'S GOING TO CONQUER THE EARTH.
THAT "BOX" IS ODIN ALL-FATHER'S "COLLECTION OF CURIOSITIES"--RELICS AND ARTIFACTS OF MYSTICAL PROPERTIES HE'S COLLECTED FOR THOUSANDS OF YEARS.
WITH THEIR LIMITLESS POWER IN MY GRASP, MIDGARD WILL NEVER KNOW WHAT HIT IT.
RRRF!
WHAT IS IT, YOU LOPSIDED POPSICLE?
RRAAGH!
YES. EVERYONE KNOWS THAT THOR IS THE ONLY ONE WORTHY TO LIFT MJOLNIR. DON'T YOU CREATURES READ?
RRRAARGH!
THE DEAL WAS THOR FOR ODIN'S TREASURE. IT'S NOT MY FAULT YOU DON'T HAVE THE MENTAL CAPACITY TO--
ACK!
THOOM

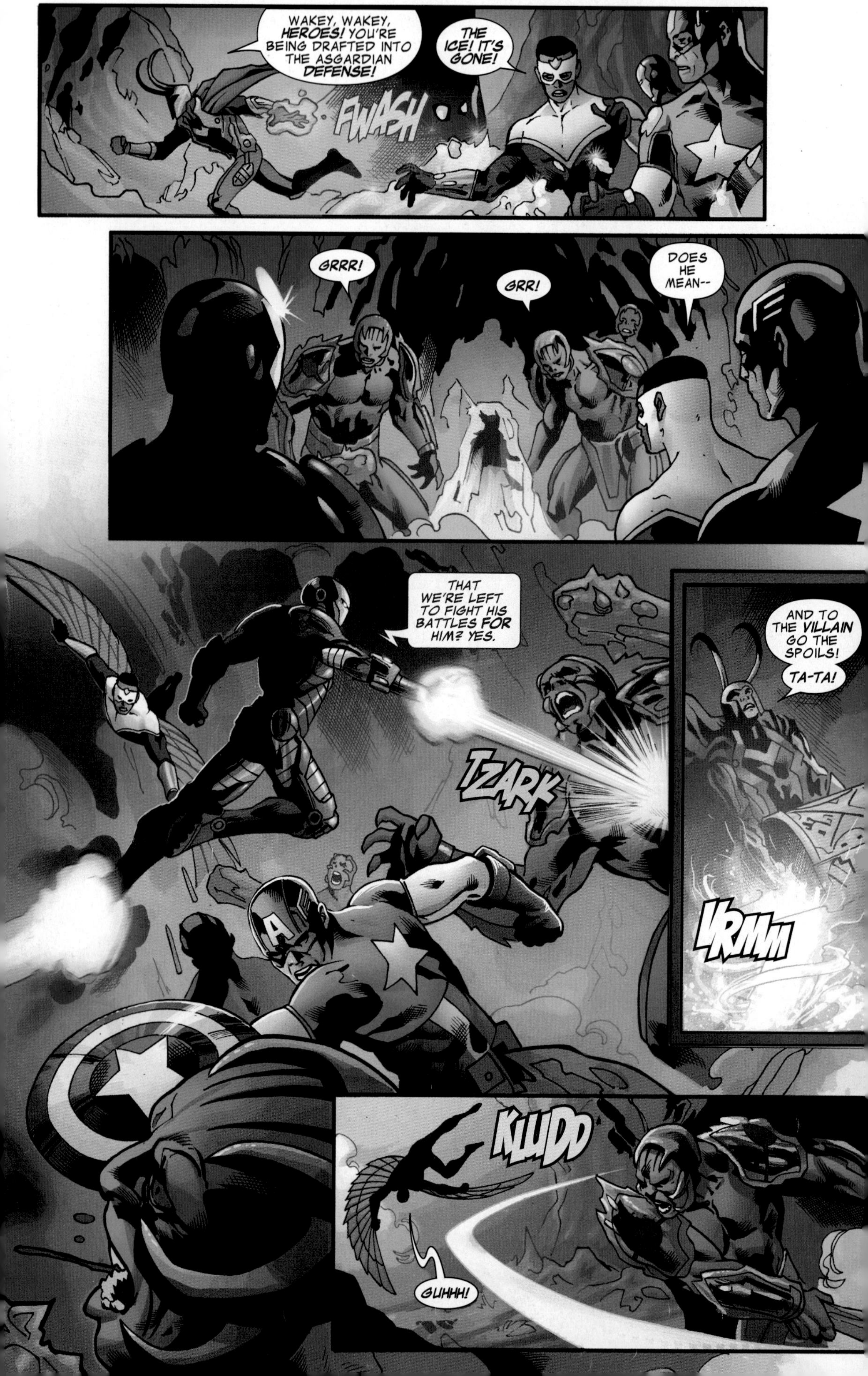

WAKEY, WAKEY, HEROES! YOU'RE BEING DRAFTED INTO THE ASGARDIAN DEFENSE!
THE ICE! IT'S GONE!
FWASH
GRRR!
GRR!
DOES HE MEAN--
THAT WE'RE LEFT TO FIGHT HIS BATTLES FOR HIM? YES.
AND TO THE VILLAIN GO THE SPOILS!
TA-TA!
TZARK
VRMM
KLUDD
GUHHH!

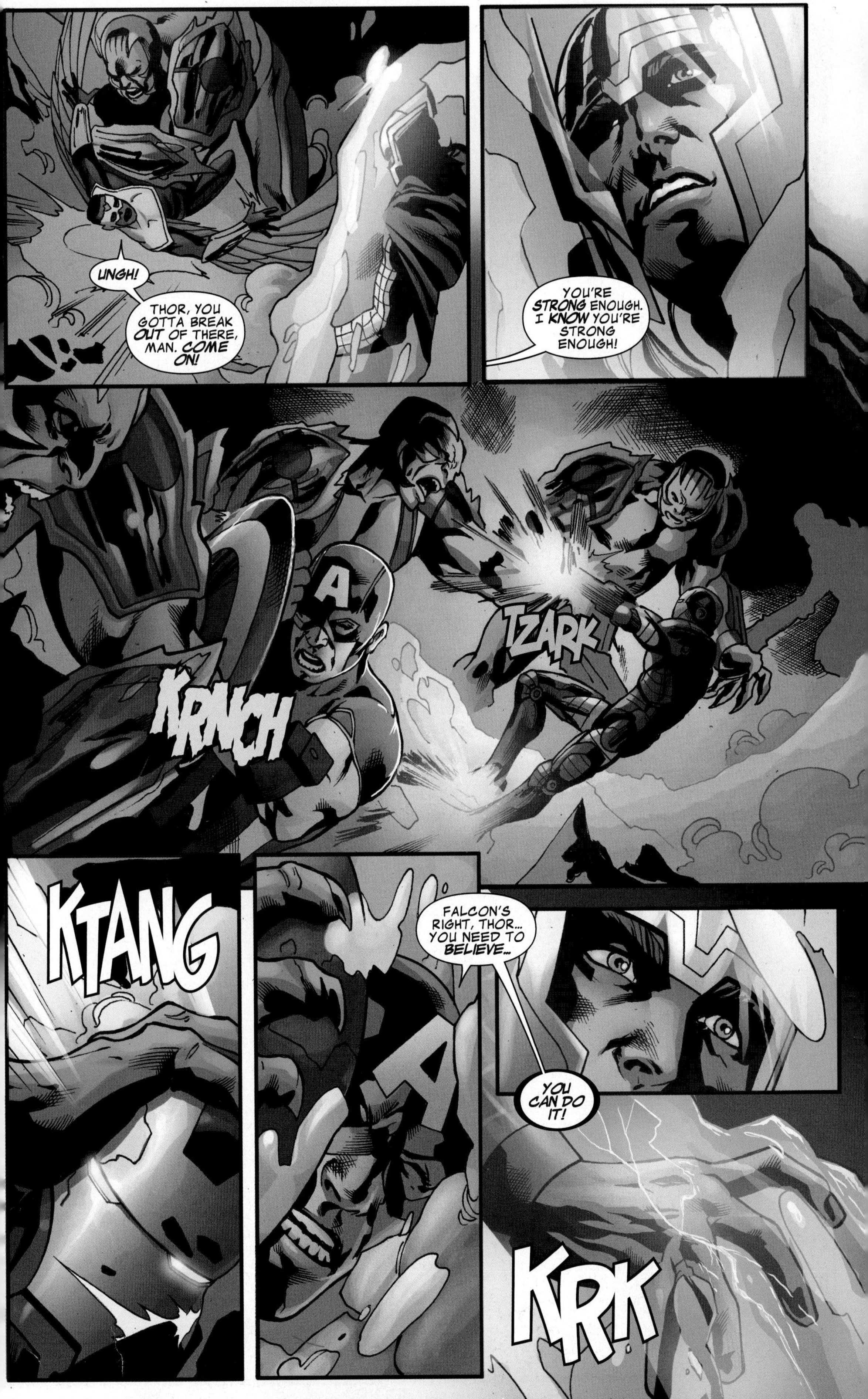
UNGH!
THOR, YOU GOTTA BREAK OUT OF THERE, MAN. COME ON!
YOU'RE STRONG ENOUGH. I KNOW YOU'RE STRONG ENOUGH!
KRNCH
TZARK
KTANG
FALCON'S RIGHT, THOR... YOU NEED TO BELIEVE...
YOU CAN DO IT!
KRK

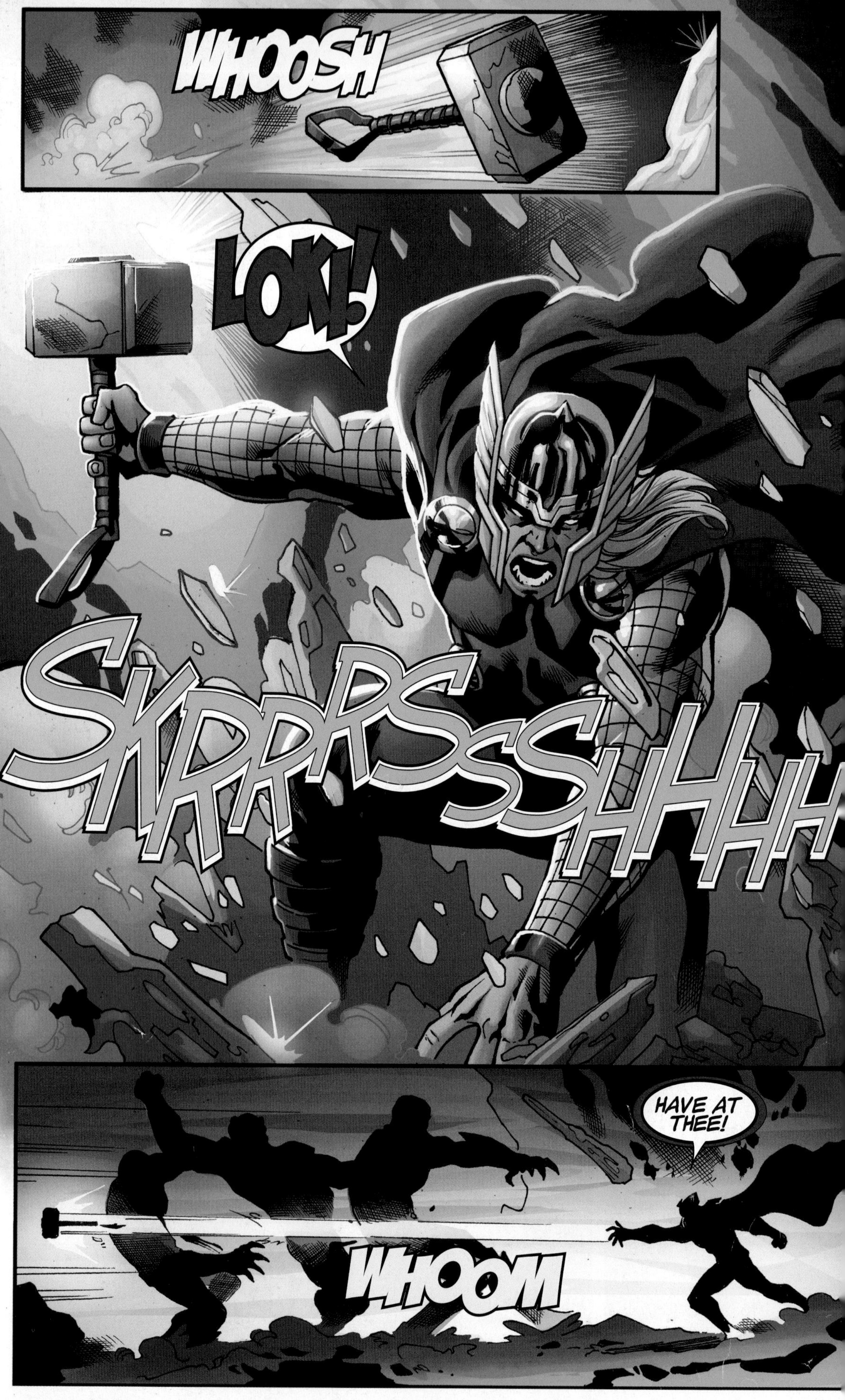
WHOOSH
LOKI!
SKRRRSSSHHHH
HAVE AT THEE!
WHOOM

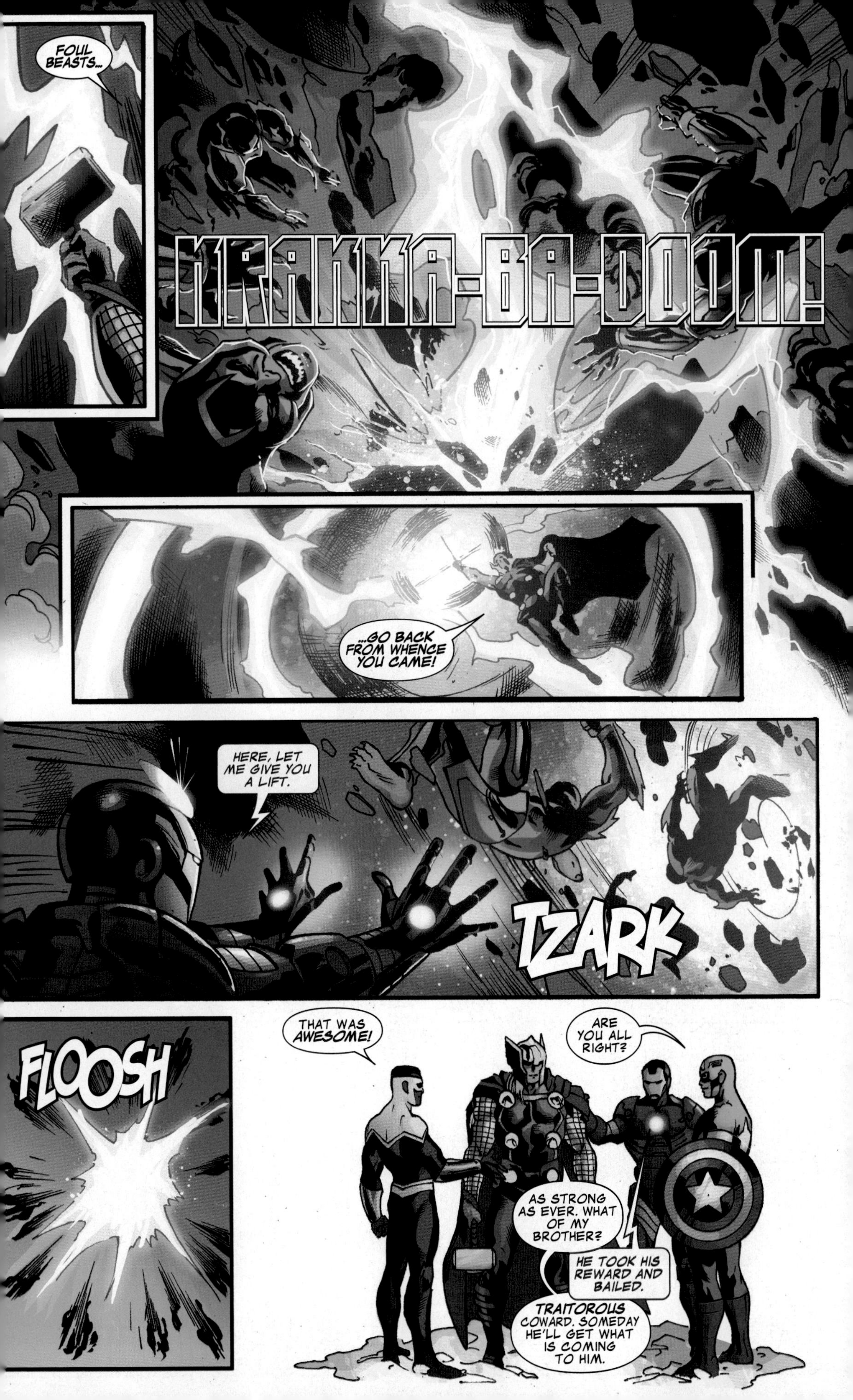
FOUL BEASTS...
KRAKKA-BA-DOOM!
...GO BACK FROM WHENCE YOU CAME!
HERE, LET ME GIVE YOU A LIFT.
TZARK
FLOOSH
THAT WAS AWESOME!
ARE YOU ALL RIGHT?
AS STRONG AS EVER. WHAT OF MY BROTHER?
HE TOOK HIS REWARD AND BAILED.
TRAITOROUS COWARD. SOMEDAY HE'LL GET WHAT IS COMING TO HIM.

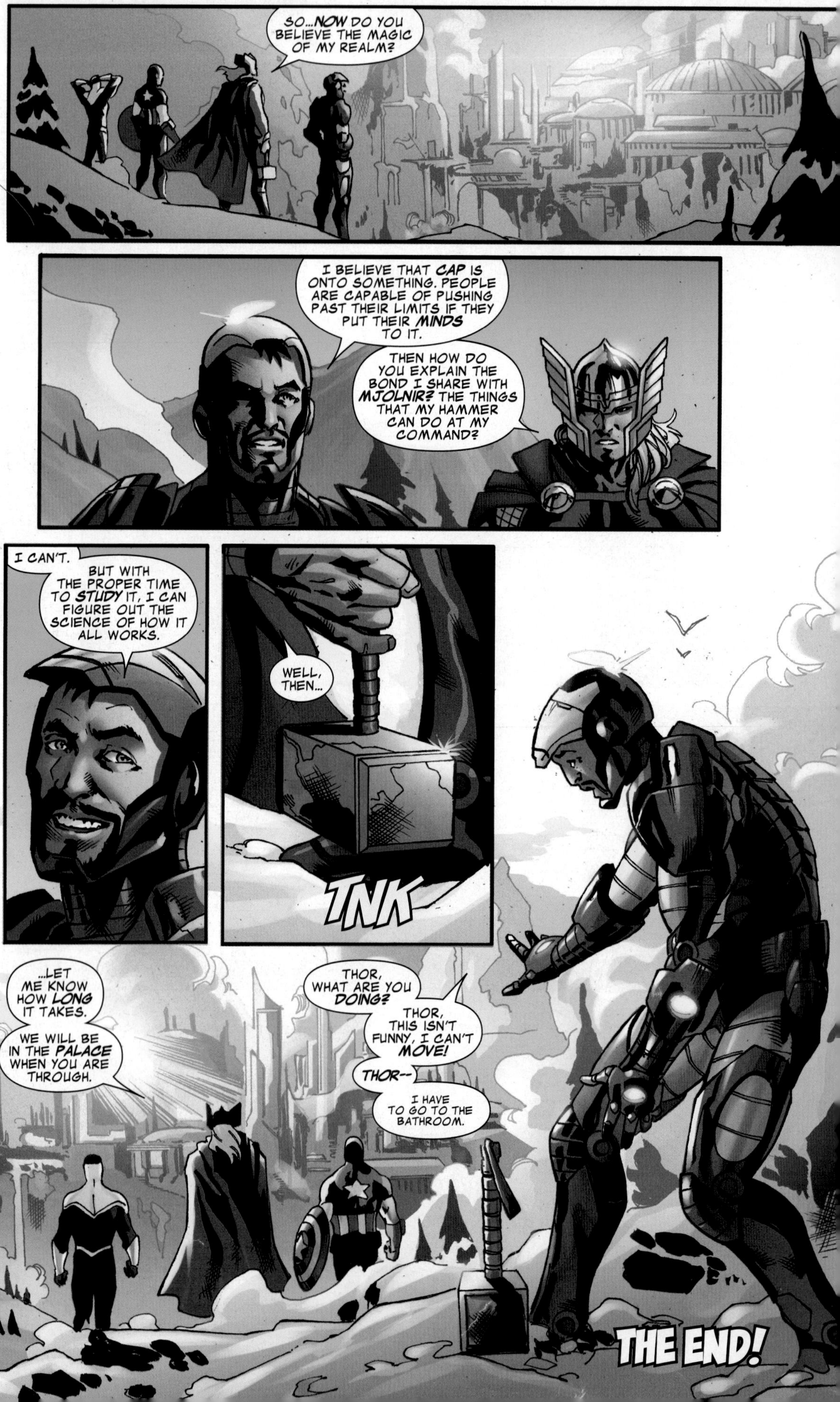

SO...NOW DO YOU BELIEVE THE MAGIC OF MY REALM?
I BELIEVE THAT CAP IS ONTO SOMETHING. PEOPLE ARE CAPABLE OF PUSHING PAST THEIR LIMITS IF THEY PUT THEIR MINDS TO IT.
THEN HOW DO YOU EXPLAIN THE BOND I SHARE WITH MJOLNIR? THE THINGS THAT MY HAMMER CAN DO AT MY COMMAND?
I CAN'T.
BUT WITH THE PROPER TIME TO STUDY IT, I CAN FIGURE OUT THE SCIENCE OF HOW IT ALL WORKS.
WELL, THEN...
TNK
...LET ME KNOW HOW LONG IT TAKES.
WE WILL BE IN THE PALACE WHEN YOU ARE THROUGH.
THOR, WHAT ARE YOU DOING?
THOR, THIS ISN'T FUNNY, I CAN'T MOVE!
THOR--
I HAVE TO GO TO THE BATHROOM.
THE END!

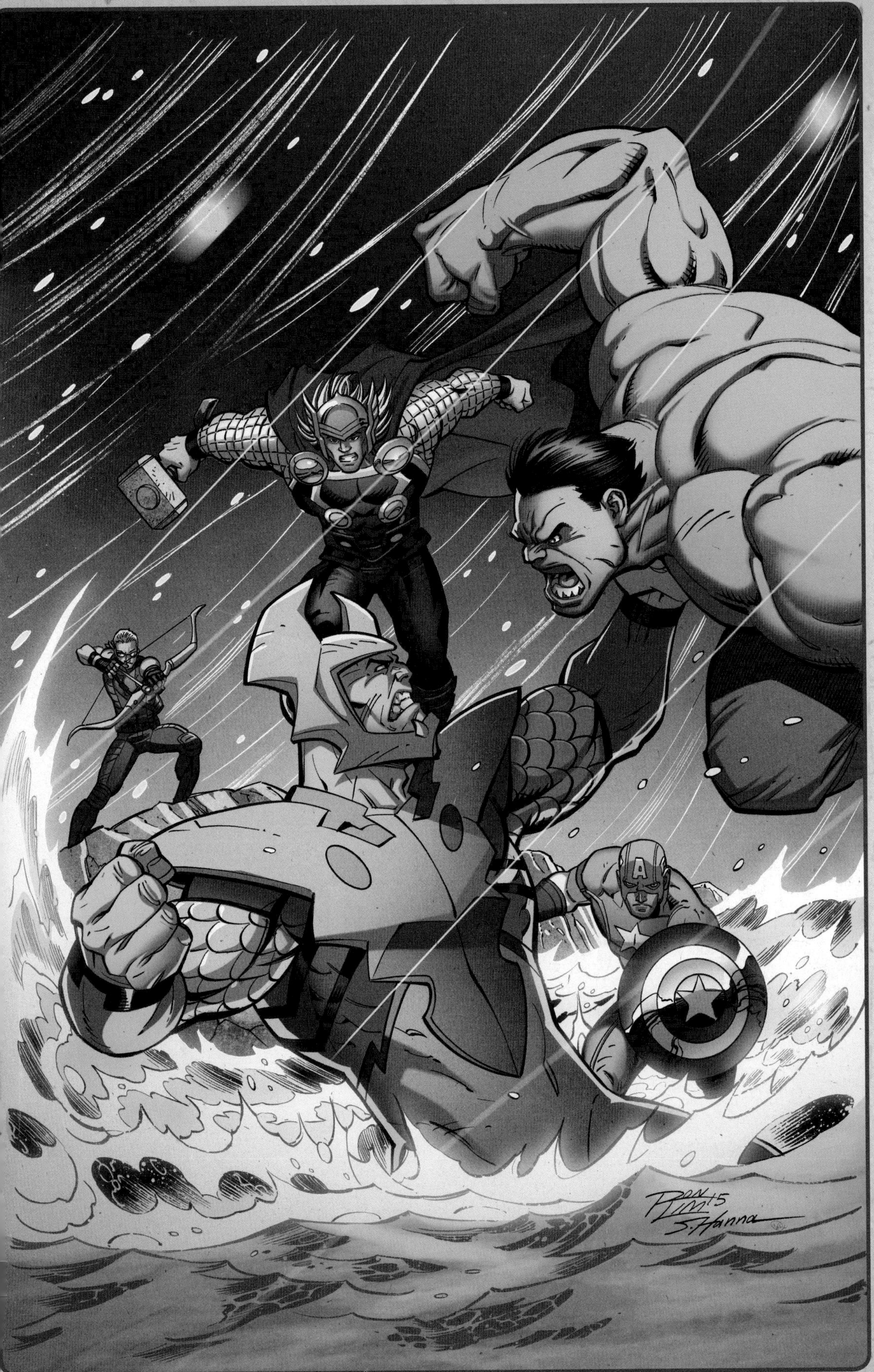

AVENGERS VS #1 : *TO TURN THE TIDE*

COVER ART BY RON LIM, SCOTT HANNA & WIL QUINTANA

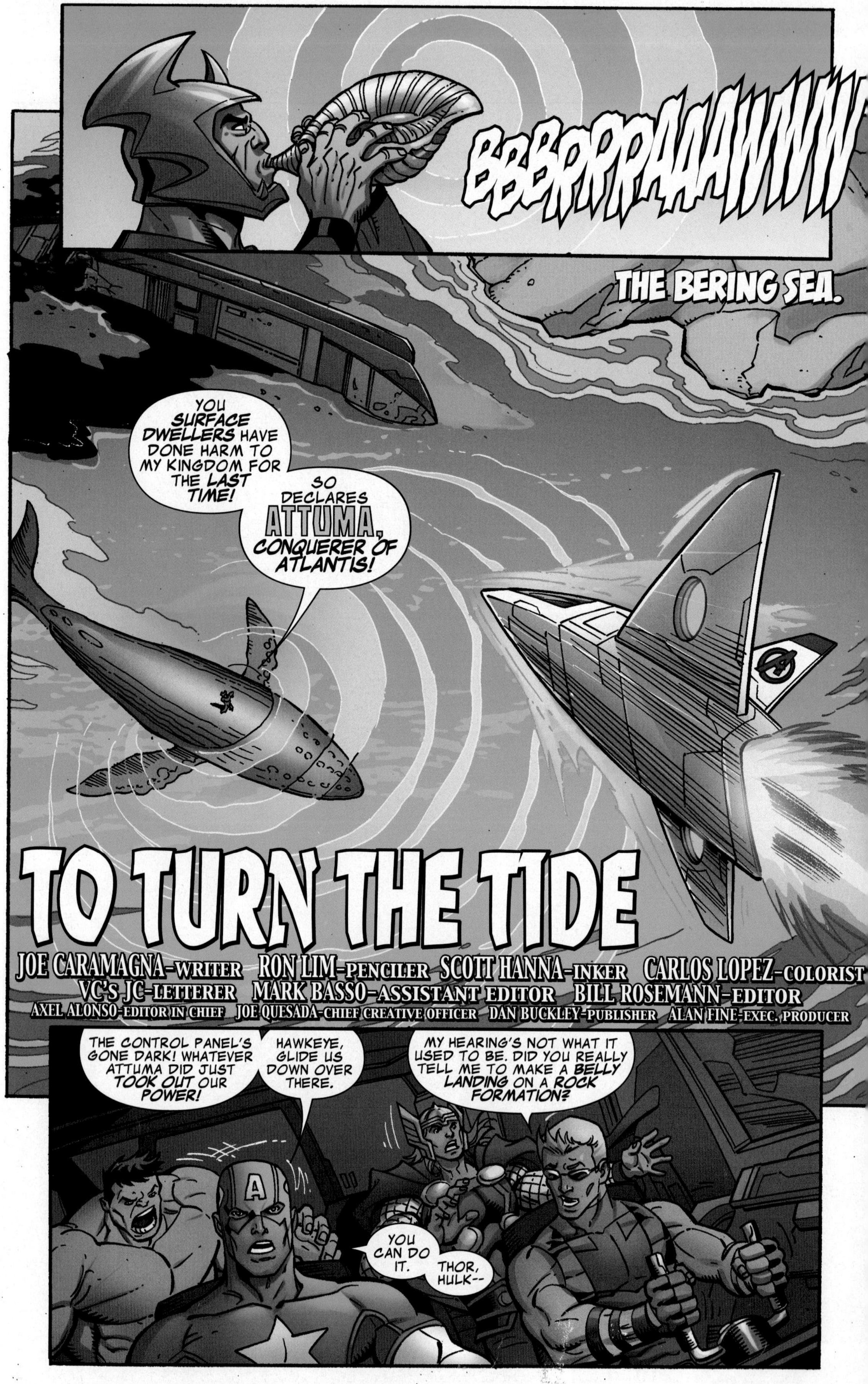
BBBRRRAAAWWW
THE BERING SEA.
YOU SURFACE DWELLERS HAVE DONE HARM TO MY KINGDOM FOR THE LAST TIME!
SO DECLARES ATTUMA, CONQUERER OF ATLANTIS!
TO TURN THE TIDE
JOE CARAMAGNA-WRITER RON LIM-PENCILER SCOTT HANNA-INKER CARLOS LOPEZ-COLORIST
VC's JC-LETTERER MARK BASSO-ASSISTANT EDITOR BILL ROSEMANN-EDITOR
AXEL ALONSO-EDITOR IN CHIEF JOE QUESADA-CHIEF CREATIVE OFFICER DAN BUCKLEY-PUBLISHER ALAN FINE-EXEC. PRODUCER
THE CONTROL PANEL'S GONE DARK! WHATEVER ATTUMA DID JUST TOOK OUT OUR POWER!
HAWKEYE, GLIDE US DOWN OVER THERE.
MY HEARING'S NOT WHAT IT USED TO BE. DID YOU REALLY TELL ME TO MAKE A BELLY LANDING ON A ROCK FORMATION?
YOU CAN DO IT.
THOR, HULK--

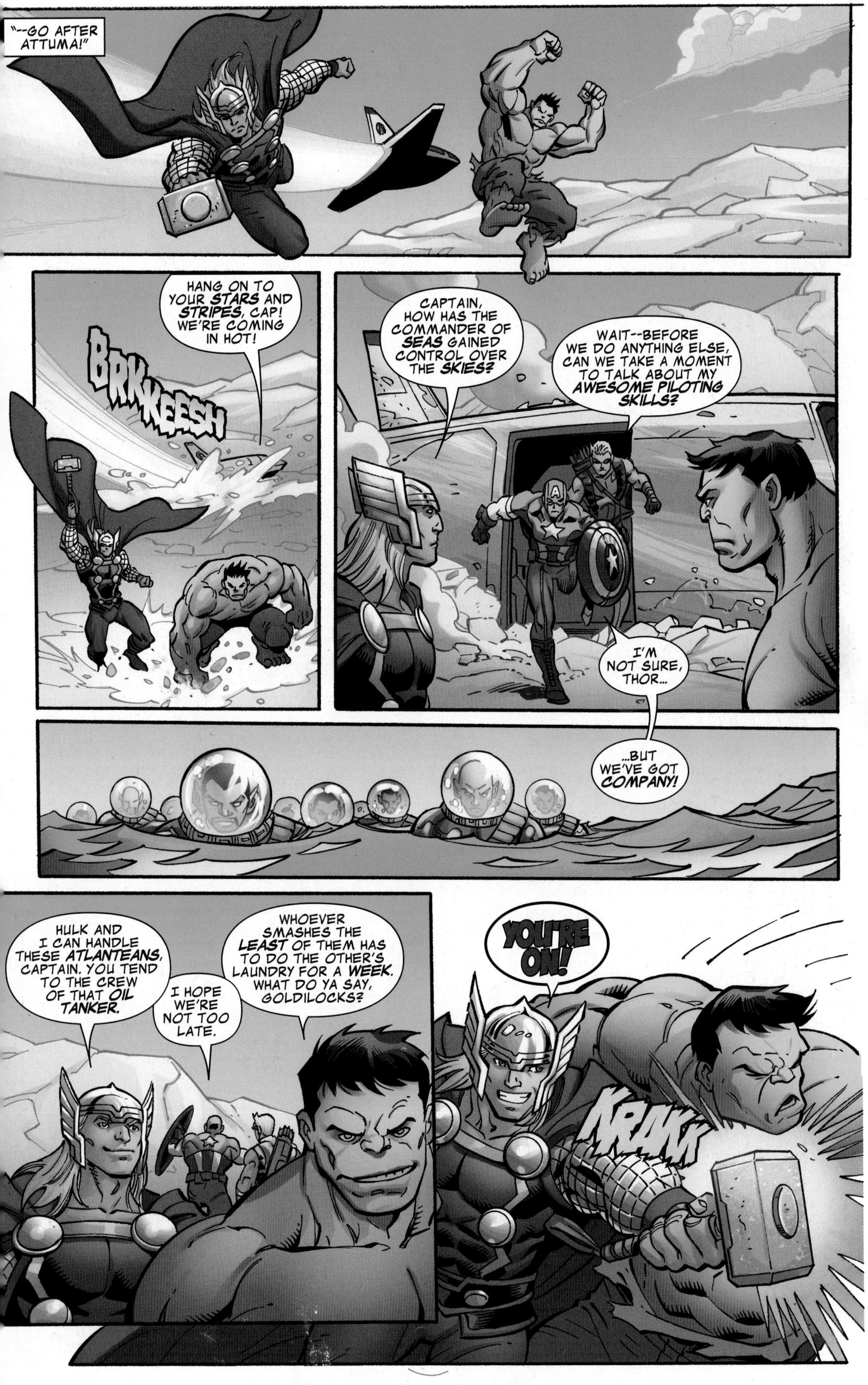
"--GO AFTER ATTUMA!"
HANG ON TO YOUR STARS AND STRIPES, CAP! WE'RE COMING IN HOT!
BRKKEESH
CAPTAIN, HOW HAS THE COMMANDER OF SEAS GAINED CONTROL OVER THE SKIES?
WAIT--BEFORE WE DO ANYTHING ELSE, CAN WE TAKE A MOMENT TO TALK ABOUT MY AWESOME PILOTING SKILLS?
I'M NOT SURE, THOR...
...BUT WE'VE GOT COMPANY!
HULK AND I CAN HANDLE THESE ATLANTEANS, CAPTAIN. YOU TEND TO THE CREW OF THAT OIL TANKER.
I HOPE WE'RE NOT TOO LATE.
WHOEVER SMASHES THE LEAST OF THEM HAS TO DO THE OTHER'S LAUNDRY FOR A WEEK. WHAT DO YA SAY, GOLDILOCKS?
YOU'RE ON!
KRAKK

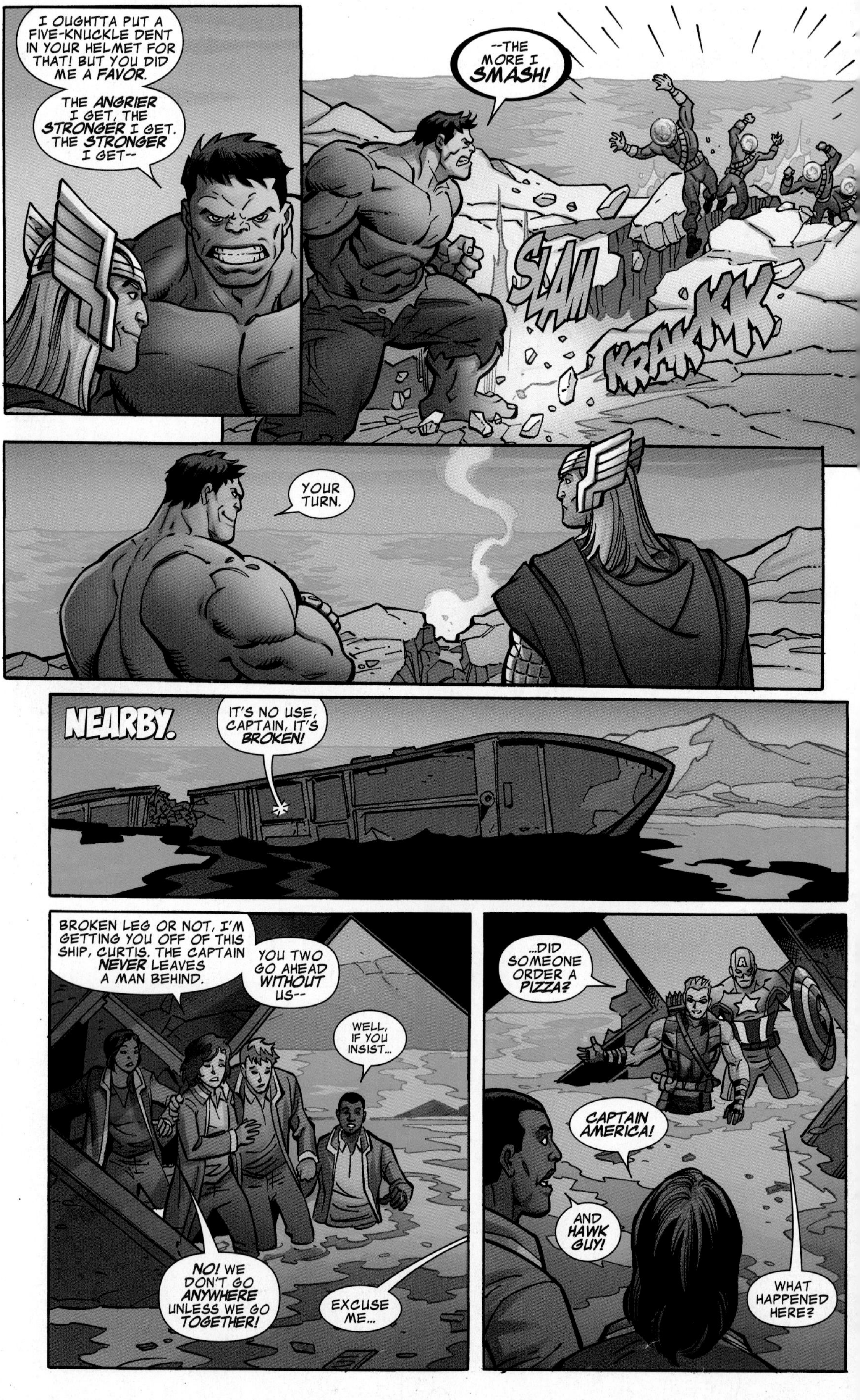

I OUGHTTA PUT A FIVE-KNUCKLE DENT IN YOUR HELMET FOR THAT! BUT YOU DID ME A FAVOR.
THE ANGRIER I GET, THE STRONGER I GET. THE STRONGER I GET--
--THE MORE I SMASH!
SLAM
KRAKKKK
YOUR TURN.
NEARBY.
IT'S NO USE, CAPTAIN, IT'S BROKEN!
BROKEN LEG OR NOT, I'M GETTING YOU OFF OF THIS SHIP, CURTIS. THE CAPTAIN NEVER LEAVES A MAN BEHIND.
YOU TWO GO AHEAD WITHOUT US--
WELL, IF YOU INSIST...
NO! WE DON'T GO ANYWHERE UNLESS WE GO TOGETHER!
EXCUSE ME...
...DID SOMEONE ORDER A PIZZA?
CAPTAIN AMERICA!
AND HAWK GUY!
WHAT HAPPENED HERE?

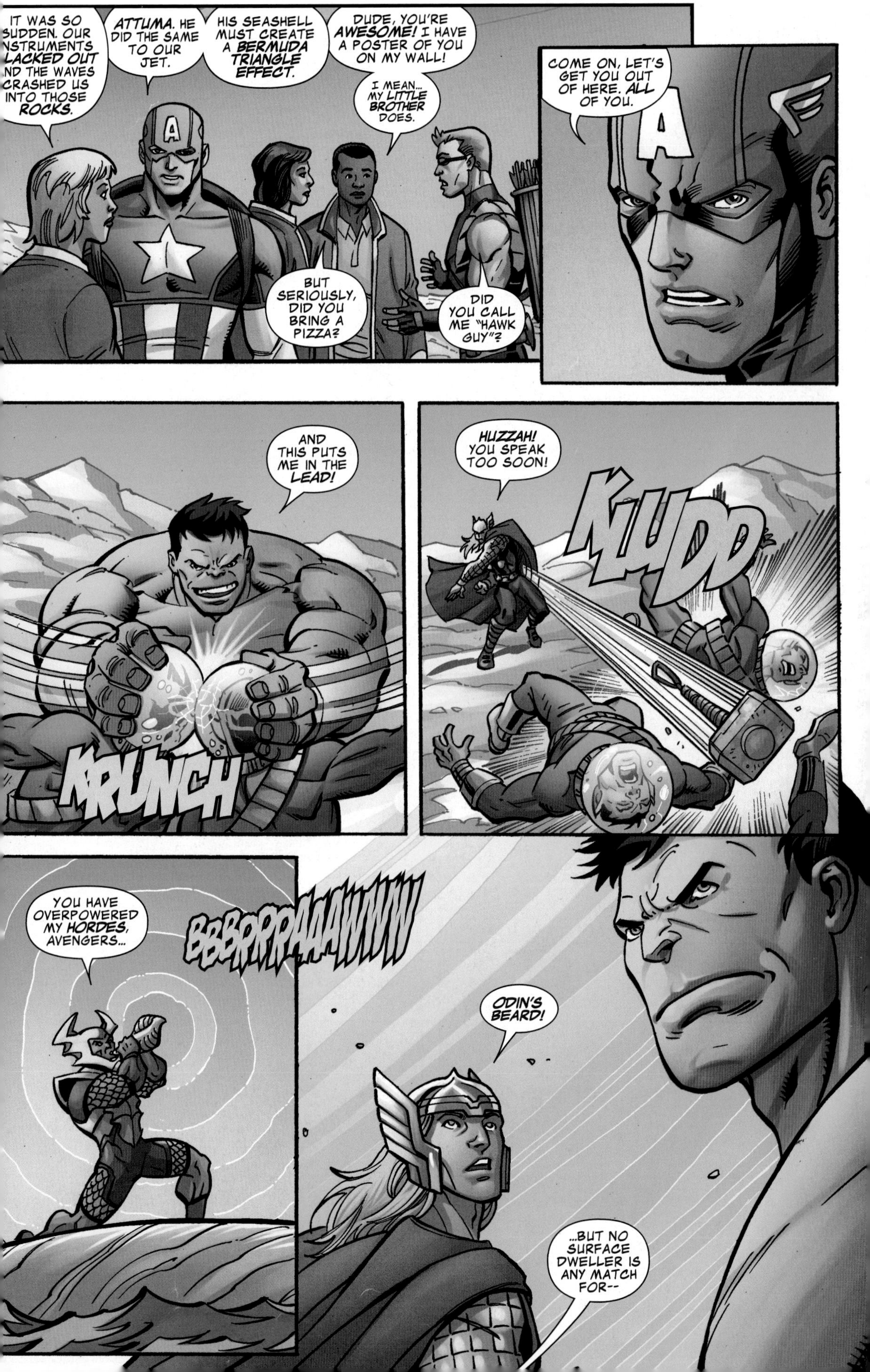

IT WAS SO SUDDEN. OUR INSTRUMENTS BLACKED OUT AND THE WAVES CRASHED US INTO THOSE ROCKS.
ATTUMA. HE DID THE SAME TO OUR JET.
HIS SEASHELL MUST CREATE A BERMUDA TRIANGLE EFFECT.
DUDE, YOU'RE AWESOME! I HAVE A POSTER OF YOU ON MY WALL!
I MEAN... MY LITTLE BROTHER DOES.
BUT SERIOUSLY, DID YOU BRING A PIZZA?
DID YOU CALL ME "HAWK GUY"?
COME ON, LET'S GET YOU OUT OF HERE. ALL OF YOU.
AND THIS PUTS ME IN THE LEAD!
KRUNCH
HUZZAH! YOU SPEAK TOO SOON!
KLUDD
YOU HAVE OVERPOWERED MY HORDES, AVENGERS...
BBBRRPPAAAWWW
ODIN'S BEARD!
...BUT NO SURFACE DWELLER IS ANY MATCH FOR--

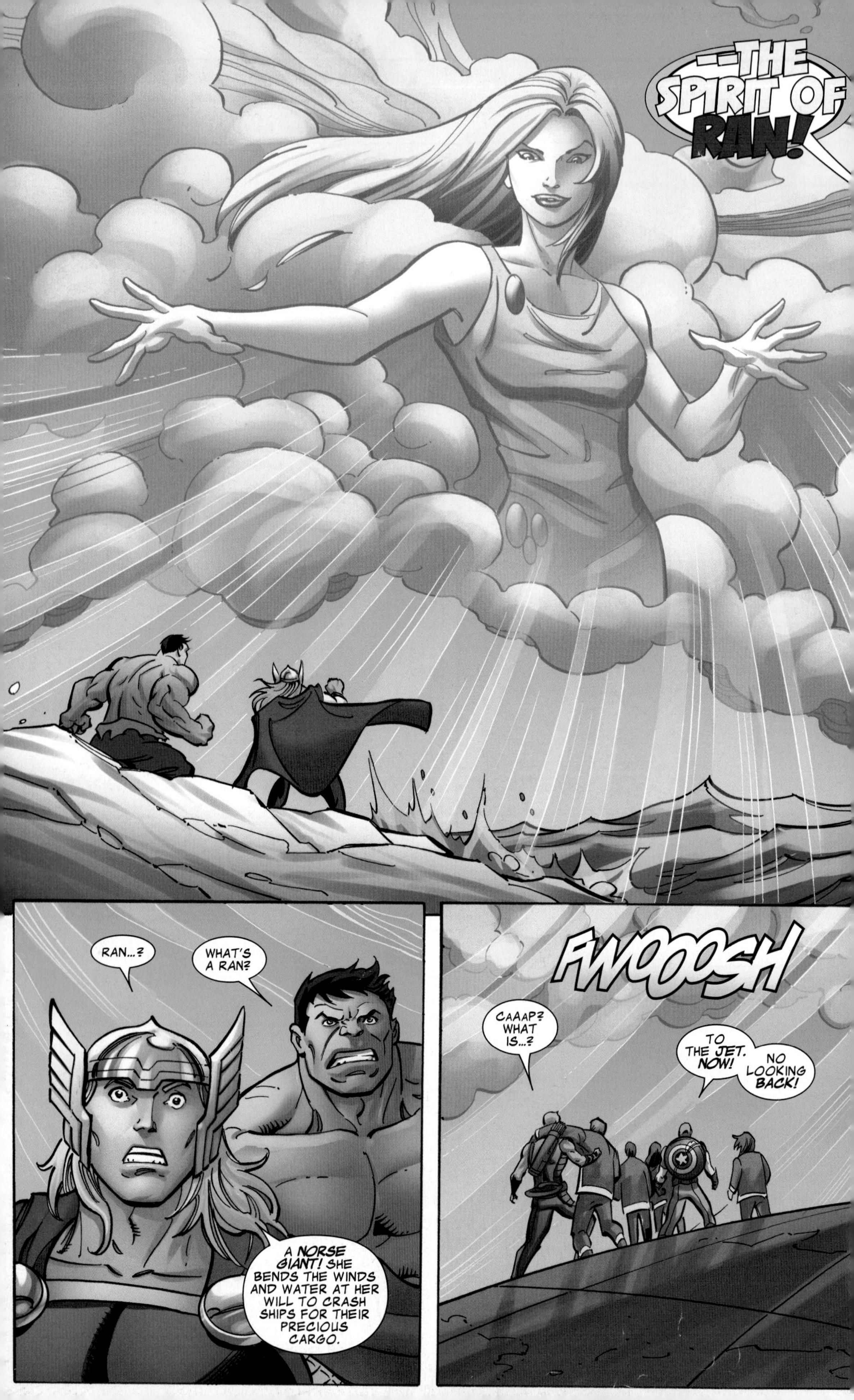

--THE SPIRIT OF RAN!
RAN...?
WHAT'S A RAN?
A NORSE GIANT! SHE BENDS THE WINDS AND WATER AT HER WILL TO CRASH SHIPS FOR THEIR PRECIOUS CARGO.
FWOOOSH
CAAAP? WHAT IS...?
TO THE JET. NOW!
NO LOOKING BACK!

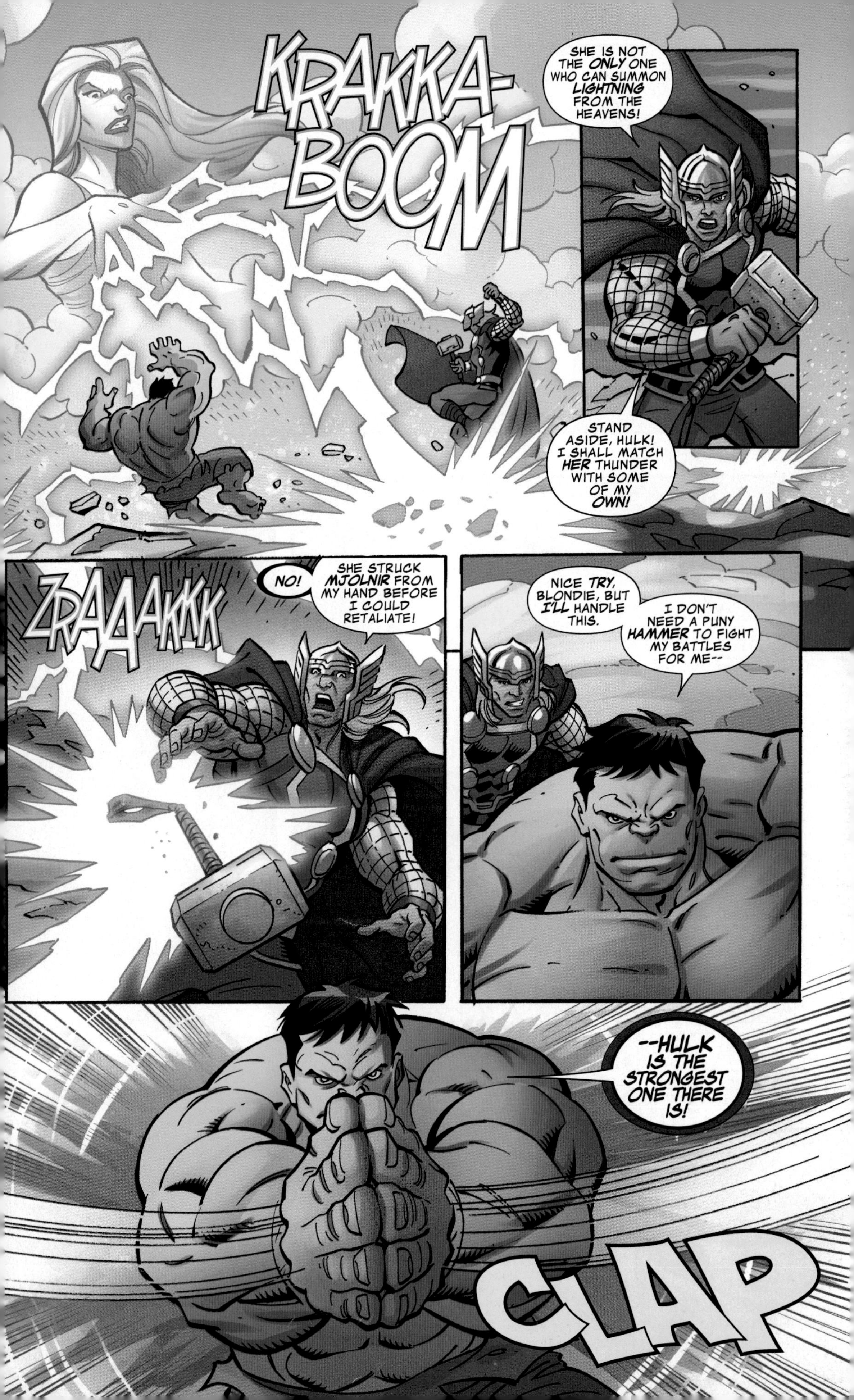
KRAKKA-BOOM
SHE IS NOT THE ONLY ONE WHO CAN SUMMON LIGHTNING FROM THE HEAVENS!
STAND ASIDE, HULK! I SHALL MATCH HER THUNDER WITH SOME OF MY OWN!
ZRAAAKKK
NO!
SHE STRUCK MJOLNIR FROM MY HAND BEFORE I COULD RETALIATE!
NICE TRY, BLONDIE, BUT I'LL HANDLE THIS.
I DON'T NEED A PUNY HAMMER TO FIGHT MY BATTLES FOR ME--
--HULK IS THE STRONGEST ONE THERE IS!
CLAP

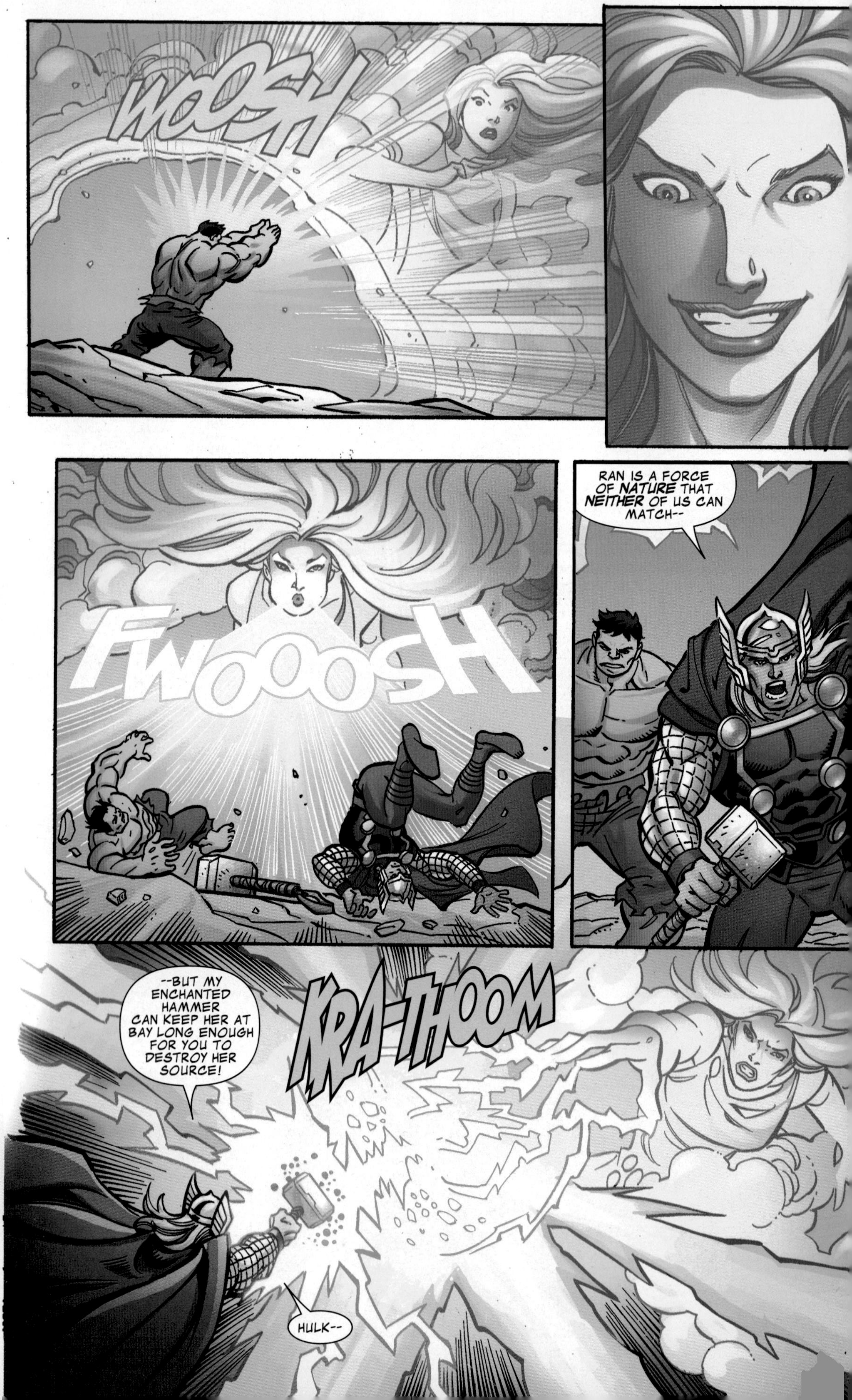
WOOSH
FWOOOSH
RAN IS A FORCE OF NATURE THAT NEITHER OF US CAN MATCH--
--BUT MY ENCHANTED HAMMER CAN KEEP HER AT BAY LONG ENOUGH FOR YOU TO DESTROY HER SOURCE!
KRA-THOOM
HULK--

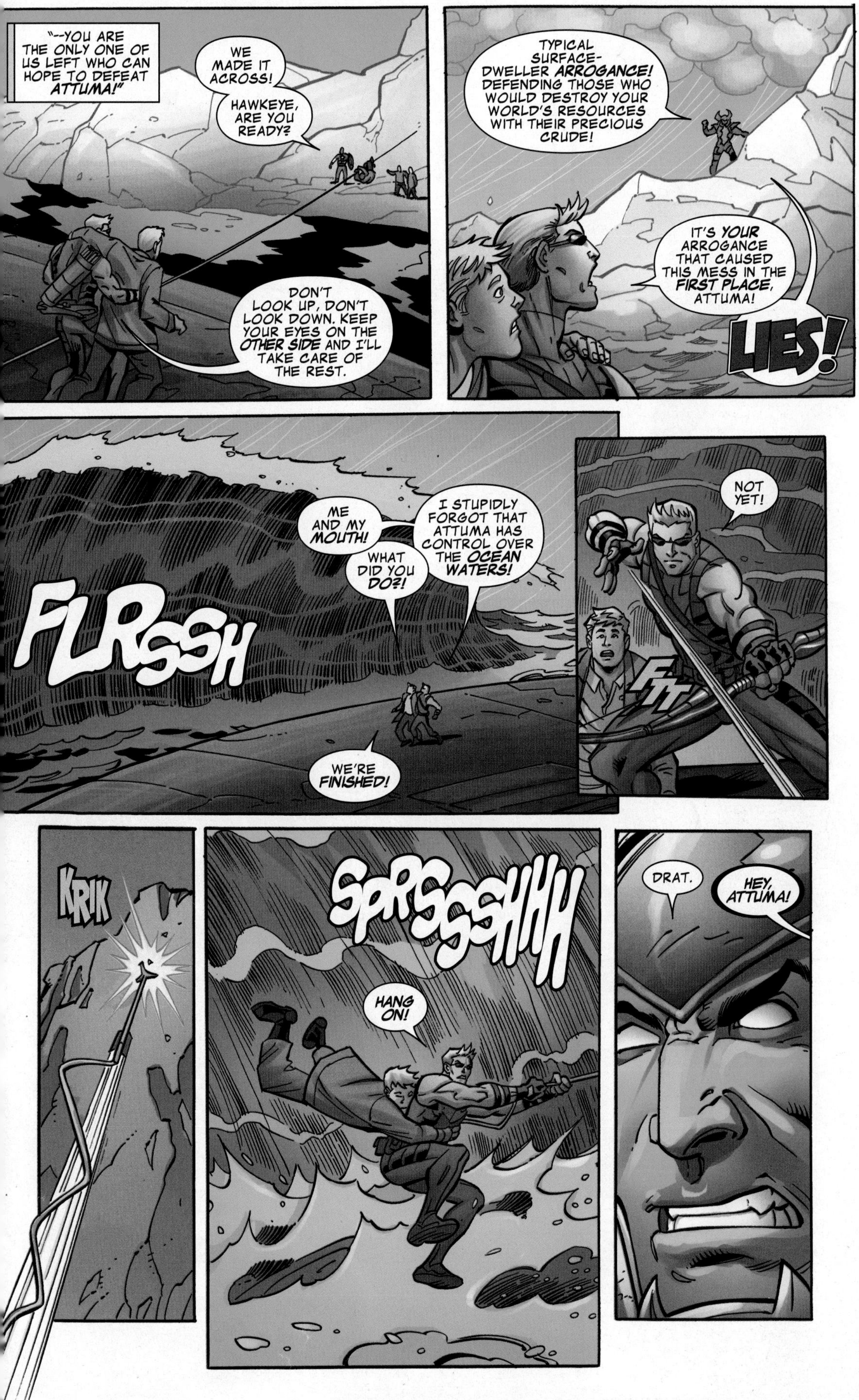
"--YOU ARE THE ONLY ONE OF US LEFT WHO CAN HOPE TO DEFEAT ATTUMA!"
WE MADE IT ACROSS!
HAWKEYE, ARE YOU READY?
DON'T LOOK UP, DON'T LOOK DOWN. KEEP YOUR EYES ON THE OTHER SIDE AND I'LL TAKE CARE OF THE REST.
TYPICAL SURFACE-DWELLER ARROGANCE! DEFENDING THOSE WHO WOULD DESTROY YOUR WORLD'S RESOURCES WITH THEIR PRECIOUS CRUDE!
IT'S YOUR ARROGANCE THAT CAUSED THIS MESS IN THE FIRST PLACE, ATTUMA!
LIES!
FLRSSH
ME AND MY MOUTH!
I STUPIDLY FORGOT THAT ATTUMA HAS CONTROL OVER THE OCEAN WATERS!
WHAT DID YOU DO?!
WE'RE FINISHED!
NOT YET!
FTT
KRIK
SPRSSSHHH
HANG ON!
DRAT.
HEY, ATTUMA!

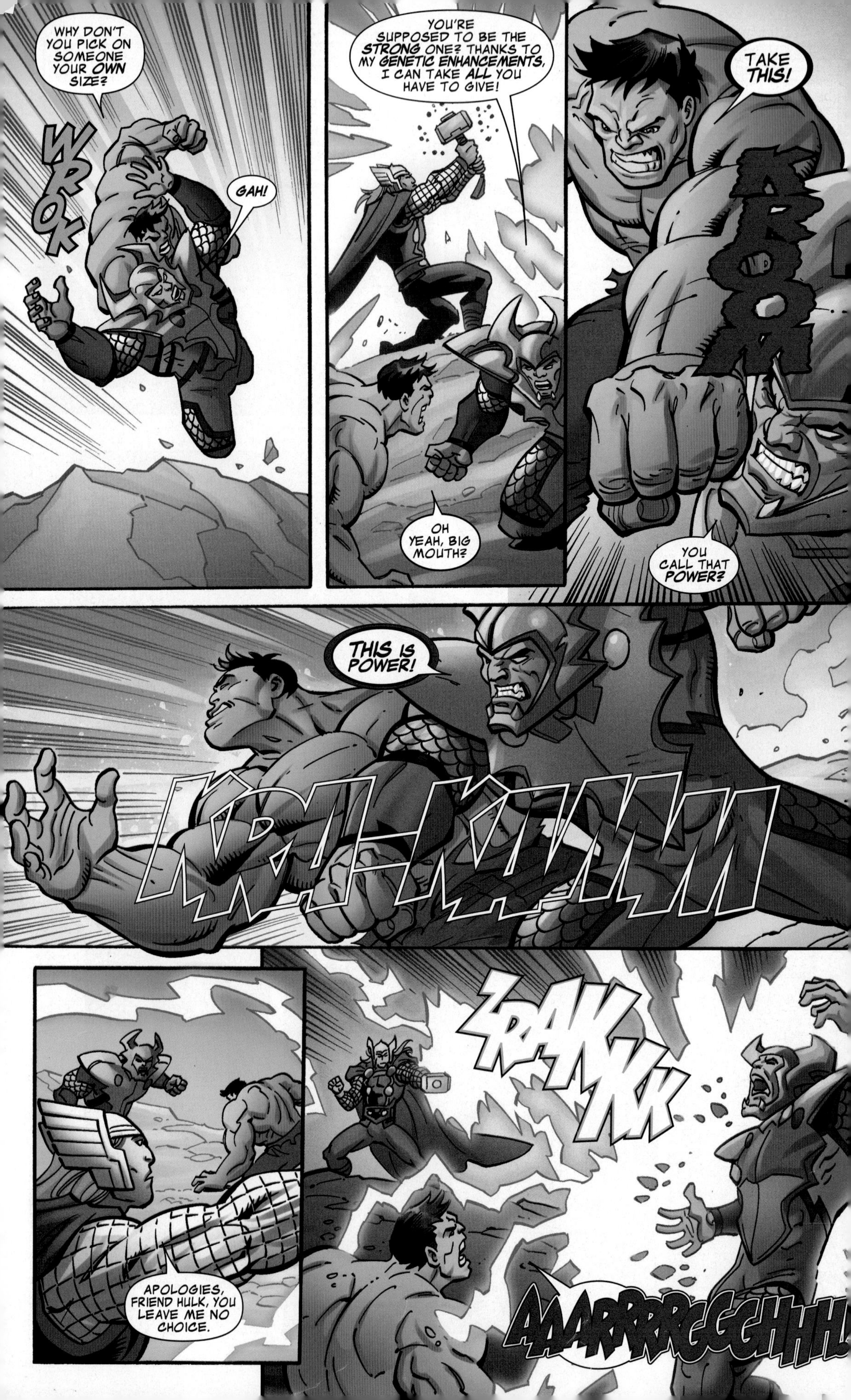
WHY DON'T YOU PICK ON SOMEONE YOUR OWN SIZE?
WROK
GAH!
YOU'RE SUPPOSED TO BE THE STRONG ONE? THANKS TO MY GENETIC ENHANCEMENTS, I CAN TAKE ALL YOU HAVE TO GIVE!
OH YEAH, BIG MOUTH?
TAKE THIS!
KROOM
YOU CALL THAT POWER?
THIS IS POWER!
KRA-KOOMM
APOLOGIES, FRIEND HULK, YOU LEAVE ME NO CHOICE.
ZRAKKK
AAARRRRGGHHH

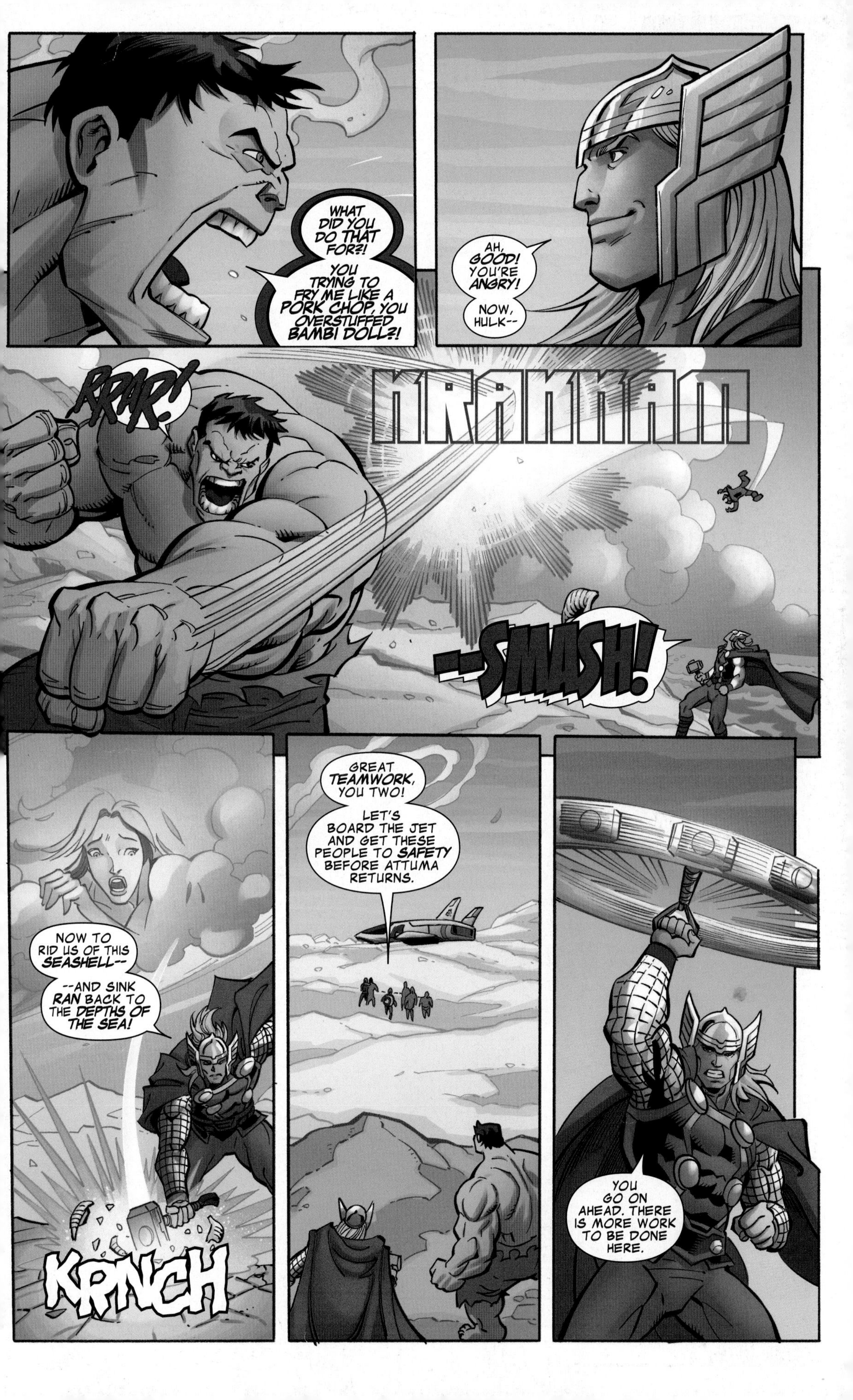
WHAT DID YOU DO THAT FOR?!
YOU TRYING TO FRY ME LIKE A PORK CHOP, YOU OVERSTUFFED BAMBI DOLL?!
AH, GOOD! YOU'RE ANGRY!
NOW, HULK--
KRAR!
KRAKKAM
--SMASH!
NOW TO RID US OF THIS SEASHELL--
--AND SINK RAN BACK TO THE DEPTHS OF THE SEA!
KRNCH
GREAT TEAMWORK, YOU TWO!
LET'S BOARD THE JET AND GET THESE PEOPLE TO SAFETY BEFORE ATTUMA RETURNS.
YOU GO ON AHEAD. THERE IS MORE WORK TO BE DONE HERE.

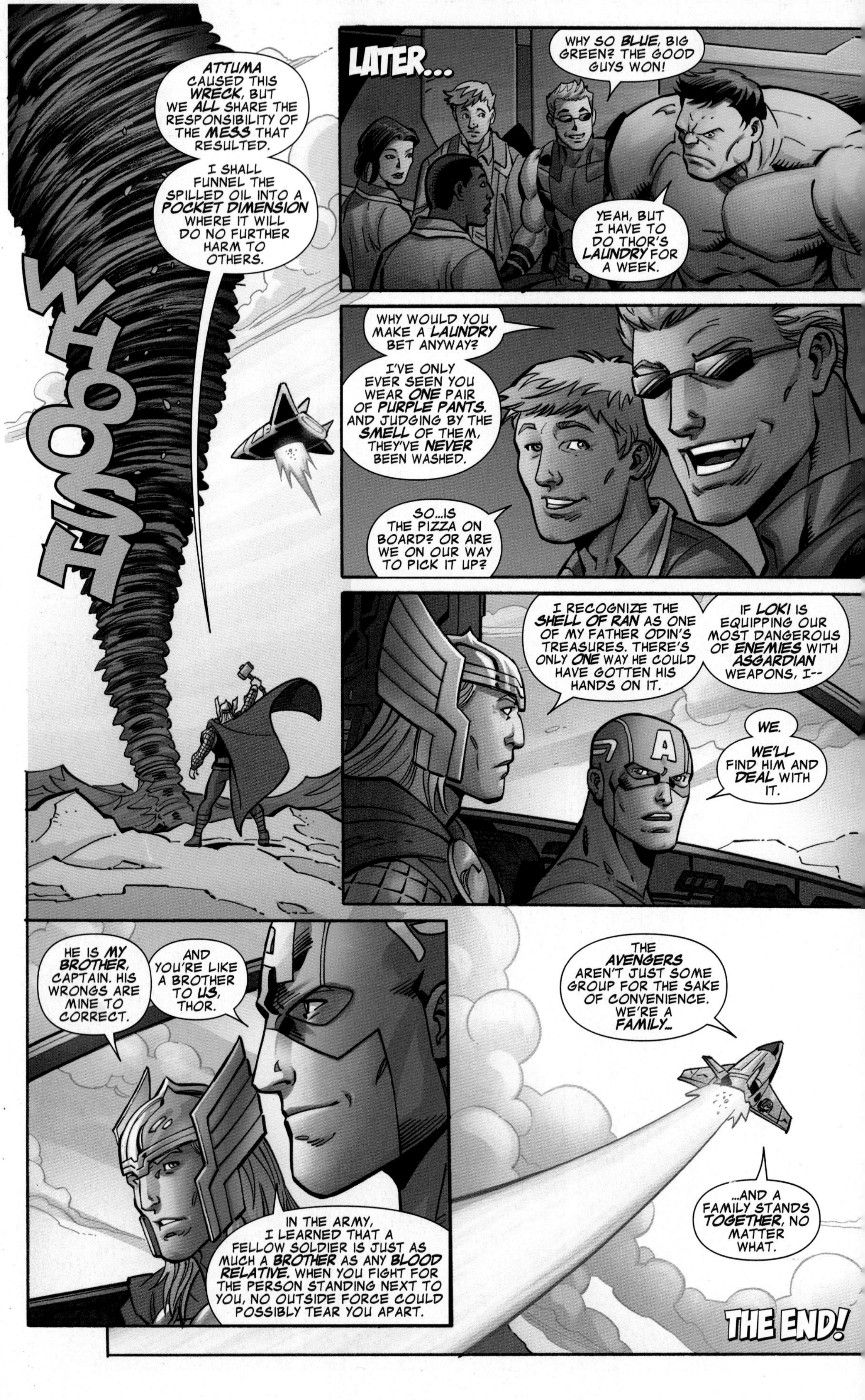

ATTUMA CAUSED THIS WRECK, BUT WE ALL SHARE THE RESPONSIBILITY OF THE MESS THAT RESULTED.
I SHALL FUNNEL THE SPILLED OIL INTO A POCKET DIMENSION WHERE IT WILL DO NO FURTHER HARM TO OTHERS.
WHOOSH
LATER...
WHY SO BLUE, BIG GREEN? THE GOOD GUYS WON!
YEAH, BUT I HAVE TO DO THOR'S LAUNDRY FOR A WEEK.
WHY WOULD YOU MAKE A LAUNDRY BET ANYWAY?
I'VE ONLY EVER SEEN YOU WEAR ONE PAIR OF PURPLE PANTS. AND JUDGING BY THE SMELL OF THEM, THEY'VE NEVER BEEN WASHED.
SO...IS THE PIZZA ON BOARD? OR ARE WE ON OUR WAY TO PICK IT UP?
I RECOGNIZE THE SHELL OF RAN AS ONE OF MY FATHER ODIN'S TREASURES. THERE'S ONLY ONE WAY HE COULD HAVE GOTTEN HIS HANDS ON IT.
IF LOKI IS EQUIPPING OUR MOST DANGEROUS OF ENEMIES WITH ASGARDIAN WEAPONS, I--
WE.
WE'LL FIND HIM AND DEAL WITH IT.
HE IS MY BROTHER, CAPTAIN. HIS WRONGS ARE MINE TO CORRECT.
AND YOU'RE LIKE A BROTHER TO US, THOR.
IN THE ARMY, I LEARNED THAT A FELLOW SOLDIER IS JUST AS MUCH A BROTHER AS ANY BLOOD RELATIVE. WHEN YOU FIGHT FOR THE PERSON STANDING NEXT TO YOU, NO OUTSIDE FORCE COULD POSSIBLY TEAR YOU APART.
THE AVENGERS AREN'T JUST SOME GROUP FOR THE SAKE OF CONVENIENCE. WE'RE A FAMILY...
...AND A FAMILY STANDS TOGETHER, NO MATTER WHAT.
THE END!

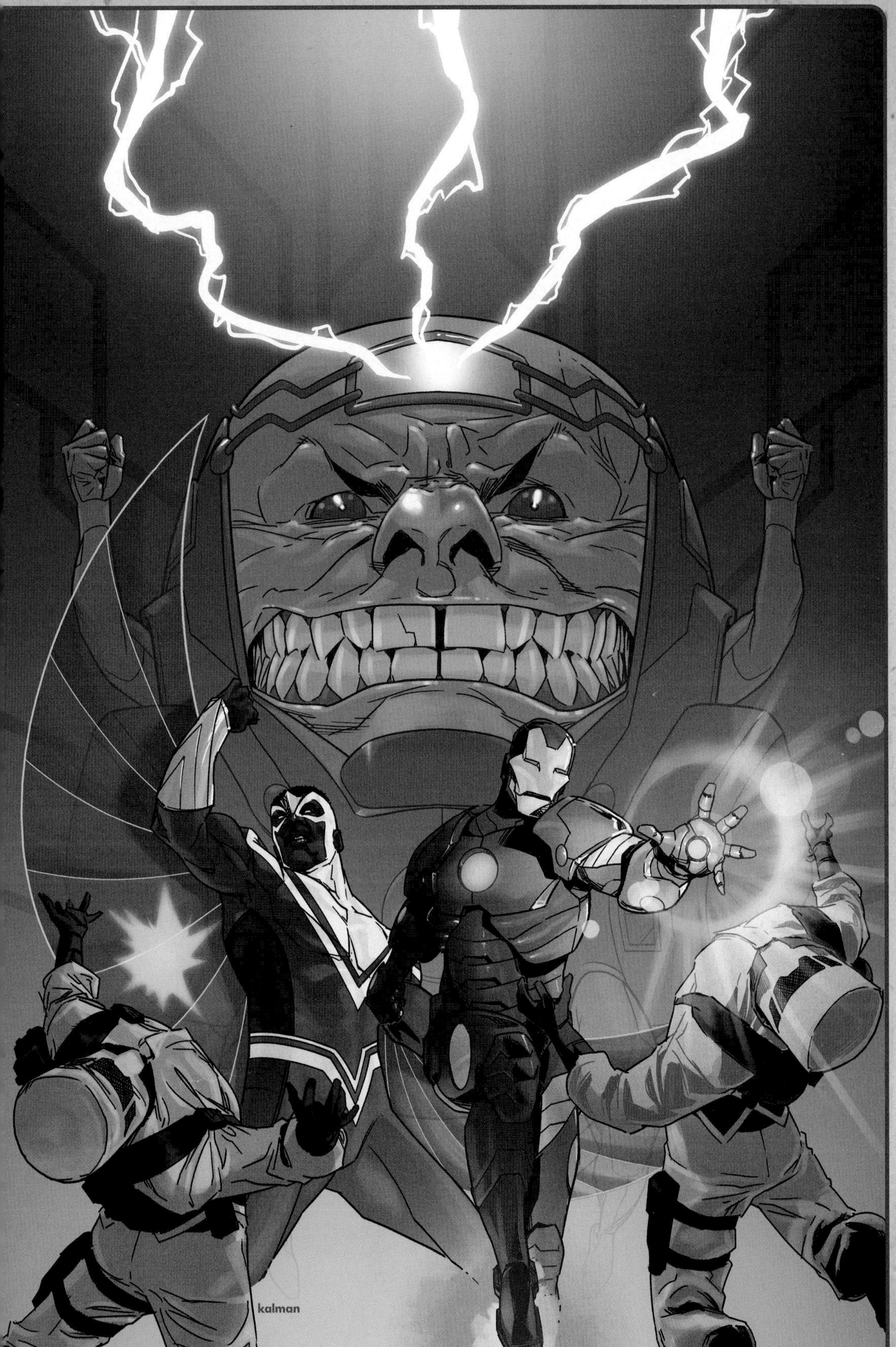
kalman

AVENGERS VS #1: *BROS BEFORE FOES*

COVER ART BY KALMAN ANDRASOFSZKY

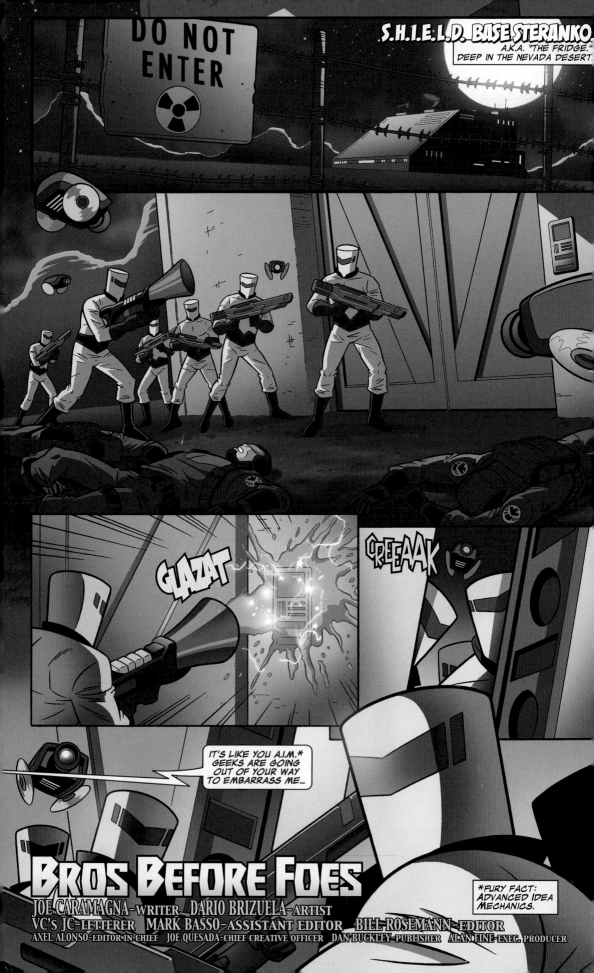

DO NOT ENTER

S.H.I.E.L.D. BASE STERANKO
A.K.A. "THE FRIDGE."
DEEP IN THE NEVADA DESERT.

GLAZAT

CREEAAK

IT'S LIKE YOU A.I.M.*
GEEKS ARE GOING
OUT OF YOUR WAY
TO EMBARRASS ME...

BROS BEFORE FOES

*FURY FACT:
ADVANCED IDEA
MECHANICS.

JOE CARAMAGNA-WRITER   DARIO BRIZUELA-ARTIST
VC'S JC-LETTERER   MARK BASSO-ASSISTANT EDITOR   BILL ROSEMANN-EDITOR
AXEL ALONSO-EDITOR-IN-CHIEF   JOE QUESADA-CHIEF CREATIVE OFFICER   DAN BUCKLEY-PUBLISHER   ALAN FINE-EXEC. PRODUCER

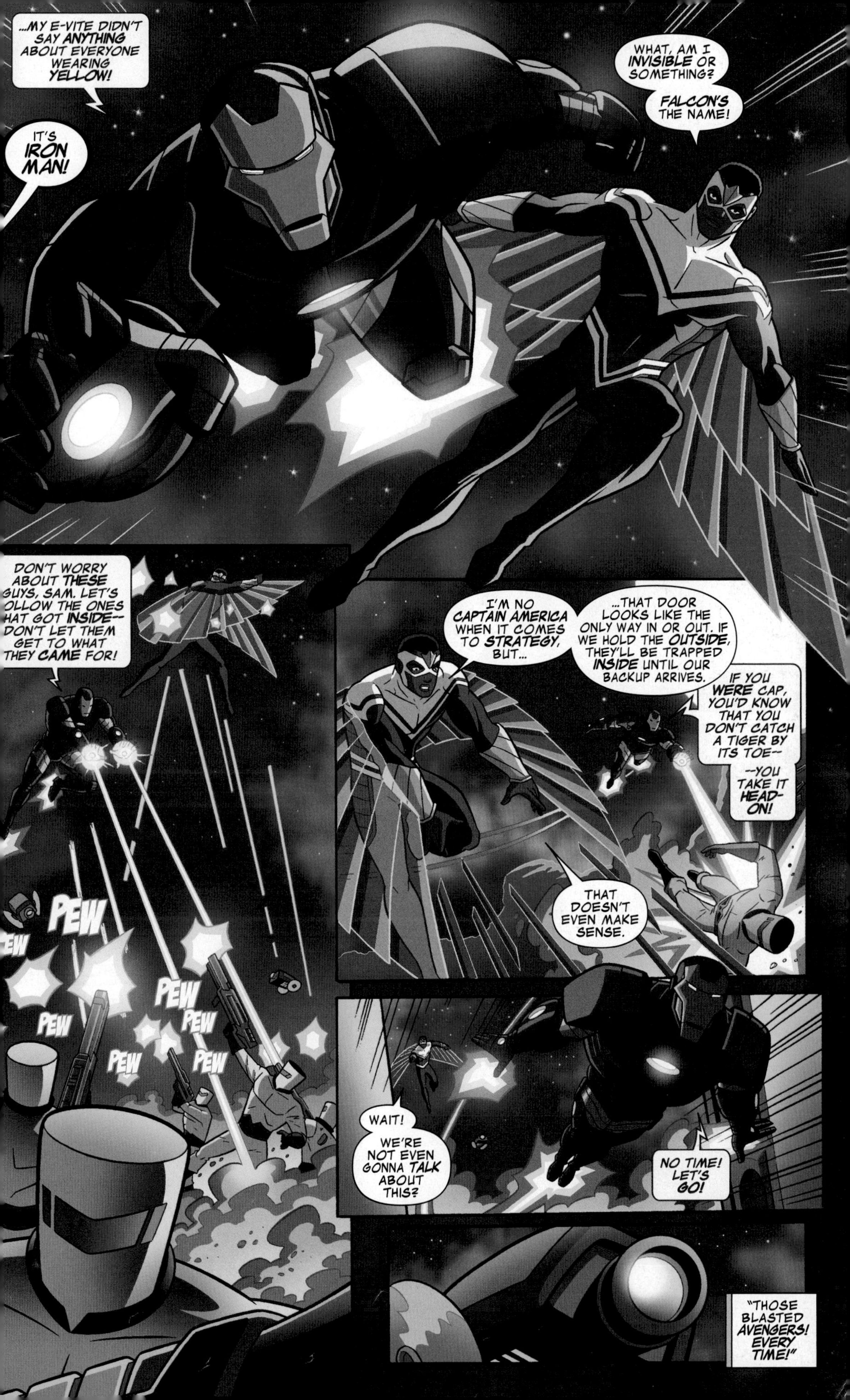
...MY E-VITE DIDN'T SAY ANYTHING ABOUT EVERYONE WEARING YELLOW!
IT'S IRON MAN!
WHAT, AM I INVISIBLE OR SOMETHING?
FALCON'S THE NAME!
DON'T WORRY ABOUT THESE GUYS, SAM. LET'S FOLLOW THE ONES THAT GOT INSIDE-- DON'T LET THEM GET TO WHAT THEY CAME FOR!
PEW
PEW
PEW
PEW
PEW
PEW
PEW
I'M NO CAPTAIN AMERICA WHEN IT COMES TO STRATEGY, BUT...
...THAT DOOR LOOKS LIKE THE ONLY WAY IN OR OUT. IF WE HOLD THE OUTSIDE, THEY'LL BE TRAPPED INSIDE UNTIL OUR BACKUP ARRIVES.
IF YOU WERE CAP, YOU'D KNOW THAT YOU DON'T CATCH A TIGER BY ITS TOE--
--YOU TAKE IT HEAD-ON!
THAT DOESN'T EVEN MAKE SENSE.
WAIT!
WE'RE NOT EVEN GONNA TALK ABOUT THIS?
NO TIME! LET'S GO!
"THOSE BLASTED AVENGERS! EVERY TIME!"

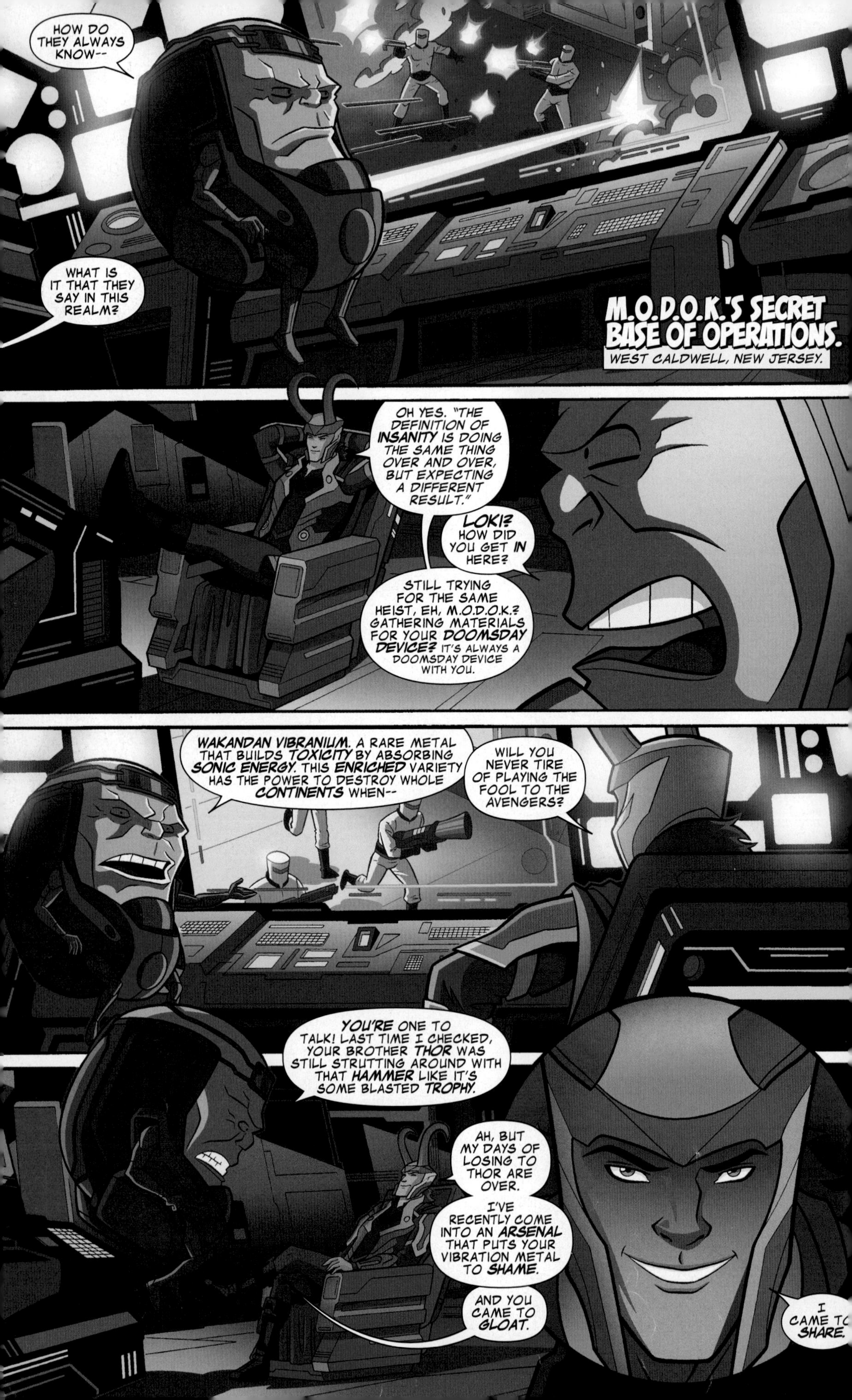
HOW DO THEY ALWAYS KNOW--
WHAT IS IT THAT THEY SAY IN THIS REALM?
M.O.D.O.K.'S SECRET BASE OF OPERATIONS.
WEST CALDWELL, NEW JERSEY.
OH YES. "THE DEFINITION OF INSANITY IS DOING THE SAME THING OVER AND OVER, BUT EXPECTING A DIFFERENT RESULT."
LOKI? HOW DID YOU GET IN HERE?
STILL TRYING FOR THE SAME HEIST, EH, M.O.D.O.K.? GATHERING MATERIALS FOR YOUR DOOMSDAY DEVICE? IT'S ALWAYS A DOOMSDAY DEVICE WITH YOU.
WAKANDAN VIBRANIUM. A RARE METAL THAT BUILDS TOXICITY BY ABSORBING SONIC ENERGY. THIS ENRICHED VARIETY HAS THE POWER TO DESTROY WHOLE CONTINENTS WHEN--
WILL YOU NEVER TIRE OF PLAYING THE FOOL TO THE AVENGERS?
YOU'RE ONE TO TALK! LAST TIME I CHECKED, YOUR BROTHER THOR WAS STILL STRUTTING AROUND WITH THAT HAMMER LIKE IT'S SOME BLASTED TROPHY.
AH, BUT MY DAYS OF LOSING TO THOR ARE OVER.
I'VE RECENTLY COME INTO AN ARSENAL THAT PUTS YOUR VIBRATION METAL TO SHAME.
AND YOU CAME TO GLOAT.
I CAME TO SHARE.

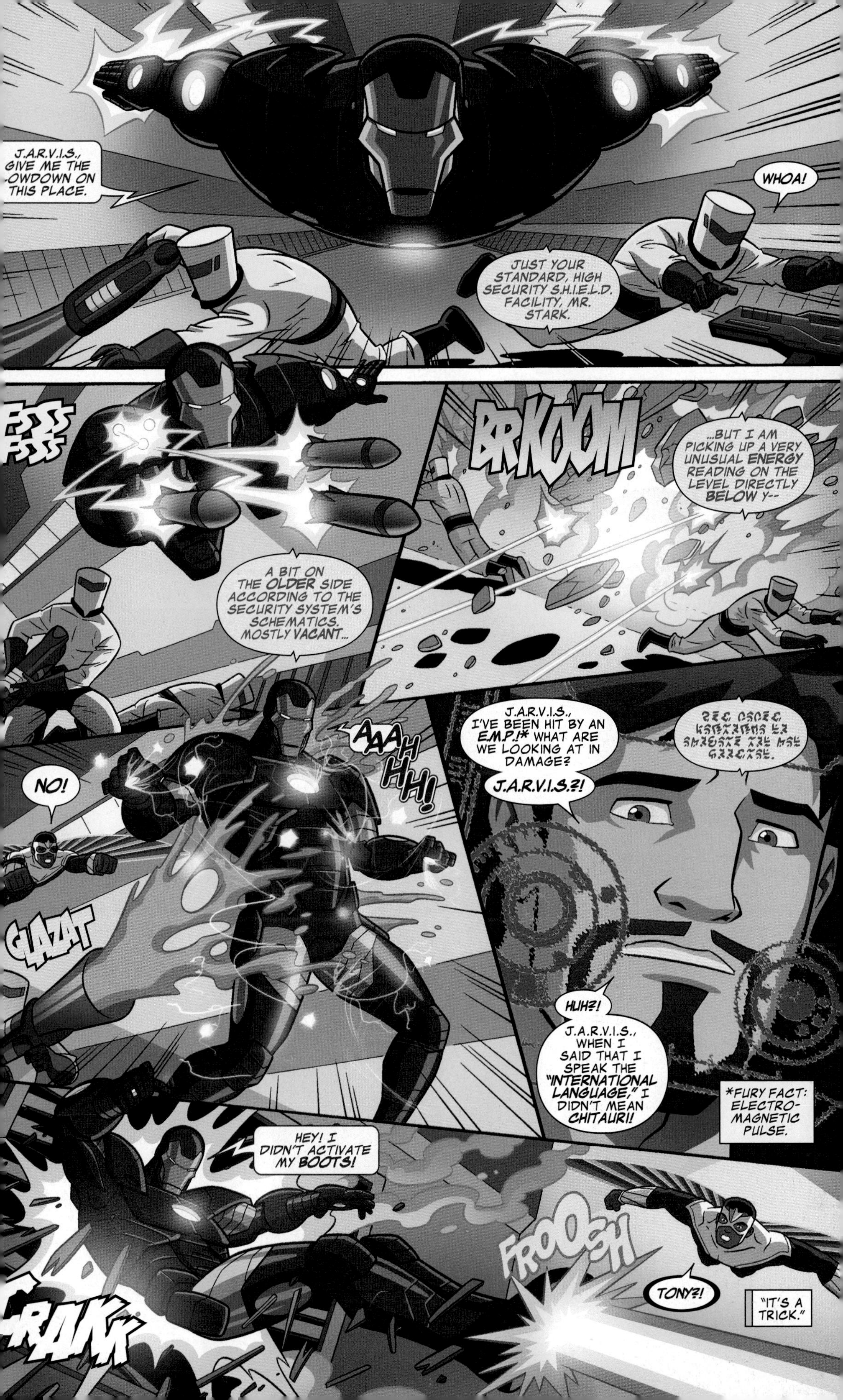
J.A.R.V.I.S., GIVE ME THE LOWDOWN ON THIS PLACE.
WHOA!
JUST YOUR STANDARD, HIGH SECURITY S.H.I.E.L.D. FACILITY, MR. STARK.
FSSS FSSS
A BIT ON THE OLDER SIDE ACCORDING TO THE SECURITY SYSTEM'S SCHEMATICS. MOSTLY VACANT...
BRKOOM
...BUT I AM PICKING UP A VERY UNUSUAL ENERGY READING ON THE LEVEL DIRECTLY BELOW Y--
NO!
AAAHHH!
GLAZAT
J.A.R.V.I.S., I'VE BEEN HIT BY AN E.M.P.!* WHAT ARE WE LOOKING AT IN DAMAGE?
J.A.R.V.I.S.?!
HUH?!
J.A.R.V.I.S., WHEN I SAID THAT I SPEAK THE "INTERNATIONAL LANGUAGE," I DIDN'T MEAN CHITAURI!
*FURY FACT: ELECTRO-MAGNETIC PULSE.
HEY! I DIDN'T ACTIVATE MY BOOTS!
FROOSH
TONY?!
"IT'S A TRICK."
RAKK

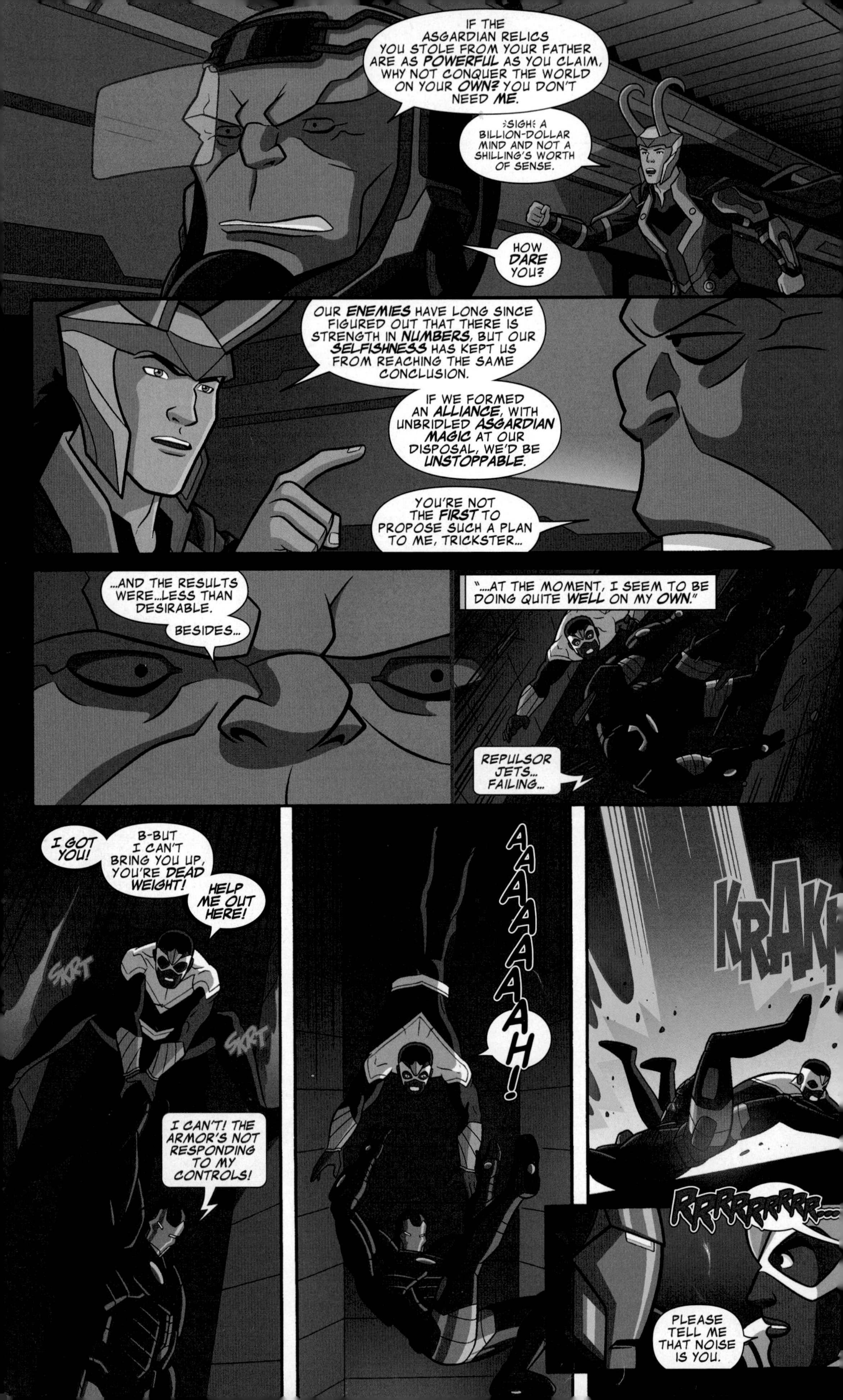

IF THE ASGARDIAN RELICS YOU STOLE FROM YOUR FATHER ARE AS POWERFUL AS YOU CLAIM, WHY NOT CONQUER THE WORLD ON YOUR OWN? YOU DON'T NEED ME.
SIGH A BILLION-DOLLAR MIND AND NOT A SHILLING'S WORTH OF SENSE.
HOW DARE YOU?
OUR ENEMIES HAVE LONG SINCE FIGURED OUT THAT THERE IS STRENGTH IN NUMBERS, BUT OUR SELFISHNESS HAS KEPT US FROM REACHING THE SAME CONCLUSION.
IF WE FORMED AN ALLIANCE, WITH UNBRIDLED ASGARDIAN MAGIC AT OUR DISPOSAL, WE'D BE UNSTOPPABLE.
YOU'RE NOT THE FIRST TO PROPOSE SUCH A PLAN TO ME, TRICKSTER...
...AND THE RESULTS WERE...LESS THAN DESIRABLE.
BESIDES...
"...AT THE MOMENT, I SEEM TO BE DOING QUITE WELL ON MY OWN."
REPULSOR JETS... FAILING...
I GOT YOU!
B-BUT I CAN'T BRING YOU UP, YOU'RE DEAD WEIGHT!
HELP ME OUT HERE!
SKRT
SKRT
I CAN'T! THE ARMOR'S NOT RESPONDING TO MY CONTROLS!
AAAAAAAH!
KRAK
RRRRRRRRR...
PLEASE TELL ME THAT NOISE IS YOU.

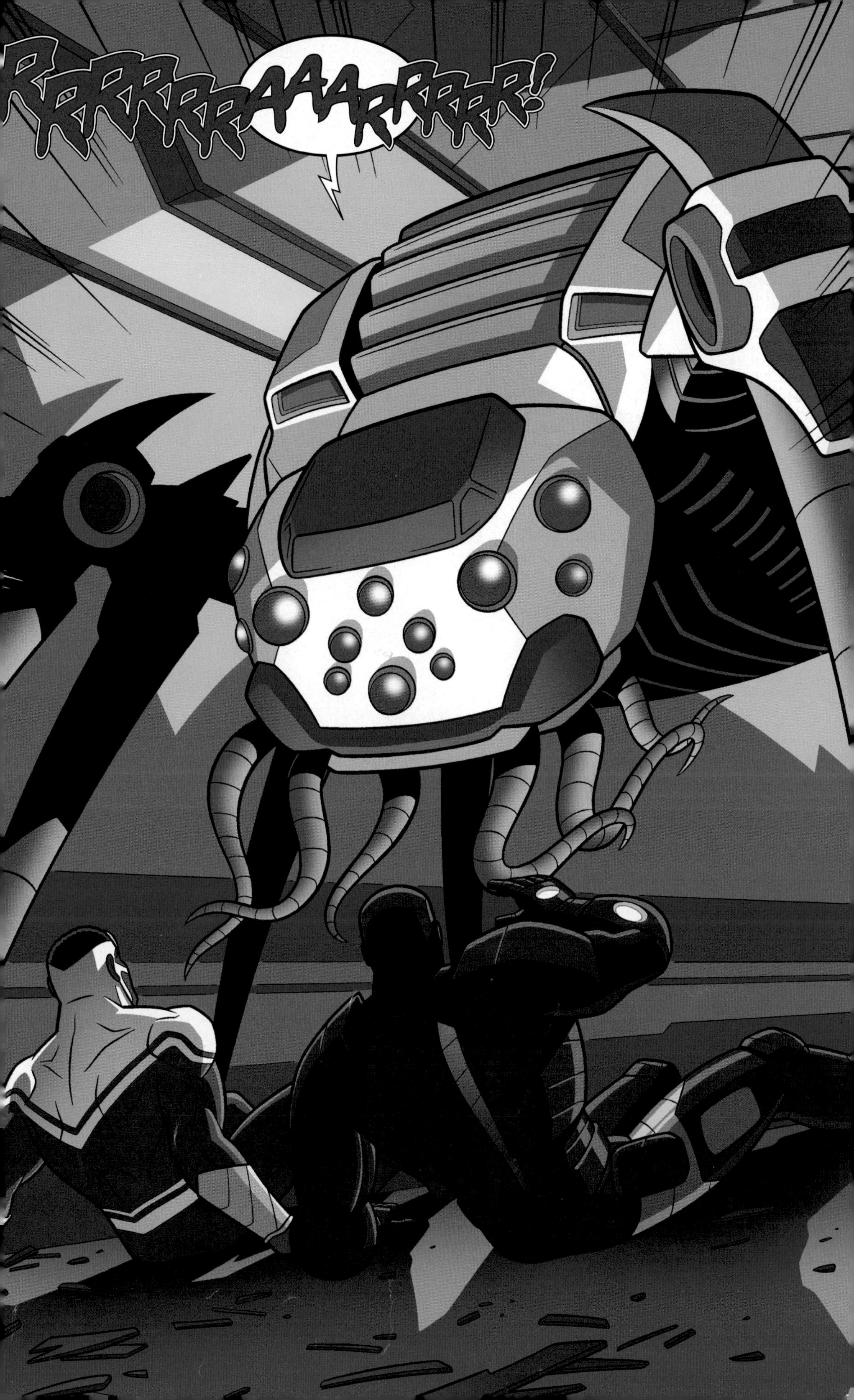
RRRRRRAAARRRR!

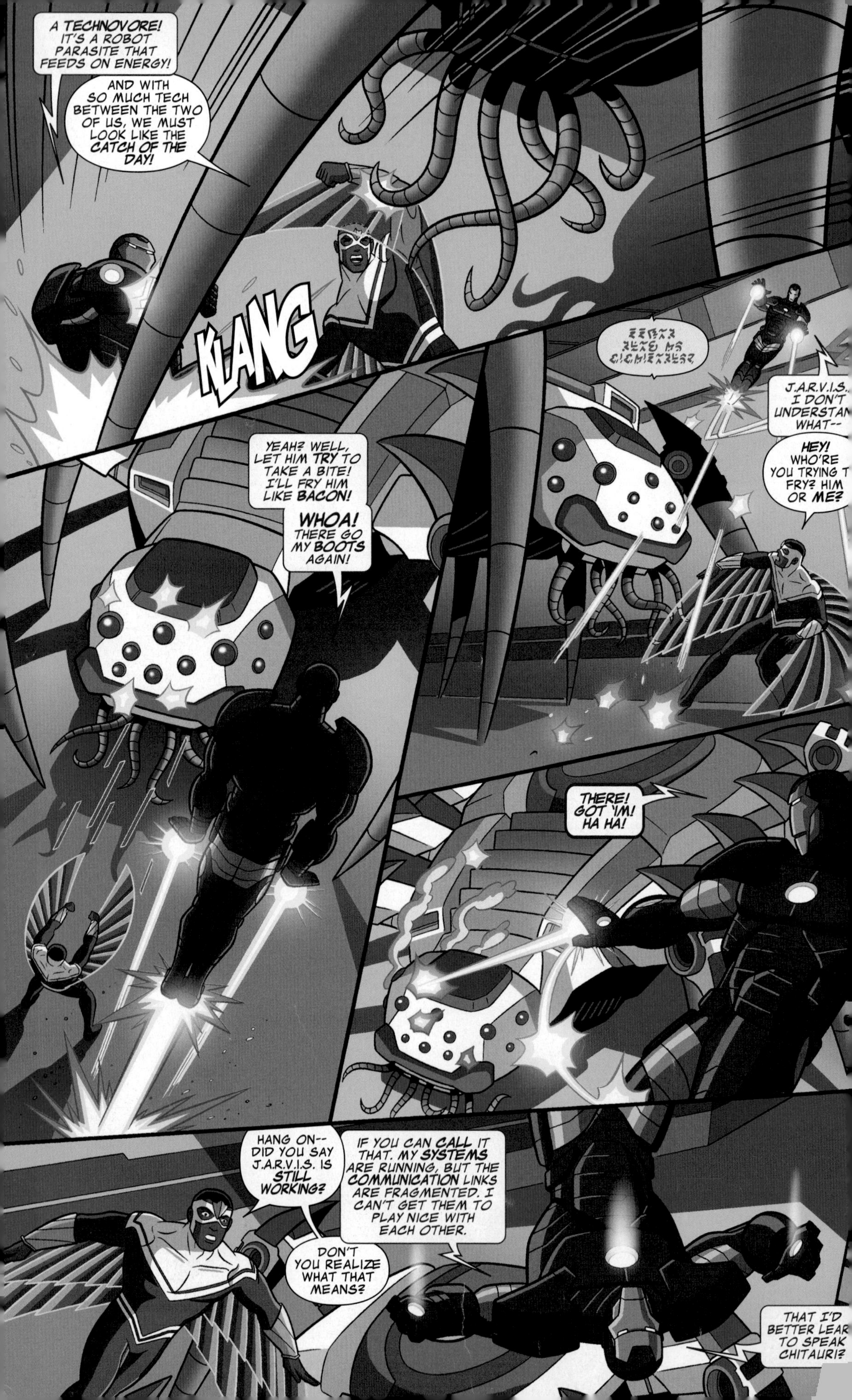
A TECHNOVORE! IT'S A ROBOT PARASITE THAT FEEDS ON ENERGY!
AND WITH SO MUCH TECH BETWEEN THE TWO OF US, WE MUST LOOK LIKE THE CATCH OF THE DAY!
KLANG
YEAH? WELL, LET HIM TRY TO TAKE A BITE! I'LL FRY HIM LIKE BACON!
WHOA! THERE GO MY BOOTS AGAIN!
J.A.R.V.I.S... I DON'T UNDERSTAN WHAT--
HEY! WHO'RE YOU TRYING T FRY? HIM OR ME?
THERE! GOT 'IM! HA HA!
HANG ON-- DID YOU SAY J.A.R.V.I.S. IS STILL WORKING?
IF YOU CAN CALL IT THAT. MY SYSTEMS ARE RUNNING, BUT THE COMMUNICATION LINKS ARE FRAGMENTED. I CAN'T GET THEM TO PLAY NICE WITH EACH OTHER.
DON'T YOU REALIZE WHAT THAT MEANS?
THAT I'D BETTER LEAR TO SPEAK CHITAURI?

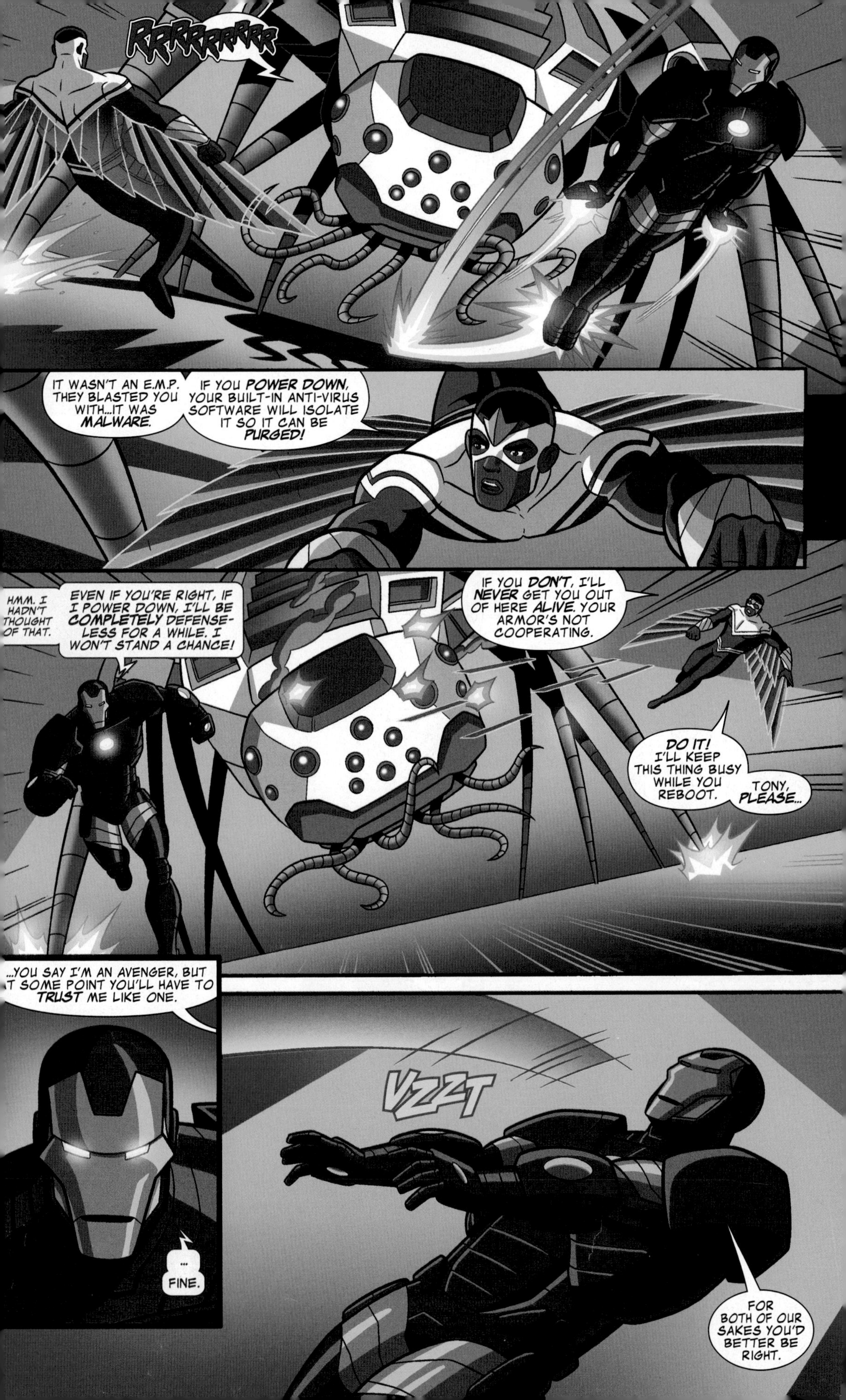
RRRRRRRRR
IT WASN'T AN E.M.P. THEY BLASTED YOU WITH...IT WAS MALWARE.
IF YOU POWER DOWN, YOUR BUILT-IN ANTI-VIRUS SOFTWARE WILL ISOLATE IT SO IT CAN BE PURGED!
HMM. I HADN'T THOUGHT OF THAT.
EVEN IF YOU'RE RIGHT, IF I POWER DOWN, I'LL BE COMPLETELY DEFENSELESS FOR A WHILE. I WON'T STAND A CHANCE!
IF YOU DON'T, I'LL NEVER GET YOU OUT OF HERE ALIVE. YOUR ARMOR'S NOT COOPERATING.
DO IT! I'LL KEEP THIS THING BUSY WHILE YOU REBOOT.
TONY, PLEASE...
...YOU SAY I'M AN AVENGER, BUT AT SOME POINT YOU'LL HAVE TO TRUST ME LIKE ONE.
...
FINE.
VZZT
FOR BOTH OF OUR SAKES YOU'D BETTER BE RIGHT.

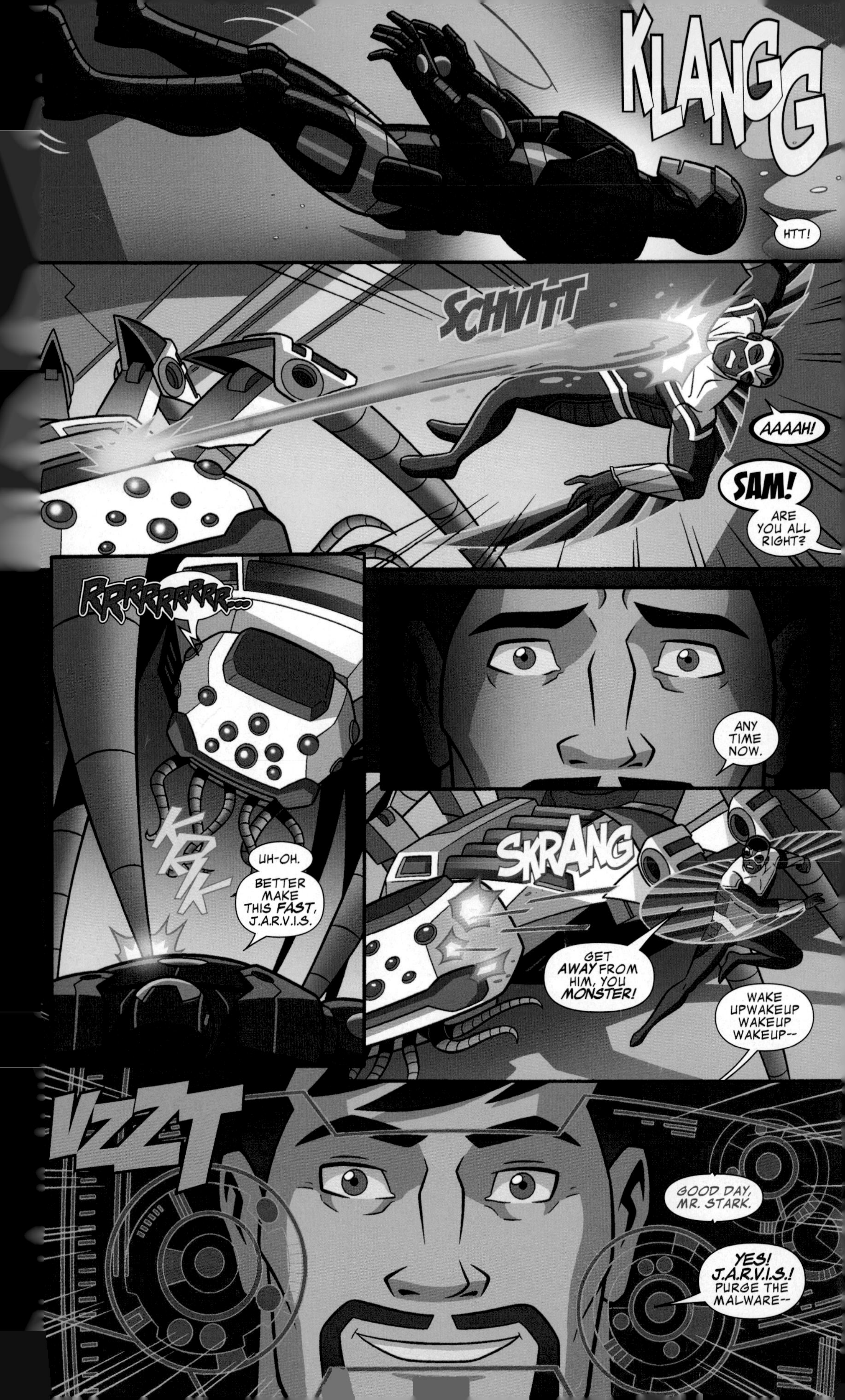
KLANGG
HTT!
SCHVITT
AAAAH!
SAM!
ARE YOU ALL RIGHT?
RRRRRRRRR...
KRIK
UH-OH.
BETTER MAKE THIS FAST, J.A.R.V.I.S.
ANY TIME NOW.
SKRANG
GET AWAY FROM HIM, YOU MONSTER!
WAKE UPWAKEUP WAKEUP WAKEUP--
VZZT
GOOD DAY, MR. STARK.
YES! J.A.R.V.I.S.! PURGE THE MALWARE--

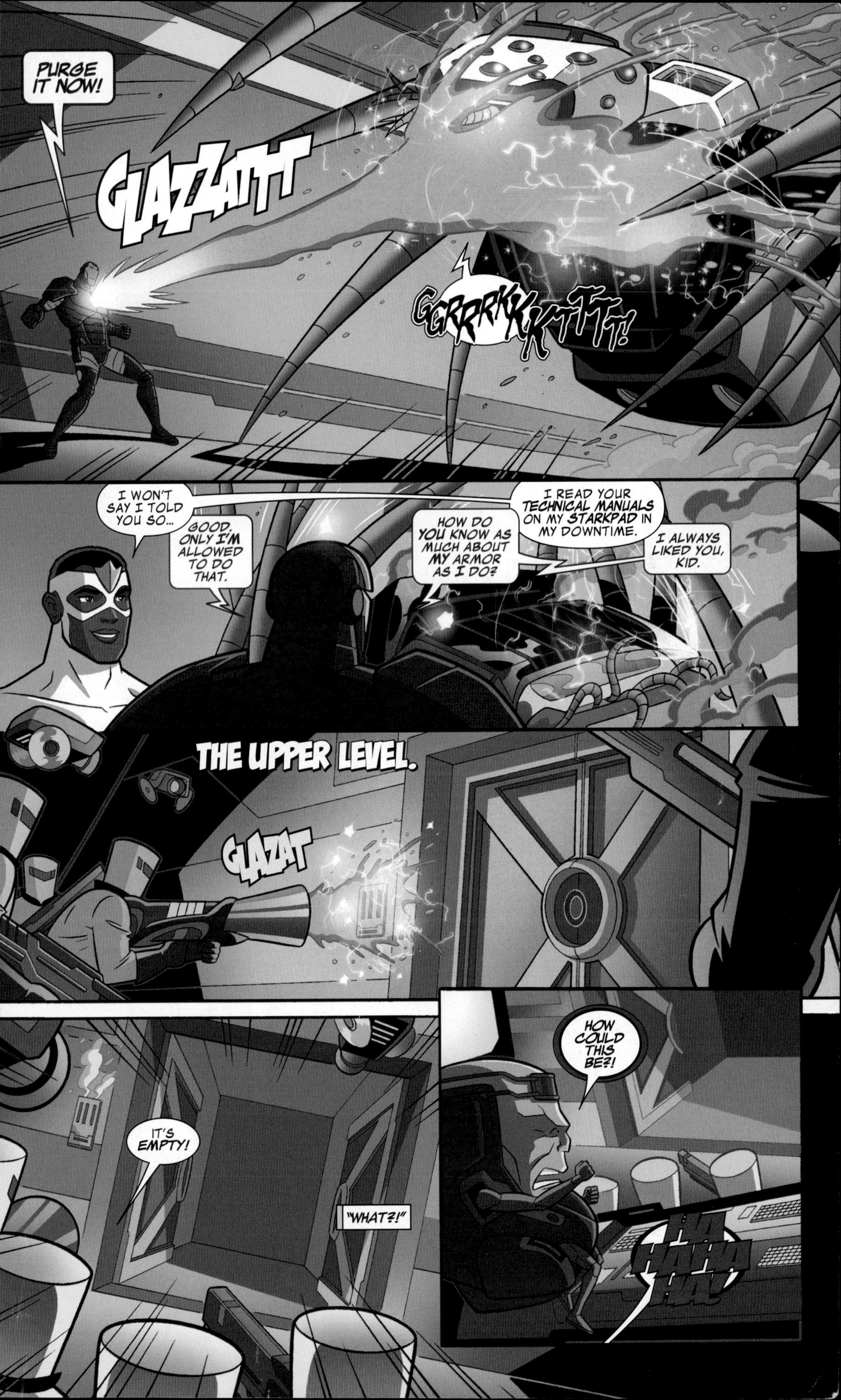
PURGE IT NOW!
GLAZZATTT
GGRRRKKKTTTT!
I WON'T SAY I TOLD YOU SO...
GOOD. ONLY I'M ALLOWED TO DO THAT.
HOW DO YOU KNOW AS MUCH ABOUT MY ARMOR AS I DO?
I READ YOUR TECHNICAL MANUALS ON MY STARKPAD IN MY DOWNTIME.
I ALWAYS LIKED YOU, KID.
THE UPPER LEVEL.
GLAZAT
IT'S EMPTY!
"WHAT?!"
HOW COULD THIS BE?!
HA HAHA HA!

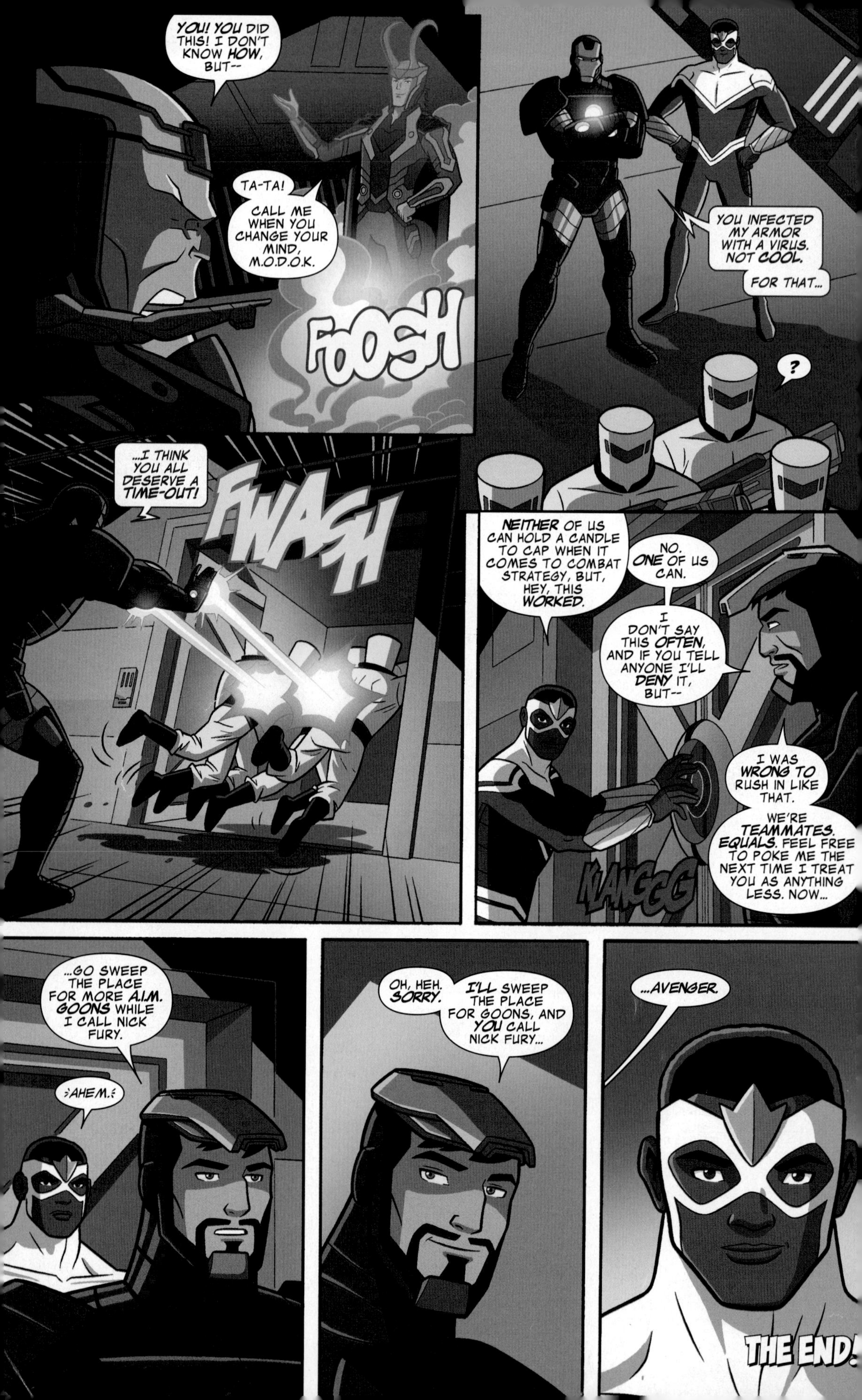
YOU! YOU DID THIS! I DON'T KNOW HOW, BUT--
TA-TA!
CALL ME WHEN YOU CHANGE YOUR MIND, M.O.D.O.K.
FOOSH
YOU INFECTED MY ARMOR WITH A VIRUS. NOT COOL.
FOR THAT...
?
...I THINK YOU ALL DESERVE A TIME-OUT!
FWASH
NEITHER OF US CAN HOLD A CANDLE TO CAP WHEN IT COMES TO COMBAT STRATEGY, BUT, HEY, THIS WORKED.
NO. ONE OF US CAN.
I DON'T SAY THIS OFTEN, AND IF YOU TELL ANYONE I'LL DENY IT, BUT--
I WAS WRONG TO RUSH IN LIKE THAT.
WE'RE TEAMMATES. EQUALS. FEEL FREE TO POKE ME THE NEXT TIME I TREAT YOU AS ANYTHING LESS. NOW...
KLANGGG
...GO SWEEP THE PLACE FOR MORE A.I.M. GOONS WHILE I CALL NICK FURY.
AHEM.
OH, HEH. SORRY.
I'LL SWEEP THE PLACE FOR GOONS, AND YOU CALL NICK FURY...
...AVENGER.
THE END!

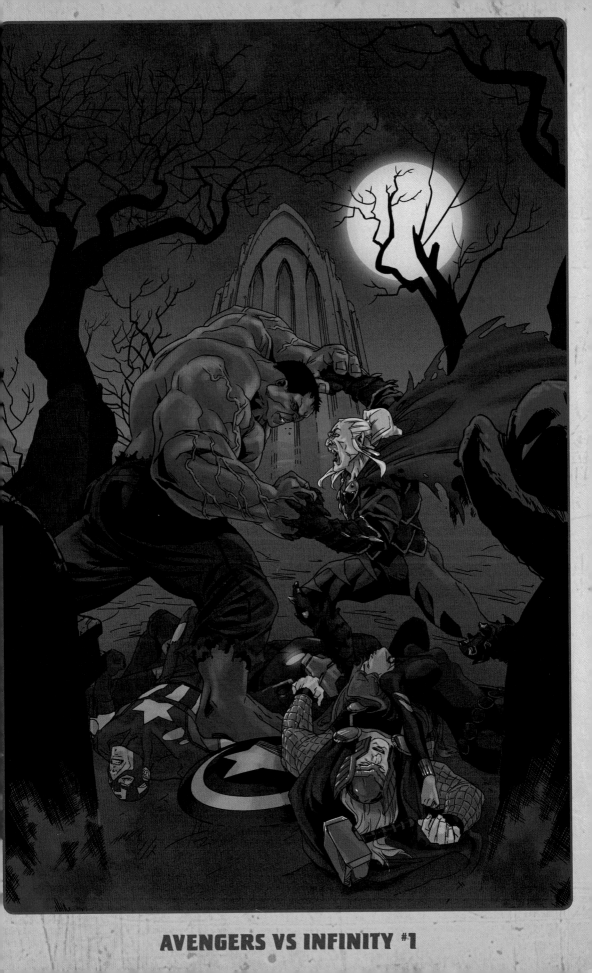

AVENGERS VS INFINITY #1

THE AVENGERS VS INFINITY

anger mismanagement

WRITER: **JOE CARAMAGNA**
PENCILER: **WELLINGTON ALVES**
INKER: **SCOTT HANNA**
COLORIST: **CARLOS LOPEZ**

DOOM EVERLASTING

WRITER: **JOE CARAMAGN**
PENCILER: **RON LIM**
INKER: **SCOTT HANN**
COLORIST: **CARLOS LOPE**

BOSSMAN SMASH!

WRITER: **JOE CARAMAGNA**
PENCILER: **RON LIM**
INKER: **SCOTT HANNA**
COLORIST: **CARLOS LOPEZ**

MIGHT OF THE LIVING DEAD!

WRITER: **JOE CARAMAGNA**
PENCILER: **RON LIM**
INKER: **SCOTT HANNA**
COLORIST: **CARLOS LOPE**

LETTERER:
VC'S JOE CARAMAGNA
COVER ARTIST:
KALMAN ANDRASOFSZKY
VARIANT COVER ARTISTS:
RON LIM AND GURU-eFX

EDITORS
BILL ROSEMANN, MARK BASSC
& EMILY SHAW
EDITOR IN CHIEF
AXEL ALONSO
CHIEF CREATIVE OFFICER
JOE QUESADA
PUBLISHER
DAN BUCKLEY
EXECUTIVE PRODUCER
ALAN FINE

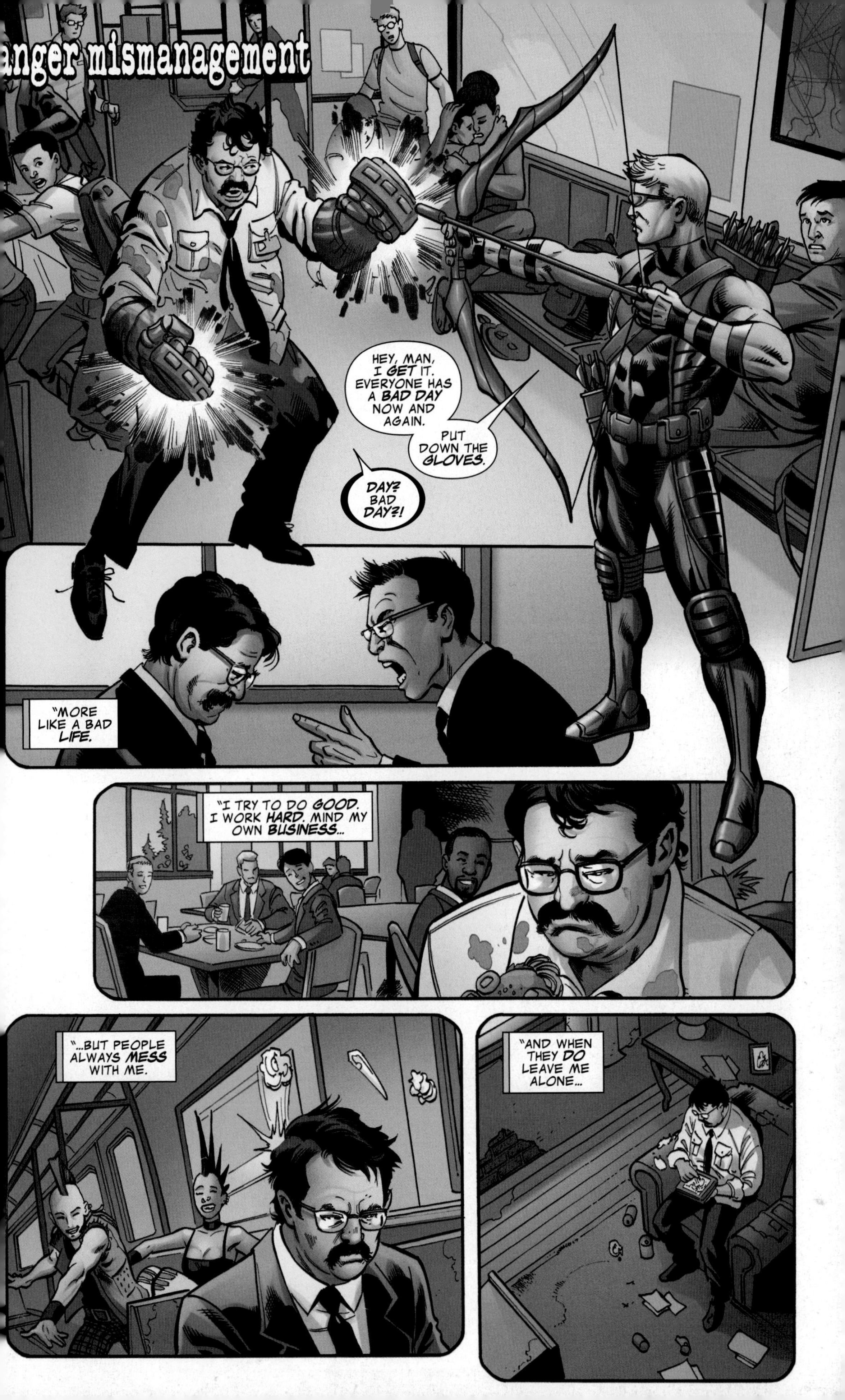
anger mismanagement
HEY, MAN, I GET IT. EVERYONE HAS A BAD DAY NOW AND AGAIN.
PUT DOWN THE GLOVES.
DAY? BAD DAY?!
"MORE LIKE A BAD LIFE.
"I TRY TO DO GOOD. I WORK HARD, MIND MY OWN BUSINESS...
"...BUT PEOPLE ALWAYS MESS WITH ME.
"AND WHEN THEY DO LEAVE ME ALONE...

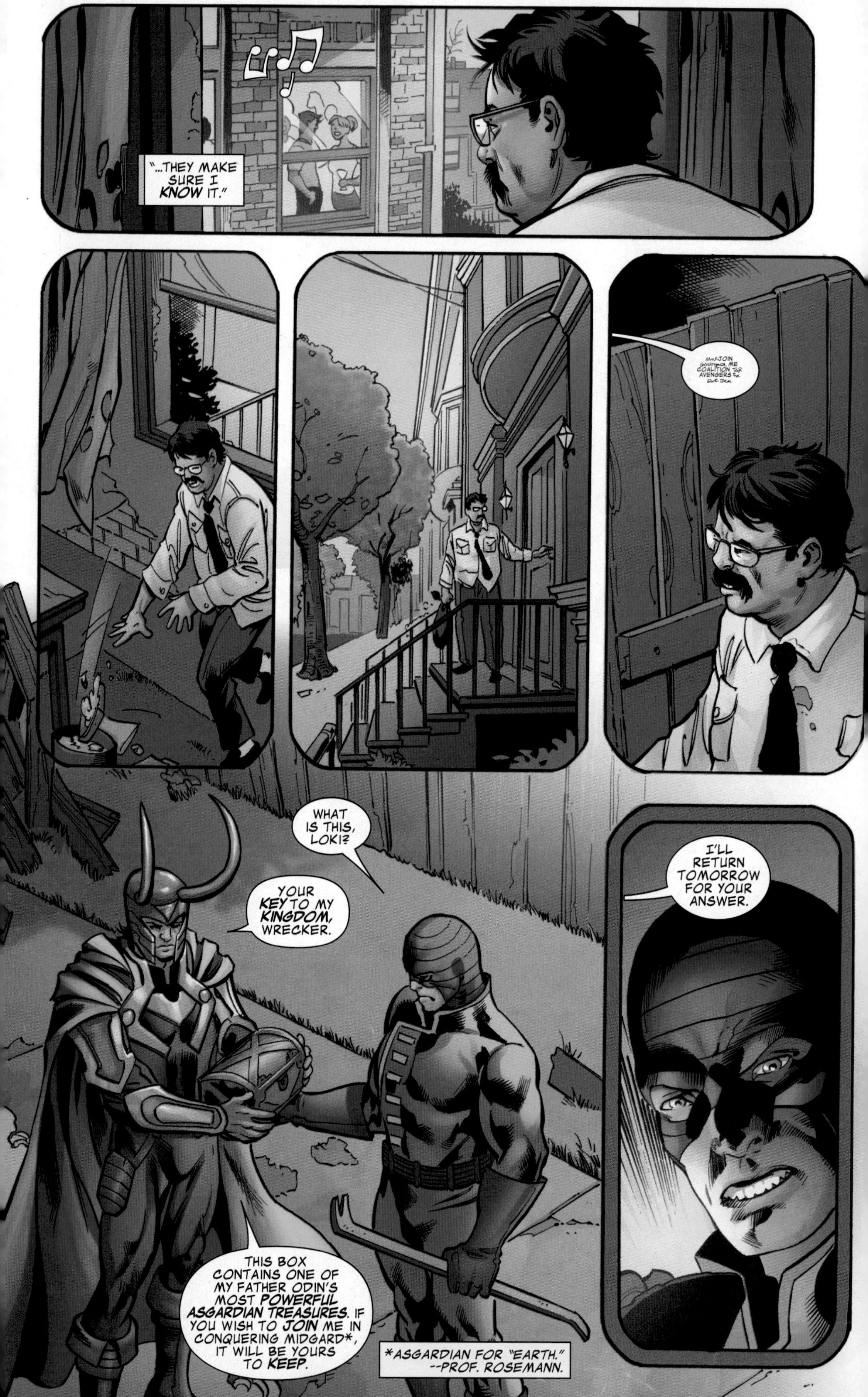

"...THEY MAKE SURE I KNOW IT."
JOIN ME COALITION AVENGERS
WHAT IS THIS, LOKI?
YOUR KEY TO MY KINGDOM, WRECKER.
I'LL RETURN TOMORROW FOR YOUR ANSWER.
THIS BOX CONTAINS ONE OF MY FATHER ODIN'S MOST POWERFUL ASGARDIAN TREASURES. IF YOU WISH TO JOIN ME IN CONQUERING MIDGARD*, IT WILL BE YOURS TO KEEP.
*ASGARDIAN FOR "EARTH." --PROF. ROSEMANN.

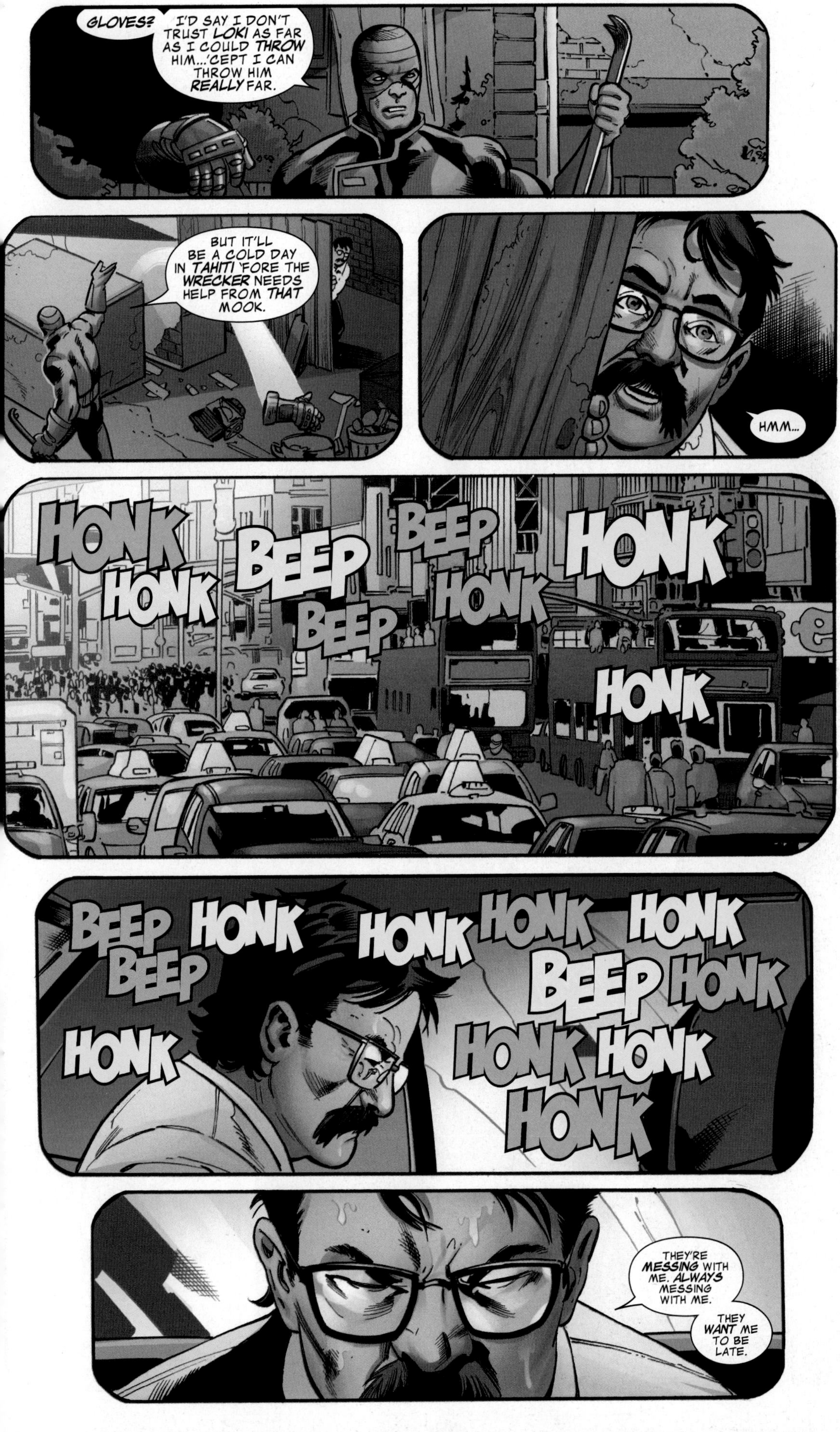
GLOVES?
I'D SAY I DON'T TRUST LOKI AS FAR AS I COULD THROW HIM...'CEPT I CAN THROW HIM REALLY FAR.
BUT IT'LL BE A COLD DAY IN TAHITI 'FORE THE WRECKER NEEDS HELP FROM THAT MOOK.
HMM...
HONK
HONK
BEEP
BEEP
BEEP
HONK
HONK
HONK
BEEP
BEEP
HONK
HONK
HONK
HONK
HONK
BEEP
HONK
HONK
HONK
HONK
THEY'RE MESSING WITH ME. ALWAYS MESSING WITH ME.
THEY WANT ME TO BE LATE.

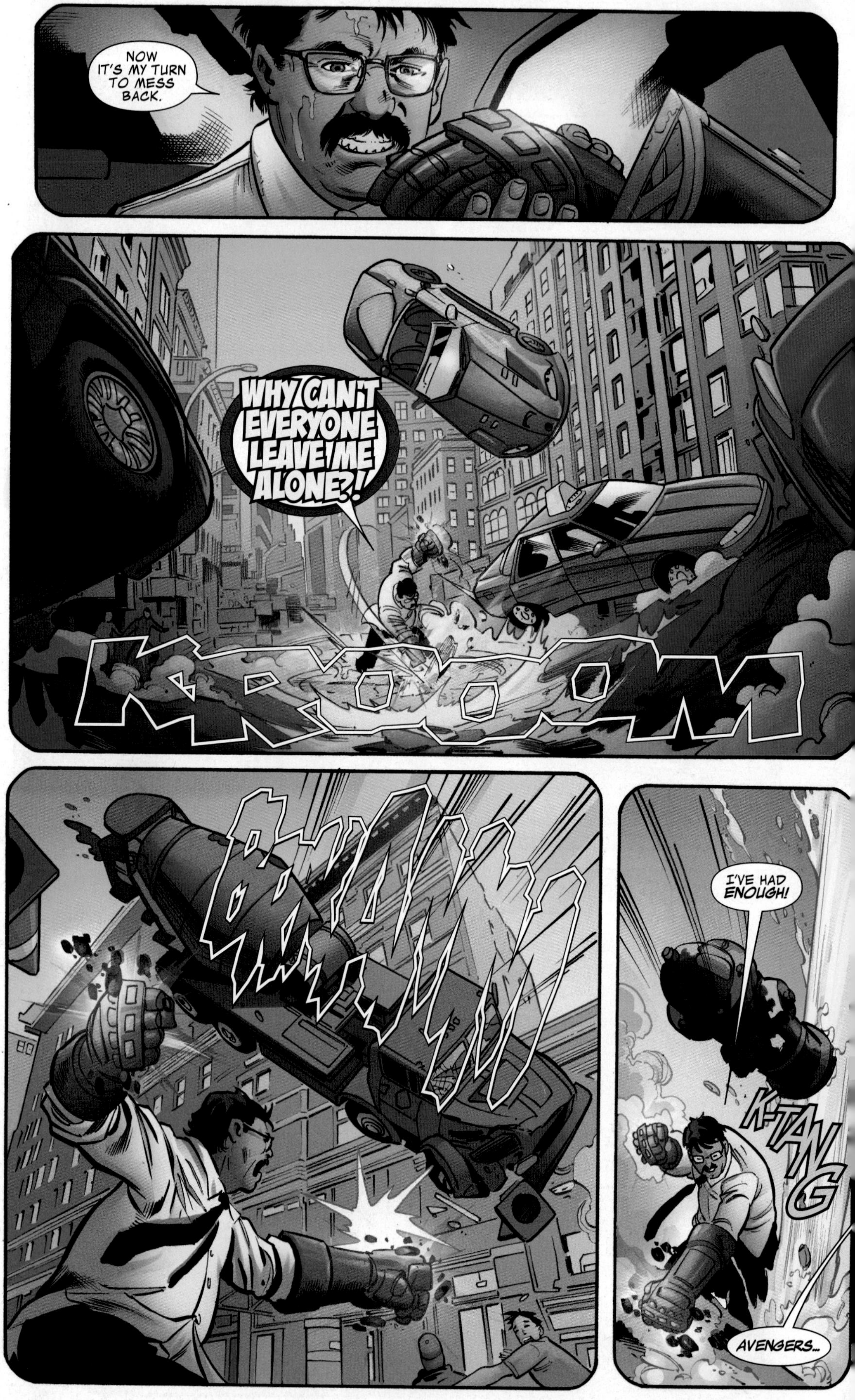
NOW IT'S MY TURN TO MESS BACK.
WHY CAN'T EVERYONE LEAVE ME ALONE?!
KRROOOM
BRAKOW
I'VE HAD ENOUGH!
K-TANG
AVENGERS...

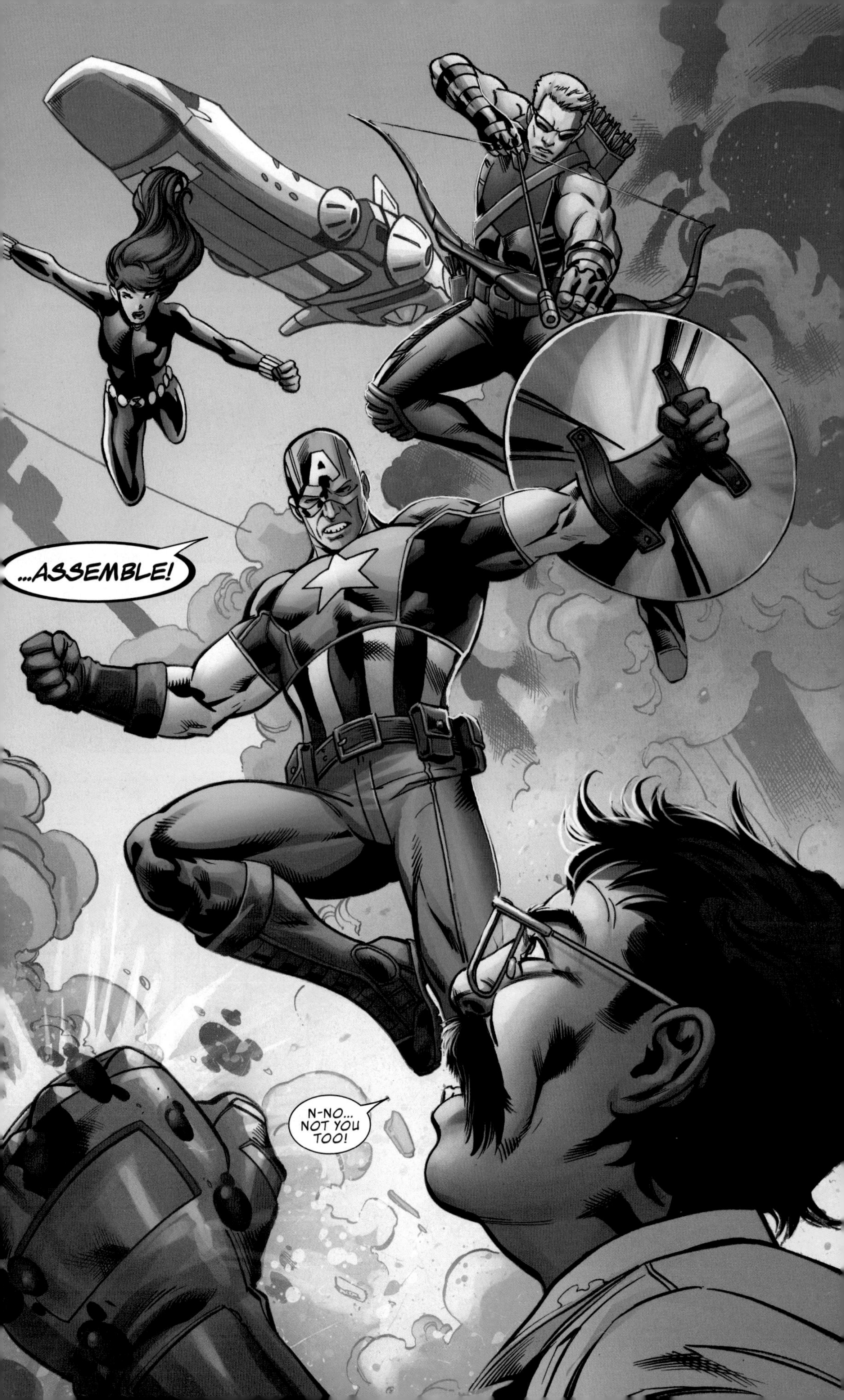
...ASSEMBLE!
N-NO... NOT YOU TOO!

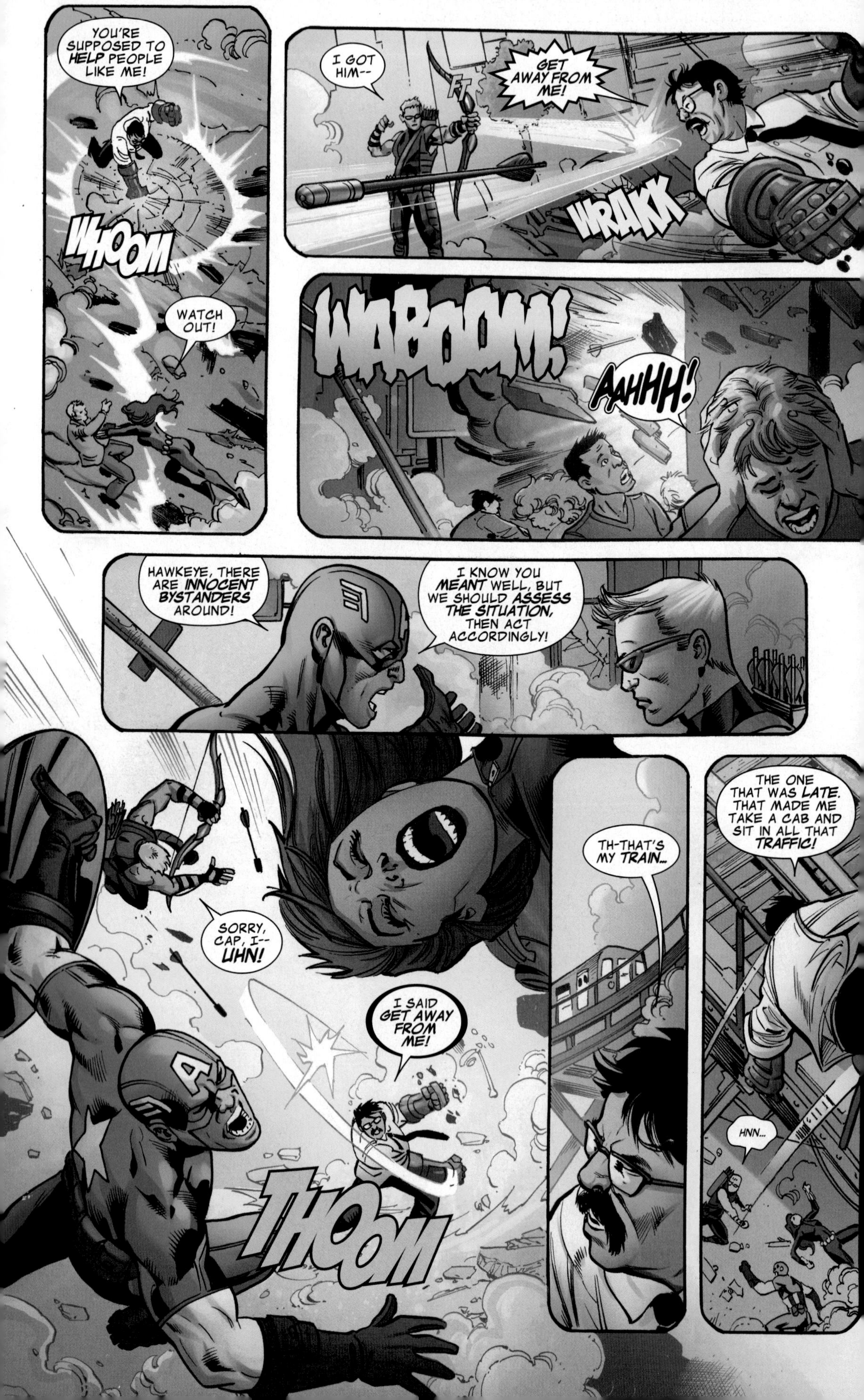
YOU'RE SUPPOSED TO HELP PEOPLE LIKE ME!
WHOOM
WATCH OUT!
I GOT HIM--
FT
GET AWAY FROM ME!
WRAKK
WABOOM!
AAHHH!
HAWKEYE, THERE ARE INNOCENT BYSTANDERS AROUND!
I KNOW YOU MEANT WELL, BUT WE SHOULD ASSESS THE SITUATION, THEN ACT ACCORDINGLY!
SORRY, CAP, I-- UHN!
I SAID GET AWAY FROM ME!
THOOM
TH-THAT'S MY TRAIN...
THE ONE THAT WAS LATE. THAT MADE ME TAKE A CAB AND SIT IN ALL THAT TRAFFIC!
HNN...

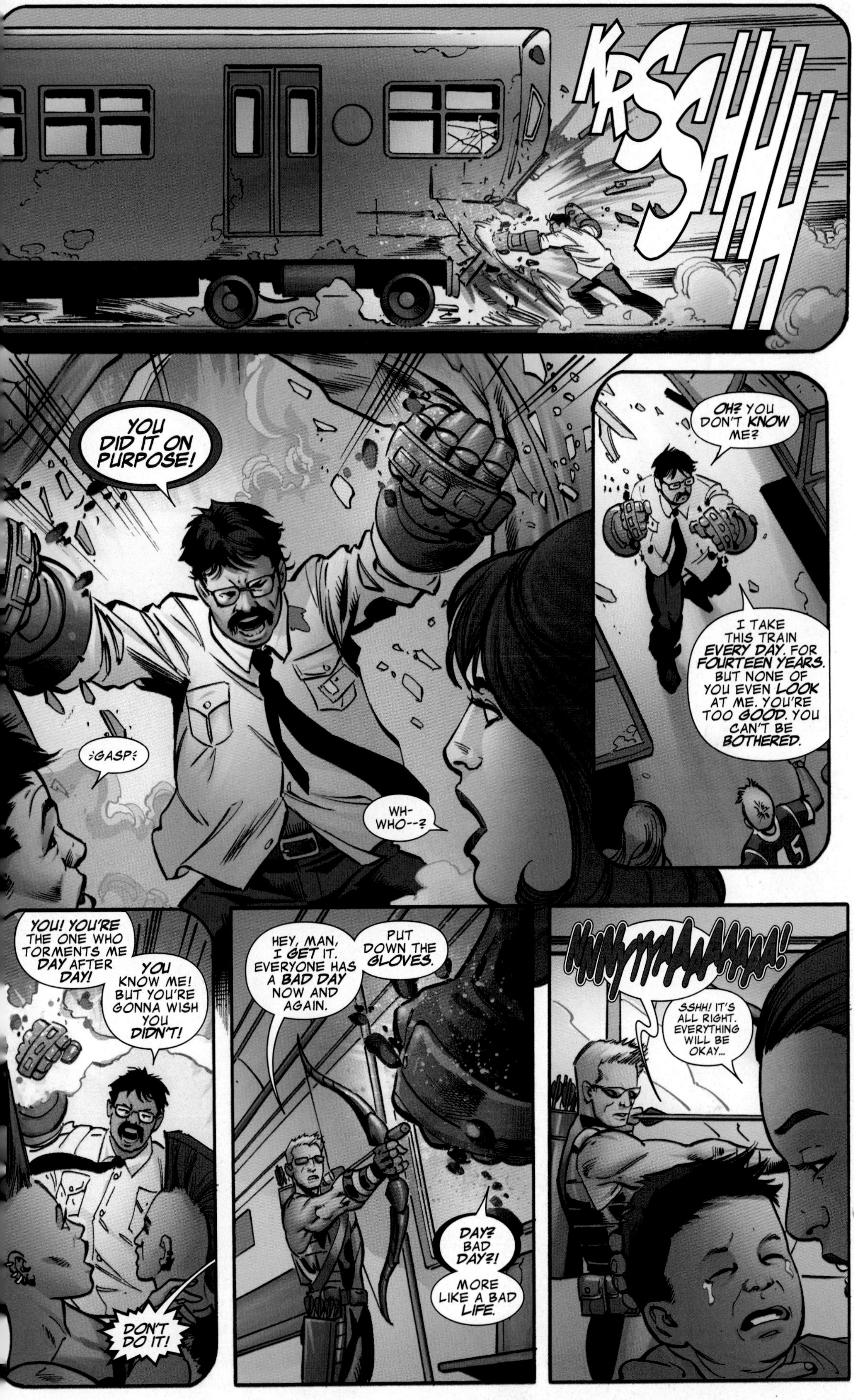
KRSCHHHH
YOU DID IT ON PURPOSE!
¡GASP!
WH-WHO--?
OH? YOU DON'T KNOW ME?
I TAKE THIS TRAIN EVERY DAY. FOR FOURTEEN YEARS. BUT NONE OF YOU EVEN LOOK AT ME. YOU'RE TOO GOOD. YOU CAN'T BE BOTHERED.
YOU! YOU'RE THE ONE WHO TORMENTS ME DAY AFTER DAY!
YOU KNOW ME! BUT YOU'RE GONNA WISH YOU DIDN'T!
DON'T DO IT!
HEY, MAN, I GET IT. EVERYONE HAS A BAD DAY NOW AND AGAIN.
PUT DOWN THE GLOVES.
DAY? BAD DAY?!
MORE LIKE A BAD LIFE.
WWNYYAAAAAAA!
SSHH! IT'S ALL RIGHT. EVERYTHING WILL BE OKAY...

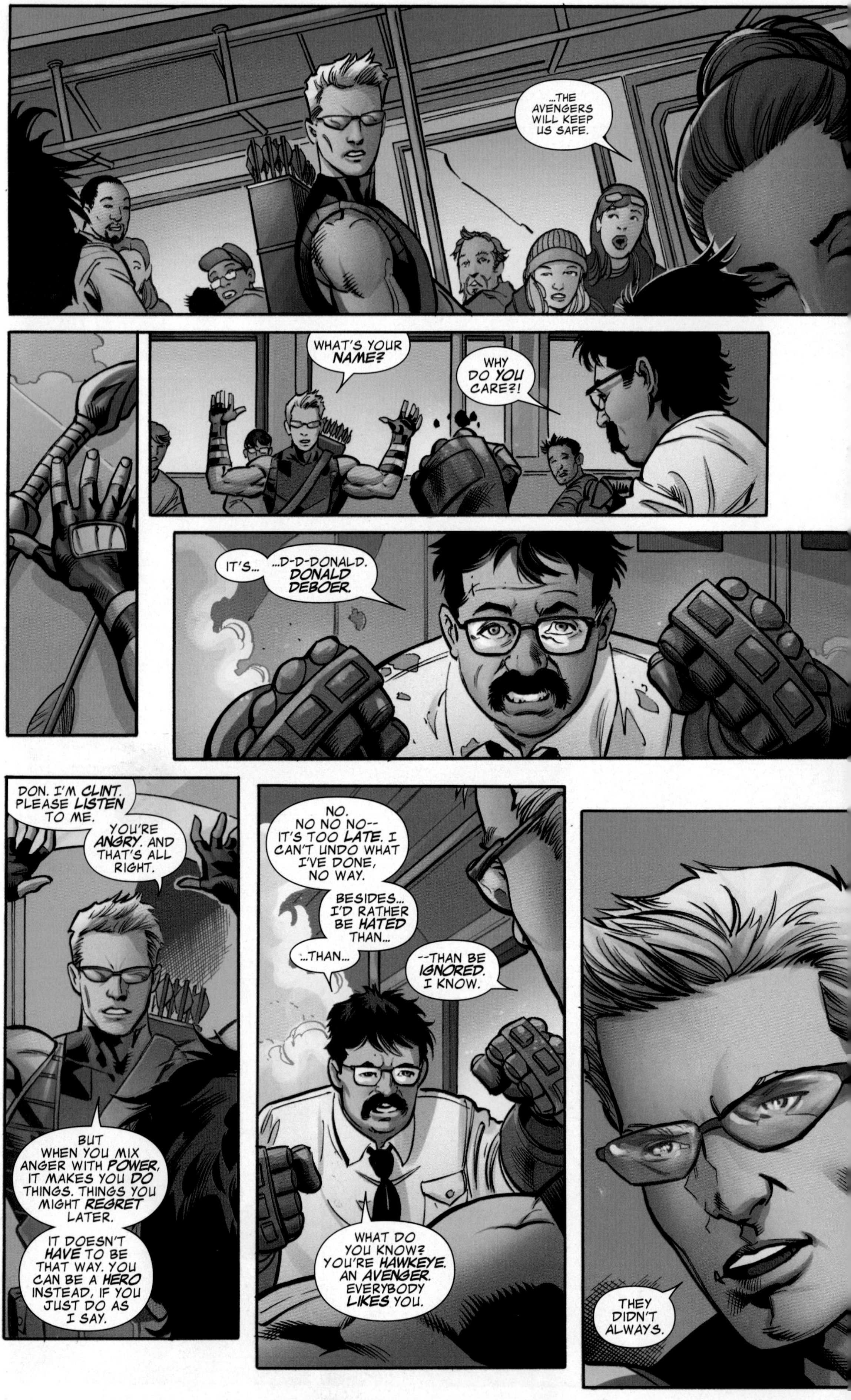
...THE AVENGERS WILL KEEP US SAFE.
WHAT'S YOUR NAME?
WHY DO YOU CARE?!
IT'S...
...D-D-DONALD. DONALD DEBOER.
DON. I'M CLINT. PLEASE LISTEN TO ME.
YOU'RE ANGRY. AND THAT'S ALL RIGHT.
BUT WHEN YOU MIX ANGER WITH POWER, IT MAKES YOU DO THINGS. THINGS YOU MIGHT REGRET LATER.
IT DOESN'T HAVE TO BE THAT WAY. YOU CAN BE A HERO INSTEAD, IF YOU JUST DO AS I SAY.
NO. NO NO NO-- IT'S TOO LATE. I CAN'T UNDO WHAT I'VE DONE, NO WAY.
BESIDES... I'D RATHER BE HATED THAN...
...THAN...
--THAN BE IGNORED. I KNOW.
WHAT DO YOU KNOW? YOU'RE HAWKEYE. AN AVENGER. EVERYBODY LIKES YOU.
THEY DIDN'T ALWAYS.

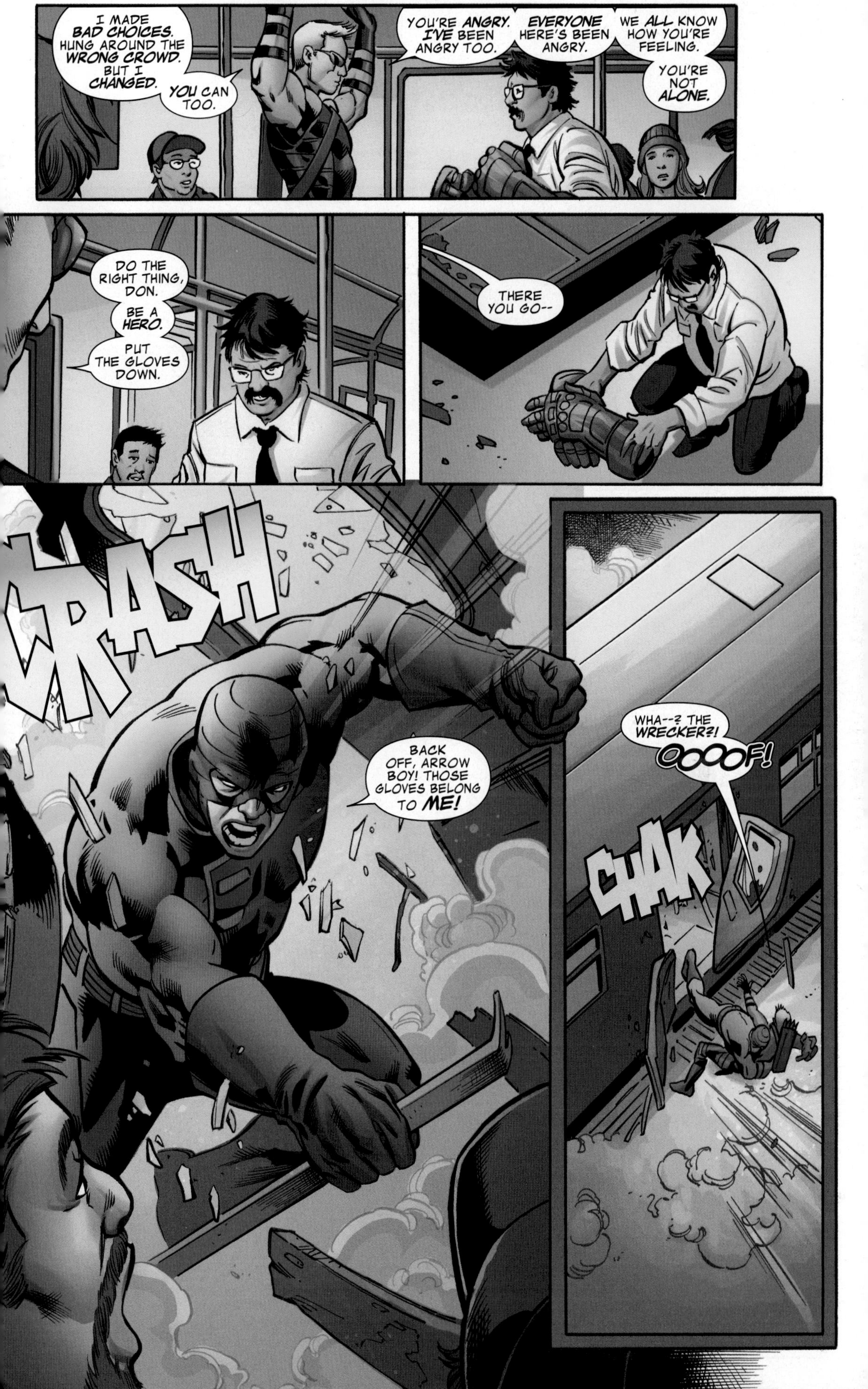
I MADE BAD CHOICES. HUNG AROUND THE WRONG CROWD. BUT I CHANGED.
YOU CAN TOO.
YOU'RE ANGRY. I'VE BEEN ANGRY TOO.
EVERYONE HERE'S BEEN ANGRY.
WE ALL KNOW HOW YOU'RE FEELING.
YOU'RE NOT ALONE.
DO THE RIGHT THING, DON.
BE A HERO.
PUT THE GLOVES DOWN.
THERE YOU GO--
CRASH
BACK OFF, ARROW BOY! THOSE GLOVES BELONG TO ME!
WHA--? THE WRECKER?!
OOOOF!
CHAK

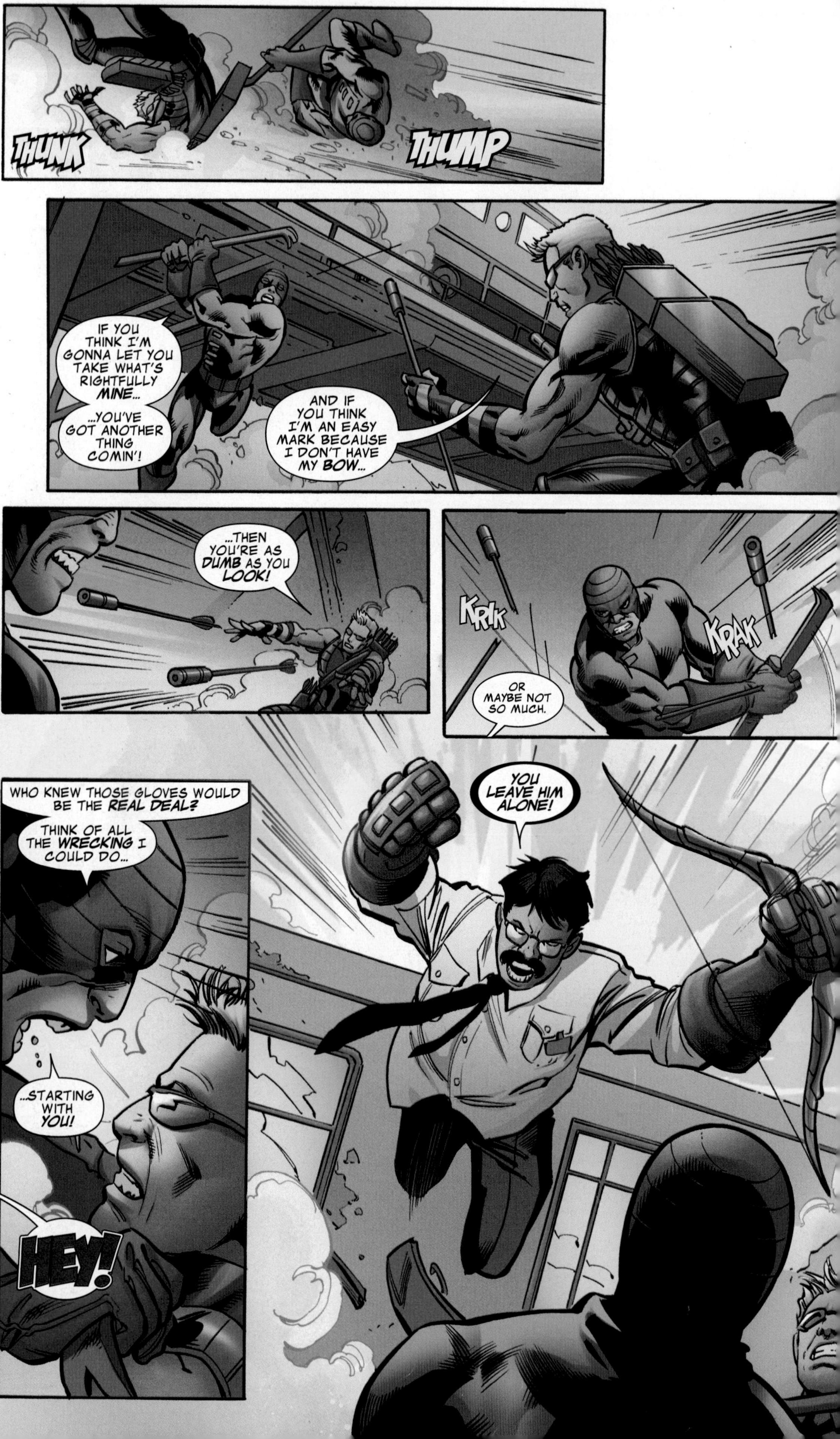
THUNK
THUMP
IF YOU THINK I'M GONNA LET YOU TAKE WHAT'S RIGHTFULLY MINE...
...YOU'VE GOT ANOTHER THING COMIN'!
AND IF YOU THINK I'M AN EASY MARK BECAUSE I DON'T HAVE MY BOW...
...THEN YOU'RE AS DUMB AS YOU LOOK!
KRIK
KRAK
OR MAYBE NOT SO MUCH.
WHO KNEW THOSE GLOVES WOULD BE THE REAL DEAL?
THINK OF ALL THE WRECKING I COULD DO...
...STARTING WITH YOU!
HEY!
YOU LEAVE HIM ALONE!

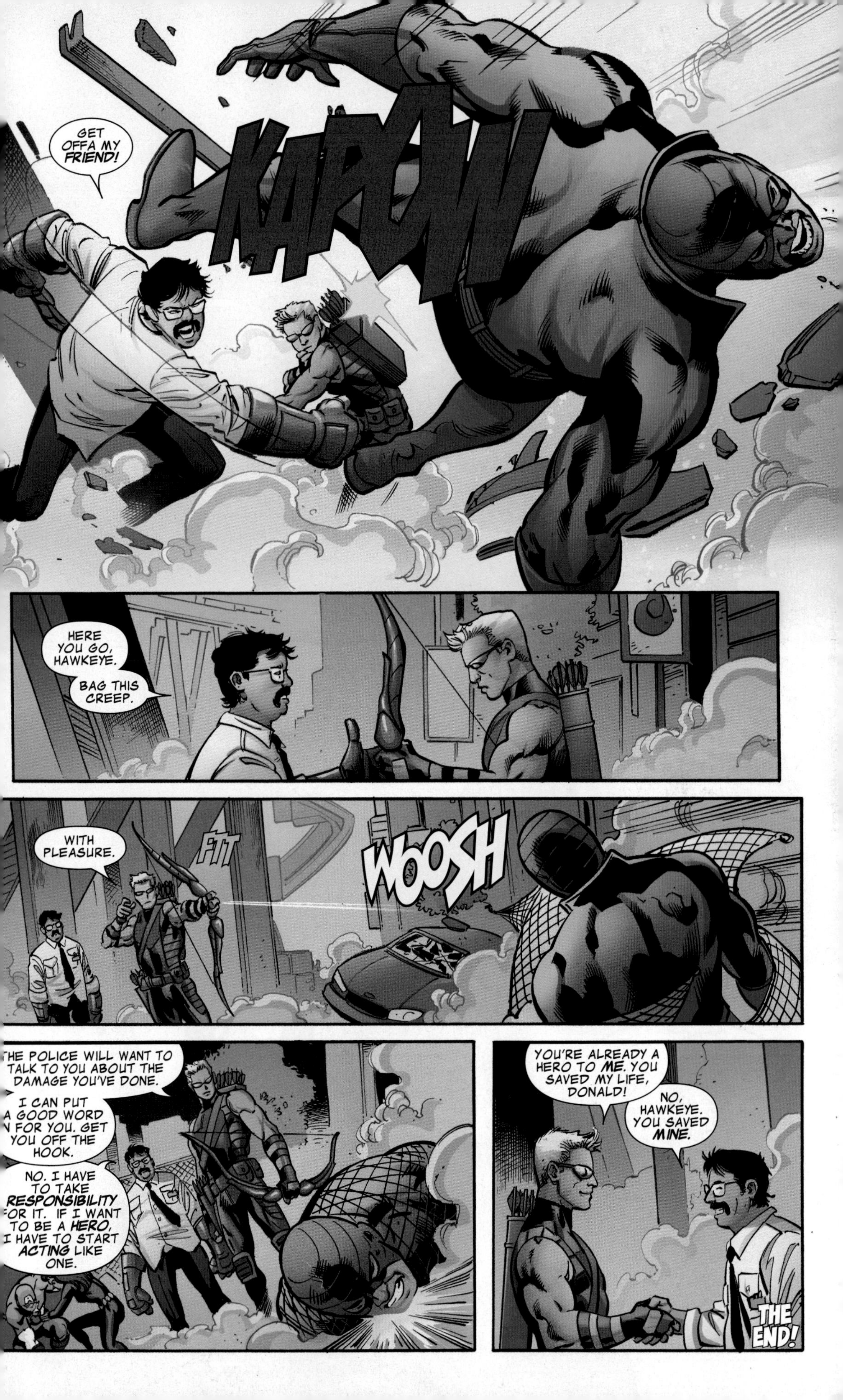
GET OFFA MY FRIEND!
KAPOW
HERE YOU GO, HAWKEYE.
BAG THIS CREEP.
WITH PLEASURE.
FTT
WOOSH
THE POLICE WILL WANT TO TALK TO YOU ABOUT THE DAMAGE YOU'VE DONE.
I CAN PUT A GOOD WORD IN FOR YOU. GET YOU OFF THE HOOK.
NO. I HAVE TO TAKE RESPONSIBILITY FOR IT. IF I WANT TO BE A HERO, I HAVE TO START ACTING LIKE ONE.
YOU'RE ALREADY A HERO TO ME. YOU SAVED MY LIFE, DONALD!
NO, HAWKEYE. YOU SAVED MINE.
THE END!

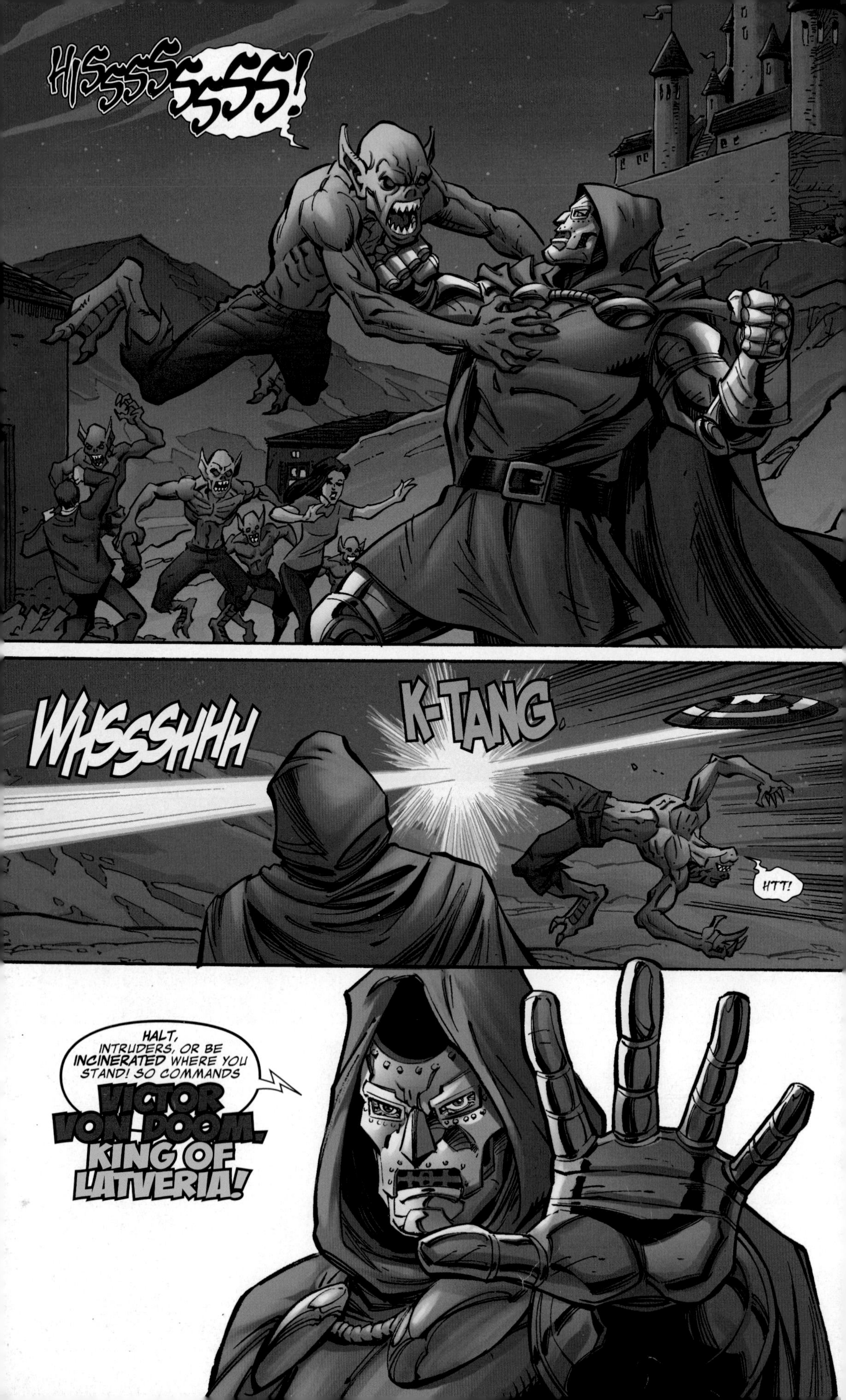
HISSSSSSSS!
WHSSSHHH
K-TANG
HTT!
HALT, INTRUDERS, OR BE INCINERATED WHERE YOU STAND! SO COMMANDS
VICTOR VON DOOM, KING OF LATVERIA!

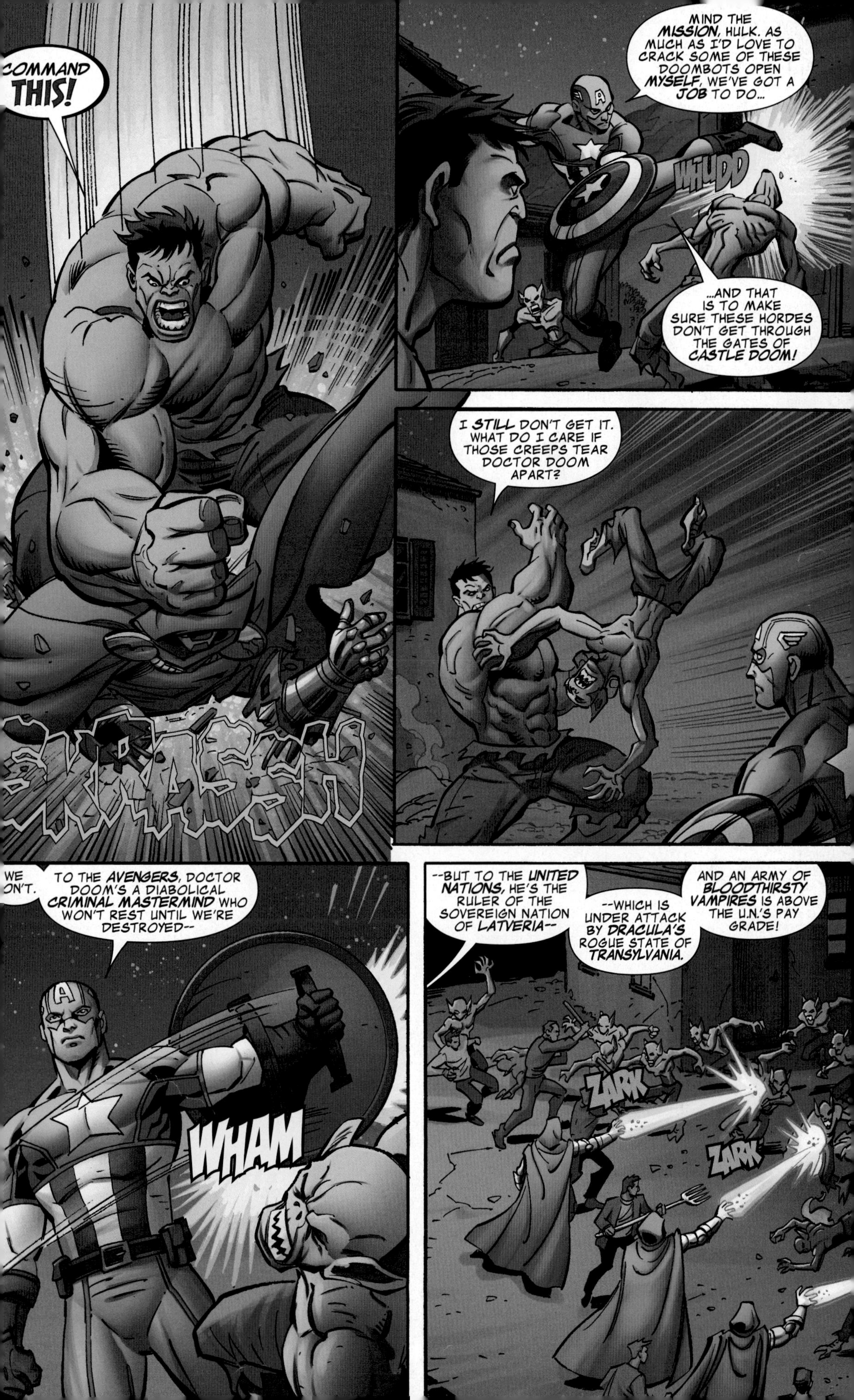

COMMAND THIS!
SKRASSH
MIND THE MISSION, HULK. AS MUCH AS I'D LOVE TO CRACK SOME OF THESE DOOMBOTS OPEN MYSELF, WE'VE GOT A JOB TO DO...
WHUDD
...AND THAT IS TO MAKE SURE THESE HORDES DON'T GET THROUGH THE GATES OF CASTLE DOOM!
I STILL DON'T GET IT. WHAT DO I CARE IF THOSE CREEPS TEAR DOCTOR DOOM APART?
WE ON'T.
TO THE AVENGERS, DOCTOR DOOM'S A DIABOLICAL CRIMINAL MASTERMIND WHO WON'T REST UNTIL WE'RE DESTROYED--
WHAM
--BUT TO THE UNITED NATIONS, HE'S THE RULER OF THE SOVEREIGN NATION OF LATVERIA--
--WHICH IS UNDER ATTACK BY DRACULA'S ROGUE STATE OF TRANSYLVANIA.
AND AN ARMY OF BLOODTHIRSTY VAMPIRES IS ABOVE THE U.N.'S PAY GRADE!
ZARK
ZARK

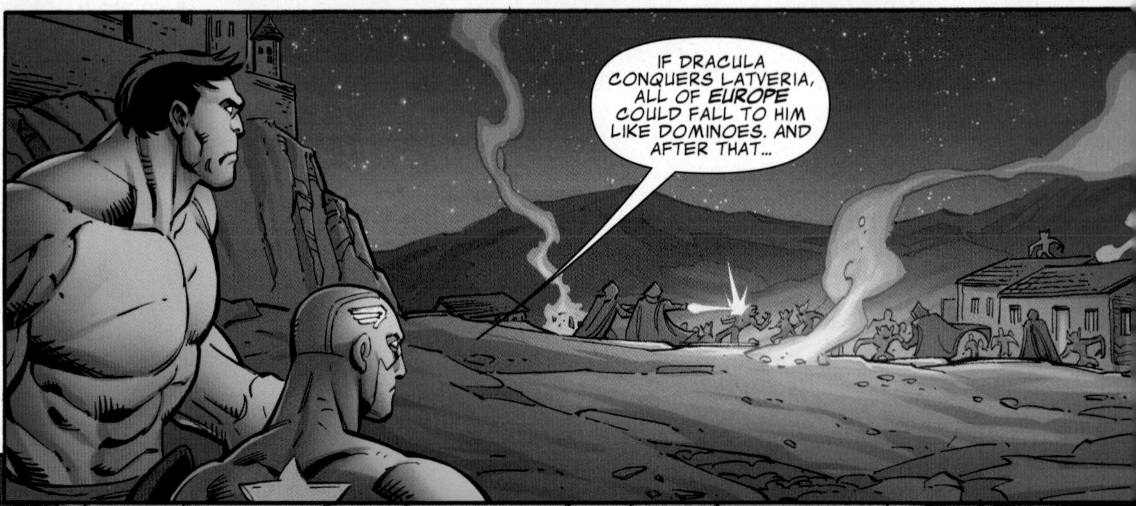
IF DRACULA CONQUERS LATVERIA, ALL OF EUROPE COULD FALL TO HIM LIKE DOMINOES. AND AFTER THAT...

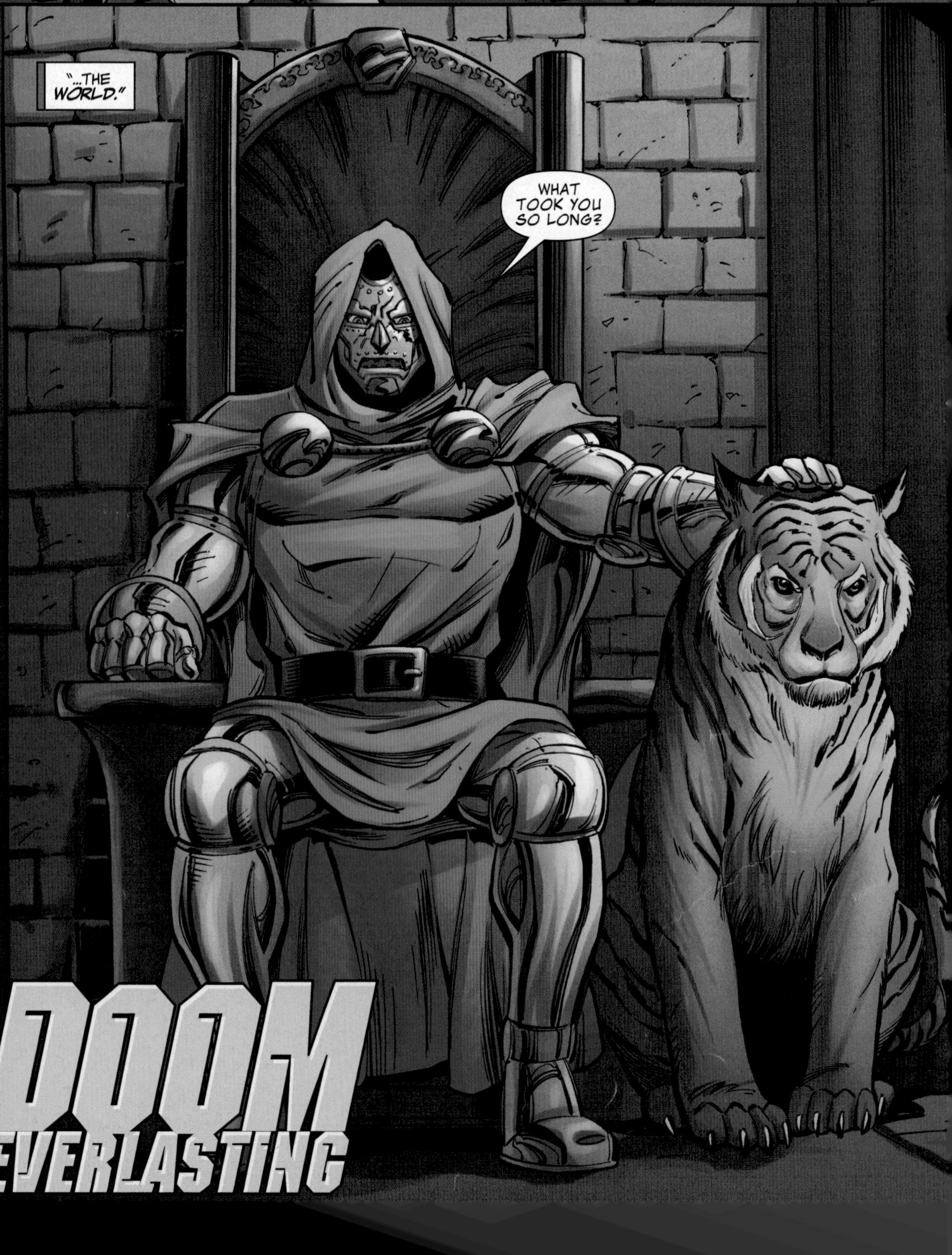
"...THE WORLD."
WHAT TOOK YOU SO LONG?
DOOM EVERLASTING

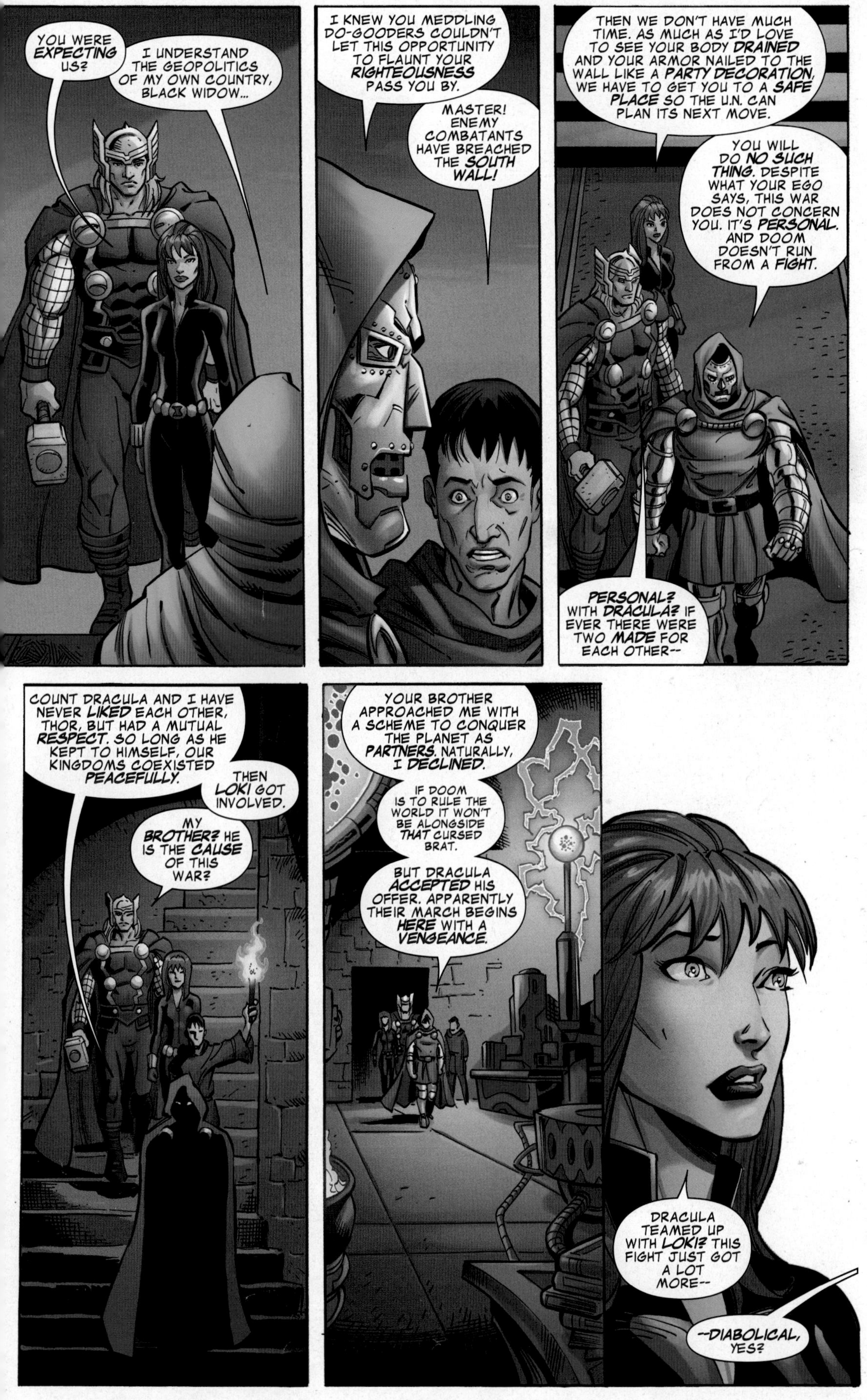
YOU WERE EXPECTING US?
I UNDERSTAND THE GEOPOLITICS OF MY OWN COUNTRY, BLACK WIDOW...
I KNEW YOU MEDDLING DO-GOODERS COULDN'T LET THIS OPPORTUNITY TO FLAUNT YOUR RIGHTEOUSNESS PASS YOU BY.
MASTER! ENEMY COMBATANTS HAVE BREACHED THE SOUTH WALL!
THEN WE DON'T HAVE MUCH TIME. AS MUCH AS I'D LOVE TO SEE YOUR BODY DRAINED AND YOUR ARMOR NAILED TO THE WALL LIKE A PARTY DECORATION, WE HAVE TO GET YOU TO A SAFE PLACE SO THE U.N. CAN PLAN ITS NEXT MOVE.
YOU WILL DO NO SUCH THING. DESPITE WHAT YOUR EGO SAYS, THIS WAR DOES NOT CONCERN YOU. IT'S PERSONAL. AND DOOM DOESN'T RUN FROM A FIGHT.
PERSONAL? WITH DRACULA? IF EVER THERE WERE TWO MADE FOR EACH OTHER--
COUNT DRACULA AND I HAVE NEVER LIKED EACH OTHER, THOR, BUT HAD A MUTUAL RESPECT. SO LONG AS HE KEPT TO HIMSELF, OUR KINGDOMS COEXISTED PEACEFULLY.
THEN LOKI GOT INVOLVED.
MY BROTHER? HE IS THE CAUSE OF THIS WAR?
YOUR BROTHER APPROACHED ME WITH A SCHEME TO CONQUER THE PLANET AS PARTNERS. NATURALLY, I DECLINED.
IF DOOM IS TO RULE THE WORLD IT WON'T BE ALONGSIDE THAT CURSED BRAT.
BUT DRACULA ACCEPTED HIS OFFER. APPARENTLY THEIR MARCH BEGINS HERE WITH A VENGEANCE.
DRACULA TEAMED UP WITH LOKI? THIS FIGHT JUST GOT A LOT MORE--
--DIABOLICAL, YES?

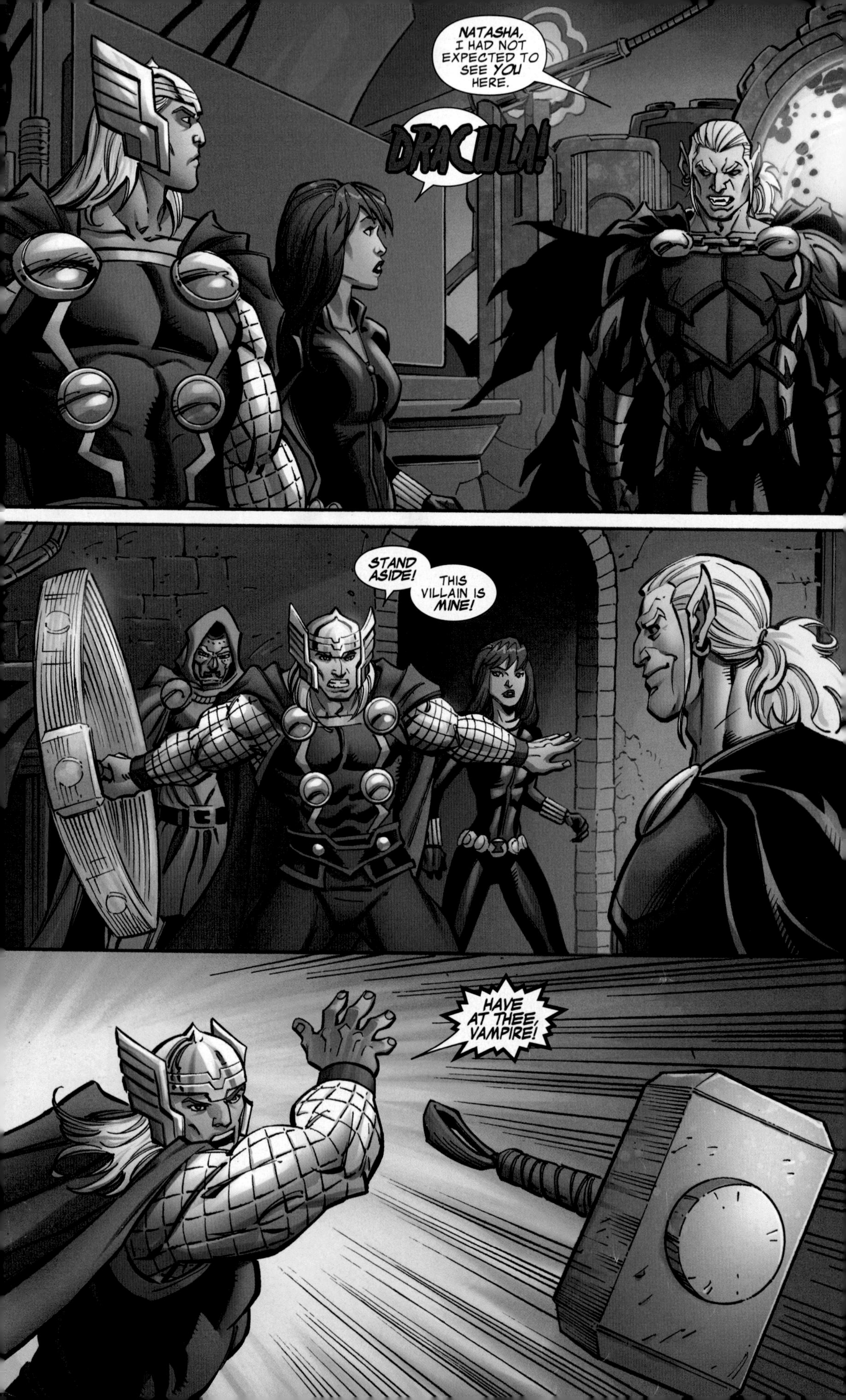

NATASHA, I HAD NOT EXPECTED TO SEE YOU HERE.
DRACULA!
STAND ASIDE!
THIS VILLAIN IS MINE!
HAVE AT THEE, VAMPIRE!

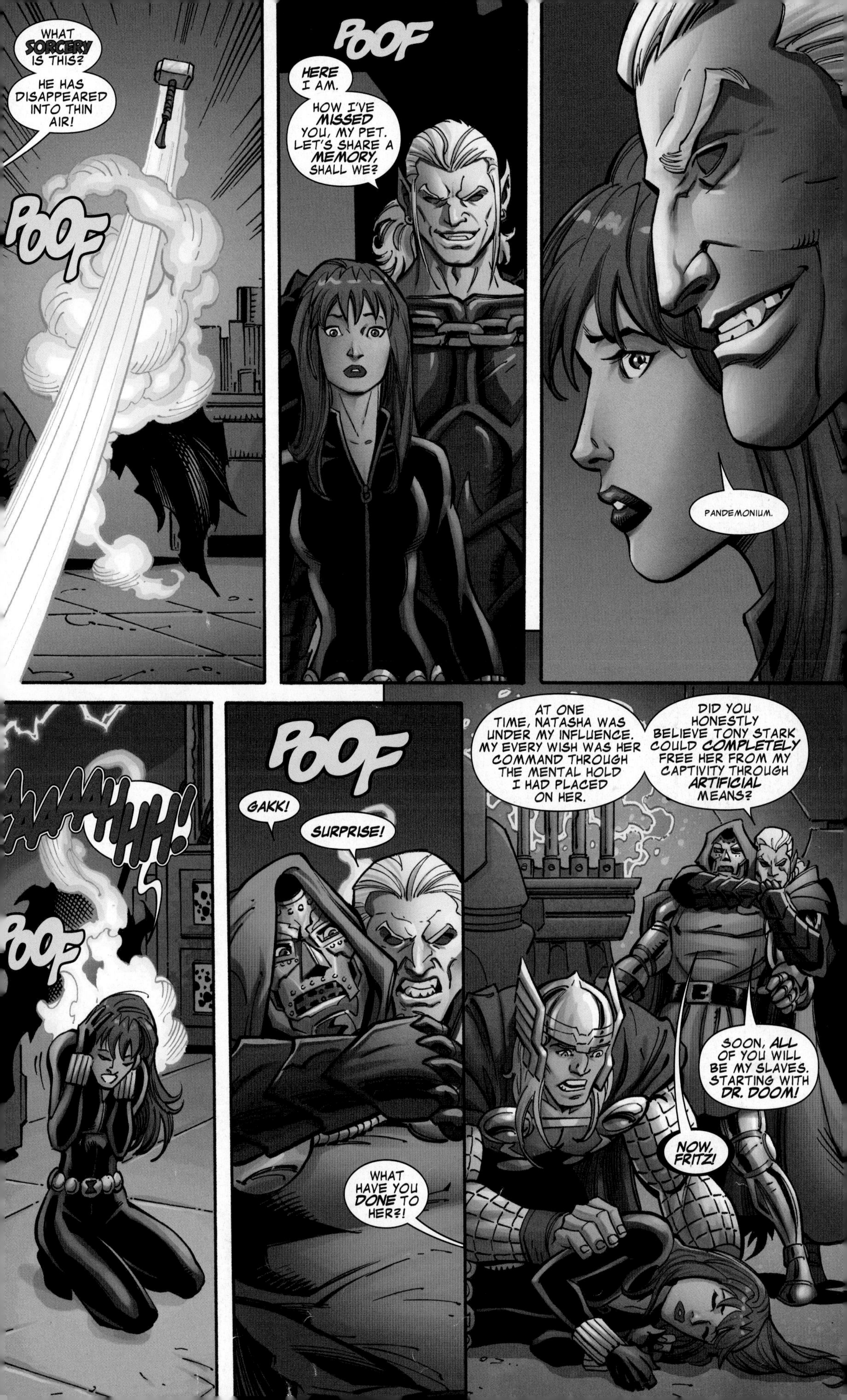
WHAT SORCERY IS THIS?
HE HAS DISAPPEARED INTO THIN AIR!
POOF
POOF
HERE I AM.
HOW I'VE MISSED YOU, MY PET. LET'S SHARE A MEMORY, SHALL WE?
PANDEMONIUM.
AAAAHHH!
POOF
POOF
GAKK!
SURPRISE!
AT ONE TIME, NATASHA WAS UNDER MY INFLUENCE. MY EVERY WISH WAS HER COMMAND THROUGH THE MENTAL HOLD I HAD PLACED ON HER.
DID YOU HONESTLY BELIEVE TONY STARK COULD COMPLETELY FREE HER FROM MY CAPTIVITY THROUGH ARTIFICIAL MEANS?
SOON, ALL OF YOU WILL BE MY SLAVES. STARTING WITH DR. DOOM!
NOW, FRITZ!
WHAT HAVE YOU DONE TO HER?!

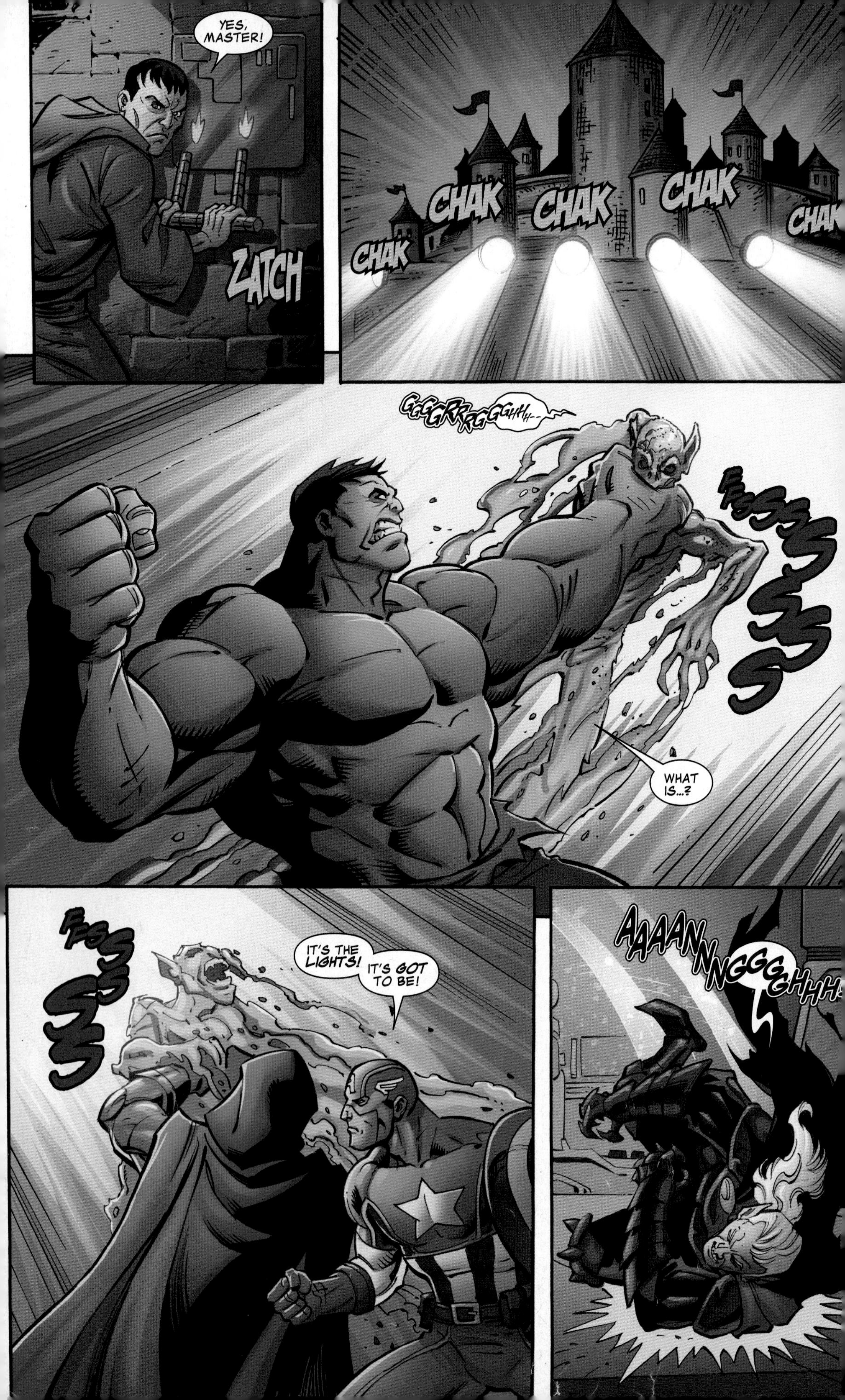
YES, MASTER!
ZATCH
CHAK
CHAK
CHAK
CHAK
CHAK
GGGGRRRRGGGHHH--
FFSSSSSSSS
WHAT IS...?
FFSSSSS
IT'S THE LIGHTS!
IT'S GOT TO BE!
AAAANNNGGGGHHHH

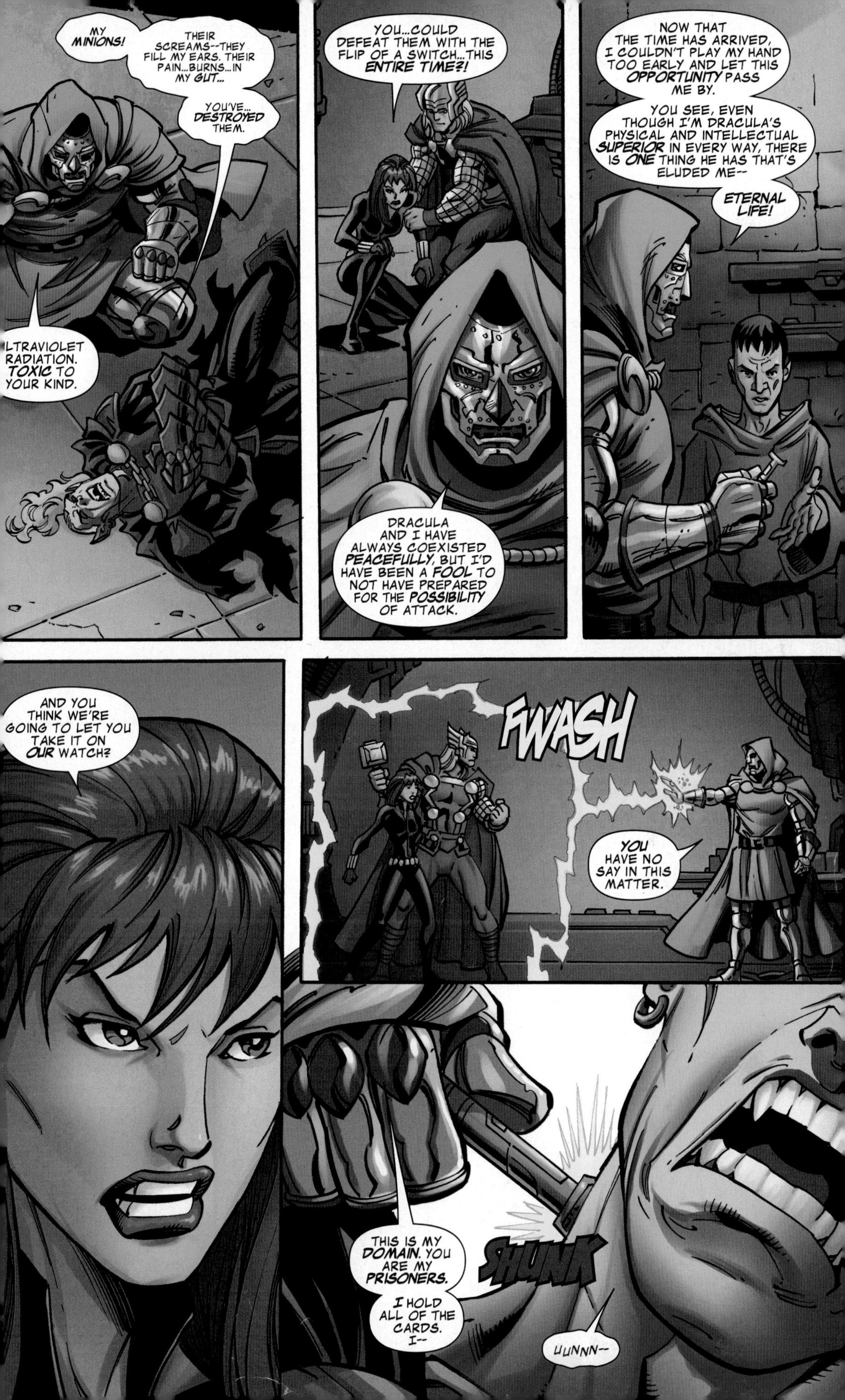
MY MINIONS!
THEIR SCREAMS--THEY FILL MY EARS. THEIR PAIN...BURNS...IN MY GUT...
YOU'VE... DESTROYED THEM.
ULTRAVIOLET RADIATION. TOXIC TO YOUR KIND.
YOU...COULD DEFEAT THEM WITH THE FLIP OF A SWITCH...THIS ENTIRE TIME?!
DRACULA AND I HAVE ALWAYS COEXISTED PEACEFULLY, BUT I'D HAVE BEEN A FOOL TO NOT HAVE PREPARED FOR THE POSSIBILITY OF ATTACK.
NOW THAT THE TIME HAS ARRIVED, I COULDN'T PLAY MY HAND TOO EARLY AND LET THIS OPPORTUNITY PASS ME BY.
YOU SEE, EVEN THOUGH I'M DRACULA'S PHYSICAL AND INTELLECTUAL SUPERIOR IN EVERY WAY, THERE IS ONE THING HE HAS THAT'S ELUDED ME--
ETERNAL LIFE!
AND YOU THINK WE'RE GOING TO LET YOU TAKE IT ON OUR WATCH?
FWASH
YOU HAVE NO SAY IN THIS MATTER.
THIS IS MY DOMAIN. YOU ARE MY PRISONERS.
I HOLD ALL OF THE CARDS. I--
SHUNK
UUNNN--

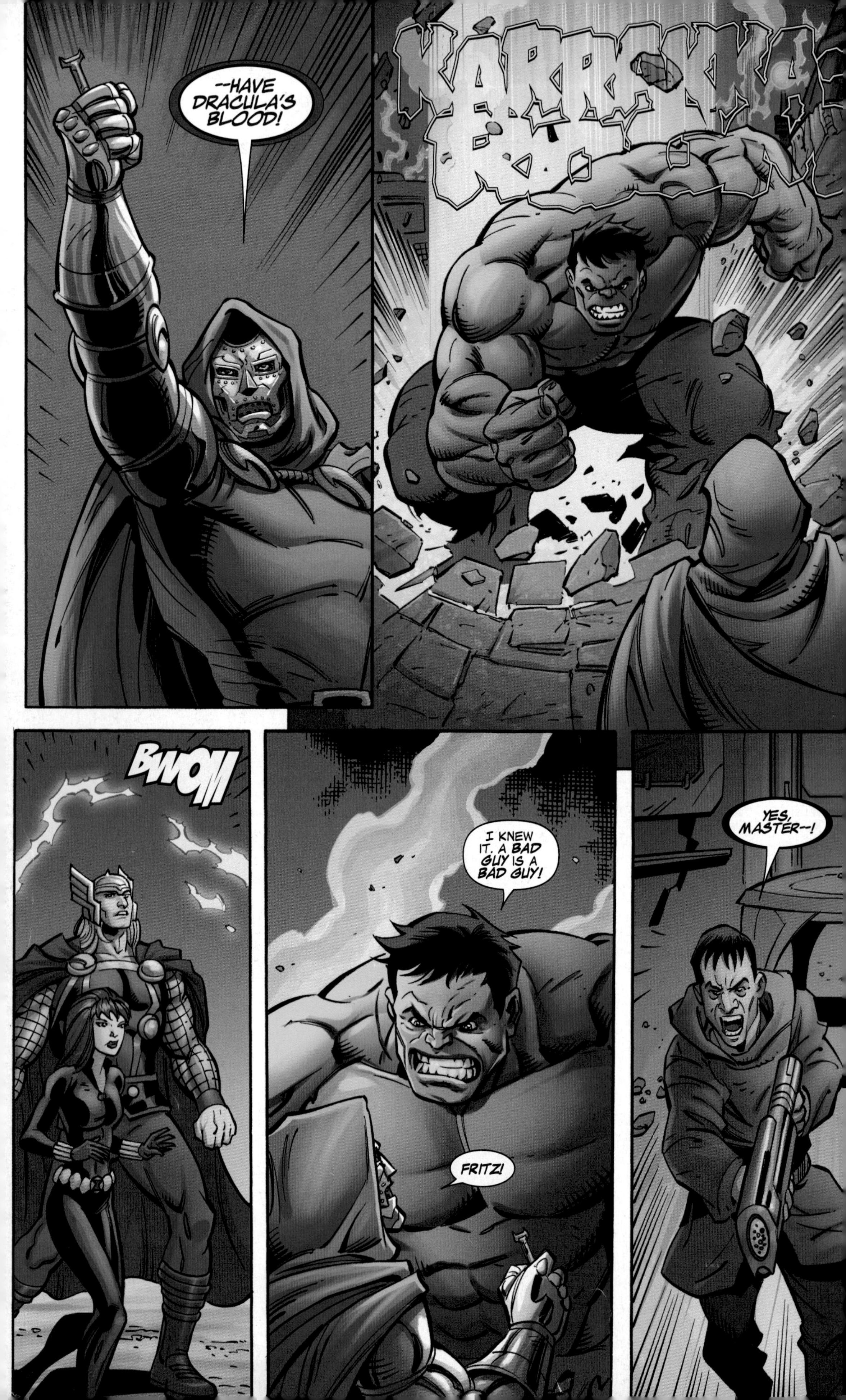
--HAVE DRACULA'S BLOOD!
BWOM
I KNEW IT. A BAD GUY IS A BAD GUY!
FRITZ!
YES, MASTER--!

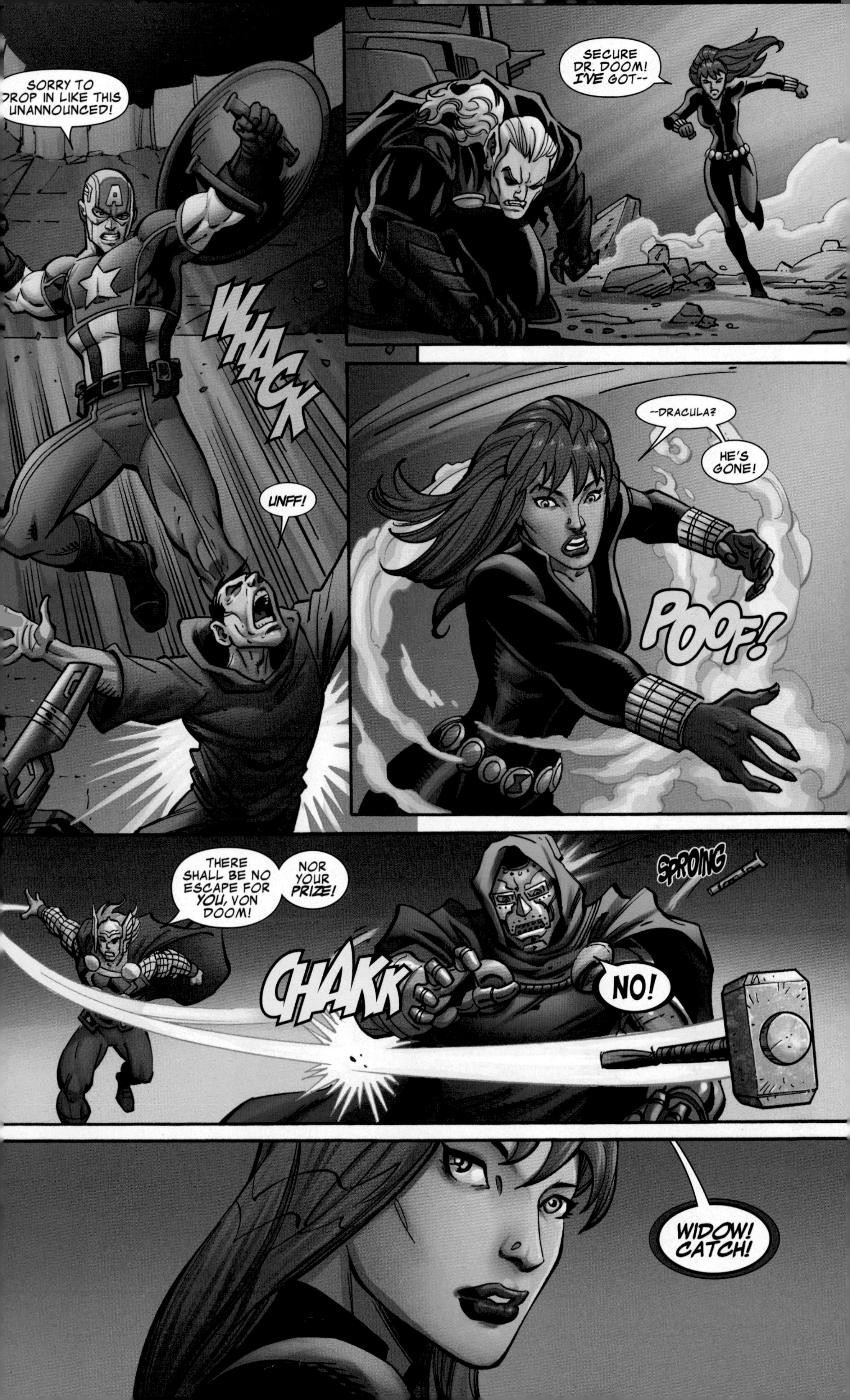
SORRY TO DROP IN LIKE THIS UNANNOUNCED!
WHACK
UNFF!
SECURE DR. DOOM! I'VE GOT--
--DRACULA?
HE'S GONE!
POOF!
THERE SHALL BE NO ESCAPE FOR YOU, VON DOOM!
NOR YOUR PRIZE!
SPROING
CHAKK
NO!
WIDOW! CATCH!

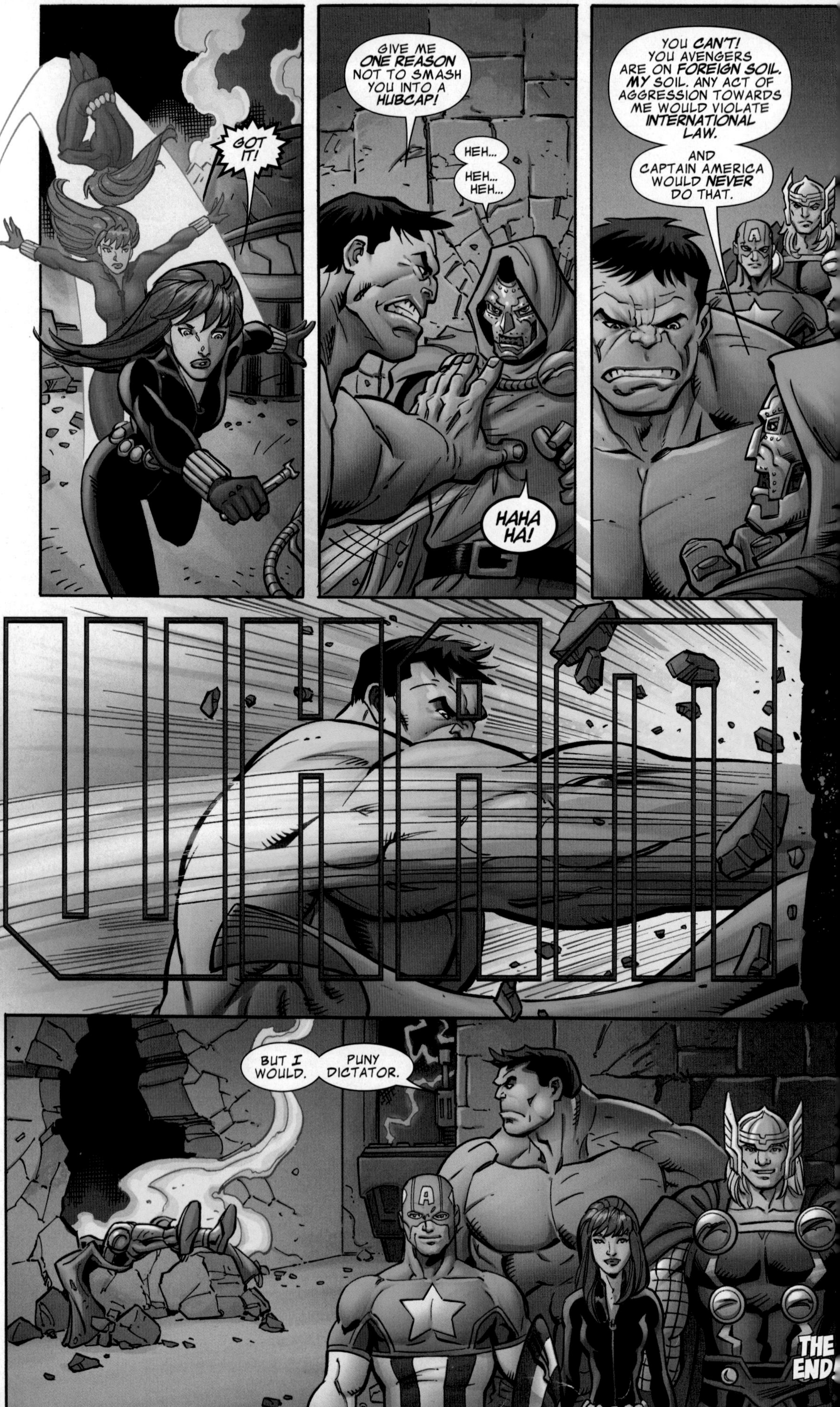
GOT IT!
GIVE ME ONE REASON NOT TO SMASH YOU INTO A HUBCAP!
HEH...
HEH... HEH...
HAHA HA!
YOU CAN'T! YOU AVENGERS ARE ON FOREIGN SOIL. MY SOIL. ANY ACT OF AGGRESSION TOWARDS ME WOULD VIOLATE INTERNATIONAL LAW.
AND CAPTAIN AMERICA WOULD NEVER DO THAT.
BUT I WOULD.
PUNY DICTATOR.
THE END.

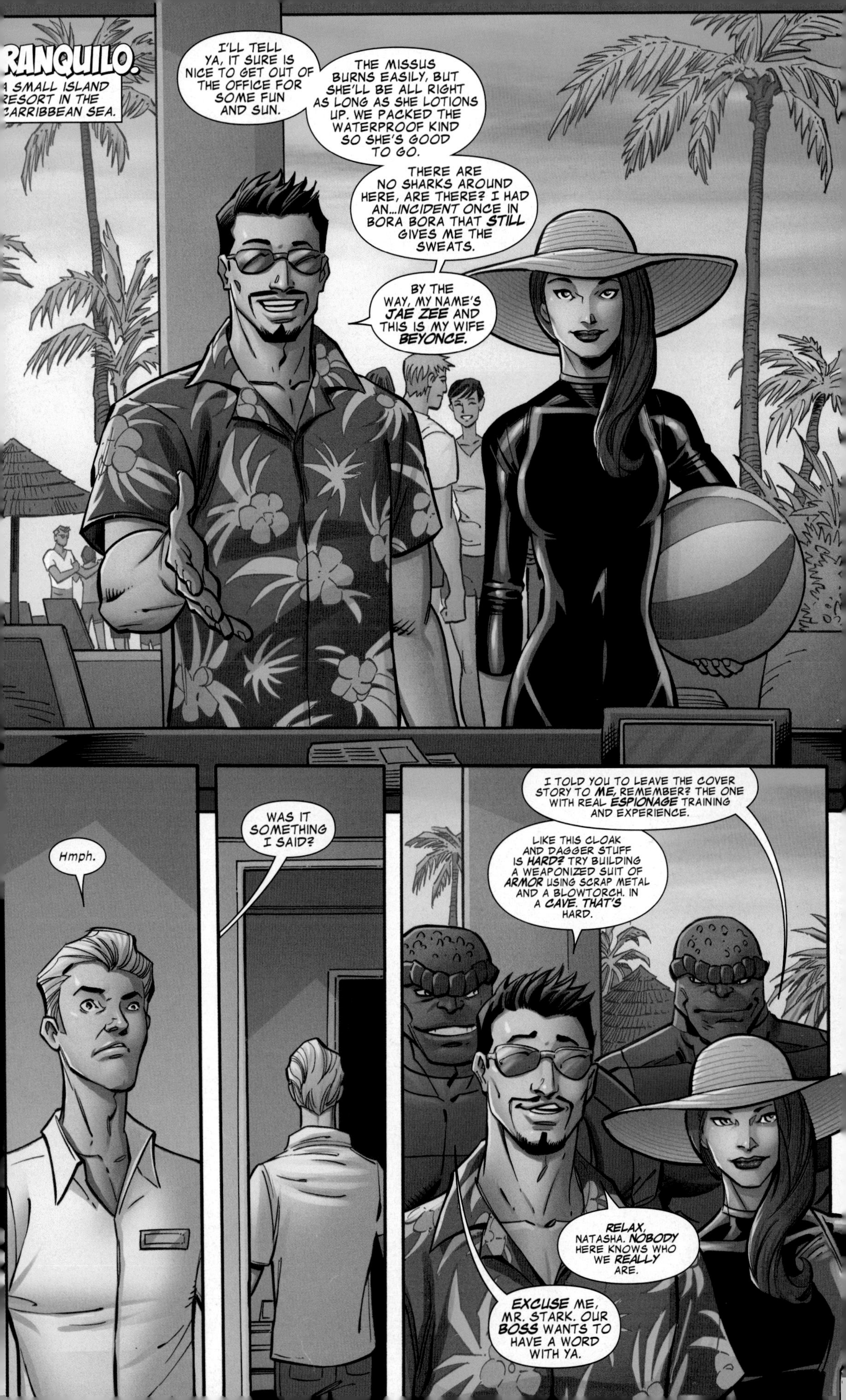
RANQUILO.
A SMALL ISLAND RESORT IN THE CARRIBBEAN SEA.
I'LL TELL YA, IT SURE IS NICE TO GET OUT OF THE OFFICE FOR SOME FUN AND SUN.
THE MISSUS BURNS EASILY, BUT SHE'LL BE ALL RIGHT AS LONG AS SHE LOTIONS UP. WE PACKED THE WATERPROOF KIND SO SHE'S GOOD TO GO.
THERE ARE NO SHARKS AROUND HERE, ARE THERE? I HAD AN...INCIDENT ONCE IN BORA BORA THAT STILL GIVES ME THE SWEATS.
BY THE WAY, MY NAME'S JAE ZEE AND THIS IS MY WIFE BEYONCE.
Hmph.
WAS IT SOMETHING I SAID?
I TOLD YOU TO LEAVE THE COVER STORY TO ME, REMEMBER? THE ONE WITH REAL ESPIONAGE TRAINING AND EXPERIENCE.
LIKE THIS CLOAK AND DAGGER STUFF IS HARD? TRY BUILDING A WEAPONIZED SUIT OF ARMOR USING SCRAP METAL AND A BLOWTORCH. IN A CAVE. THAT'S HARD.
RELAX, NATASHA. NOBODY HERE KNOWS WHO WE REALLY ARE.
EXCUSE ME, MR. STARK. OUR BOSS WANTS TO HAVE A WORD WITH YA.

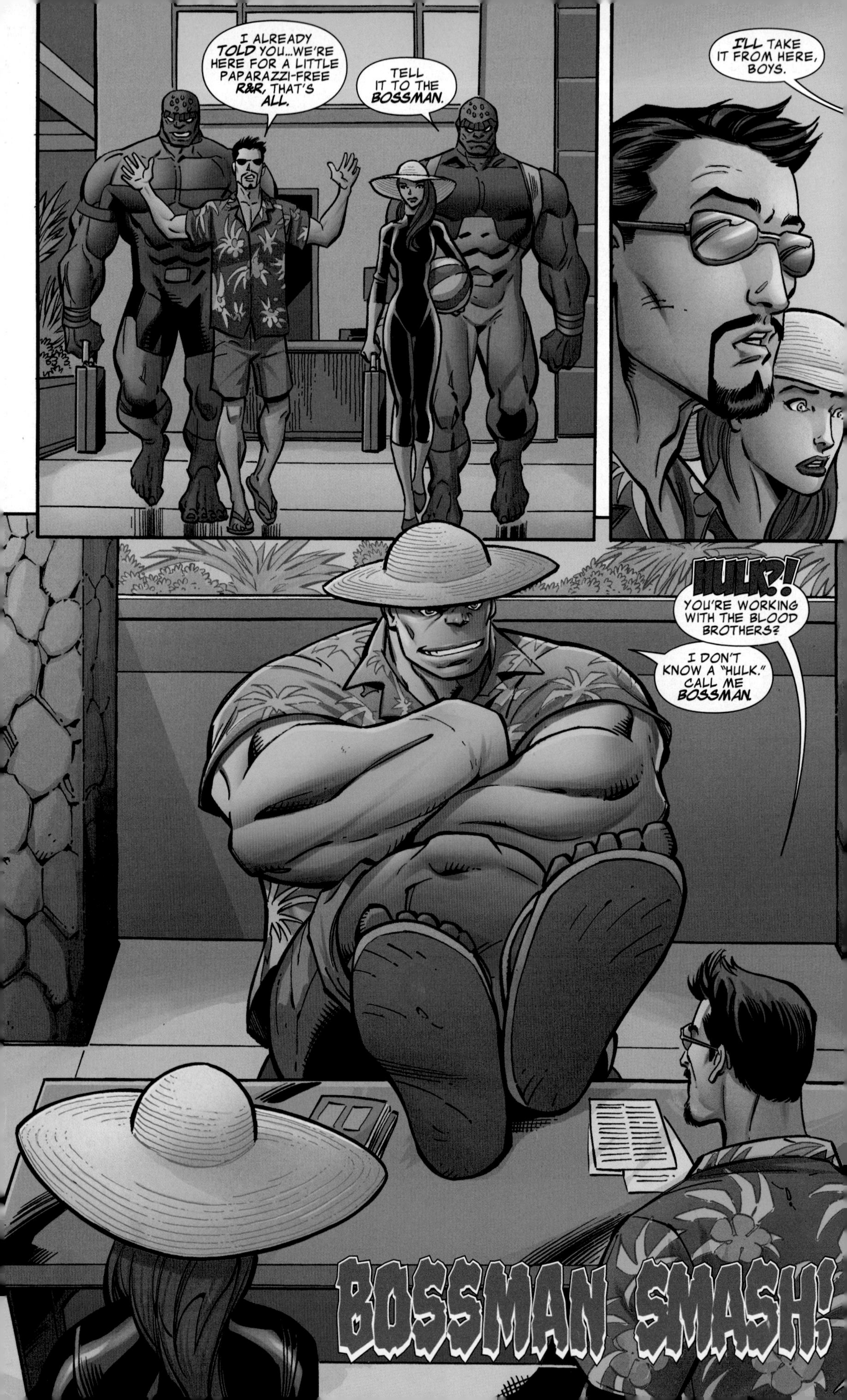
I ALREADY TOLD YOU...WE'RE HERE FOR A LITTLE PAPARAZZI-FREE R&R, THAT'S ALL.
TELL IT TO THE BOSSMAN.
I'LL TAKE IT FROM HERE, BOYS.
HULK?!
YOU'RE WORKING WITH THE BLOOD BROTHERS?
I DON'T KNOW A "HULK." CALL ME BOSSMAN.
BOSSMAN SMASH!

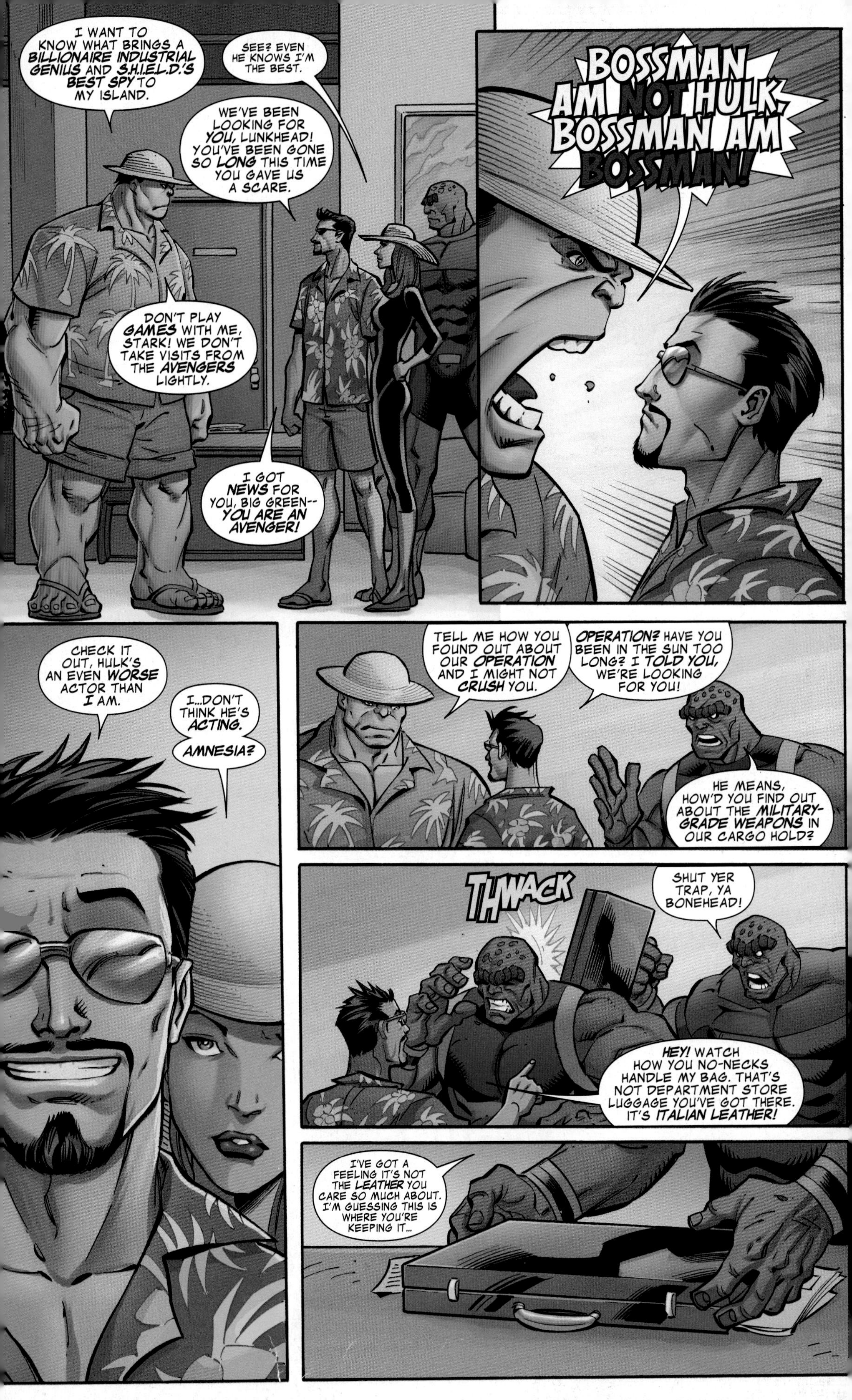
I WANT TO KNOW WHAT BRINGS A BILLIONAIRE INDUSTRIAL GENIUS AND S.H.I.E.L.D.'S BEST SPY TO MY ISLAND.
SEE? EVEN HE KNOWS I'M THE BEST.
WE'VE BEEN LOOKING FOR YOU, LUNKHEAD! YOU'VE BEEN GONE SO LONG THIS TIME YOU GAVE US A SCARE.
DON'T PLAY GAMES WITH ME, STARK! WE DON'T TAKE VISITS FROM THE AVENGERS LIGHTLY.
I GOT NEWS FOR YOU, BIG GREEN-- YOU ARE AN AVENGER!
BOSSMAN AM NOT HULK. BOSSMAN AM BOSSMAN!
CHECK IT OUT, HULK'S AN EVEN WORSE ACTOR THAN I AM.
I...DON'T THINK HE'S ACTING.
AMNESIA?
TELL ME HOW YOU FOUND OUT ABOUT OUR OPERATION AND I MIGHT NOT CRUSH YOU.
OPERATION? HAVE YOU BEEN IN THE SUN TOO LONG? I TOLD YOU, WE'RE LOOKING FOR YOU!
HE MEANS, HOW'D YOU FIND OUT ABOUT THE MILITARY-GRADE WEAPONS IN OUR CARGO HOLD?
THWACK
SHUT YER TRAP, YA BONEHEAD!
HEY! WATCH HOW YOU NO-NECKS HANDLE MY BAG. THAT'S NOT DEPARTMENT STORE LUGGAGE YOU'VE GOT THERE. IT'S ITALIAN LEATHER!
I'VE GOT A FEELING IT'S NOT THE LEATHER YOU CARE SO MUCH ABOUT. I'M GUESSING THIS IS WHERE YOU'RE KEEPING IT...

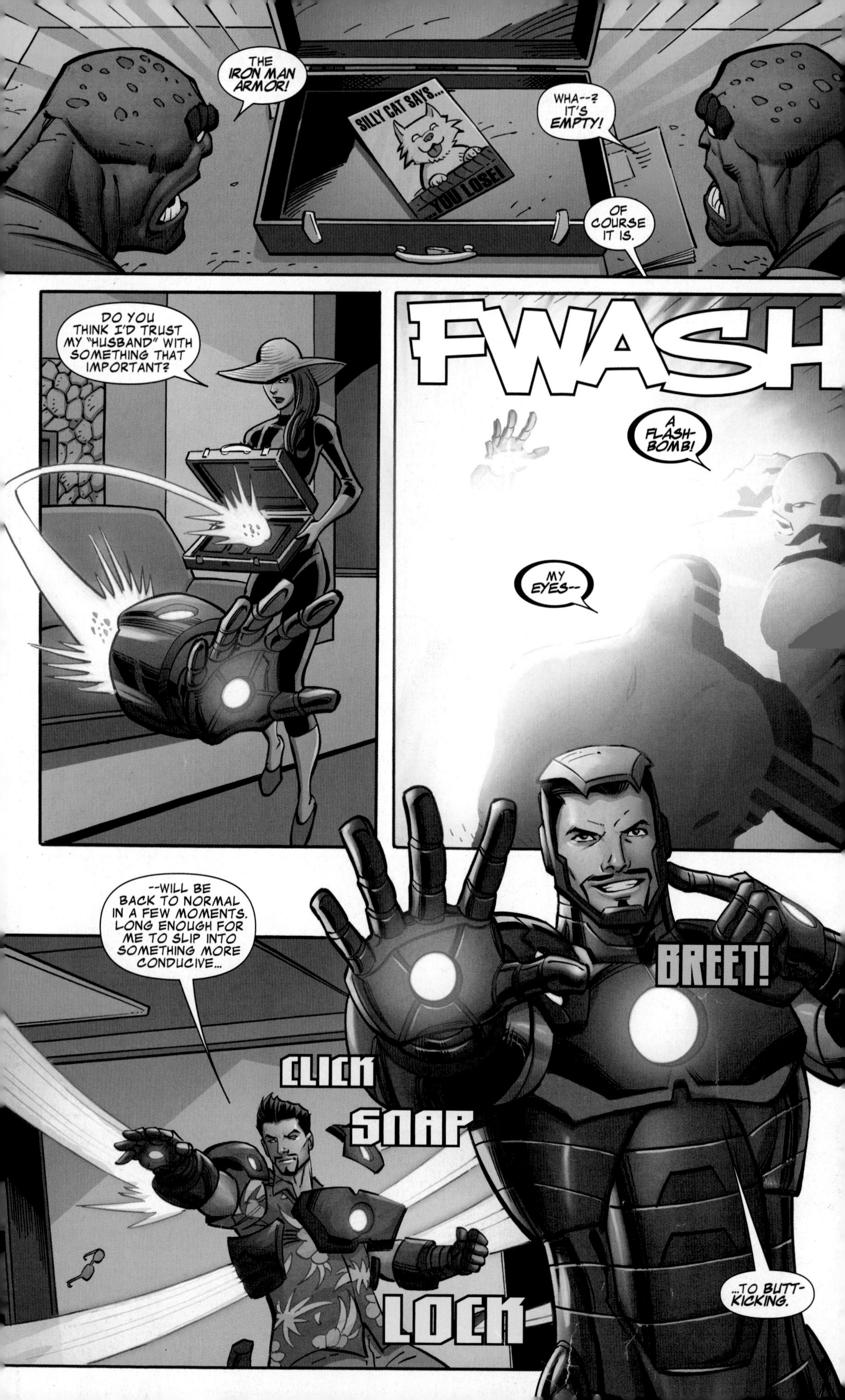
THE IRON MAN ARMOR!
SILLY CAT SAYS...
...YOU LOSE!
WHA--? IT'S EMPTY!
OF COURSE IT IS.
DO YOU THINK I'D TRUST MY "HUSBAND" WITH SOMETHING THAT IMPORTANT?
FWASH
A FLASH-BOMB!
MY EYES--
--WILL BE BACK TO NORMAL IN A FEW MOMENTS. LONG ENOUGH FOR ME TO SLIP INTO SOMETHING MORE CONDUCIVE...
CLICK
SNAP
LOCK
BREET!
...TO BUTT-KICKING.

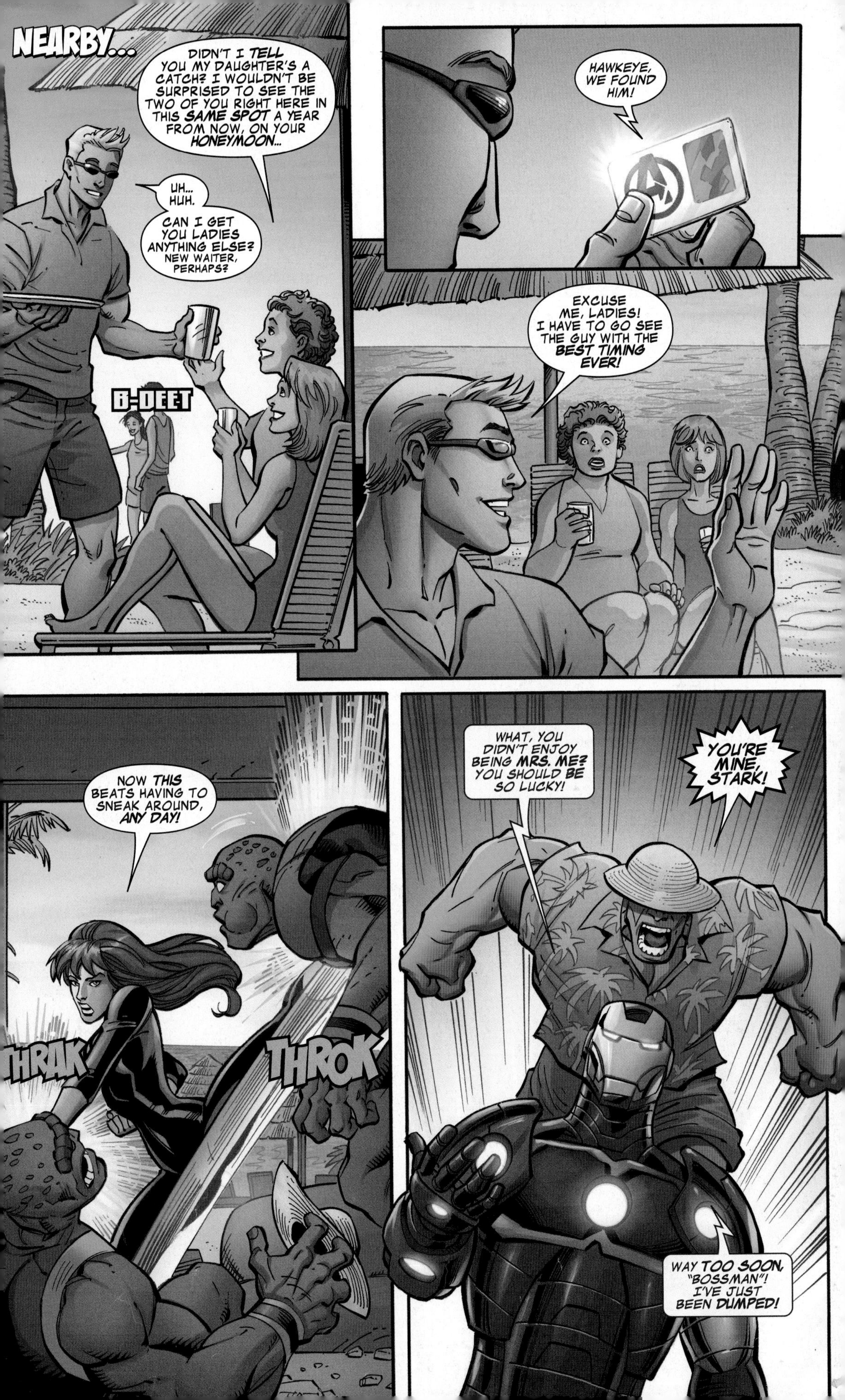
NEARBY...
DIDN'T I TELL YOU MY DAUGHTER'S A CATCH? I WOULDN'T BE SURPRISED TO SEE THE TWO OF YOU RIGHT HERE IN THIS SAME SPOT A YEAR FROM NOW, ON YOUR HONEYMOON...
UH... HUH.
CAN I GET YOU LADIES ANYTHING ELSE? NEW WAITER, PERHAPS?
B-DEET
HAWKEYE, WE FOUND HIM!
EXCUSE ME, LADIES! I HAVE TO GO SEE THE GUY WITH THE BEST TIMING EVER!
NOW THIS BEATS HAVING TO SNEAK AROUND, ANY DAY!
THRAK
THROK
WHAT, YOU DIDN'T ENJOY BEING MRS. ME? YOU SHOULD BE SO LUCKY!
YOU'RE MINE, STARK!
WAY TOO SOON, "BOSSMAN"! I'VE JUST BEEN DUMPED!

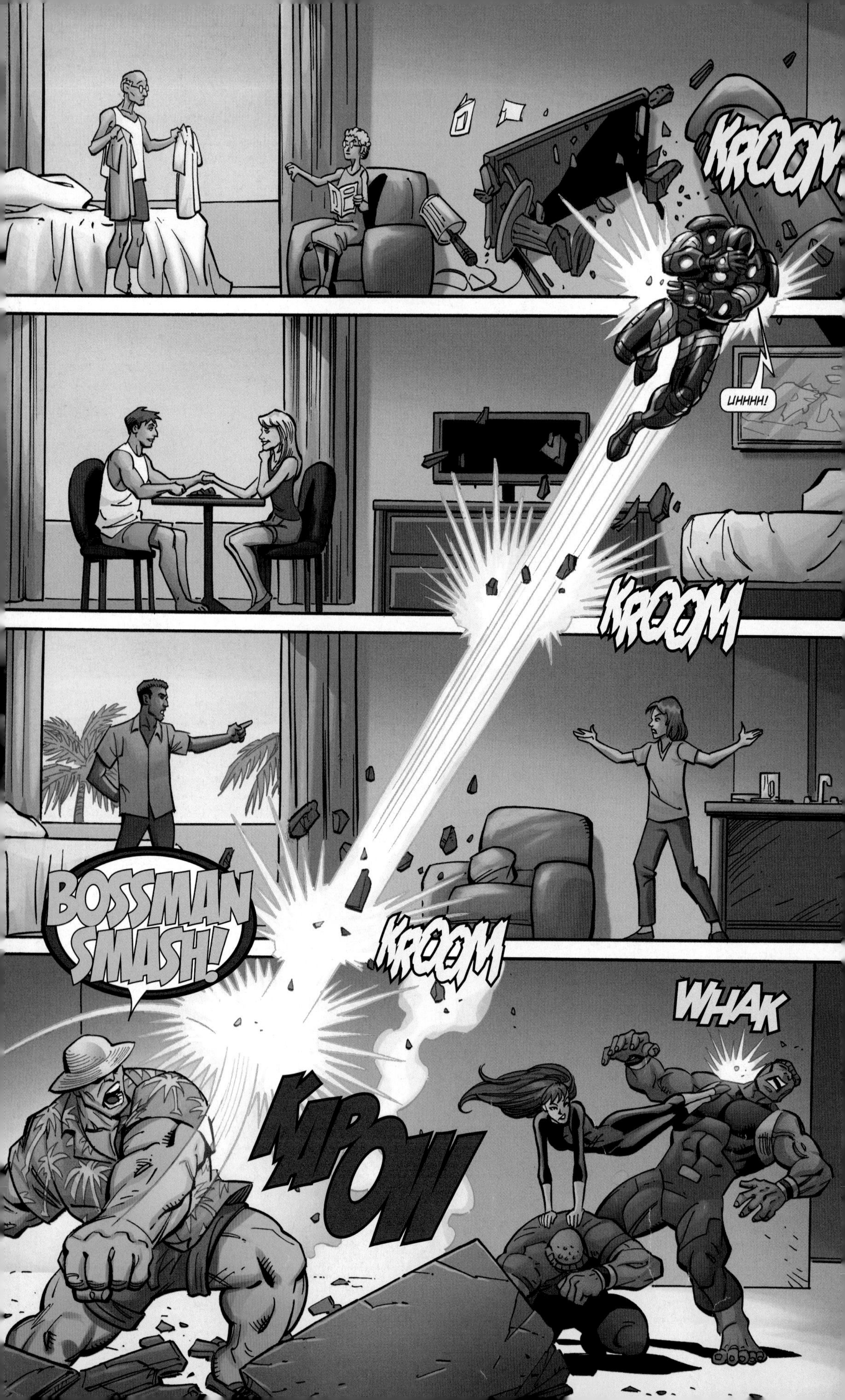
KROOM
UHHHH!
KROOM
KROOM
BOSSMAN SMASH!
WHAK
KPOW

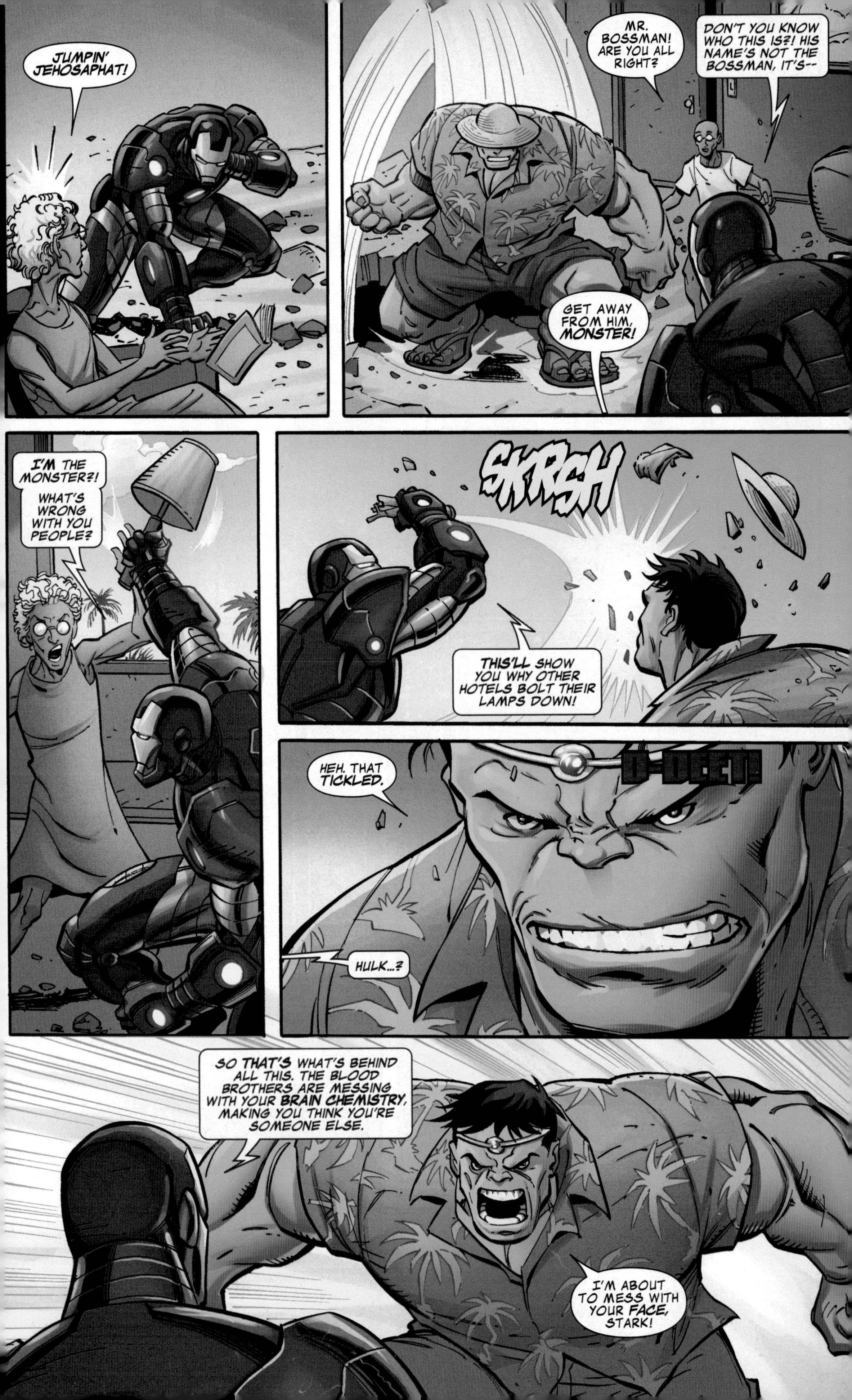
JUMPIN' JEHOSAPHAT!
MR. BOSSMAN! ARE YOU ALL RIGHT?
DON'T YOU KNOW WHO THIS IS?! HIS NAME'S NOT THE BOSSMAN, IT'S--
GET AWAY FROM HIM, MONSTER!
I'M THE MONSTER?!
WHAT'S WRONG WITH YOU PEOPLE?
SKRSH
THIS'LL SHOW YOU WHY OTHER HOTELS BOLT THEIR LAMPS DOWN!
HEH. THAT TICKLED.
D-DEET!
HULK...?
SO THAT'S WHAT'S BEHIND ALL THIS. THE BLOOD BROTHERS ARE MESSING WITH YOUR BRAIN CHEMISTRY, MAKING YOU THINK YOU'RE SOMEONE ELSE.
I'M ABOUT TO MESS WITH YOUR FACE, STARK!

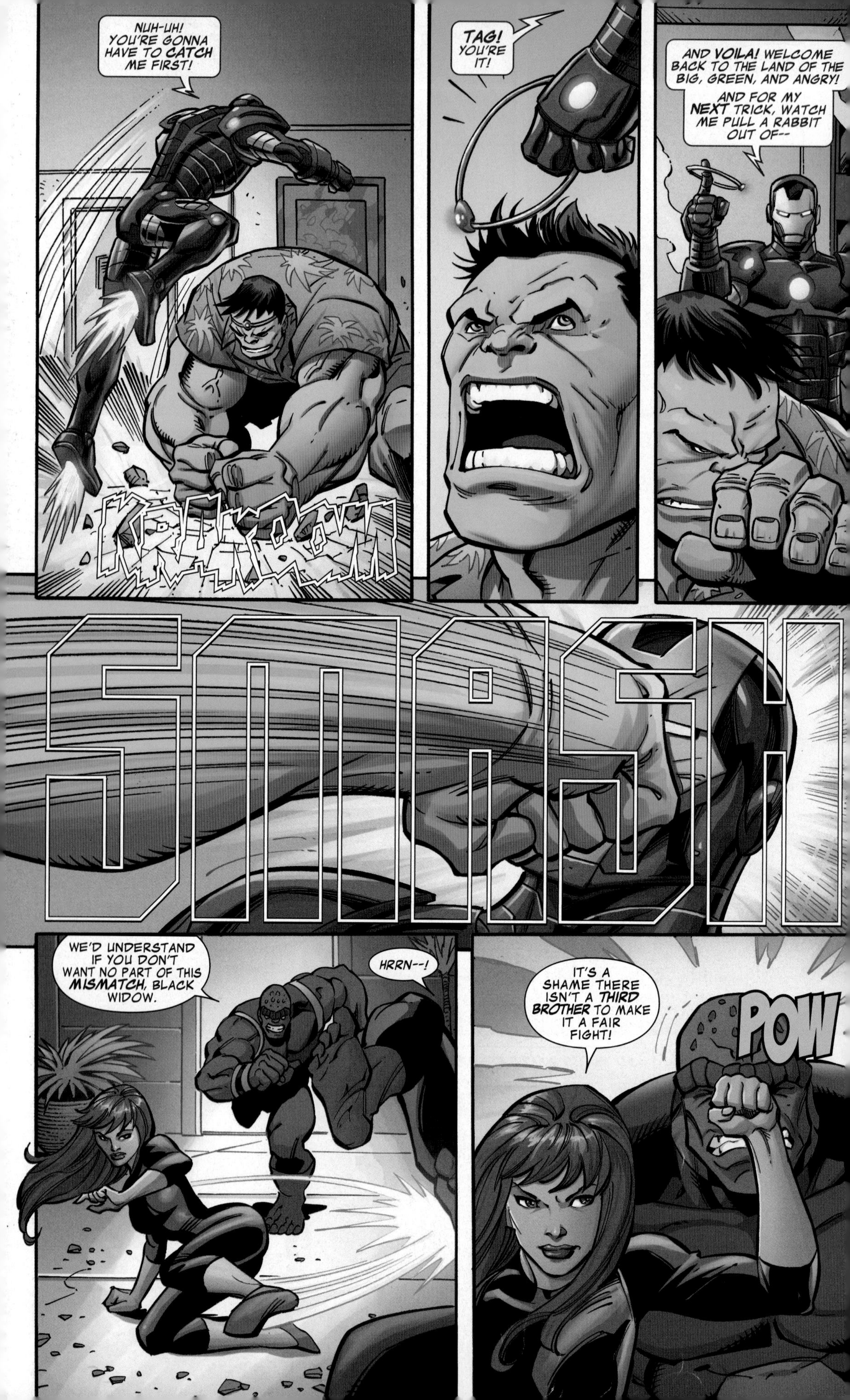
NUH-UH! YOU'RE GONNA HAVE TO CATCH ME FIRST!
TAG! YOU'RE IT!
AND VOILA! WELCOME BACK TO THE LAND OF THE BIG, GREEN, AND ANGRY!
AND FOR MY NEXT TRICK, WATCH ME PULL A RABBIT OUT OF--
SMASH
WE'D UNDERSTAND IF YOU DON'T WANT NO PART OF THIS MISMATCH, BLACK WIDOW.
HRRN--!
IT'S A SHAME THERE ISN'T A THIRD BROTHER TO MAKE IT A FAIR FIGHT!
POW

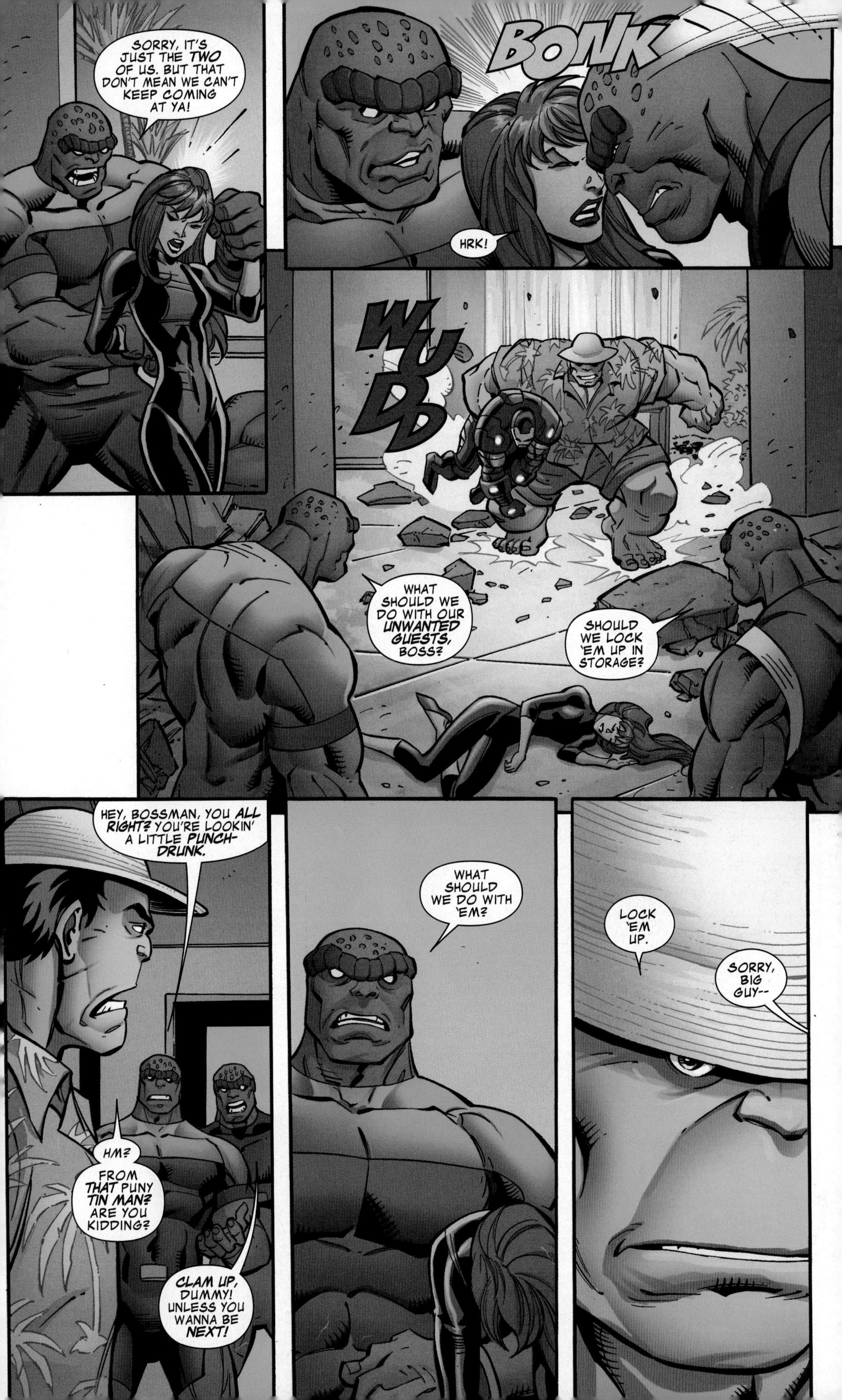
SORRY, IT'S JUST THE TWO OF US. BUT THAT DON'T MEAN WE CAN'T KEEP COMING AT YA!
BONK
HRK!
WUDD
WHAT SHOULD WE DO WITH OUR UNWANTED GUESTS, BOSS?
SHOULD WE LOCK 'EM UP IN STORAGE?
HEY, BOSSMAN, YOU ALL RIGHT? YOU'RE LOOKIN' A LITTLE PUNCH-DRUNK.
HM?
FROM THAT PUNY TIN MAN? ARE YOU KIDDING?
CLAM UP, DUMMY! UNLESS YOU WANNA BE NEXT!
WHAT SHOULD WE DO WITH 'EM?
LOCK 'EM UP.
SORRY, BIG GUY--

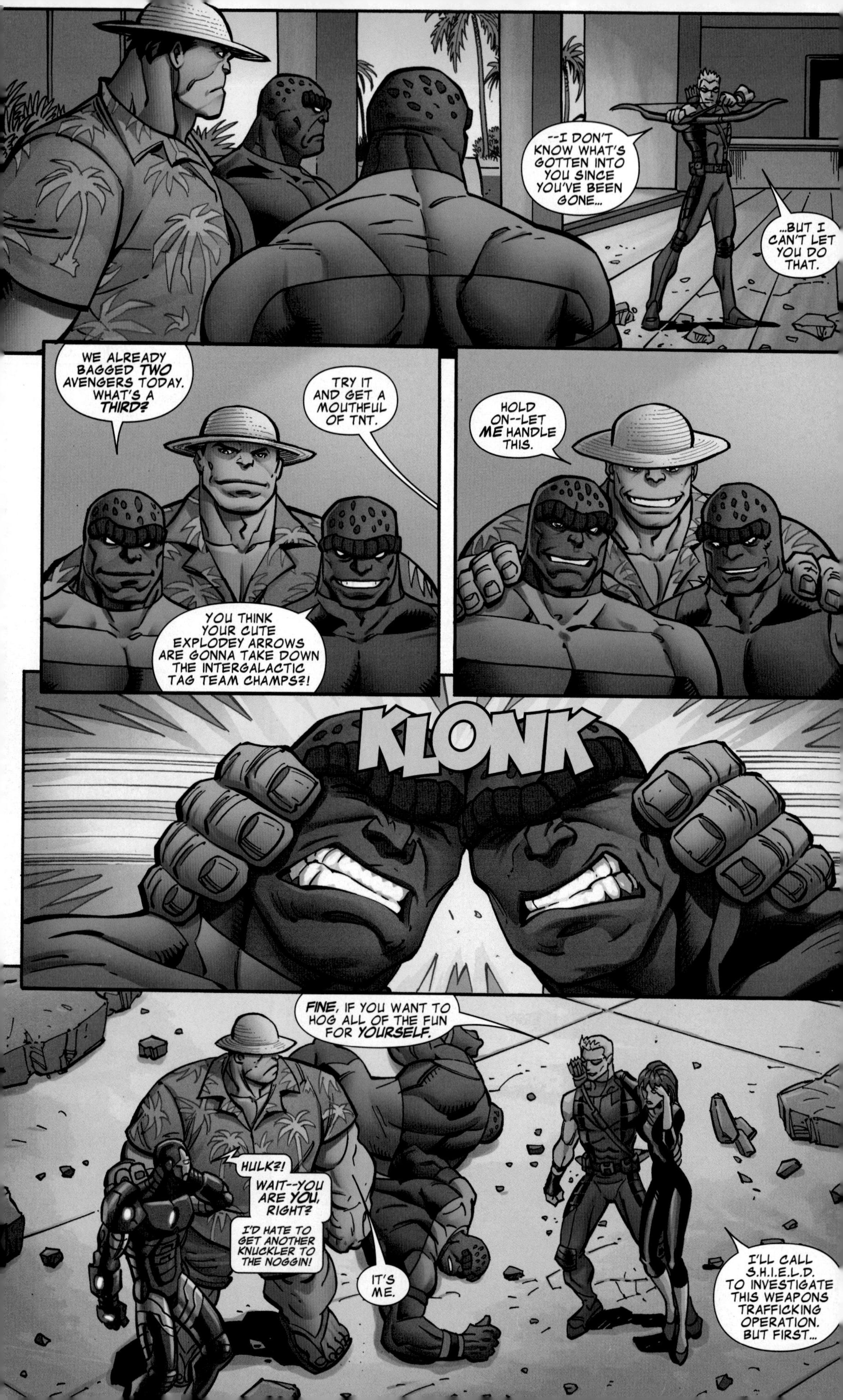
--I DON'T KNOW WHAT'S GOTTEN INTO YOU SINCE YOU'VE BEEN GONE...
...BUT I CAN'T LET YOU DO THAT.
WE ALREADY BAGGED TWO AVENGERS TODAY. WHAT'S A THIRD?
TRY IT AND GET A MOUTHFUL OF TNT.
YOU THINK YOUR CUTE EXPLODEY ARROWS ARE GONNA TAKE DOWN THE INTERGALACTIC TAG TEAM CHAMPS?!
HOLD ON--LET ME HANDLE THIS.
KLONK
FINE, IF YOU WANT TO HOG ALL OF THE FUN FOR YOURSELF.
HULK?!
WAIT--YOU ARE YOU, RIGHT?
I'D HATE TO GET ANOTHER KNUCKLER TO THE NOGGIN!
IT'S ME.
I'LL CALL S.H.I.E.L.D. TO INVESTIGATE THIS WEAPONS TRAFFICKING OPERATION. BUT FIRST...

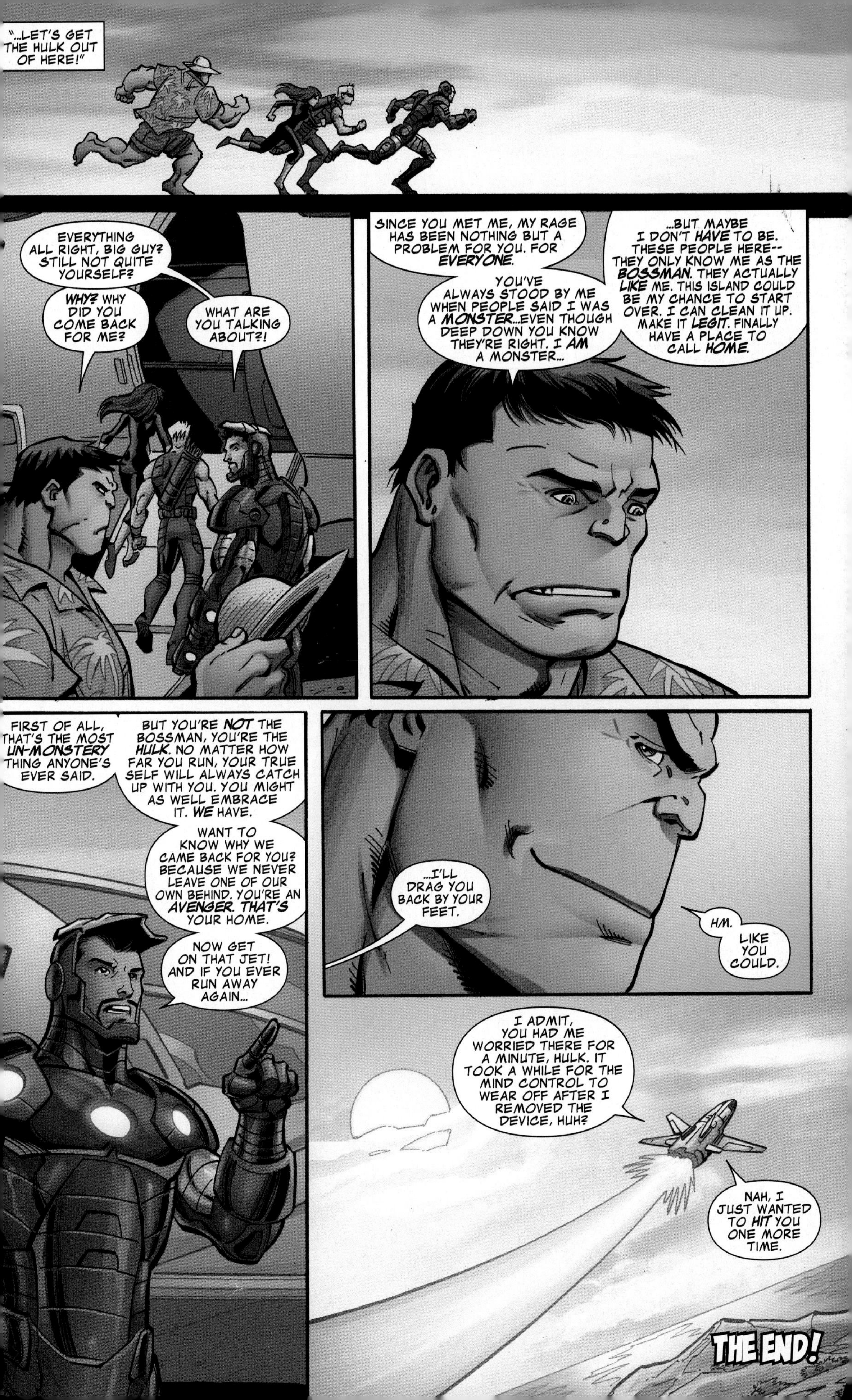

"...LET'S GET THE HULK OUT OF HERE!"
EVERYTHING ALL RIGHT, BIG GUY? STILL NOT QUITE YOURSELF?
WHY? WHY DID YOU COME BACK FOR ME?
WHAT ARE YOU TALKING ABOUT?!
SINCE YOU MET ME, MY RAGE HAS BEEN NOTHING BUT A PROBLEM FOR YOU. FOR EVERYONE.
YOU'VE ALWAYS STOOD BY ME WHEN PEOPLE SAID I WAS A MONSTER...EVEN THOUGH DEEP DOWN YOU KNOW THEY'RE RIGHT. I AM A MONSTER...
...BUT MAYBE I DON'T HAVE TO BE. THESE PEOPLE HERE--THEY ONLY KNOW ME AS THE BOSSMAN. THEY ACTUALLY LIKE ME. THIS ISLAND COULD BE MY CHANCE TO START OVER. I CAN CLEAN IT UP. MAKE IT LEGIT. FINALLY HAVE A PLACE TO CALL HOME.
FIRST OF ALL, THAT'S THE MOST UN-MONSTERY THING ANYONE'S EVER SAID.
BUT YOU'RE NOT THE BOSSMAN, YOU'RE THE HULK. NO MATTER HOW FAR YOU RUN, YOUR TRUE SELF WILL ALWAYS CATCH UP WITH YOU. YOU MIGHT AS WELL EMBRACE IT. WE HAVE.
WANT TO KNOW WHY WE CAME BACK FOR YOU? BECAUSE WE NEVER LEAVE ONE OF OUR OWN BEHIND. YOU'RE AN AVENGER. THAT'S YOUR HOME.
NOW GET ON THAT JET! AND IF YOU EVER RUN AWAY AGAIN...
...I'LL DRAG YOU BACK BY YOUR FEET.
HM.
LIKE YOU COULD.
I ADMIT, YOU HAD ME WORRIED THERE FOR A MINUTE, HULK. IT TOOK A WHILE FOR THE MIND CONTROL TO WEAR OFF AFTER I REMOVED THE DEVICE, HUH?
NAH, I JUST WANTED TO HIT YOU ONE MORE TIME.
THE END!

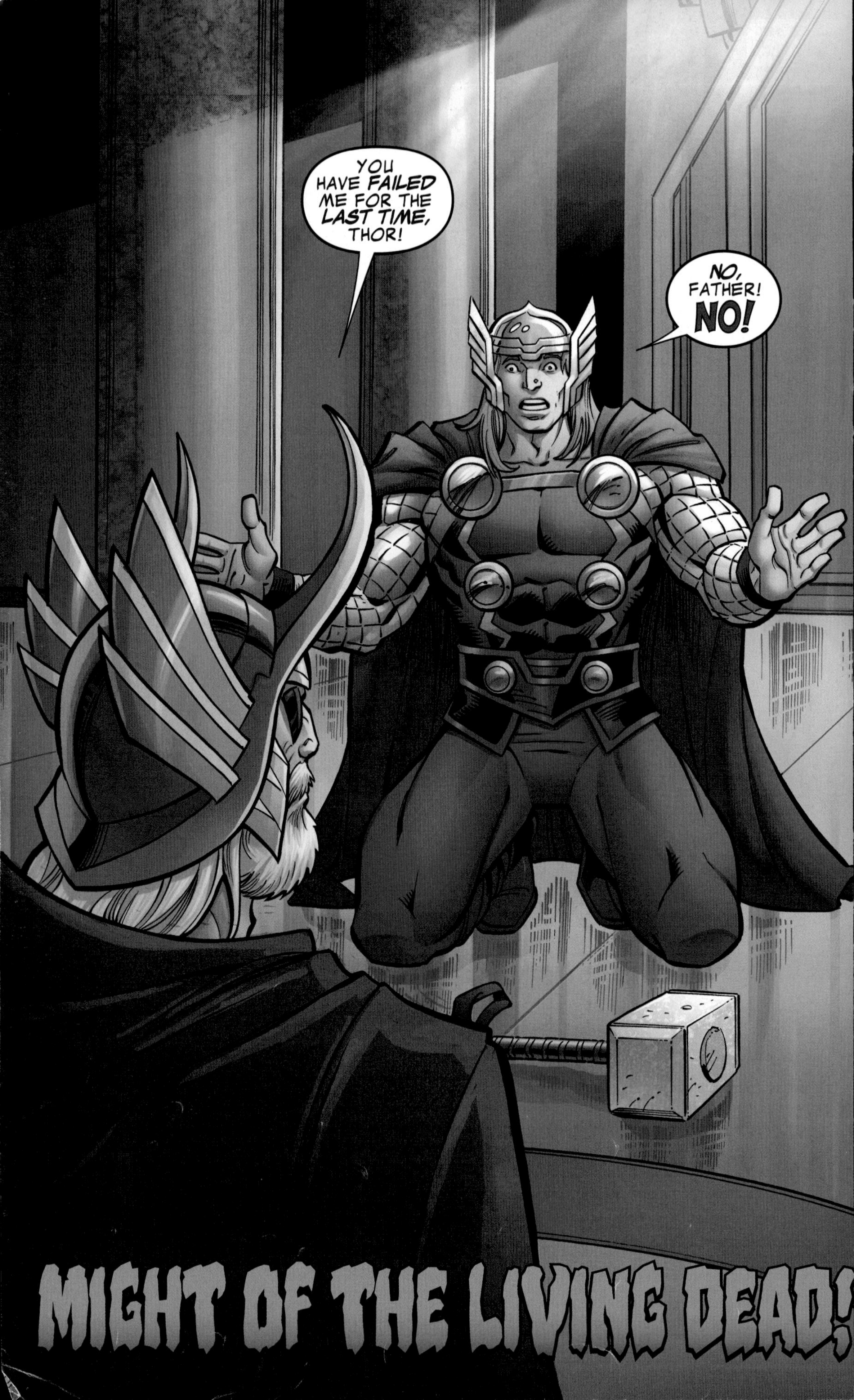
YOU HAVE FAILED ME FOR THE LAST TIME, THOR!
NO, FATHER! NO!
MIGHT OF THE LIVING DEAD!

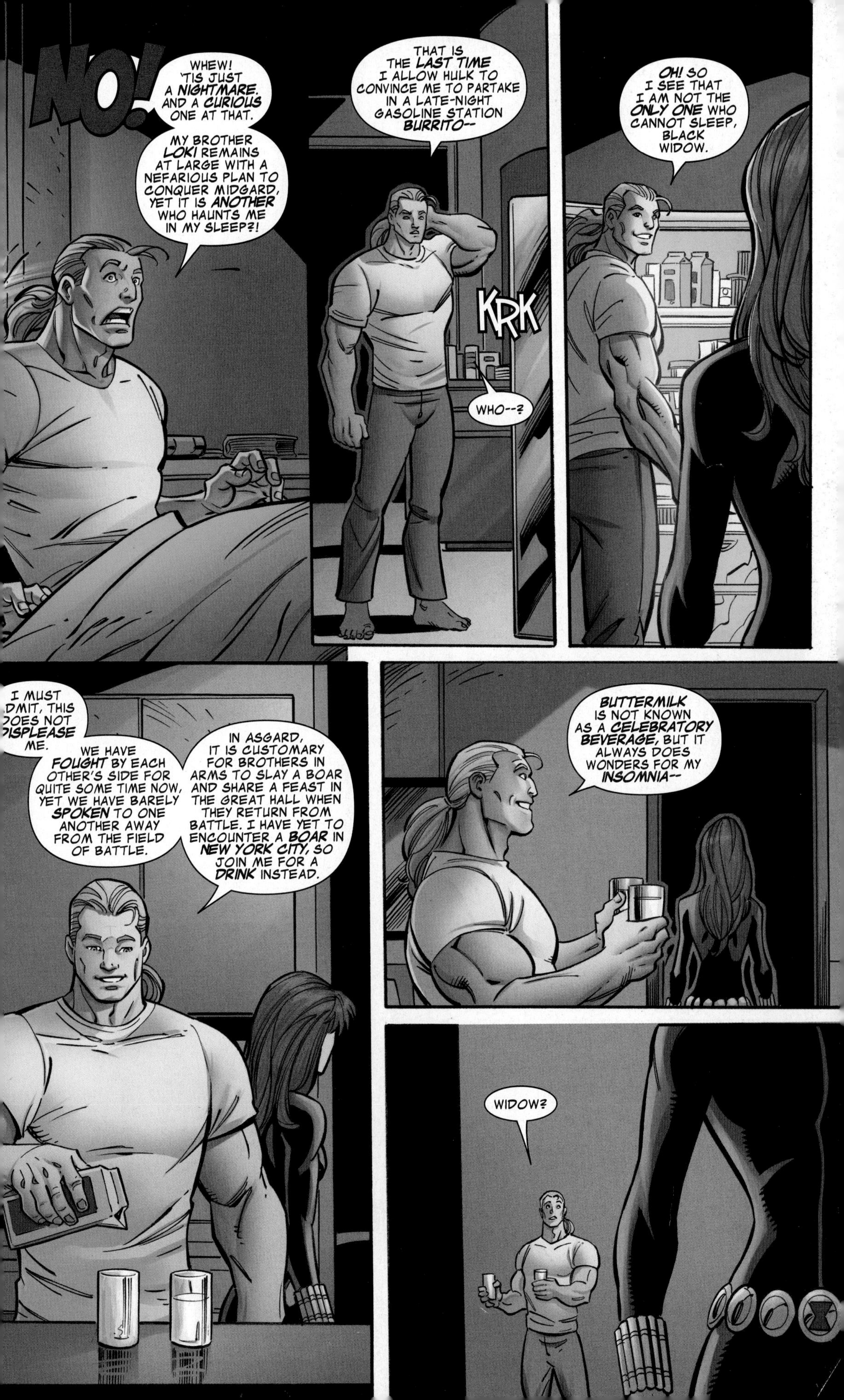
NO!
WHEW! 'TIS JUST A NIGHTMARE. AND A CURIOUS ONE AT THAT.
MY BROTHER LOKI REMAINS AT LARGE WITH A NEFARIOUS PLAN TO CONQUER MIDGARD, YET IT IS ANOTHER WHO HAUNTS ME IN MY SLEEP?!
THAT IS THE LAST TIME I ALLOW HULK TO CONVINCE ME TO PARTAKE IN A LATE-NIGHT GASOLINE STATION BURRITO--
KRK
WHO--?
OH! SO I SEE THAT I AM NOT THE ONLY ONE WHO CANNOT SLEEP, BLACK WIDOW.
I MUST ADMIT, THIS DOES NOT DISPLEASE ME.
WE HAVE FOUGHT BY EACH OTHER'S SIDE FOR QUITE SOME TIME NOW, YET WE HAVE BARELY SPOKEN TO ONE ANOTHER AWAY FROM THE FIELD OF BATTLE.
IN ASGARD, IT IS CUSTOMARY FOR BROTHERS IN ARMS TO SLAY A BOAR AND SHARE A FEAST IN THE GREAT HALL WHEN THEY RETURN FROM BATTLE. I HAVE YET TO ENCOUNTER A BOAR IN NEW YORK CITY, SO JOIN ME FOR A DRINK INSTEAD.
BUTTERMILK IS NOT KNOWN AS A CELEBRATORY BEVERAGE, BUT IT ALWAYS DOES WONDERS FOR MY INSOMNIA--
WIDOW?

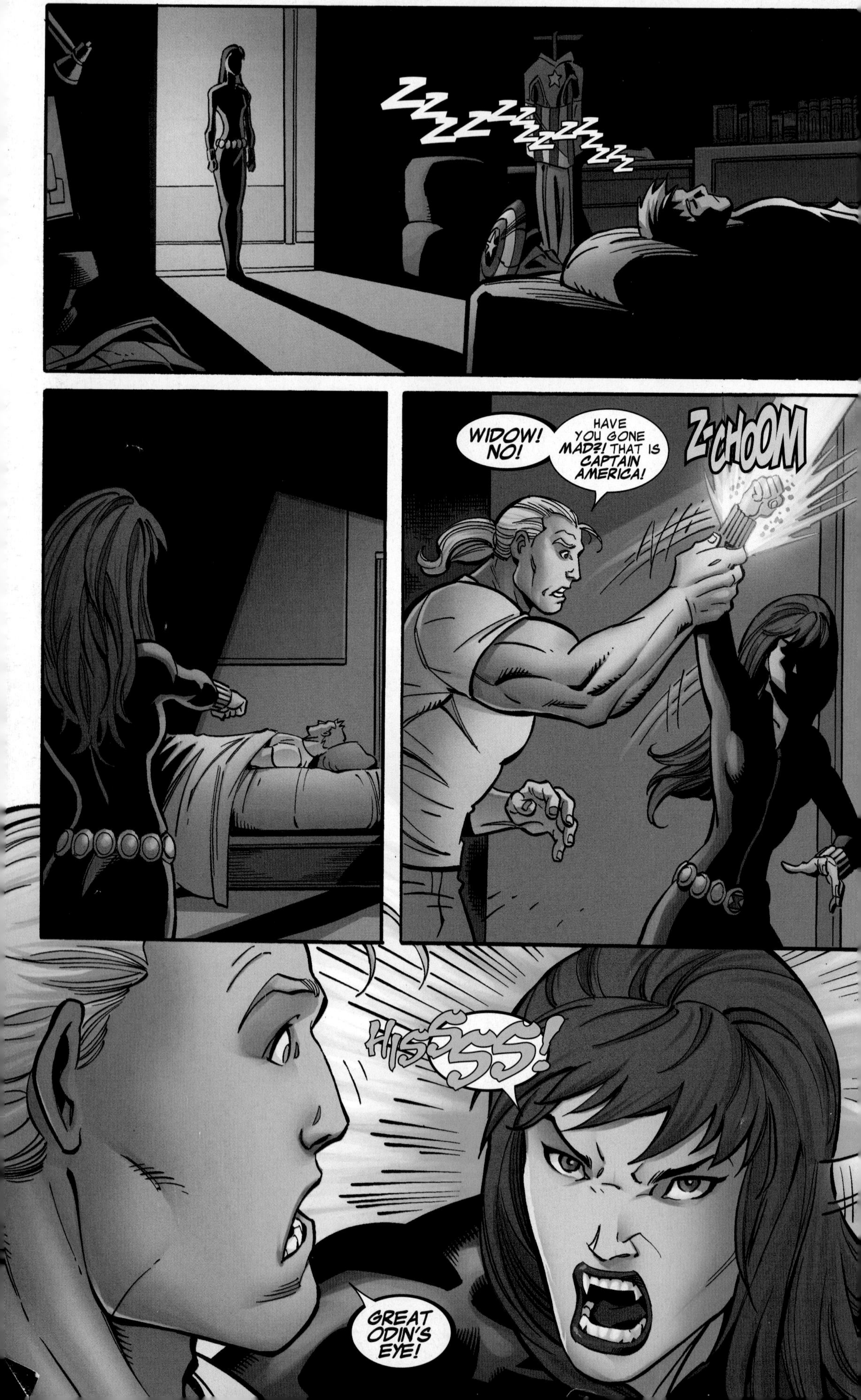

ZZZZZZZZZZZZ
WIDOW! NO!
HAVE YOU GONE MAD?! THAT IS CAPTAIN AMERICA!
Z-CHOOM
HISSSS!
GREAT ODIN'S EYE!

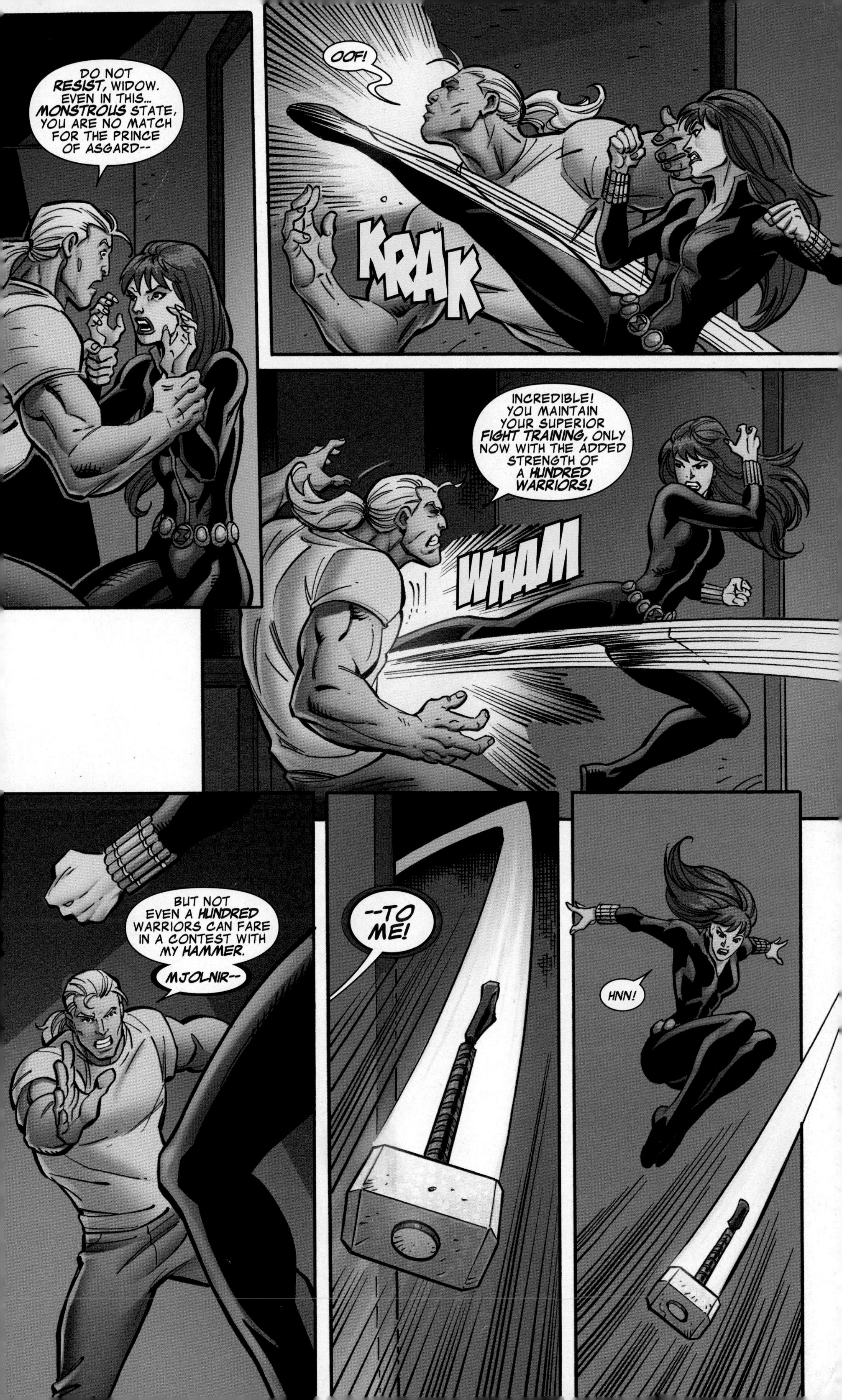
DO NOT RESIST, WIDOW. EVEN IN THIS... MONSTROUS STATE, YOU ARE NO MATCH FOR THE PRINCE OF ASGARD--
OOF!
KRAK
INCREDIBLE! YOU MAINTAIN YOUR SUPERIOR FIGHT TRAINING, ONLY NOW WITH THE ADDED STRENGTH OF A HUNDRED WARRIORS!
WHAM
BUT NOT EVEN A HUNDRED WARRIORS CAN FARE IN A CONTEST WITH MY HAMMER.
MJOLNIR--
--TO ME!
HNN!

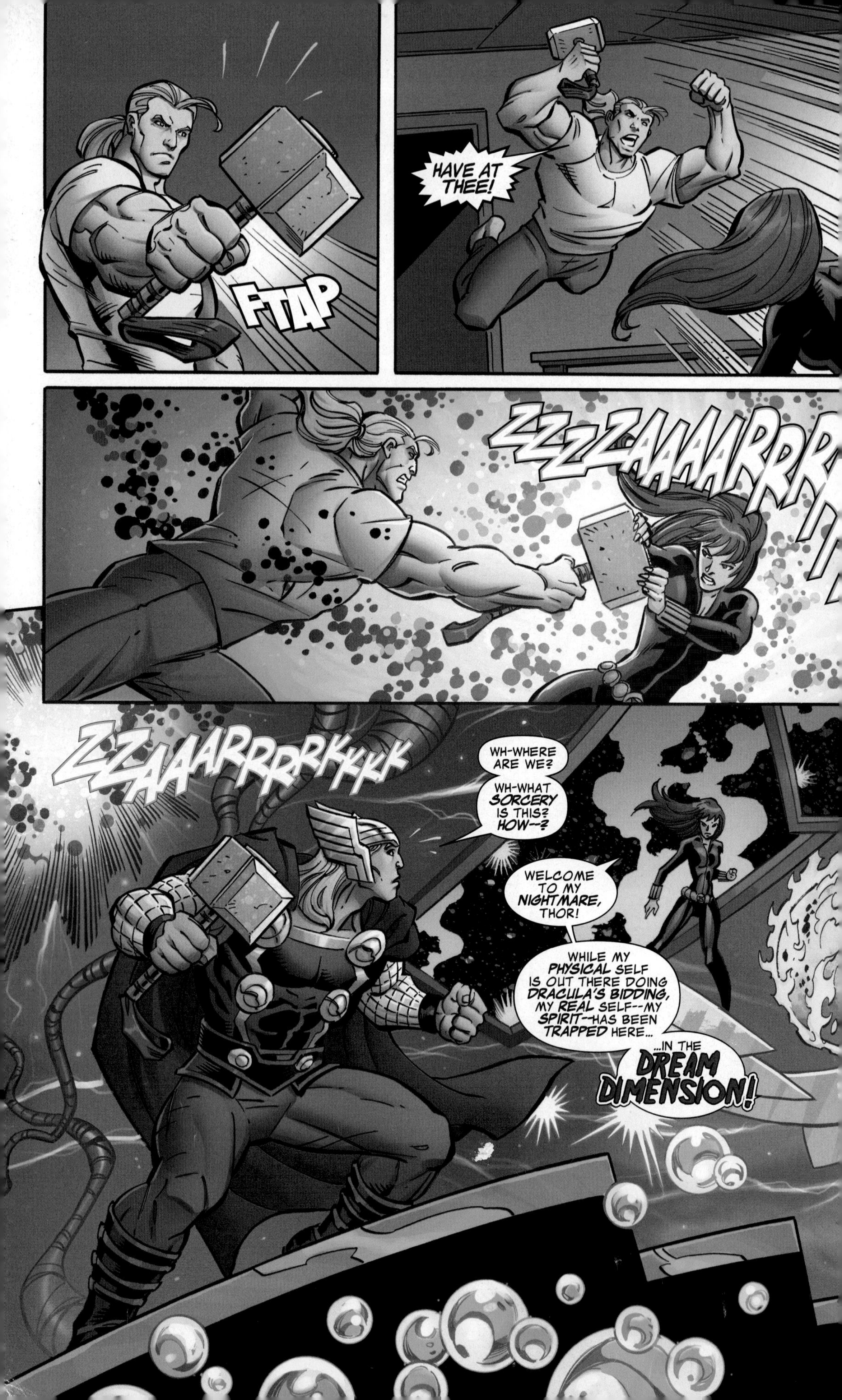
FTAP
HAVE AT THEE!
ZZZZAAAARRRR
ZZAAARRRRKKKK
WH-WHERE ARE WE?
WH-WHAT SORCERY IS THIS? HOW--?
WELCOME TO MY NIGHTMARE, THOR!
WHILE MY PHYSICAL SELF IS OUT THERE DOING DRACULA'S BIDDING, MY REAL SELF--MY SPIRIT--HAS BEEN TRAPPED HERE...
...IN THE DREAM DIMENSION!

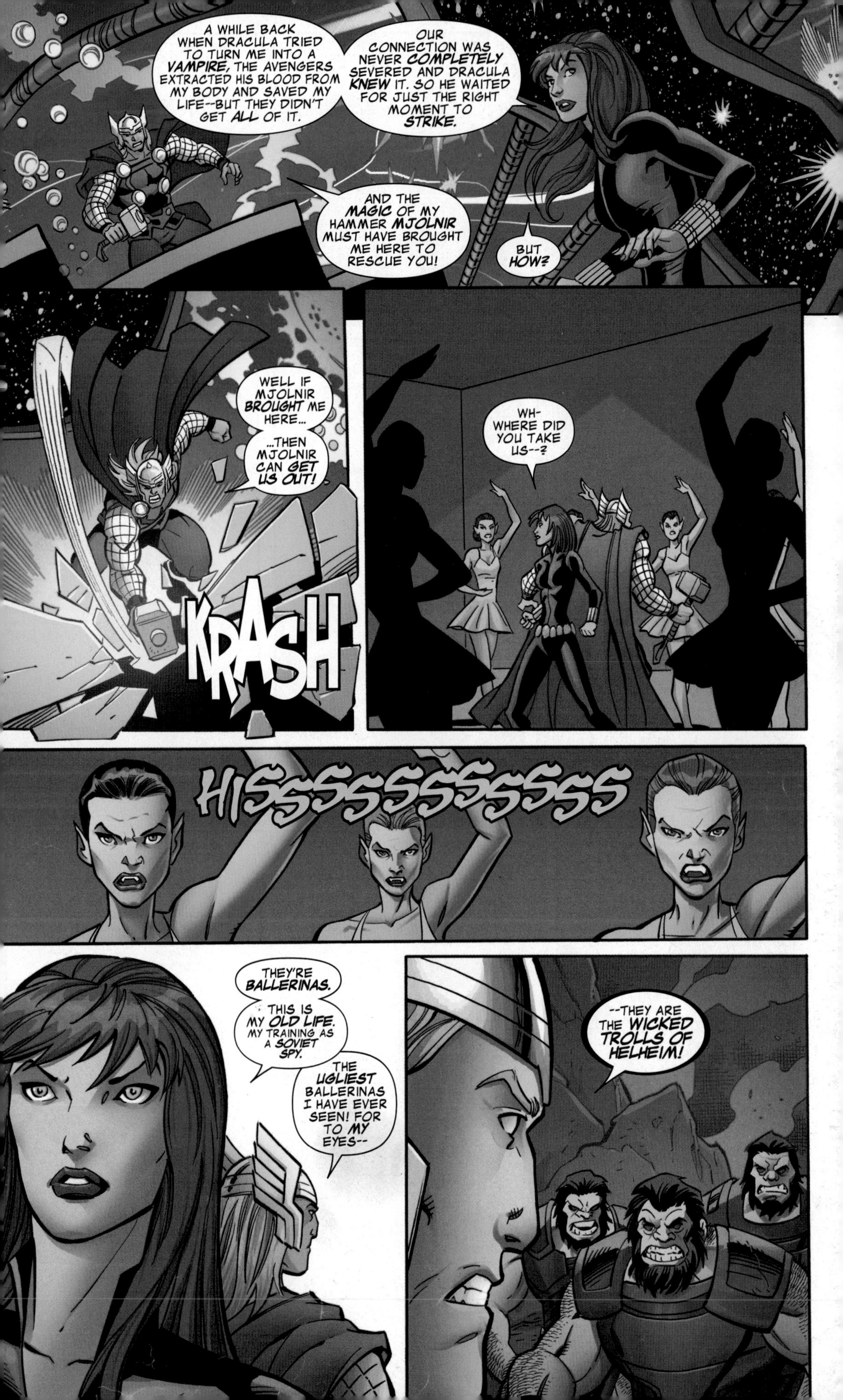

A WHILE BACK WHEN DRACULA TRIED TO TURN ME INTO A VAMPIRE, THE AVENGERS EXTRACTED HIS BLOOD FROM MY BODY AND SAVED MY LIFE--BUT THEY DIDN'T GET ALL OF IT.
OUR CONNECTION WAS NEVER COMPLETELY SEVERED AND DRACULA KNEW IT. SO HE WAITED FOR JUST THE RIGHT MOMENT TO STRIKE.
AND THE MAGIC OF MY HAMMER MJOLNIR MUST HAVE BROUGHT ME HERE TO RESCUE YOU!
BUT HOW?
WELL IF MJOLNIR BROUGHT ME HERE...
...THEN MJOLNIR CAN GET US OUT!
KRASH
WH- WHERE DID YOU TAKE US--?
HISSSSSSSSSSSS
THEY'RE BALLERINAS.
THIS IS MY OLD LIFE. MY TRAINING AS A SOVIET SPY.
THE UGLIEST BALLERINAS I HAVE EVER SEEN! FOR TO MY EYES--
--THEY ARE THE WICKED TROLLS OF HELHEIM!

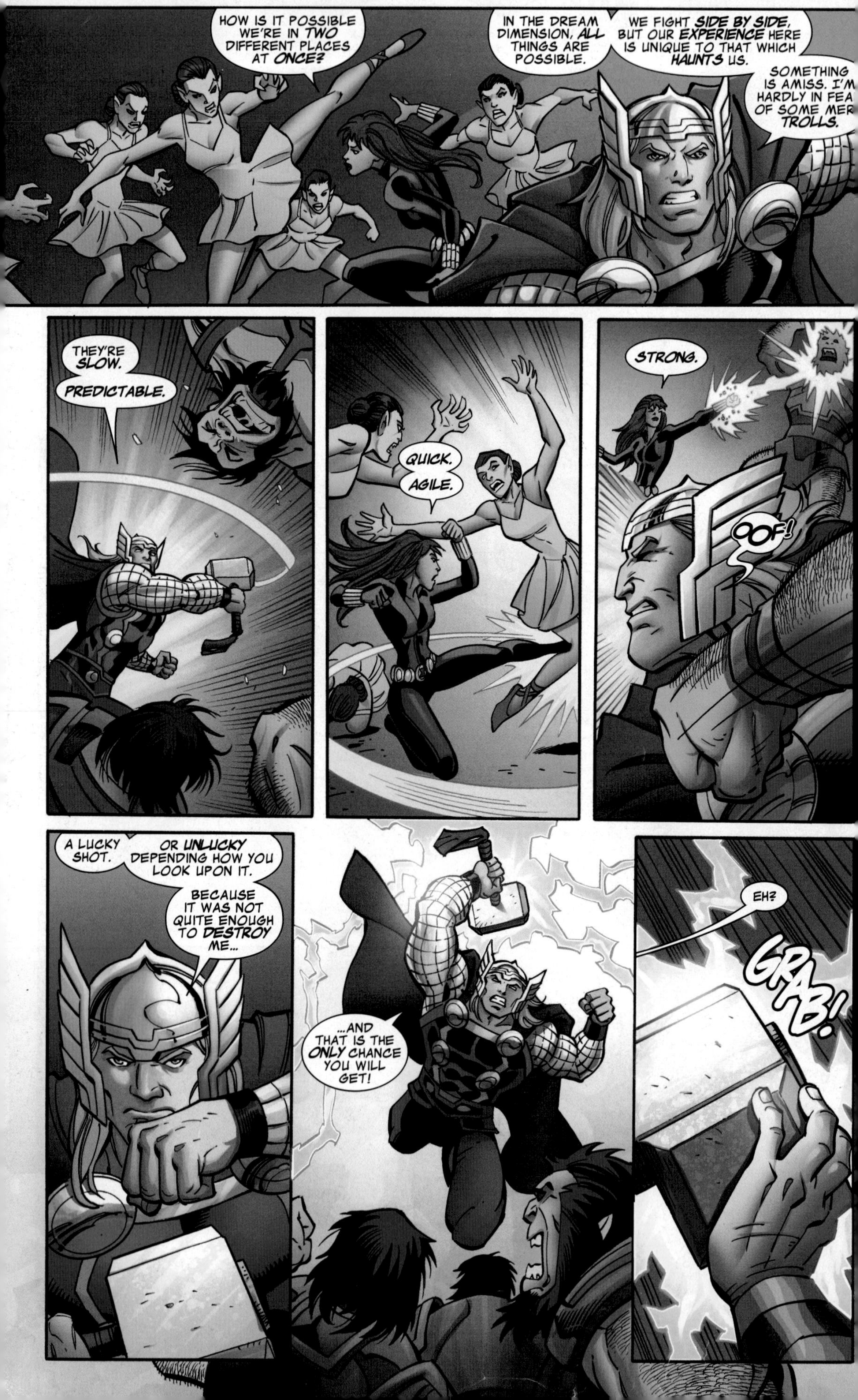

HOW IS IT POSSIBLE WE'RE IN TWO DIFFERENT PLACES AT ONCE?
IN THE DREAM DIMENSION, ALL THINGS ARE POSSIBLE.
WE FIGHT SIDE BY SIDE, BUT OUR EXPERIENCE HERE IS UNIQUE TO THAT WHICH HAUNTS US.
THEY'RE SLOW.
PREDICTABLE.
QUICK.
AGILE.
STRONG.
OOF!
A LUCKY SHOT.
OR UNLUCKY DEPENDING HOW YOU LOOK UPON IT.
BECAUSE IT WAS NOT QUITE ENOUGH TO DESTROY ME...
...AND THAT IS THE ONLY CHANCE YOU WILL GET!
EH?
GRAB!

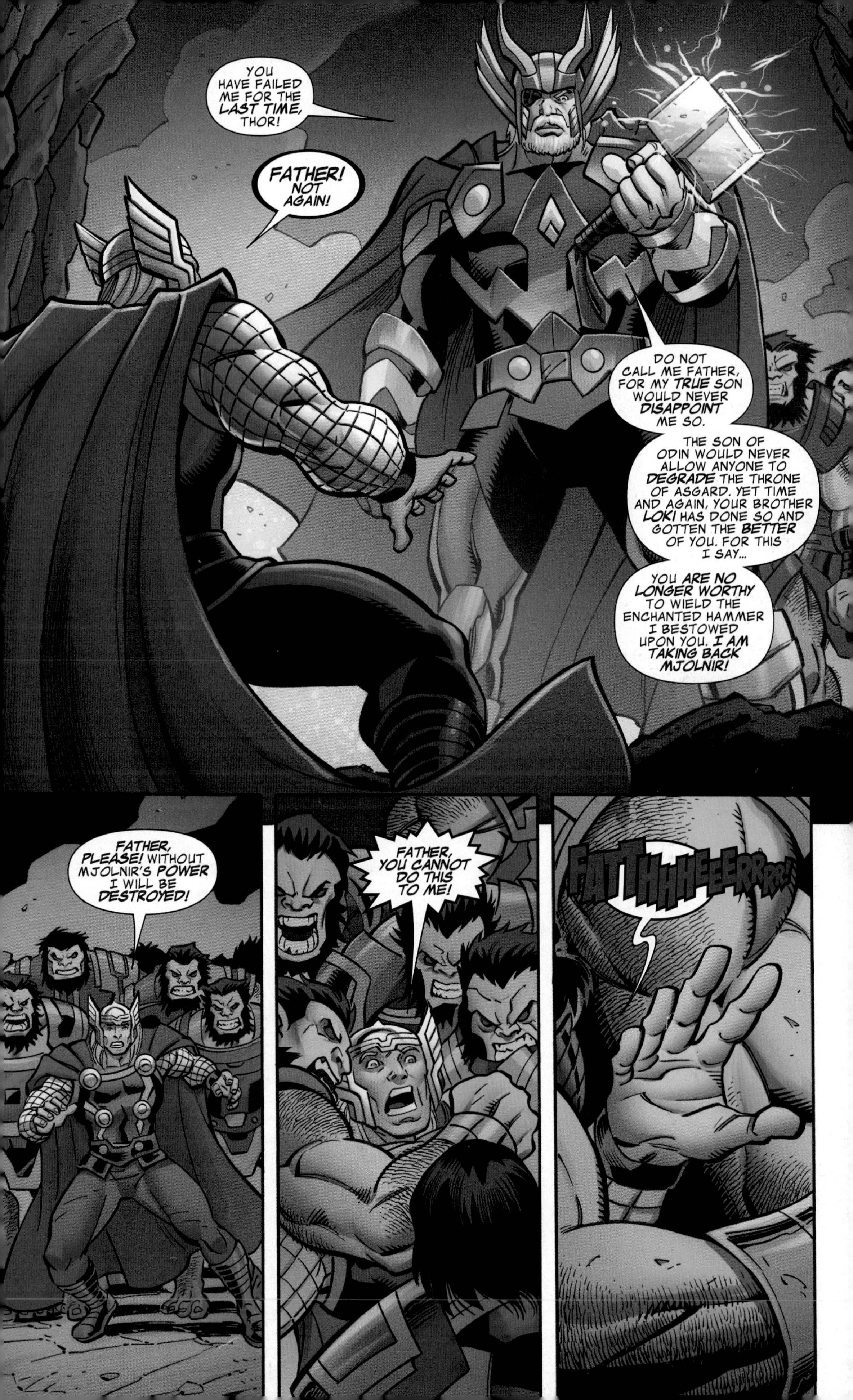
YOU HAVE FAILED ME FOR THE LAST TIME, THOR!
FATHER! NOT AGAIN!
DO NOT CALL ME FATHER, FOR MY TRUE SON WOULD NEVER DISAPPOINT ME SO.
THE SON OF ODIN WOULD NEVER ALLOW ANYONE TO DEGRADE THE THRONE OF ASGARD. YET TIME AND AGAIN, YOUR BROTHER LOKI HAS DONE SO AND GOTTEN THE BETTER OF YOU. FOR THIS I SAY...
YOU ARE NO LONGER WORTHY TO WIELD THE ENCHANTED HAMMER I BESTOWED UPON YOU. I AM TAKING BACK MJOLNIR!
FATHER, PLEASE! WITHOUT MJOLNIR'S POWER I WILL BE DESTROYED!
FATHER, YOU CANNOT DO THIS TO ME!
FATTHHHHEEERRRR!

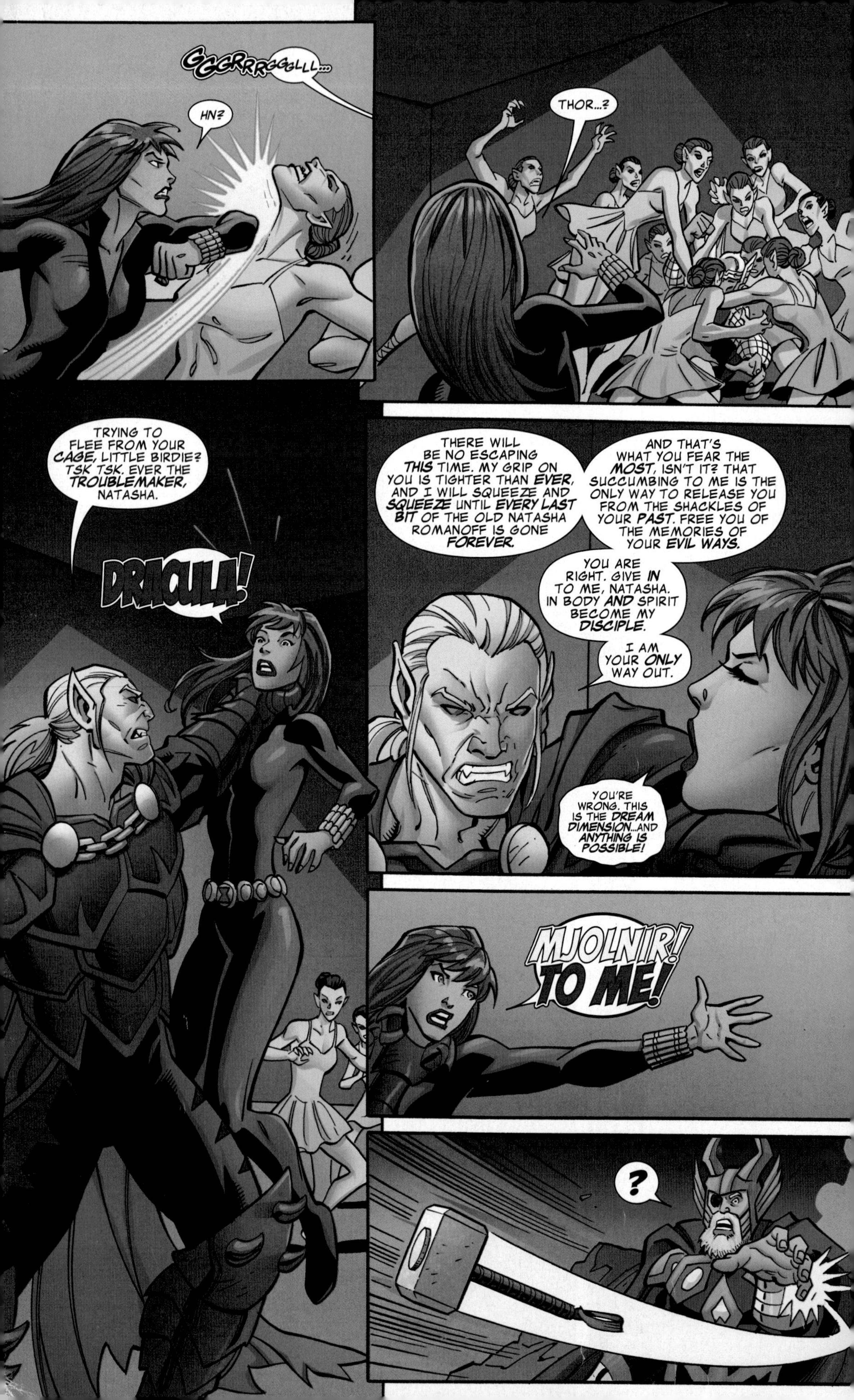

GGGRRRGGGLLL...
HN?
THOR...?
TRYING TO FLEE FROM YOUR CAGE, LITTLE BIRDIE? TSK TSK. EVER THE TROUBLEMAKER, NATASHA.
DRACULA!
THERE WILL BE NO ESCAPING THIS TIME. MY GRIP ON YOU IS TIGHTER THAN EVER, AND I WILL SQUEEZE AND SQUEEZE UNTIL EVERY LAST BIT OF THE OLD NATASHA ROMANOFF IS GONE FOREVER.
AND THAT'S WHAT YOU FEAR THE MOST, ISN'T IT? THAT SUCCUMBING TO ME IS THE ONLY WAY TO RELEASE YOU FROM THE SHACKLES OF YOUR PAST. FREE YOU OF THE MEMORIES OF YOUR EVIL WAYS.
YOU ARE RIGHT. GIVE IN TO ME, NATASHA. IN BODY AND SPIRIT BECOME MY DISCIPLE.
I AM YOUR ONLY WAY OUT.
YOU'RE WRONG. THIS IS THE DREAM DIMENSION...AND ANYTHING IS POSSIBLE!
MJOLNIR! TO ME!
?

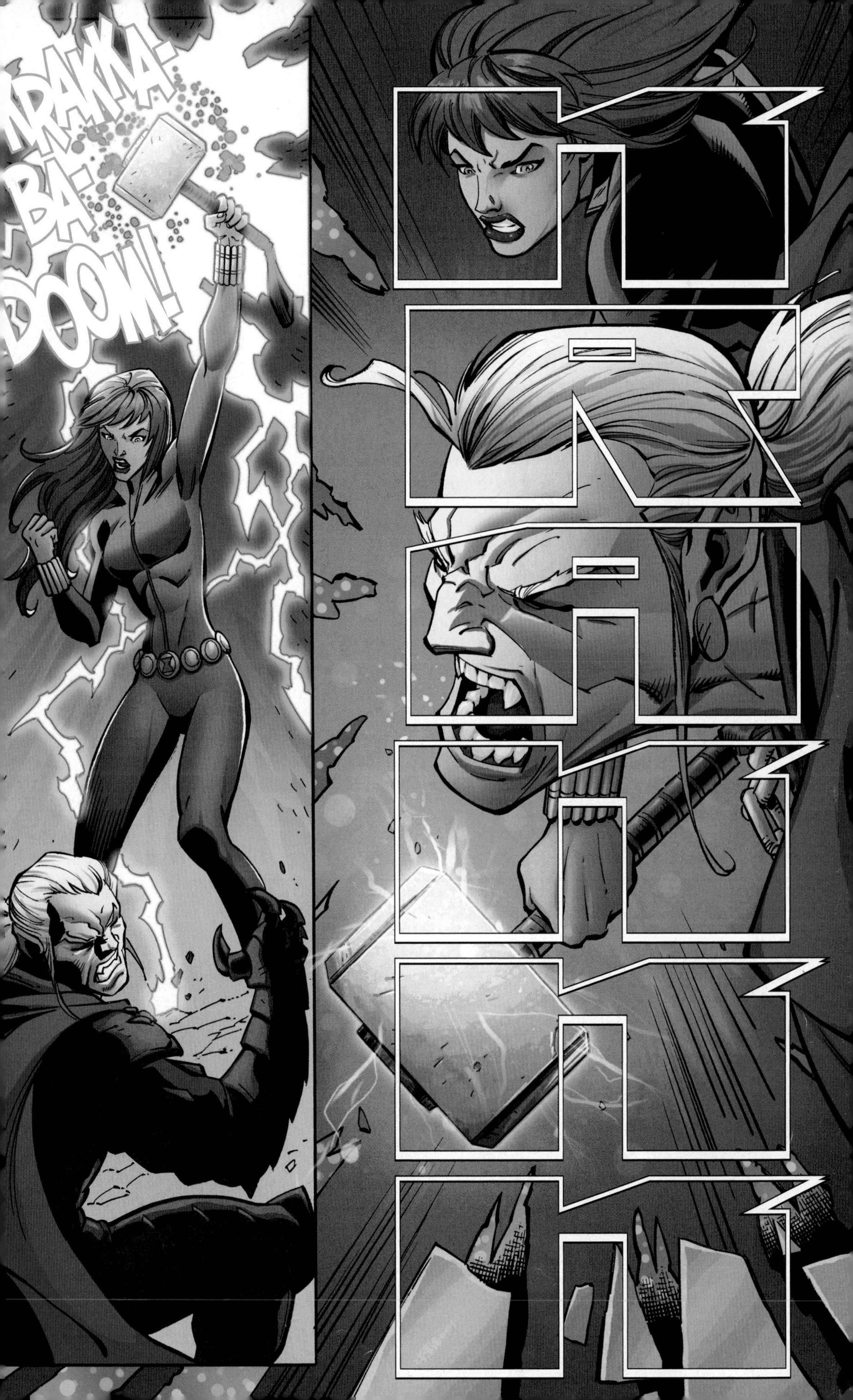
RAKKA-
BA-
DOOM!

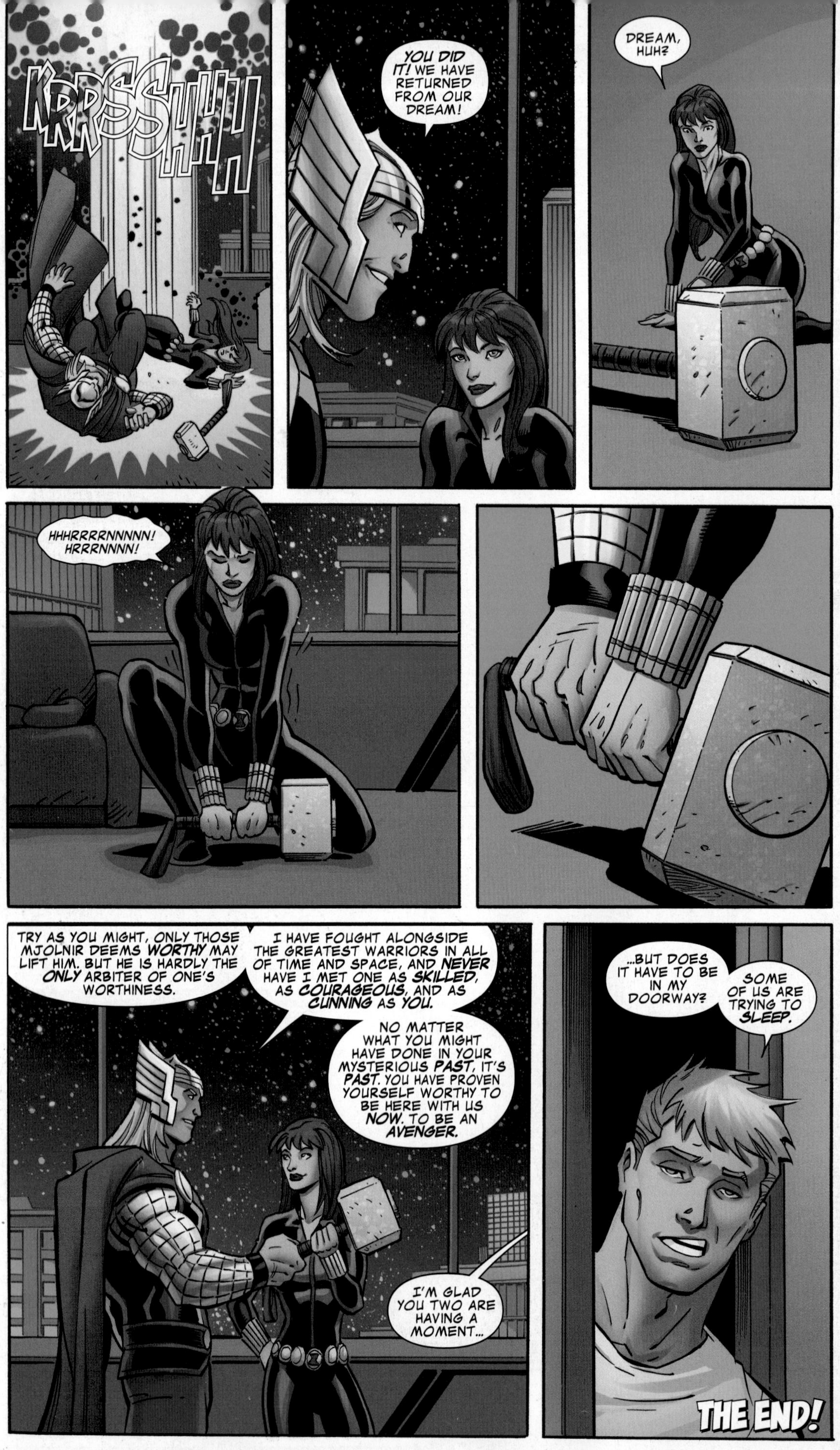
KRRSSHHH
YOU DID IT! WE HAVE RETURNED FROM OUR DREAM!
DREAM, HUH?
HHHRRRRNNNNN! HRRRNNNN!
TRY AS YOU MIGHT, ONLY THOSE MJOLNIR DEEMS WORTHY MAY LIFT HIM. BUT HE IS HARDLY THE ONLY ARBITER OF ONE'S WORTHINESS.
I HAVE FOUGHT ALONGSIDE THE GREATEST WARRIORS IN ALL OF TIME AND SPACE, AND NEVER HAVE I MET ONE AS SKILLED, AS COURAGEOUS, AND AS CUNNING AS YOU.
NO MATTER WHAT YOU MIGHT HAVE DONE IN YOUR MYSTERIOUS PAST, IT'S PAST. YOU HAVE PROVEN YOURSELF WORTHY TO BE HERE WITH US NOW. TO BE AN AVENGER.
I'M GLAD YOU TWO ARE HAVING A MOMENT...
...BUT DOES IT HAVE TO BE IN MY DOORWAY?
SOME OF US ARE TRYING TO SLEEP.
THE END!

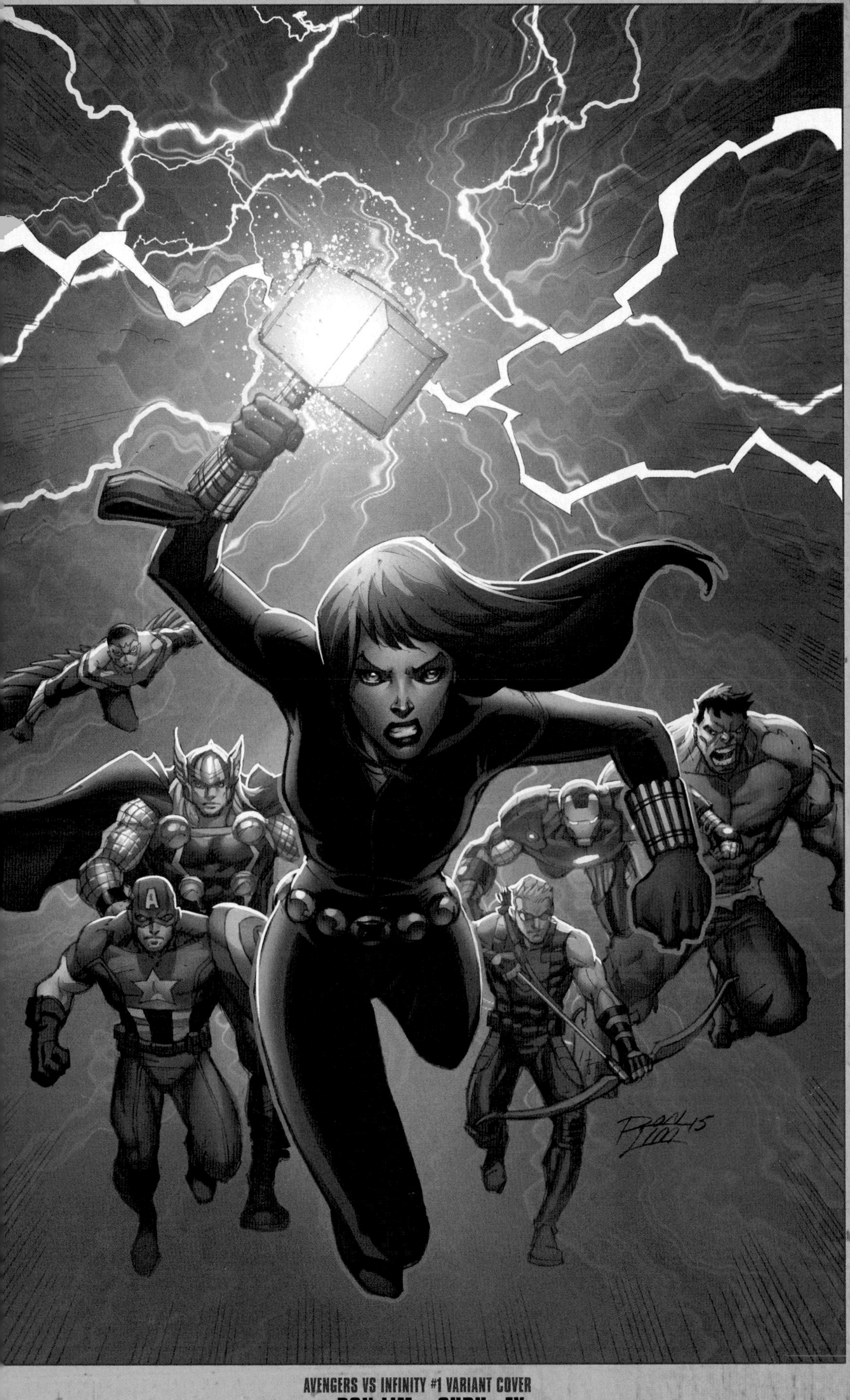

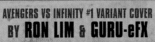

AVENGERS VS INFINITY #1 VARIANT COVER
BY **RON LIM & GURU-eFX**

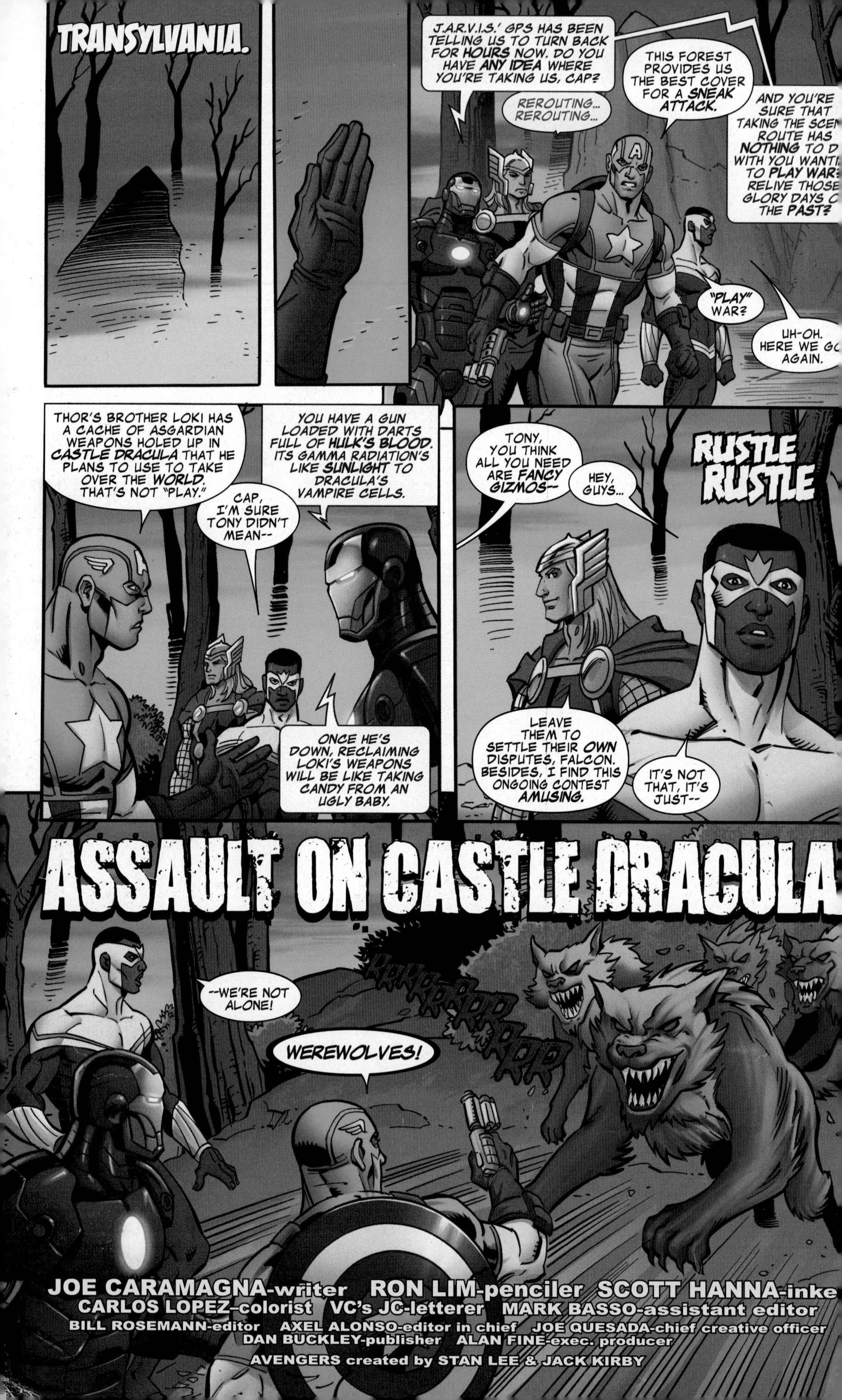
TRANSYLVANIA.
J.A.R.V.I.S.' GPS HAS BEEN TELLING US TO TURN BACK FOR HOURS NOW. DO YOU HAVE ANY IDEA WHERE YOU'RE TAKING US, CAP?
REROUTING... REROUTING...
THIS FOREST PROVIDES US THE BEST COVER FOR A SNEAK ATTACK.
AND YOU'RE SURE THAT TAKING THE SCEN ROUTE HAS NOTHING TO D WITH YOU WANTI TO PLAY WAR RELIVE THOSE GLORY DAYS O THE PAST?
"PLAY" WAR?
UH-OH. HERE WE G AGAIN.
THOR'S BROTHER LOKI HAS A CACHE OF ASGARDIAN WEAPONS HOLED UP IN CASTLE DRACULA THAT HE PLANS TO USE TO TAKE OVER THE WORLD. THAT'S NOT "PLAY."
CAP, I'M SURE TONY DIDN'T MEAN--
YOU HAVE A GUN LOADED WITH DARTS FULL OF HULK'S BLOOD. ITS GAMMA RADIATION'S LIKE SUNLIGHT TO DRACULA'S VAMPIRE CELLS.
ONCE HE'S DOWN, RECLAIMING LOKI'S WEAPONS WILL BE LIKE TAKING CANDY FROM AN UGLY BABY.
TONY, YOU THINK ALL YOU NEED ARE FANCY GIZMOS--
HEY, GUYS...
RUSTLE RUSTLE
LEAVE THEM TO SETTLE THEIR OWN DISPUTES, FALCON. BESIDES, I FIND THIS ONGOING CONTEST AMUSING.
IT'S NOT THAT, IT'S JUST--
ASSAULT ON CASTLE DRACULA
--WE'RE NOT ALONE!
WEREWOLVES!
JOE CARAMAGNA-writer RON LIM-penciler SCOTT HANNA-inke
CARLOS LOPEZ-colorist VC's JC-letterer MARK BASSO-assistant editor
BILL ROSEMANN-editor AXEL ALONSO-editor in chief JOE QUESADA-chief creative officer
DAN BUCKLEY-publisher ALAN FINE-exec. producer
AVENGERS created by STAN LEE & JACK KIRBY

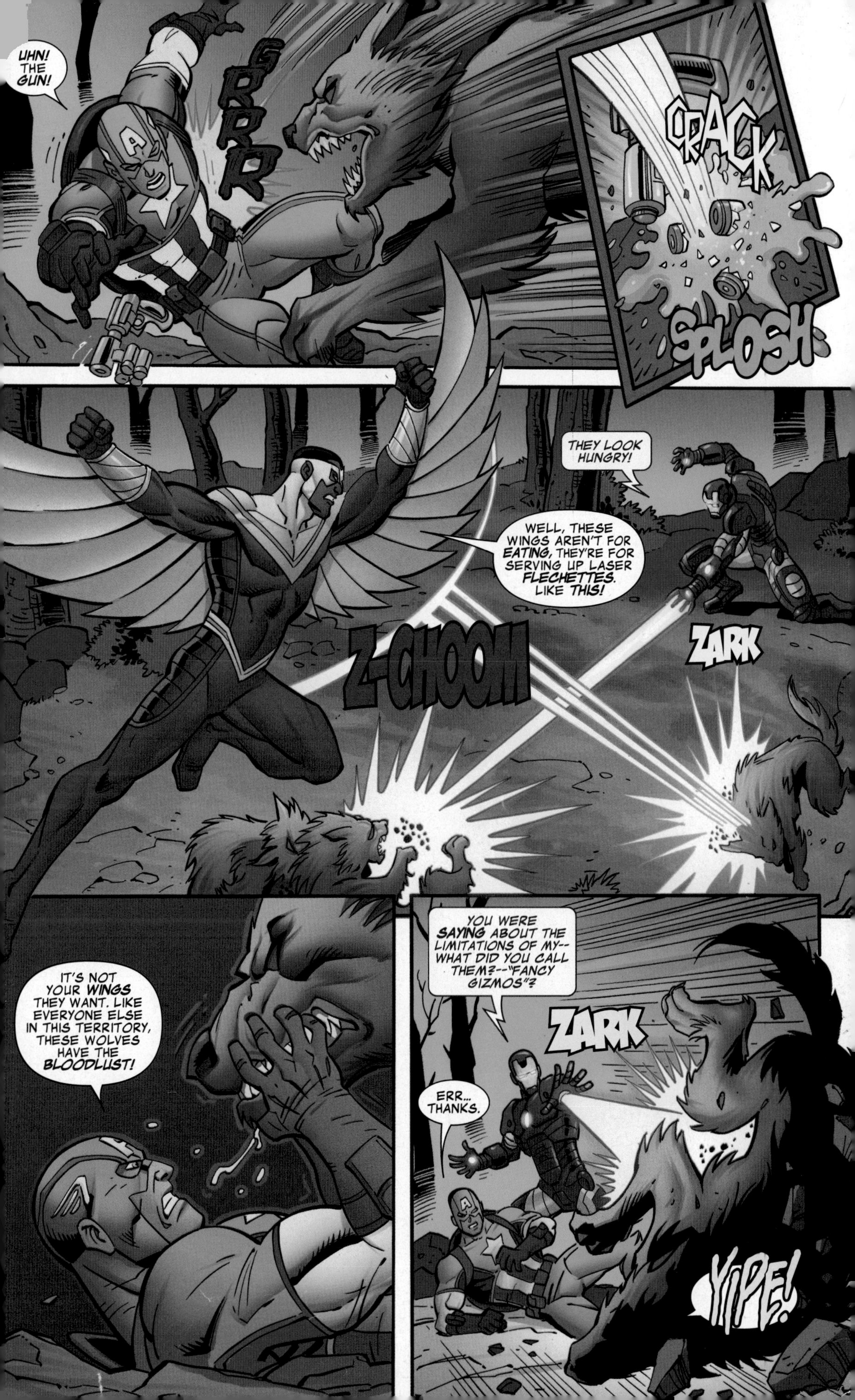
UHN! THE GUN!
GRRR
CRACK
SPLOSH
THEY LOOK HUNGRY!
WELL, THESE WINGS AREN'T FOR EATING, THEY'RE FOR SERVING UP LASER FLECHETTES. LIKE THIS!
Z-CHOOM
ZARK
IT'S NOT YOUR WINGS THEY WANT. LIKE EVERYONE ELSE IN THIS TERRITORY, THESE WOLVES HAVE THE BLOODLUST!
YOU WERE SAYING ABOUT THE LIMITATIONS OF MY-- WHAT DID YOU CALL THEM?--"FANCY GIZMOS"?
ZARK
ERR... THANKS.
YIPE!

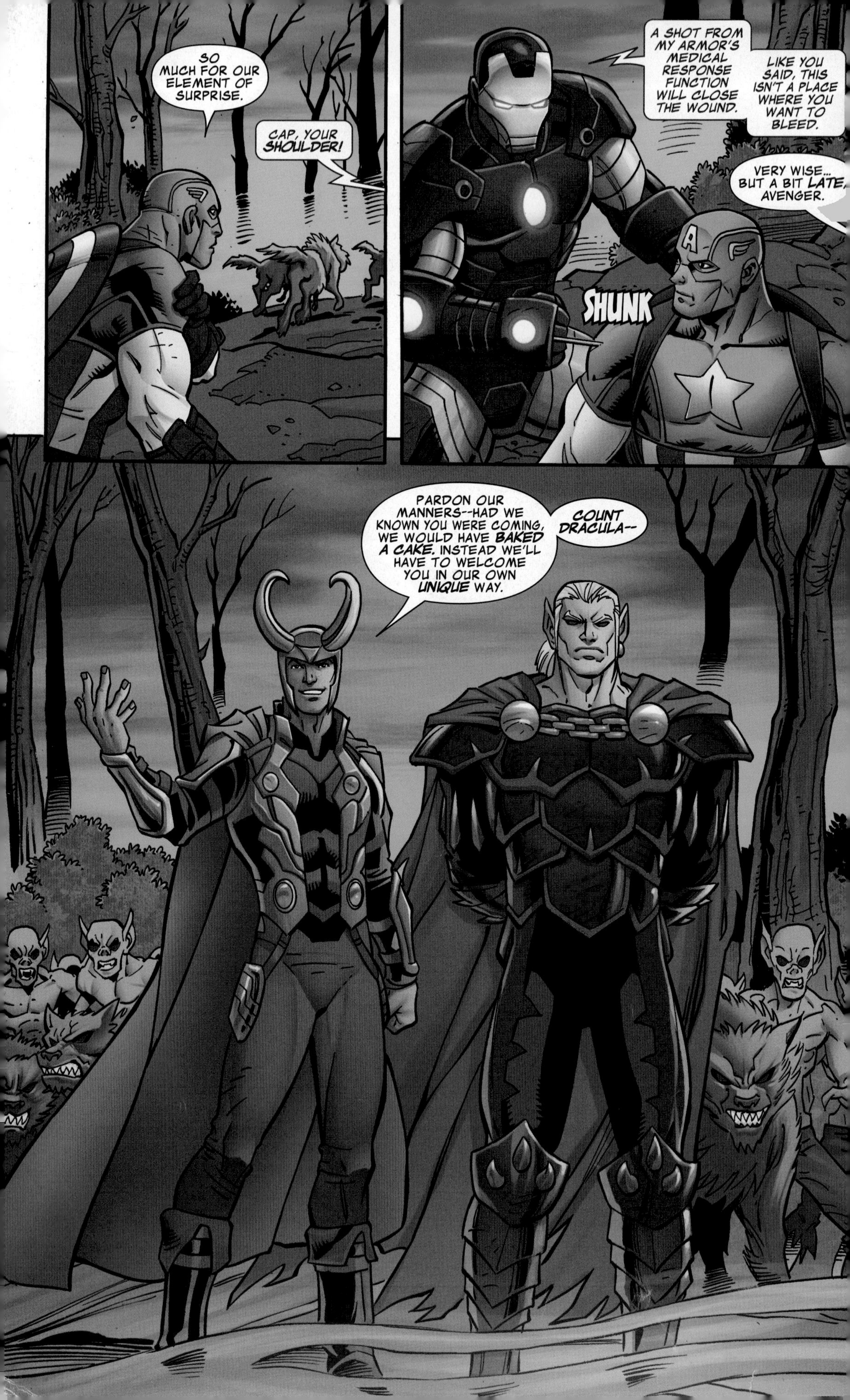
SO MUCH FOR OUR ELEMENT OF SURPRISE.
CAP, YOUR SHOULDER!
A SHOT FROM MY ARMOR'S MEDICAL RESPONSE FUNCTION WILL CLOSE THE WOUND.
LIKE YOU SAID, THIS ISN'T A PLACE WHERE YOU WANT TO BLEED.
VERY WISE... BUT A BIT LATE, AVENGER.
SHUNK
PARDON OUR MANNERS--HAD WE KNOWN YOU WERE COMING, WE WOULD HAVE BAKED A CAKE. INSTEAD WE'LL HAVE TO WELCOME YOU IN OUR OWN UNIQUE WAY.
COUNT DRACULA--

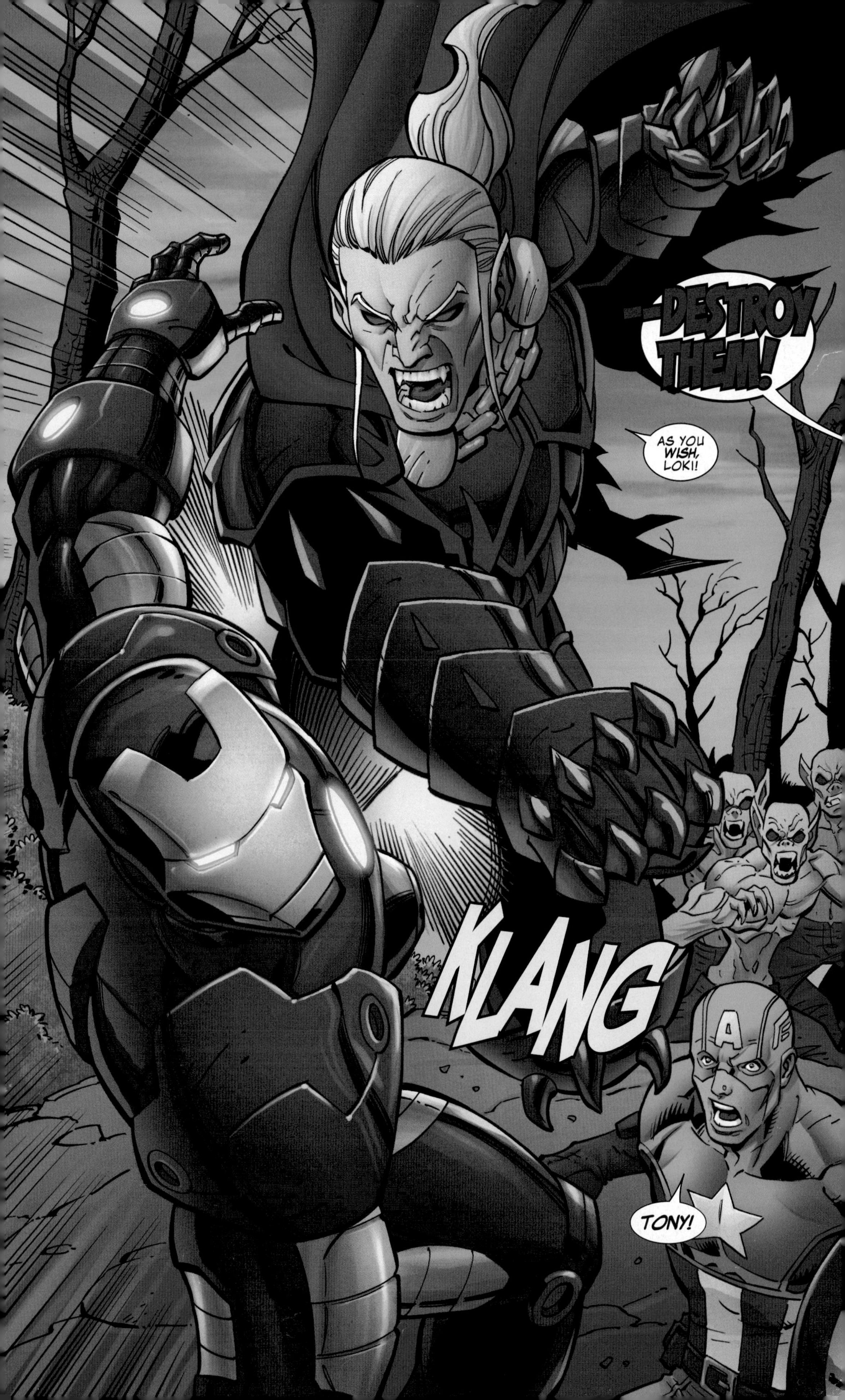
—DESTROY THEM!
AS YOU WISH, LOKI!
KLANG
TONY!

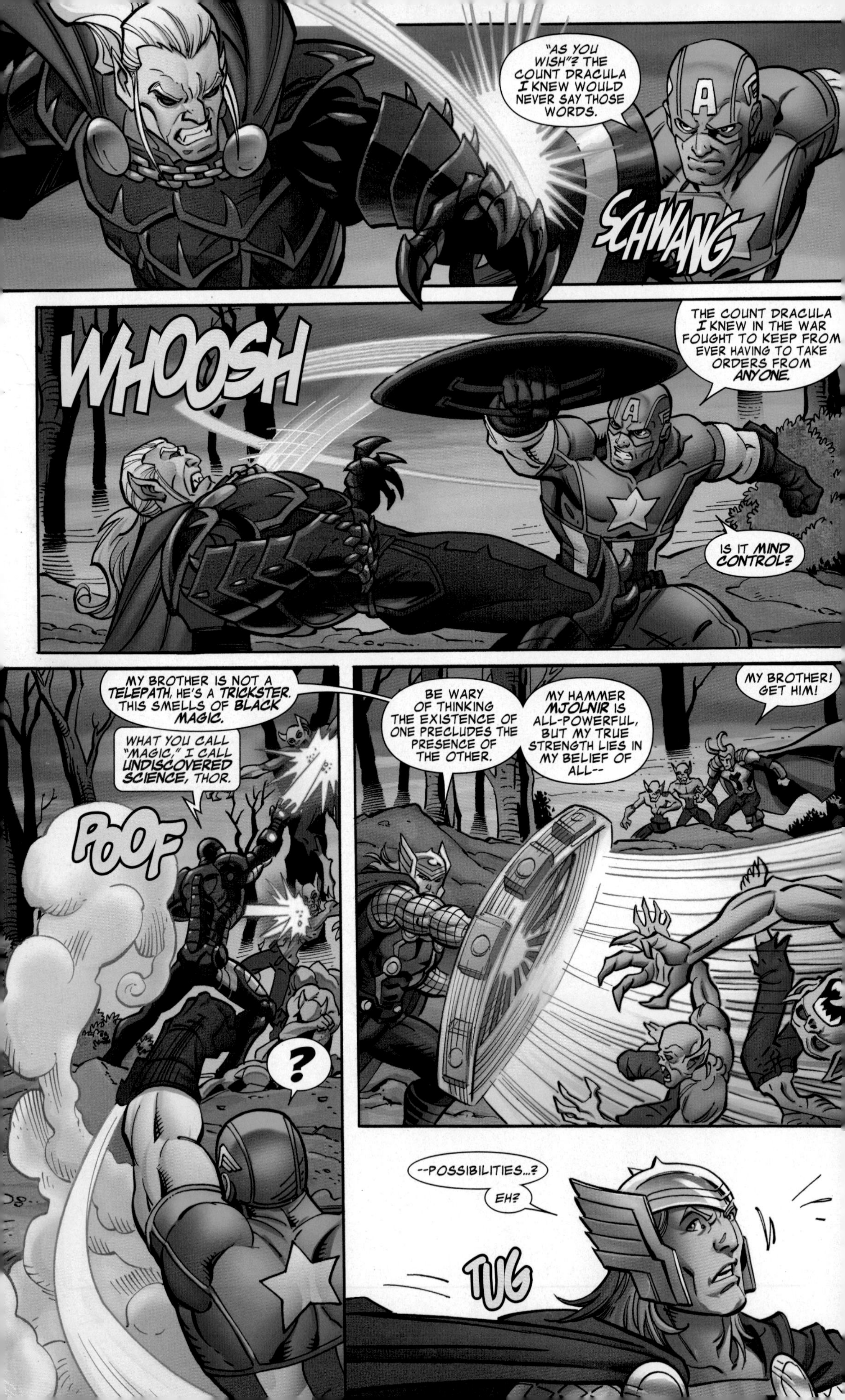
"AS YOU WISH"? THE COUNT DRACULA I KNEW WOULD NEVER SAY THOSE WORDS.
SCHWANG
WHOOSH
THE COUNT DRACULA I KNEW IN THE WAR FOUGHT TO KEEP FROM EVER HAVING TO TAKE ORDERS FROM ANYONE.
IS IT MIND CONTROL?
MY BROTHER IS NOT A TELEPATH, HE'S A TRICKSTER. THIS SMELLS OF BLACK MAGIC.
WHAT YOU CALL "MAGIC," I CALL UNDISCOVERED SCIENCE, THOR.
POOF
?
BE WARY OF THINKING THE EXISTENCE OF ONE PRECLUDES THE PRESENCE OF THE OTHER.
MY HAMMER MJOLNIR IS ALL-POWERFUL, BUT MY TRUE STRENGTH LIES IN MY BELIEF OF ALL--
MY BROTHER! GET HIM!
--POSSIBILITIES...?
EH?
TUG

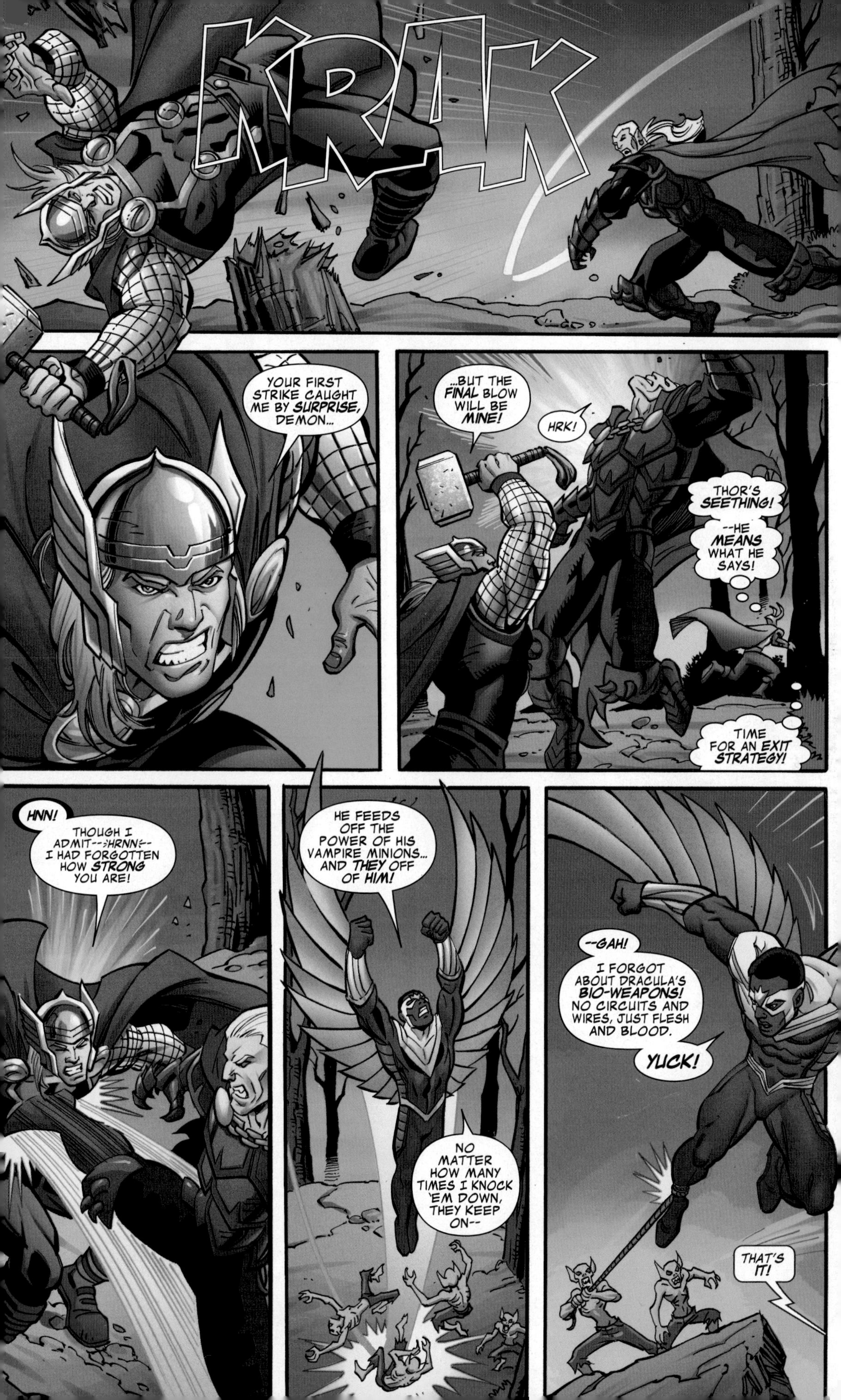
KRAK
YOUR FIRST STRIKE CAUGHT ME BY SURPRISE, DEMON...
...BUT THE FINAL BLOW WILL BE MINE!
HRK!
THOR'S SEETHING! --HE MEANS WHAT HE SAYS!
TIME FOR AN EXIT STRATEGY!
HNN!
THOUGH I ADMIT-- HRNN --I HAD FORGOTTEN HOW STRONG YOU ARE!
HE FEEDS OFF THE POWER OF HIS VAMPIRE MINIONS... AND THEY OFF OF HIM!
NO MATTER HOW MANY TIMES I KNOCK 'EM DOWN, THEY KEEP ON--
--GAH!
I FORGOT ABOUT DRACULA'S BIO-WEAPONS! NO CIRCUITS AND WIRES, JUST FLESH AND BLOOD.
YUCK!
THAT'S IT!

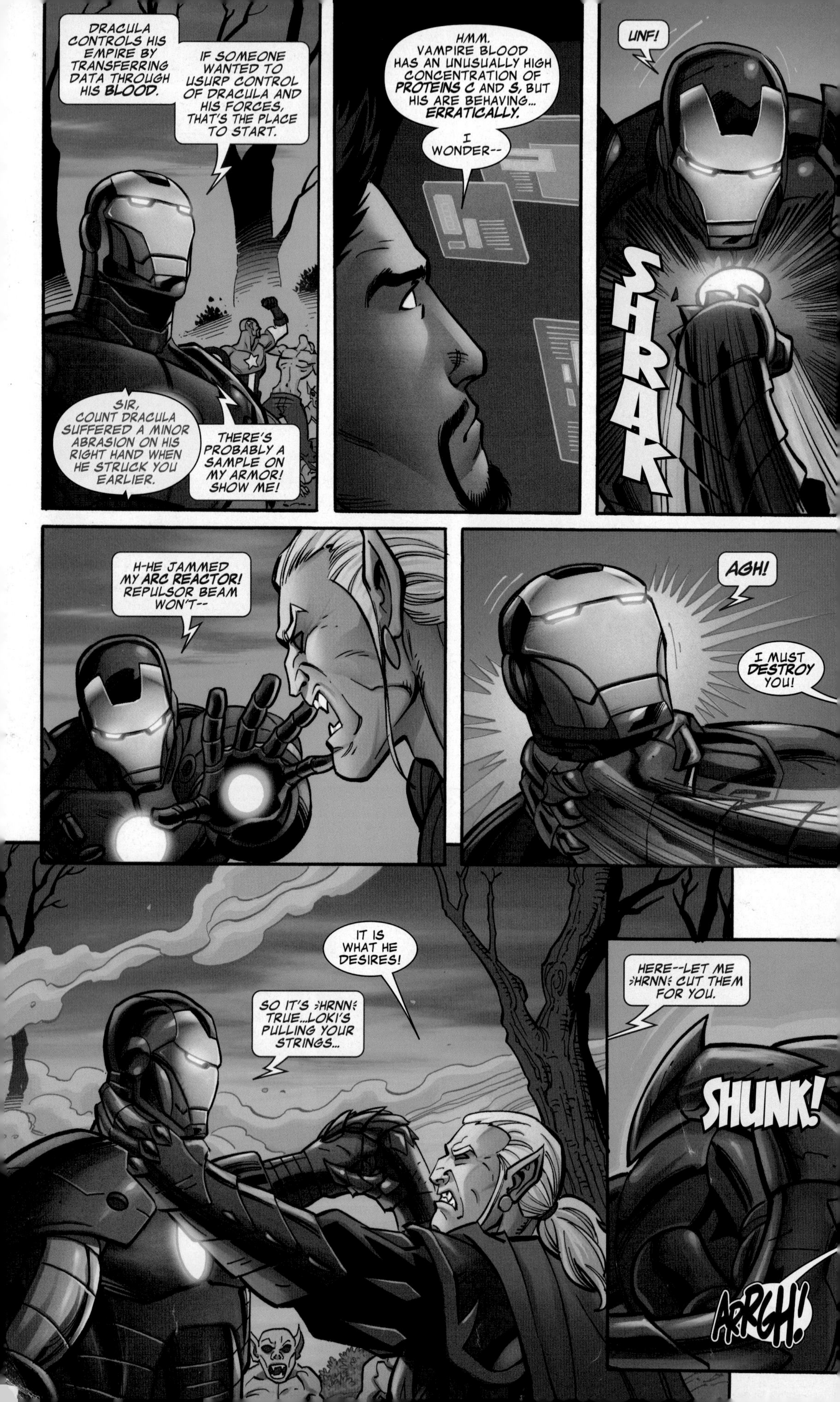
DRACULA CONTROLS HIS EMPIRE BY TRANSFERRING DATA THROUGH HIS BLOOD.
IF SOMEONE WANTED TO USURP CONTROL OF DRACULA AND HIS FORCES, THAT'S THE PLACE TO START.
SIR, COUNT DRACULA SUFFERED A MINOR ABRASION ON HIS RIGHT HAND WHEN HE STRUCK YOU EARLIER.
THERE'S PROBABLY A SAMPLE ON MY ARMOR! SHOW ME!
HMM. VAMPIRE BLOOD HAS AN UNUSUALLY HIGH CONCENTRATION OF PROTEINS C AND S, BUT HIS ARE BEHAVING... ERRATICALLY.
I WONDER--
UNF!
SHRAK
H-HE JAMMED MY ARC REACTOR! REPULSOR BEAM WON'T--
AGH!
I MUST DESTROY YOU!
IT IS WHAT HE DESIRES!
SO IT'S >HRNN< TRUE...LOKI'S PULLING YOUR STRINGS...
HERE--LET ME >HRNN< CUT THEM FOR YOU.
SHUNK!
ARRGH!

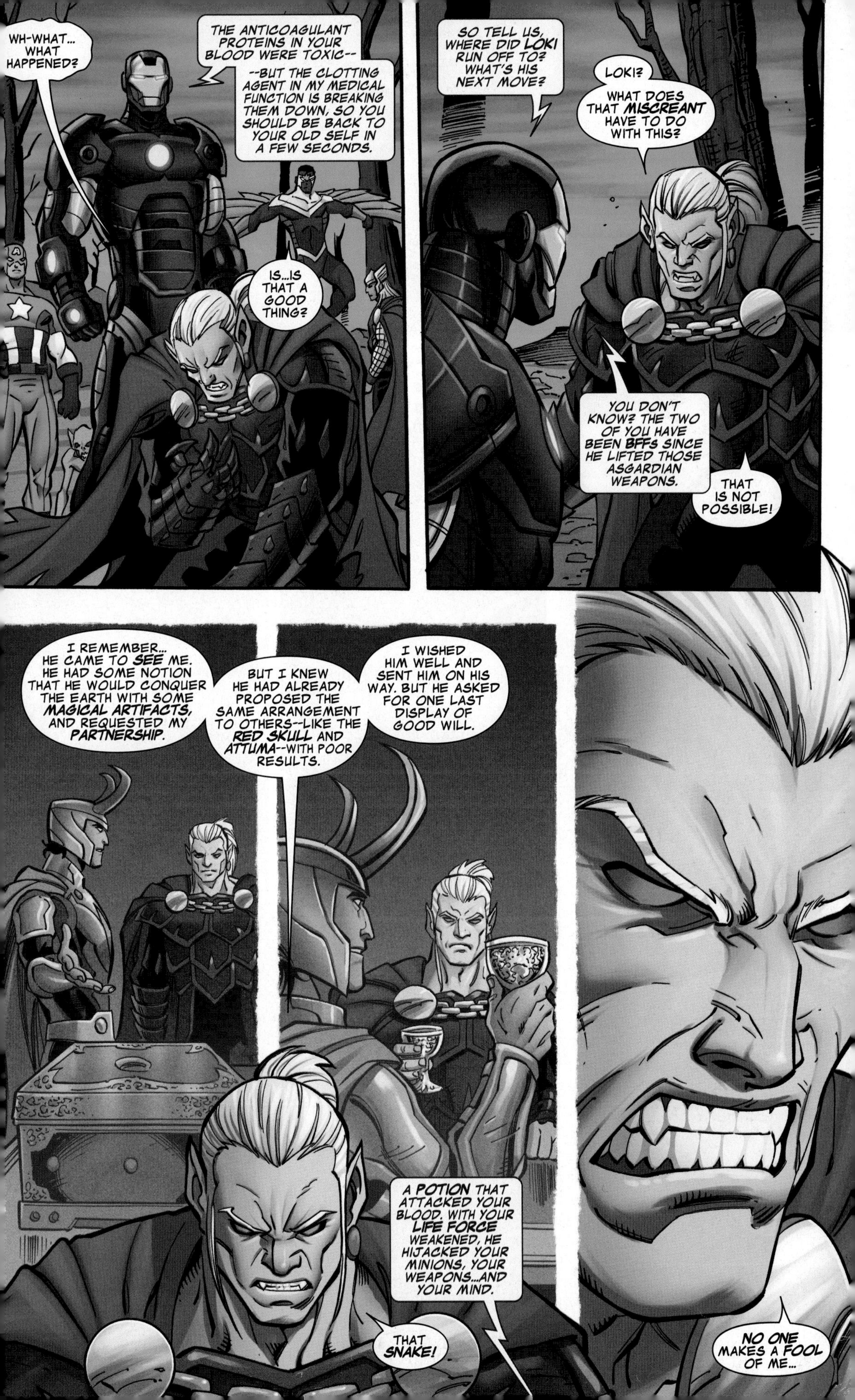
WH-WHAT... WHAT HAPPENED?
THE ANTICOAGULANT PROTEINS IN YOUR BLOOD WERE TOXIC--
--BUT THE CLOTTING AGENT IN MY MEDICAL FUNCTION IS BREAKING THEM DOWN, SO YOU SHOULD BE BACK TO YOUR OLD SELF IN A FEW SECONDS.
IS...IS THAT A GOOD THING?
SO TELL US, WHERE DID LOKI RUN OFF TO? WHAT'S HIS NEXT MOVE?
LOKI?
WHAT DOES THAT MISCREANT HAVE TO DO WITH THIS?
YOU DON'T KNOW? THE TWO OF YOU HAVE BEEN BFFs SINCE HE LIFTED THOSE ASGARDIAN WEAPONS.
THAT IS NOT POSSIBLE!
I REMEMBER... HE CAME TO SEE ME. HE HAD SOME NOTION THAT HE WOULD CONQUER THE EARTH WITH SOME MAGICAL ARTIFACTS, AND REQUESTED MY PARTNERSHIP.
BUT I KNEW HE HAD ALREADY PROPOSED THE SAME ARRANGEMENT TO OTHERS--LIKE THE RED SKULL AND ATTUMA--WITH POOR RESULTS.
I WISHED HIM WELL AND SENT HIM ON HIS WAY. BUT HE ASKED FOR ONE LAST DISPLAY OF GOOD WILL.
A POTION THAT ATTACKED YOUR BLOOD. WITH YOUR LIFE FORCE WEAKENED, HE HIJACKED YOUR MINIONS, YOUR WEAPONS...AND YOUR MIND.
THAT SNAKE!
NO ONE MAKES A FOOL OF ME...

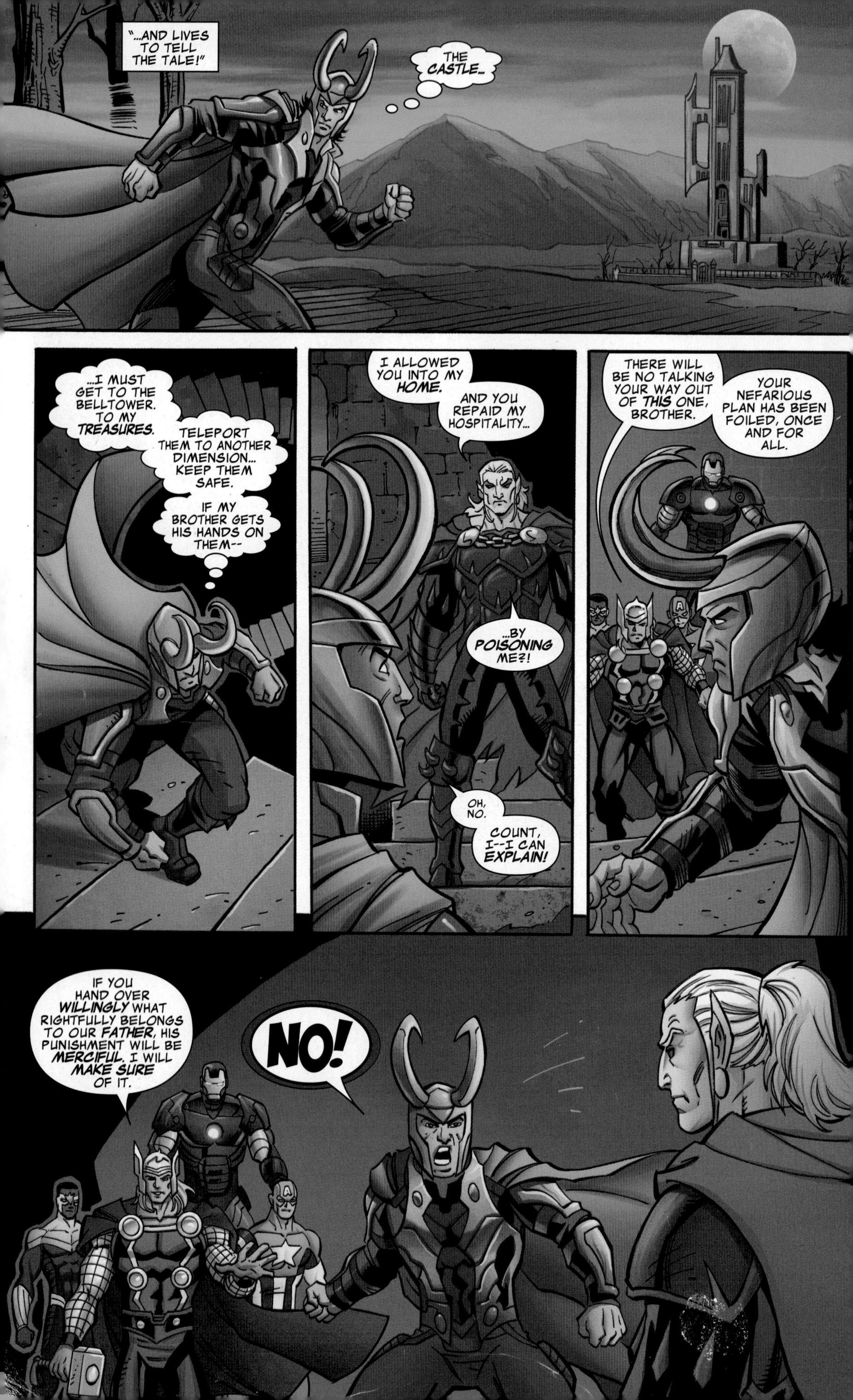
"...AND LIVES TO TELL THE TALE!"
THE CASTLE...
...I MUST GET TO THE BELLTOWER. TO MY TREASURES.
TELEPORT THEM TO ANOTHER DIMENSION... KEEP THEM SAFE.
IF MY BROTHER GETS HIS HANDS ON THEM--
I ALLOWED YOU INTO MY HOME.
AND YOU REPAID MY HOSPITALITY...
...BY POISONING ME?!
OH, NO.
COUNT, I--I CAN EXPLAIN!
THERE WILL BE NO TALKING YOUR WAY OUT OF THIS ONE, BROTHER.
YOUR NEFARIOUS PLAN HAS BEEN FOILED, ONCE AND FOR ALL.
IF YOU HAND OVER WILLINGLY WHAT RIGHTFULLY BELONGS TO OUR FATHER, HIS PUNISHMENT WILL BE MERCIFUL. I WILL MAKE SURE OF IT.
NO!

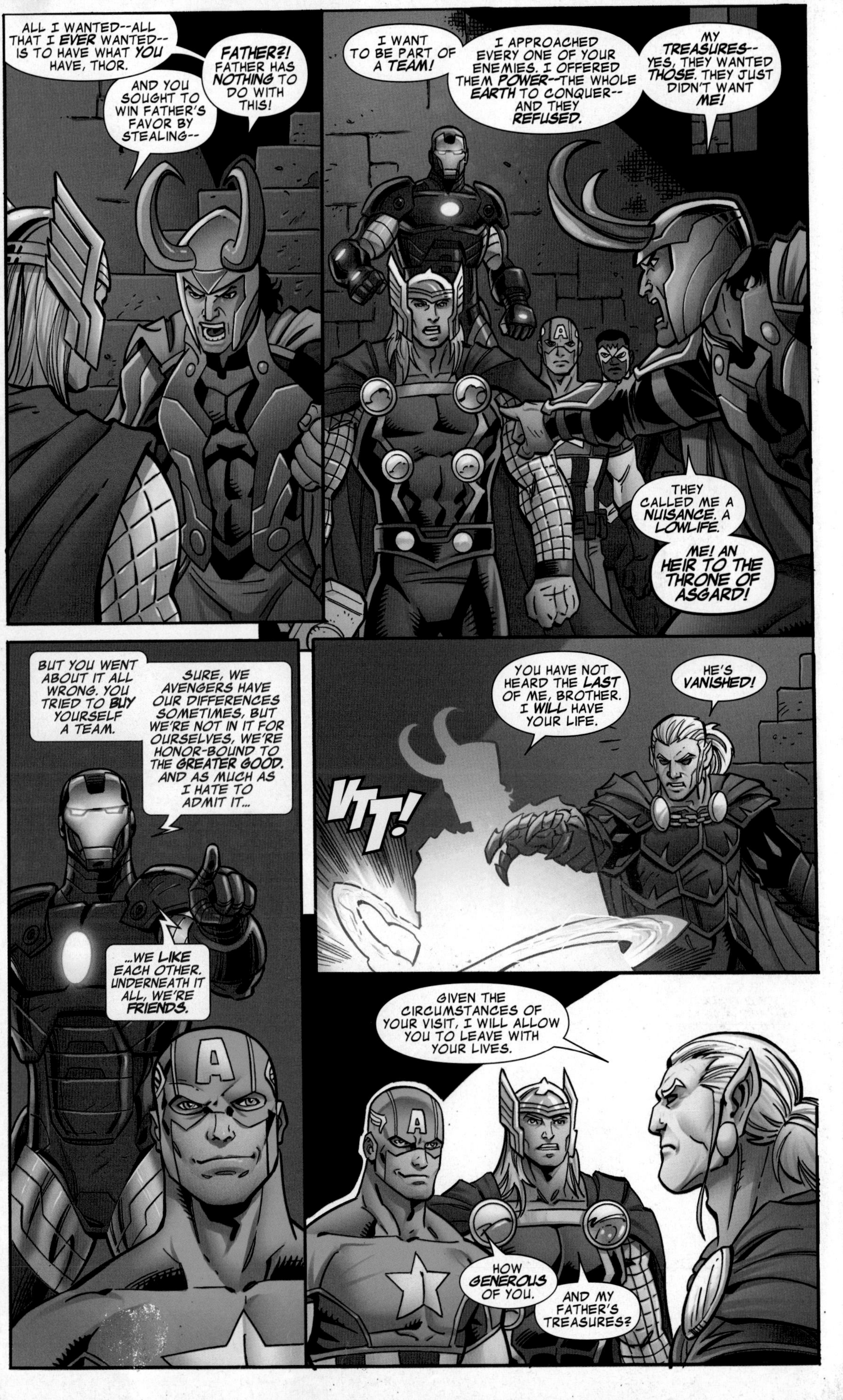
ALL I WANTED--ALL THAT I **EVER** WANTED--IS TO HAVE WHAT **YOU** HAVE, THOR.
AND YOU SOUGHT TO WIN FATHER'S FAVOR BY STEALING--
FATHER?! FATHER HAS **NOTHING** TO DO WITH THIS!
I WANT TO BE PART OF A **TEAM!**
I APPROACHED EVERY ONE OF YOUR ENEMIES. I OFFERED THEM **POWER**--THE WHOLE **EARTH** TO CONQUER--AND THEY **REFUSED.**
MY **TREASURES**--YES, THEY WANTED **THOSE**. THEY JUST DIDN'T WANT **ME!**
THEY CALLED ME A **NUISANCE**. A **LOWLIFE**.
ME! AN HEIR TO THE THRONE OF ASGARD!
BUT YOU WENT ABOUT IT ALL WRONG. YOU TRIED TO **BUY** YOURSELF A TEAM.
SURE, WE AVENGERS HAVE OUR DIFFERENCES SOMETIMES, BUT WE'RE NOT IN IT FOR OURSELVES, WE'RE HONOR-BOUND TO THE **GREATER GOOD**. AND AS MUCH AS I HATE TO ADMIT IT...
...WE **LIKE** EACH OTHER. UNDERNEATH IT ALL, WE'RE **FRIENDS**.
YOU HAVE NOT HEARD THE **LAST** OF ME, BROTHER. I **WILL** HAVE YOUR LIFE.
VTT!
HE'S **VANISHED!**
GIVEN THE CIRCUMSTANCES OF YOUR VISIT, I WILL ALLOW YOU TO LEAVE WITH YOUR LIVES.
HOW **GENEROUS** OF YOU.
AND MY FATHER'S TREASURES?

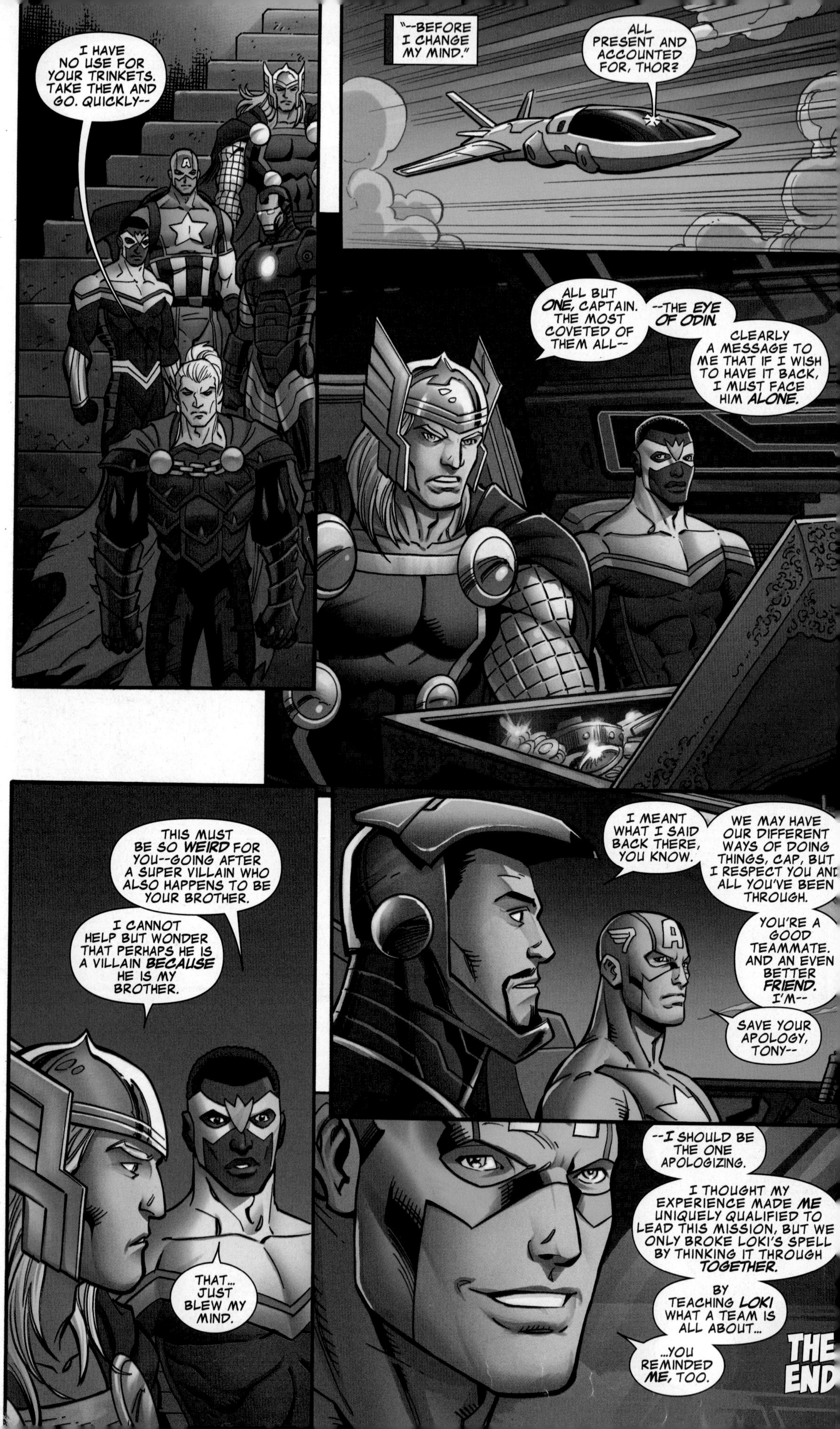
I HAVE NO USE FOR YOUR TRINKETS. TAKE THEM AND GO. QUICKLY--
"--BEFORE I CHANGE MY MIND."
ALL PRESENT AND ACCOUNTED FOR, THOR?
ALL BUT ONE, CAPTAIN. THE MOST COVETED OF THEM ALL--
--THE EYE OF ODIN.
CLEARLY A MESSAGE TO ME THAT IF I WISH TO HAVE IT BACK, I MUST FACE HIM ALONE.
THIS MUST BE SO WEIRD FOR YOU--GOING AFTER A SUPER VILLAIN WHO ALSO HAPPENS TO BE YOUR BROTHER.
I CANNOT HELP BUT WONDER THAT PERHAPS HE IS A VILLAIN BECAUSE HE IS MY BROTHER.
THAT... JUST BLEW MY MIND.
I MEANT WHAT I SAID BACK THERE, YOU KNOW.
WE MAY HAVE OUR DIFFERENT WAYS OF DOING THINGS, CAP, BUT I RESPECT YOU AND ALL YOU'VE BEEN THROUGH.
YOU'RE A GOOD TEAMMATE. AND AN EVEN BETTER FRIEND. I'M--
SAVE YOUR APOLOGY, TONY--
--I SHOULD BE THE ONE APOLOGIZING.
I THOUGHT MY EXPERIENCE MADE ME UNIQUELY QUALIFIED TO LEAD THIS MISSION, BUT WE ONLY BROKE LOKI'S SPELL BY THINKING IT THROUGH TOGETHER.
BY TEACHING LOKI WHAT A TEAM IS ALL ABOUT...
...YOU REMINDED ME, TOO.
THE END

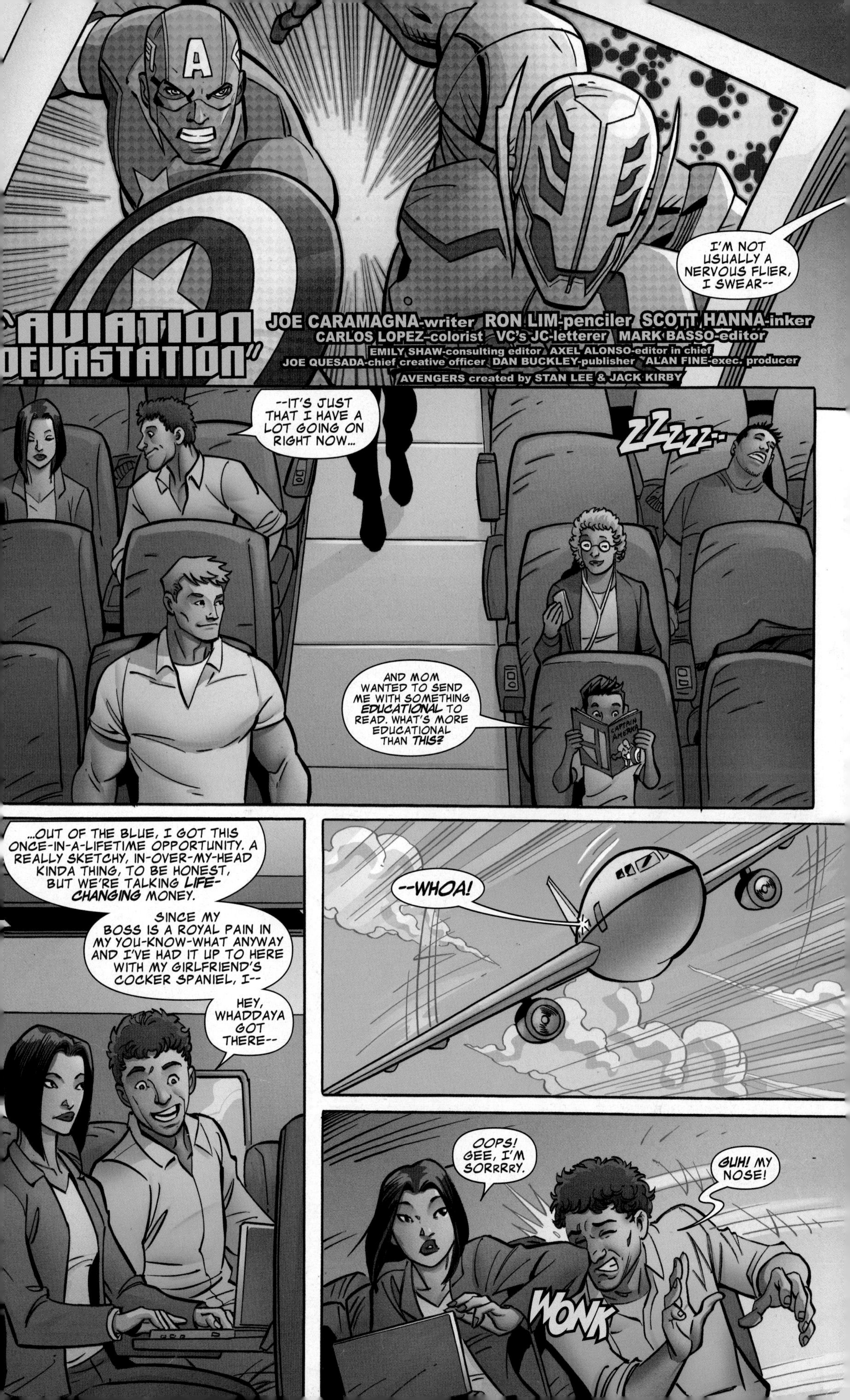
I'M NOT USUALLY A NERVOUS FLIER, I SWEAR--
"AVIATION DEVASTATION"
JOE CARAMAGNA-writer RON LIM-penciler SCOTT HANNA-inker
CARLOS LOPEZ-colorist VC's JC-letterer MARK BASSO-editor
EMILY SHAW-consulting editor AXEL ALONSO-editor in chief
JOE QUESADA-chief creative officer DAN BUCKLEY-publisher ALAN FINE-exec. producer
AVENGERS created by STAN LEE & JACK KIRBY
--IT'S JUST THAT I HAVE A LOT GOING ON RIGHT NOW...
ZZZZZ--
AND MOM WANTED TO SEND ME WITH SOMETHING EDUCATIONAL TO READ. WHAT'S MORE EDUCATIONAL THAN THIS?
CAPTAIN AMERICA
...OUT OF THE BLUE, I GOT THIS ONCE-IN-A-LIFETIME OPPORTUNITY. A REALLY SKETCHY, IN-OVER-MY-HEAD KINDA THING, TO BE HONEST, BUT WE'RE TALKING LIFE-CHANGING MONEY.
SINCE MY BOSS IS A ROYAL PAIN IN MY YOU-KNOW-WHAT ANYWAY AND I'VE HAD IT UP TO HERE WITH MY GIRLFRIEND'S COCKER SPANIEL, I--
HEY, WHADDAYA GOT THERE--
--WHOA!
OOPS! GEE, I'M SORRRRY.
GUH! MY NOSE!
WONK

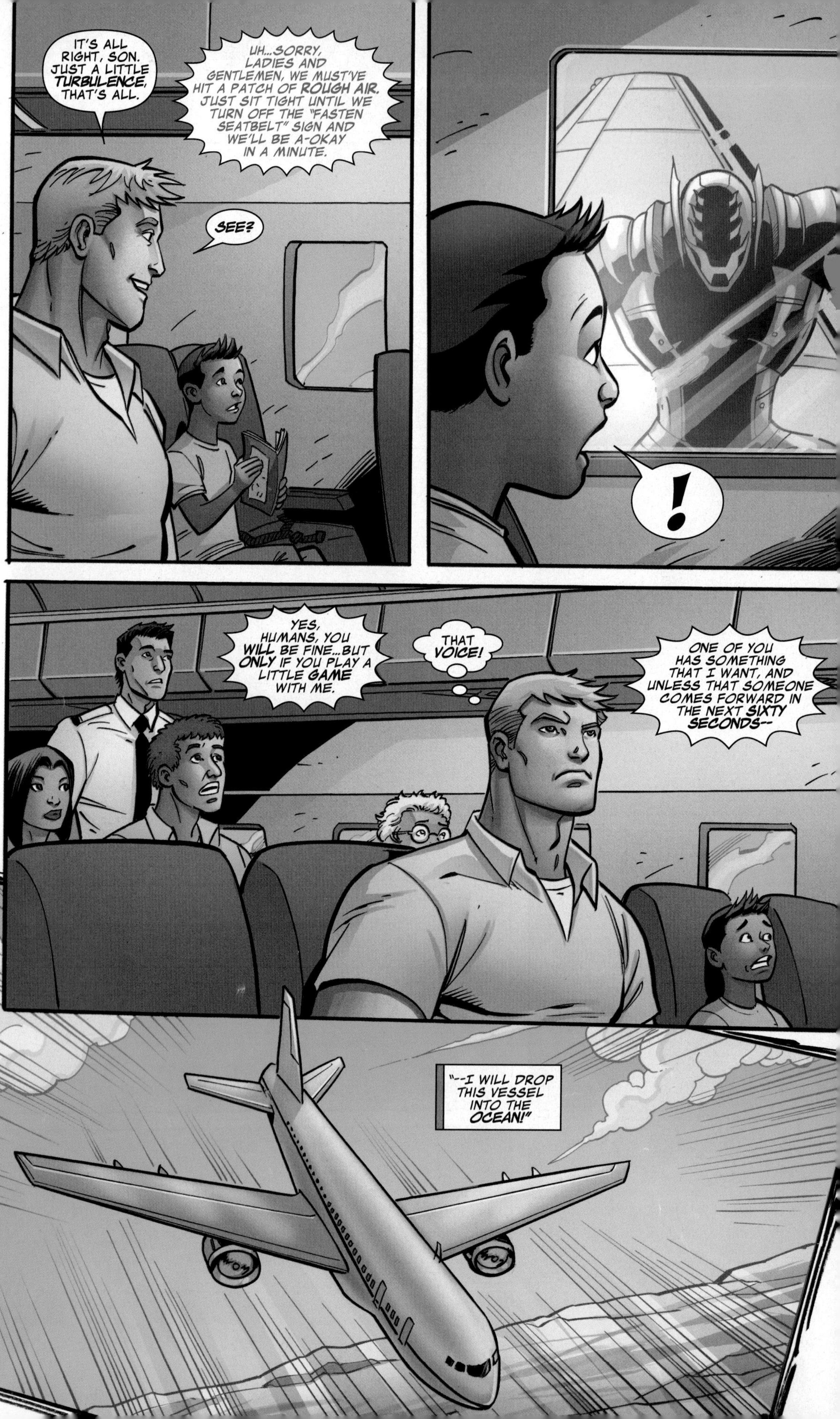
IT'S ALL RIGHT, SON. JUST A LITTLE TURBULENCE, THAT'S ALL.
UH...SORRY, LADIES AND GENTLEMEN, WE MUST'VE HIT A PATCH OF ROUGH AIR. JUST SIT TIGHT UNTIL WE TURN OFF THE "FASTEN SEATBELT" SIGN AND WE'LL BE A-OKAY IN A MINUTE.
SEE?
!
YES, HUMANS, YOU WILL BE FINE...BUT ONLY IF YOU PLAY A LITTLE GAME WITH ME.
THAT VOICE!
ONE OF YOU HAS SOMETHING THAT I WANT, AND UNLESS THAT SOMEONE COMES FORWARD IN THE NEXT SIXTY SECONDS--
"--I WILL DROP THIS VESSEL INTO THE OCEAN!"

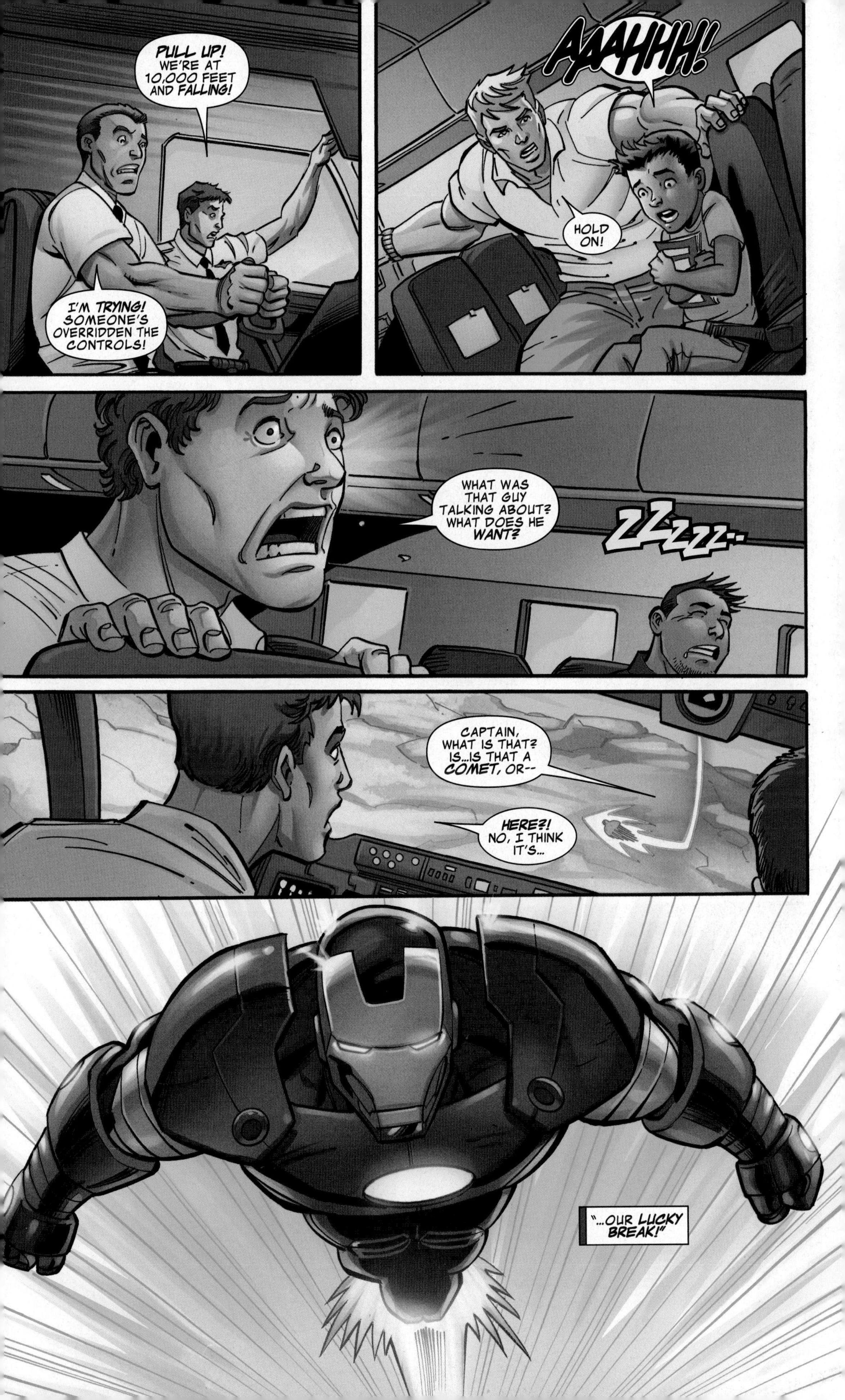
PULL UP! WE'RE AT 10,000 FEET AND FALLING!
I'M TRYING! SOMEONE'S OVERRIDDEN THE CONTROLS!
AAAHHH!
HOLD ON!
WHAT WAS THAT GUY TALKING ABOUT? WHAT DOES HE WANT?
ZZZZZ--
CAPTAIN, WHAT IS THAT? IS...IS THAT A COMET, OR--
HERE?! NO, I THINK IT'S...
"...OUR LUCKY BREAK!"

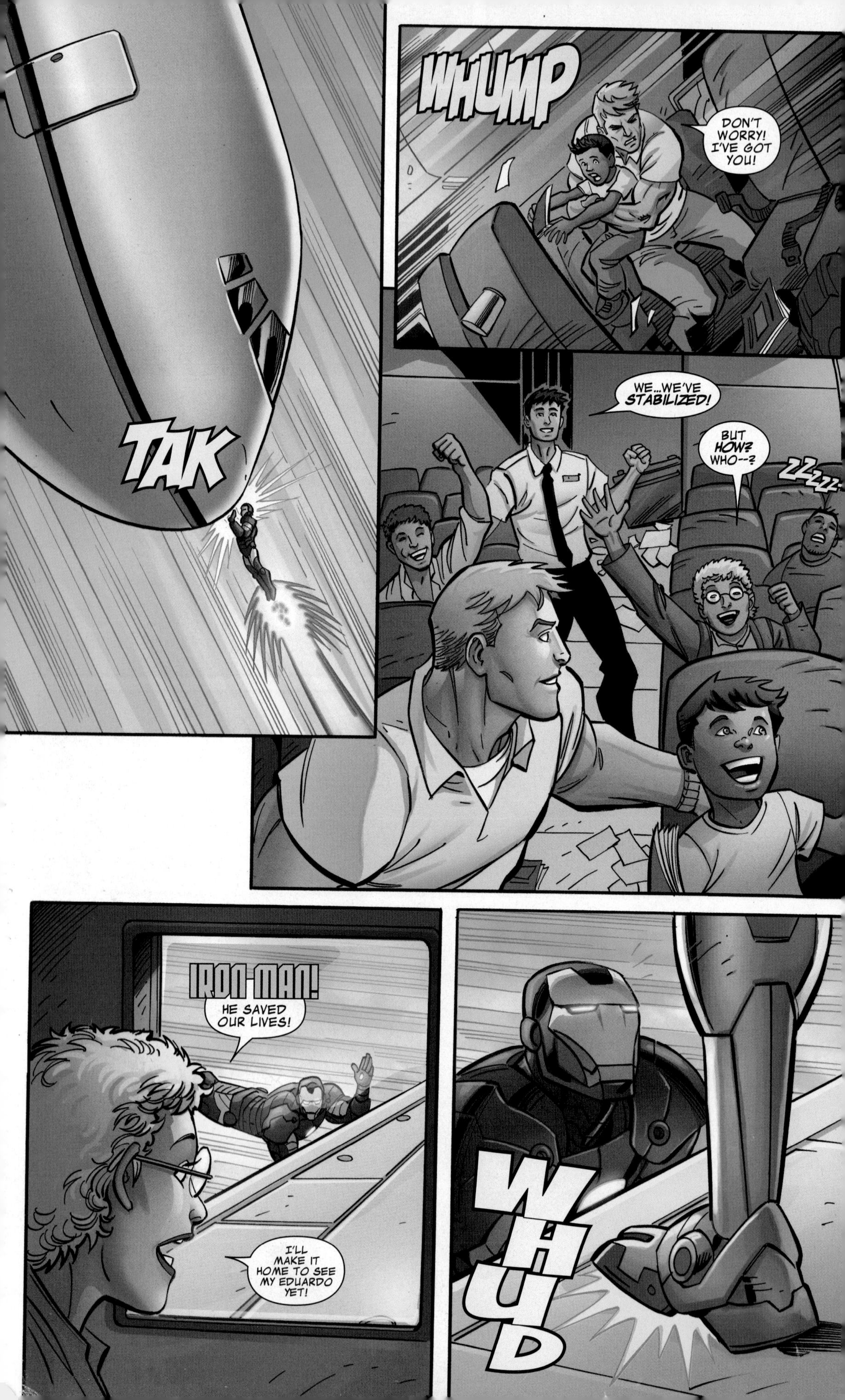
TAK
WHUMP
DON'T WORRY! I'VE GOT YOU!
WE...WE'VE STABILIZED!
BUT HOW? WHO--?
ZZZZZ-
IRON MAN!
HE SAVED OUR LIVES!
I'LL MAKE IT HOME TO SEE MY EDUARDO YET!
WHUD

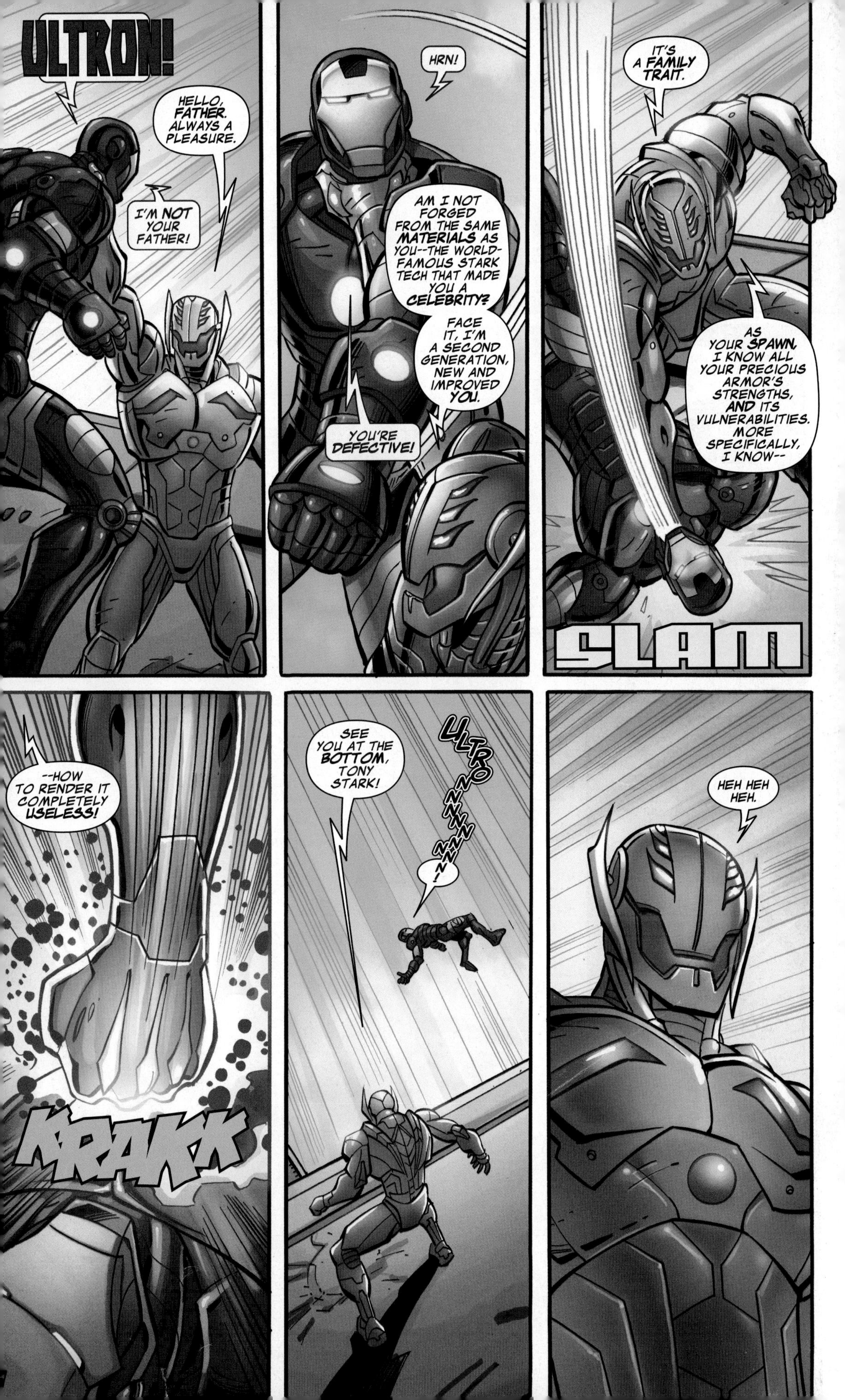
ULTRON!
HELLO, FATHER. ALWAYS A PLEASURE.
I'M NOT YOUR FATHER!
HRN!
AM I NOT FORGED FROM THE SAME MATERIALS AS YOU--THE WORLD-FAMOUS STARK TECH THAT MADE YOU A CELEBRITY?
FACE IT, I'M A SECOND GENERATION, NEW AND IMPROVED YOU.
YOU'RE DEFECTIVE!
IT'S A FAMILY TRAIT.
AS YOUR SPAWN, I KNOW ALL YOUR PRECIOUS ARMOR'S STRENGTHS, AND ITS VULNERABILITIES. MORE SPECIFICALLY, I KNOW--
SLAM
--HOW TO RENDER IT COMPLETELY USELESS!
KRAKK
SEE YOU AT THE BOTTOM, TONY STARK!
ULTRONNNNNNNN!
HEH HEH HEH.

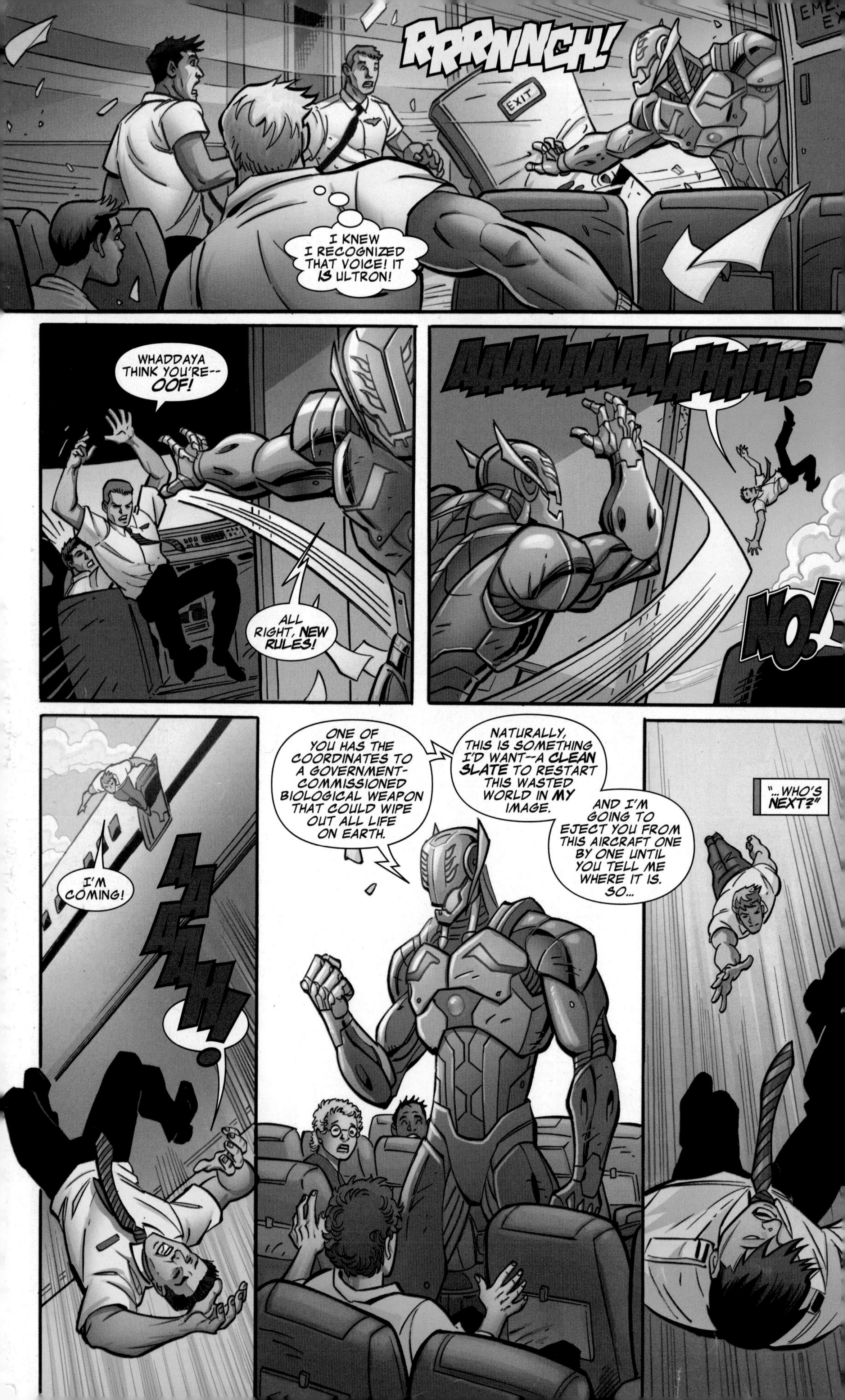
RRRNNCH!
EXIT
I KNEW I RECOGNIZED THAT VOICE! IT **IS** ULTRON!
WHADDAYA THINK YOU'RE-- **OOF!**
ALL RIGHT, **NEW RULES!**
AAAAAAAAAAHHHH!
NO!
I'M COMING!
AAAAHH!
ONE OF YOU HAS THE COORDINATES TO A GOVERNMENT-COMMISSIONED BIOLOGICAL WEAPON THAT COULD WIPE OUT ALL LIFE ON EARTH.
NATURALLY, THIS IS SOMETHING I'D WANT--A **CLEAN SLATE** TO RESTART THIS WASTED WORLD IN **MY** IMAGE.
AND I'M GOING TO EJECT YOU FROM THIS AIRCRAFT ONE BY ONE UNTIL YOU TELL ME WHERE IT IS. SO...
"...WHO'S **NEXT?**"

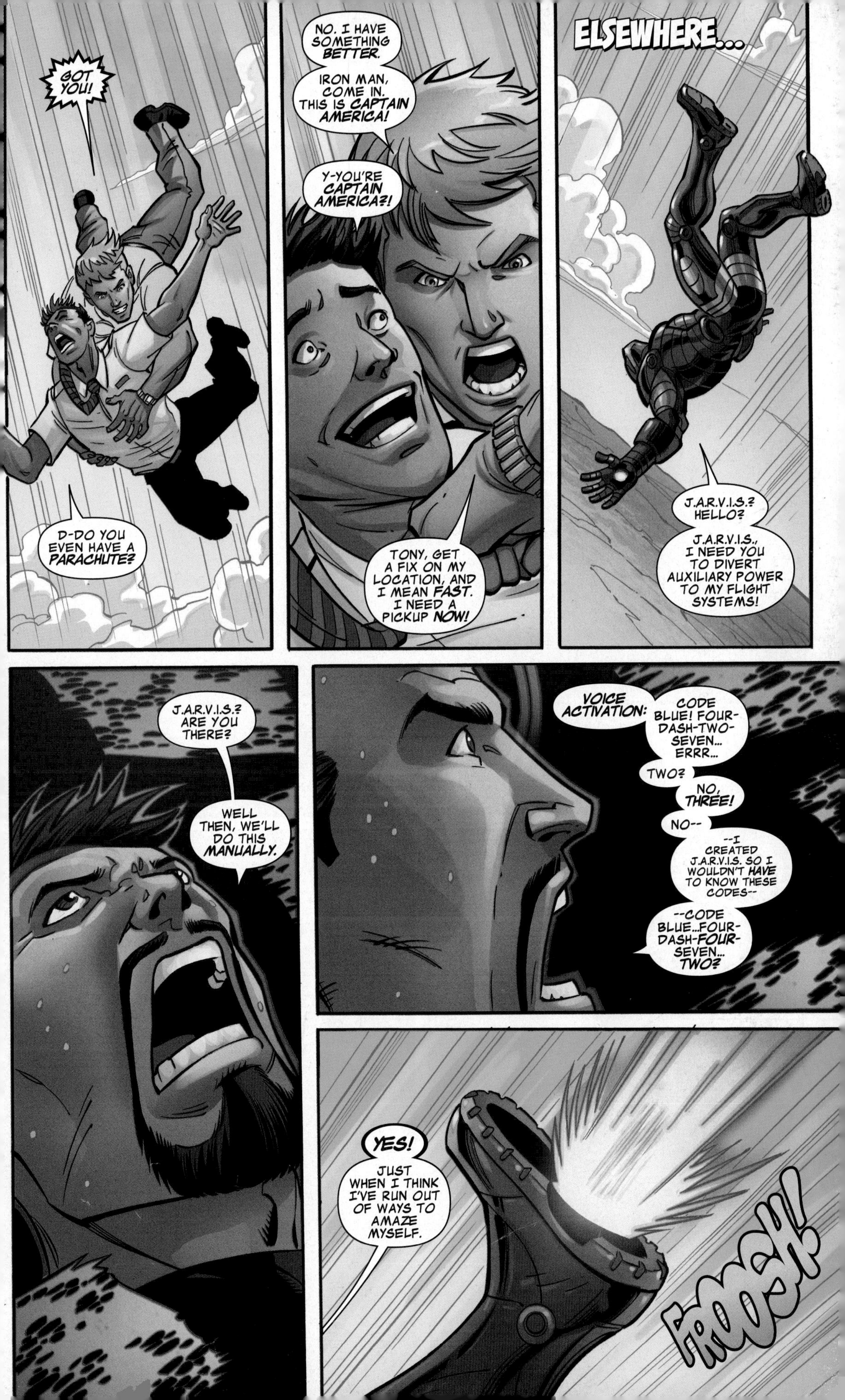
GOT YOU!
D-DO YOU EVEN HAVE A PARACHUTE?
NO. I HAVE SOMETHING BETTER.
IRON MAN, COME IN. THIS IS CAPTAIN AMERICA!
Y-YOU'RE CAPTAIN AMERICA?!
TONY, GET A FIX ON MY LOCATION, AND I MEAN FAST. I NEED A PICKUP NOW!
ELSEWHERE...
J.A.R.V.I.S.? HELLO?
J.A.R.V.I.S., I NEED YOU TO DIVERT AUXILIARY POWER TO MY FLIGHT SYSTEMS!
J.A.R.V.I.S.? ARE YOU THERE?
WELL THEN, WE'LL DO THIS MANUALLY.
VOICE ACTIVATION:
CODE BLUE! FOUR-DASH-TWO-SEVEN... ERRR...
TWO?
NO, THREE!
NO--
--I CREATED J.A.R.V.I.S. SO I WOULDN'T HAVE TO KNOW THESE CODES--
--CODE BLUE...FOUR-DASH-FOUR-SEVEN... TWO?
YES!
JUST WHEN I THINK I'VE RUN OUT OF WAYS TO AMAZE MYSELF.
FROOSH!

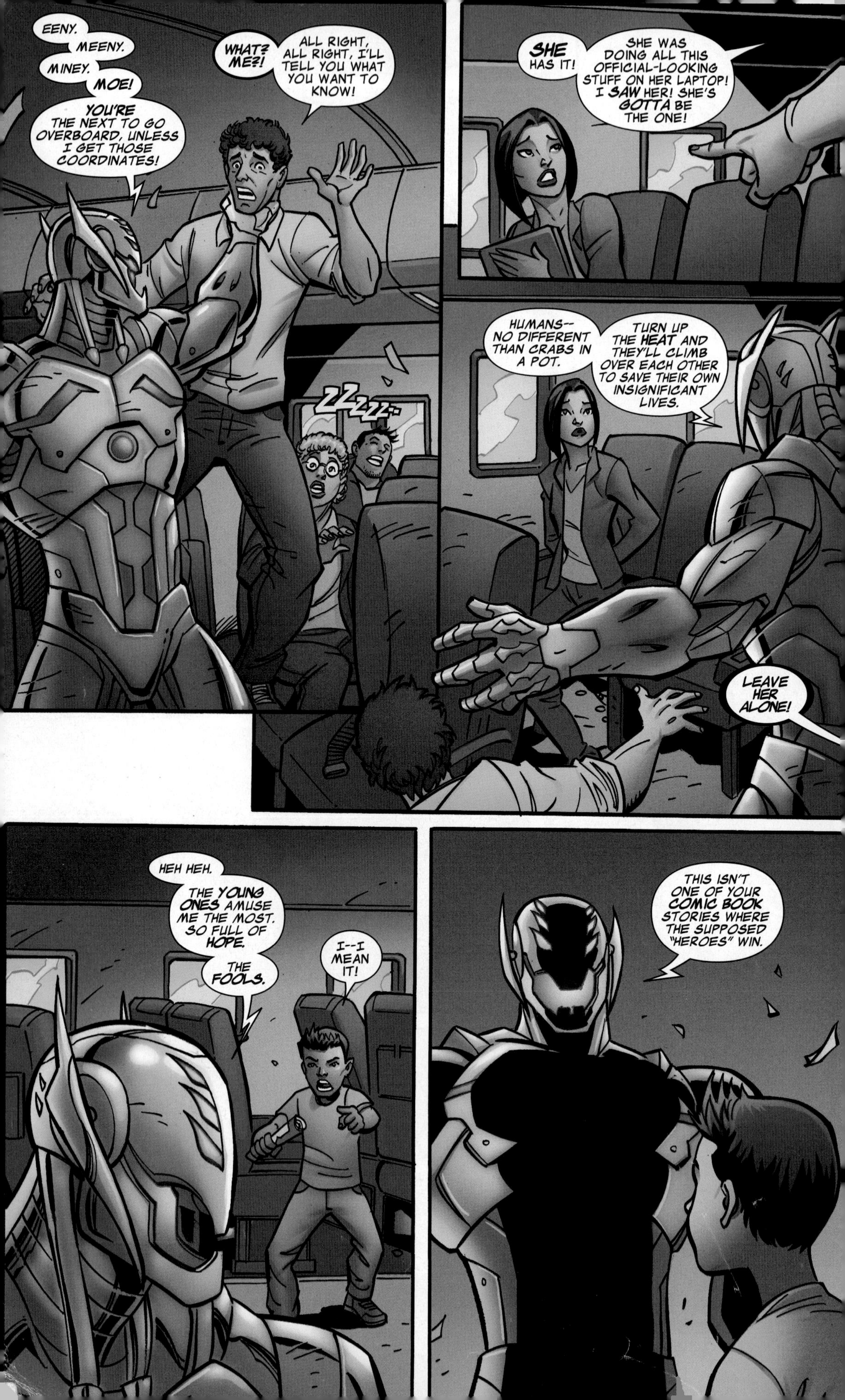
EENY.
MEENY.
MINEY.
MOE!
YOU'RE THE NEXT TO GO OVERBOARD, UNLESS I GET THOSE COORDINATES!
WHAT? ME?!
ALL RIGHT, ALL RIGHT, I'LL TELL YOU WHAT YOU WANT TO KNOW!
ZZZZZ--
SHE HAS IT!
SHE WAS DOING ALL THIS OFFICIAL-LOOKING STUFF ON HER LAPTOP! I SAW HER! SHE'S GOTTA BE THE ONE!
HUMANS-- NO DIFFERENT THAN CRABS IN A POT.
TURN UP THE HEAT AND THEY'LL CLIMB OVER EACH OTHER TO SAVE THEIR OWN INSIGNIFICANT LIVES.
LEAVE HER ALONE!
HEH HEH.
THE YOUNG ONES AMUSE ME THE MOST. SO FULL OF HOPE.
THE FOOLS.
I--I MEAN IT!
THIS ISN'T ONE OF YOUR COMIC BOOK STORIES WHERE THE SUPPOSED "HEROES" WIN.

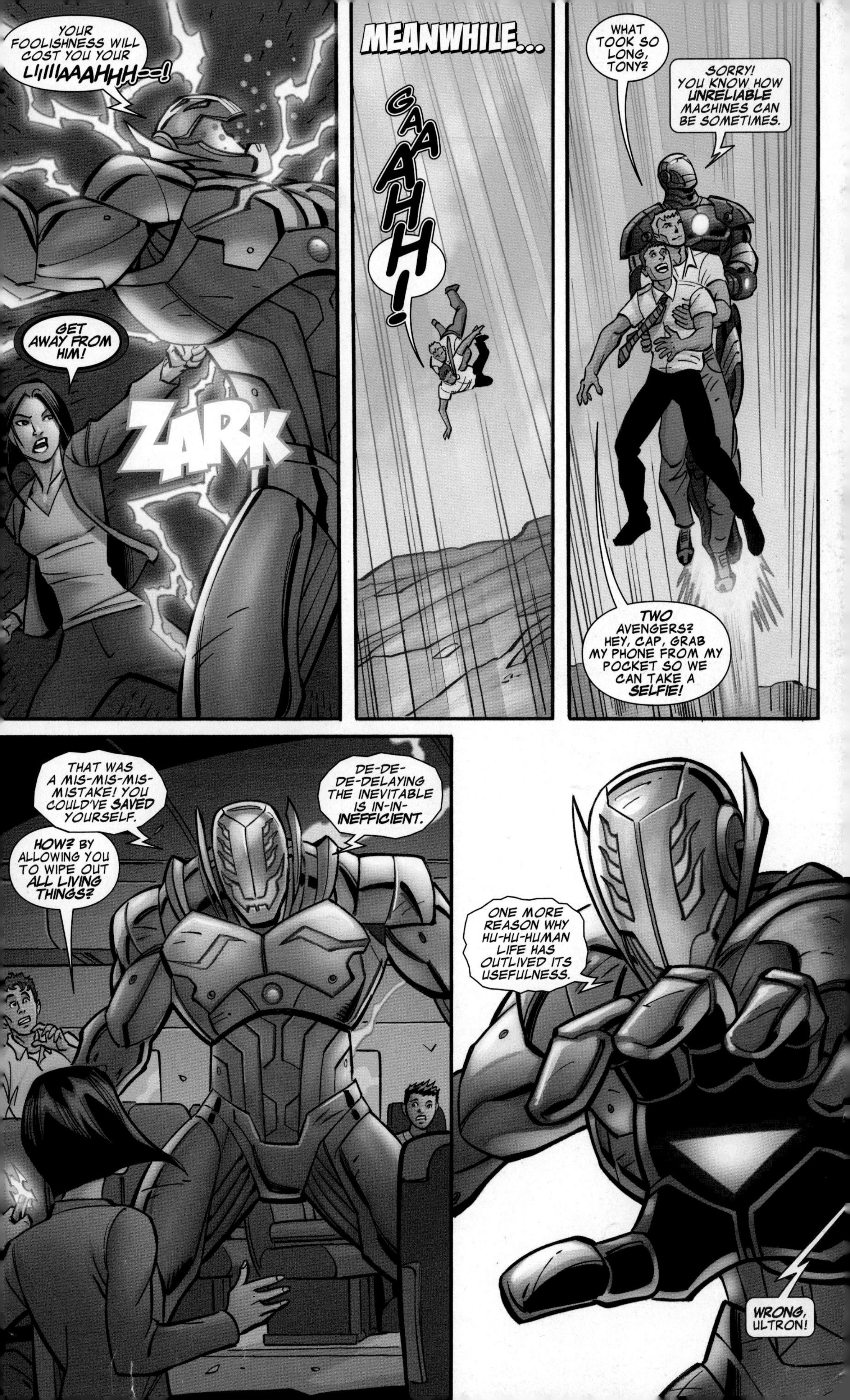
YOUR FOOLISHNESS WILL COST YOU YOUR LIIIIAAAHHH--!
GET AWAY FROM HIM!
ZARK
MEANWHILE...
GAAAAHHH!
WHAT TOOK SO LONG, TONY?
SORRY! YOU KNOW HOW UNRELIABLE MACHINES CAN BE SOMETIMES.
TWO AVENGERS? HEY, CAP, GRAB MY PHONE FROM MY POCKET SO WE CAN TAKE A SELFIE!
THAT WAS A MIS-MIS-MIS-MISTAKE! YOU COULD'VE SAVED YOURSELF.
DE-DE-DE-DELAYING THE INEVITABLE IS IN-IN-INEFFICIENT.
HOW? BY ALLOWING YOU TO WIPE OUT ALL LIVING THINGS?
ONE MORE REASON WHY HU-HU-HUMAN LIFE HAS OUTLIVED ITS USEFULNESS.
WRONG, ULTRON!

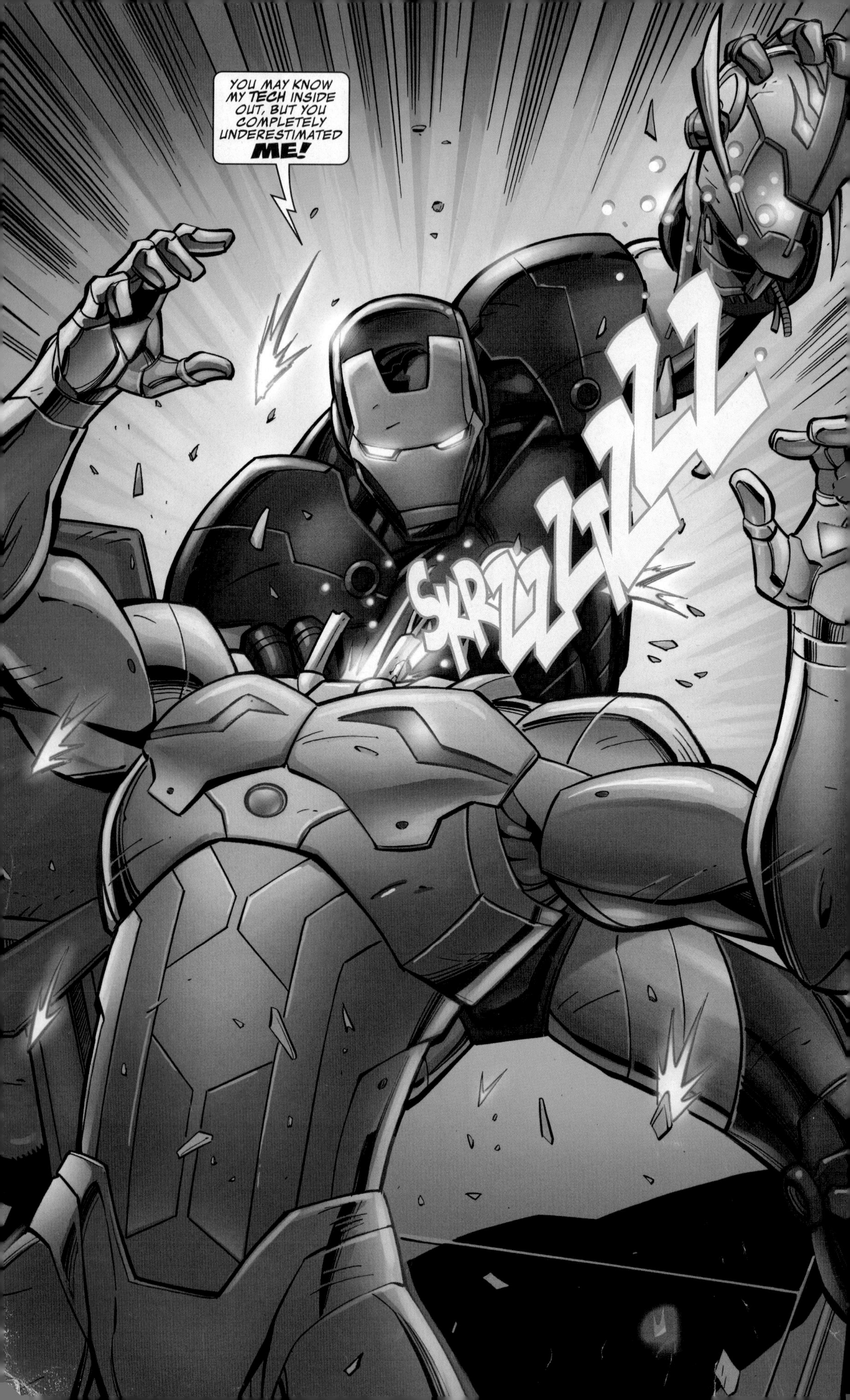
YOU MAY KNOW MY TECH INSIDE OUT, BUT YOU COMPLETELY UNDERESTIMATED ME!
SKRZZZZZZ

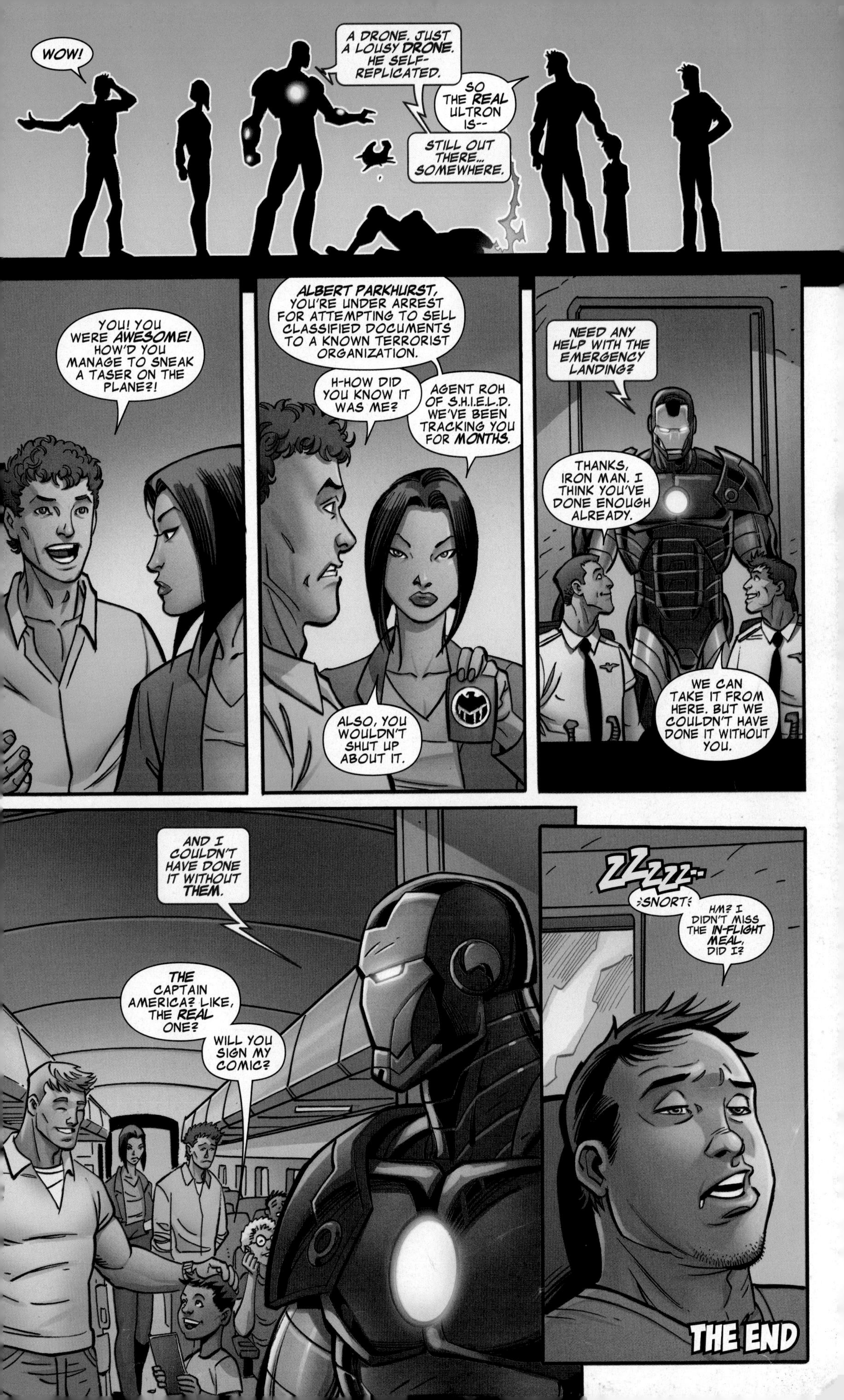
WOW!
A DRONE. JUST A LOUSY DRONE. HE SELF-REPLICATED.
SO THE REAL ULTRON IS--
STILL OUT THERE... SOMEWHERE.
YOU! YOU WERE AWESOME! HOW'D YOU MANAGE TO SNEAK A TASER ON THE PLANE?!
ALBERT PARKHURST, YOU'RE UNDER ARREST FOR ATTEMPTING TO SELL CLASSIFIED DOCUMENTS TO A KNOWN TERRORIST ORGANIZATION.
H-HOW DID YOU KNOW IT WAS ME?
AGENT ROH OF S.H.I.E.L.D. WE'VE BEEN TRACKING YOU FOR MONTHS.
ALSO, YOU WOULDN'T SHUT UP ABOUT IT.
NEED ANY HELP WITH THE EMERGENCY LANDING?
THANKS, IRON MAN. I THINK YOU'VE DONE ENOUGH ALREADY.
WE CAN TAKE IT FROM HERE. BUT WE COULDN'T HAVE DONE IT WITHOUT YOU.
AND I COULDN'T HAVE DONE IT WITHOUT THEM.
THE CAPTAIN AMERICA? LIKE, THE REAL ONE?
WILL YOU SIGN MY COMIC?
ZZZZZ--
SNORT
HM? I DIDN'T MISS THE IN-FLIGHT MEAL, DID I?
THE END

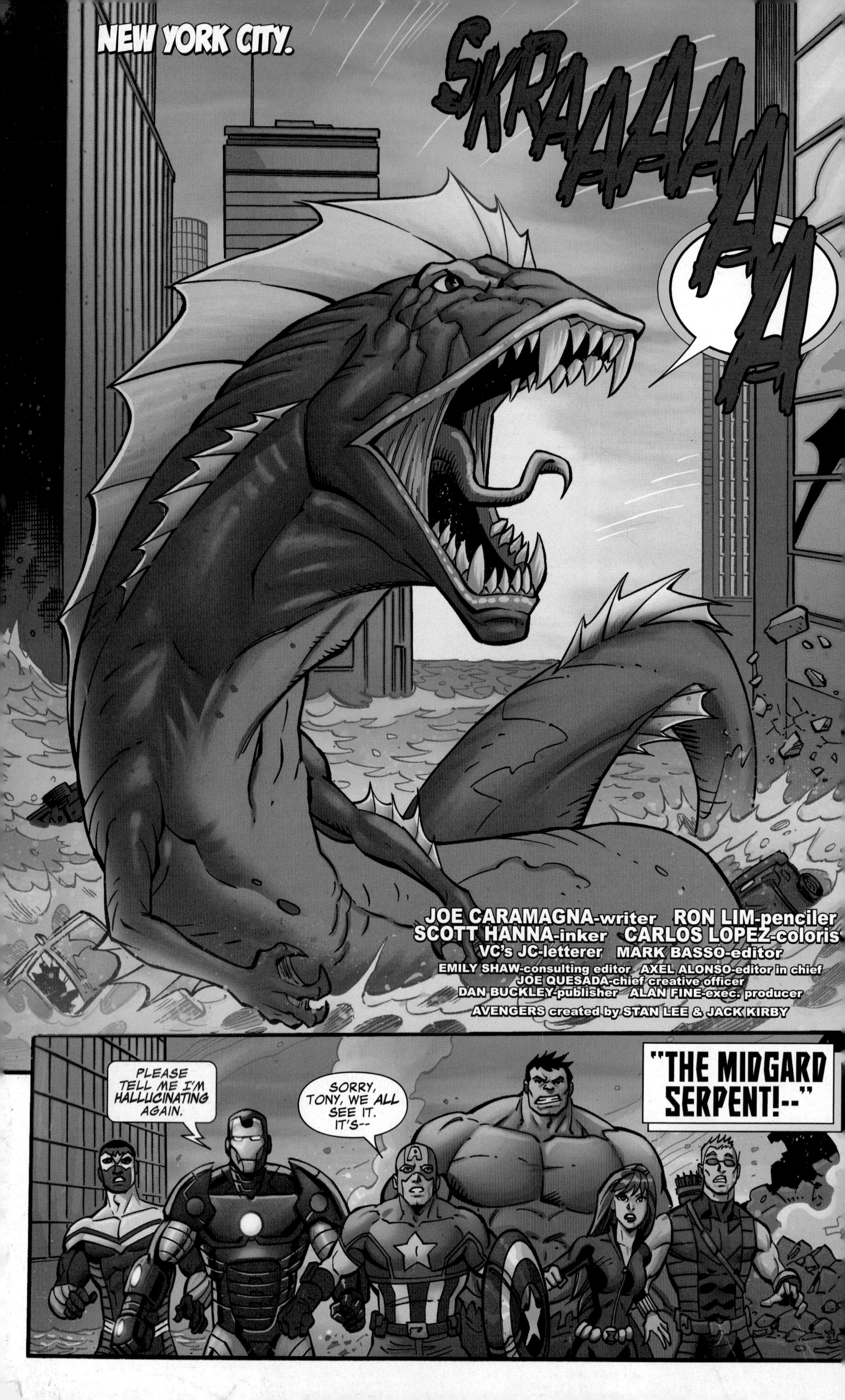

NEW YORK CITY.
SKRAAAAAAAA
JOE CARAMAGNA-writer RON LIM-penciler
SCOTT HANNA-inker CARLOS LOPEZ-coloris
VC's JC-letterer MARK BASSO-editor
EMILY SHAW-consulting editor AXEL ALONSO-editor in chief
JOE QUESADA-chief creative officer
DAN BUCKLEY-publisher ALAN FINE-exec. producer
AVENGERS created by STAN LEE & JACK KIRBY
"THE MIDGARD SERPENT!--"
PLEASE TELL ME I'M HALLUCINATING AGAIN.
SORRY, TONY, WE ALL SEE IT. IT'S--

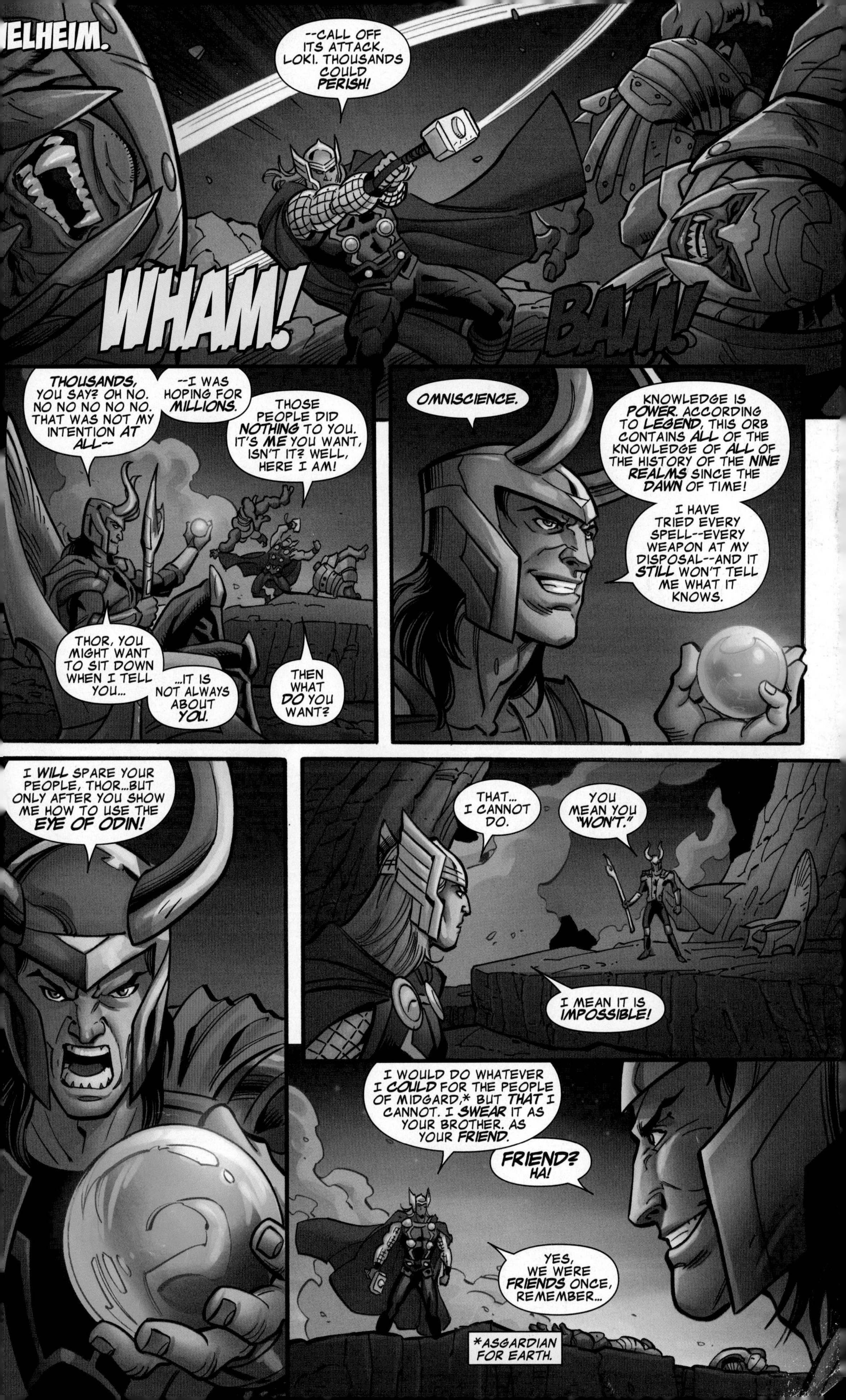

ELHEIM.
--CALL OFF ITS ATTACK, LOKI. THOUSANDS COULD PERISH!
WHAM!
BAM!
THOUSANDS, YOU SAY? OH NO. NO NO NO NO NO. THAT WAS NOT MY INTENTION AT ALL--
--I WAS HOPING FOR MILLIONS.
THOSE PEOPLE DID NOTHING TO YOU. IT'S ME YOU WANT, ISN'T IT? WELL, HERE I AM!
THOR, YOU MIGHT WANT TO SIT DOWN WHEN I TELL YOU...
...IT IS NOT ALWAYS ABOUT YOU.
THEN WHAT DO YOU WANT?
OMNISCIENCE.
KNOWLEDGE IS POWER. ACCORDING TO LEGEND, THIS ORB CONTAINS ALL OF THE KNOWLEDGE OF ALL OF THE HISTORY OF THE NINE REALMS SINCE THE DAWN OF TIME!
I HAVE TRIED EVERY SPELL--EVERY WEAPON AT MY DISPOSAL--AND IT STILL WON'T TELL ME WHAT IT KNOWS.
I WILL SPARE YOUR PEOPLE, THOR...BUT ONLY AFTER YOU SHOW ME HOW TO USE THE EYE OF ODIN!
THAT... I CANNOT DO.
YOU MEAN YOU "WON'T."
I MEAN IT IS IMPOSSIBLE!
I WOULD DO WHATEVER I COULD FOR THE PEOPLE OF MIDGARD,* BUT THAT I CANNOT. I SWEAR IT AS YOUR BROTHER. AS YOUR FRIEND.
FRIEND? HA!
YES, WE WERE FRIENDS ONCE, REMEMBER...
*ASGARDIAN FOR EARTH.

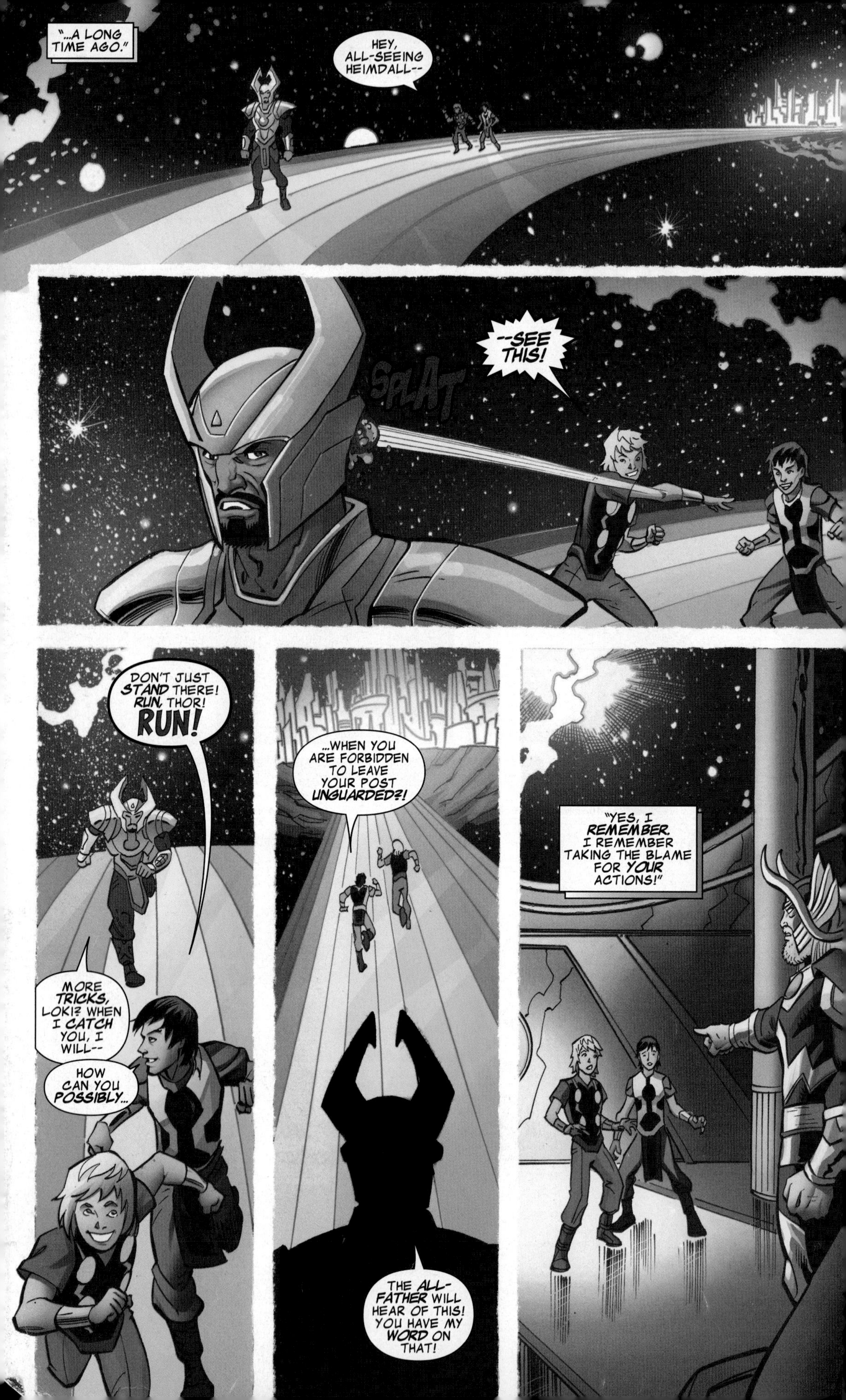
"...A LONG TIME AGO."
HEY, ALL-SEEING HEIMDALL--
SPLAT
--SEE THIS!
DON'T JUST STAND THERE! RUN, THOR! RUN!
MORE TRICKS, LOKI? WHEN I CATCH YOU, I WILL--
HOW CAN YOU POSSIBLY...
...WHEN YOU ARE FORBIDDEN TO LEAVE YOUR POST UNGUARDED?!
THE ALL-FATHER WILL HEAR OF THIS! YOU HAVE MY WORD ON THAT!
"YES, I REMEMBER. I REMEMBER TAKING THE BLAME FOR YOUR ACTIONS!"

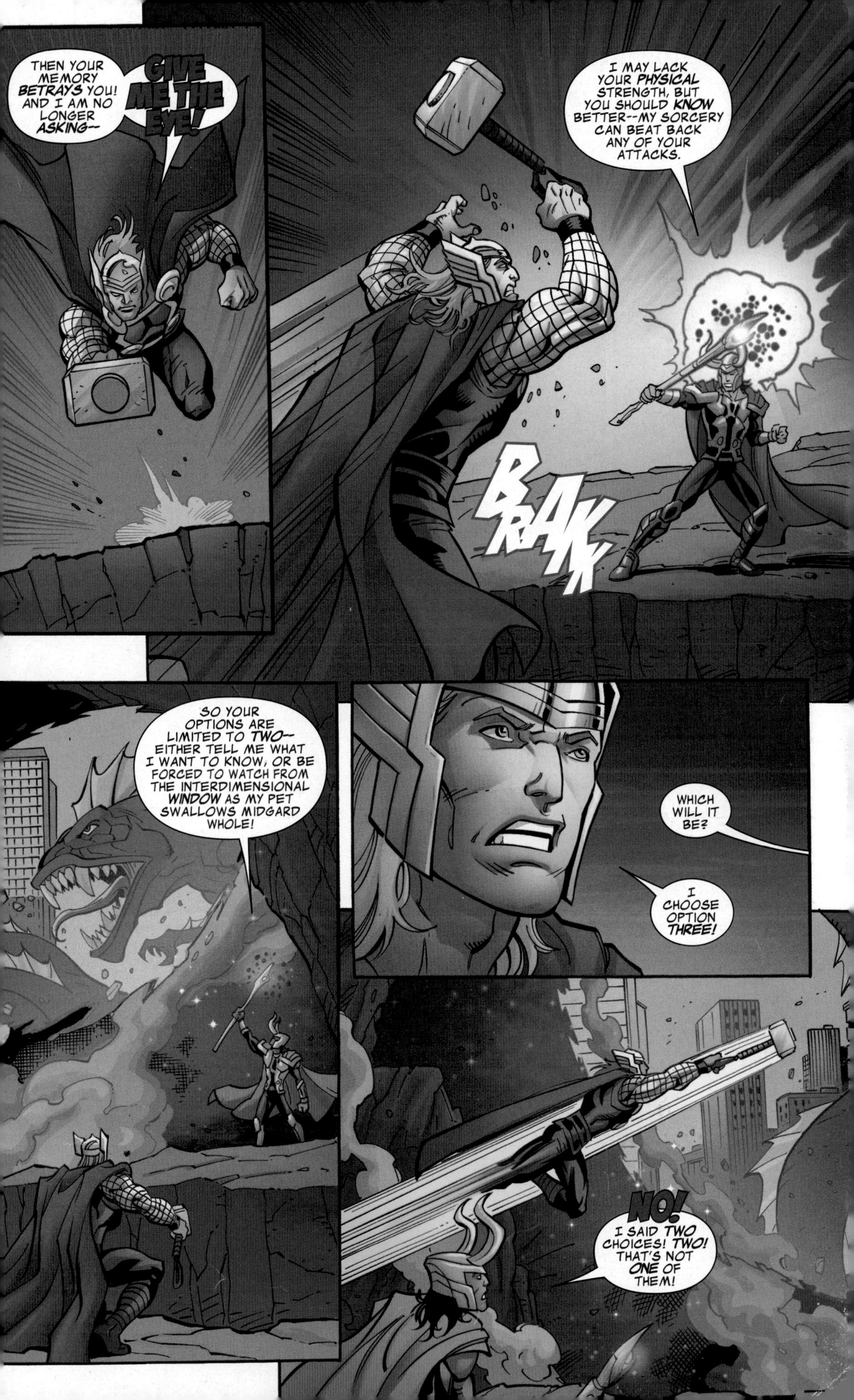
THEN YOUR MEMORY BETRAYS YOU! AND I AM NO LONGER ASKING--
GIVE ME THE EYE!
I MAY LACK YOUR PHYSICAL STRENGTH, BUT YOU SHOULD KNOW BETTER--MY SORCERY CAN BEAT BACK ANY OF YOUR ATTACKS.
BRAKK
SO YOUR OPTIONS ARE LIMITED TO TWO-- EITHER TELL ME WHAT I WANT TO KNOW, OR BE FORCED TO WATCH FROM THE INTERDIMENSIONAL WINDOW AS MY PET SWALLOWS MIDGARD WHOLE!
WHICH WILL IT BE?
I CHOOSE OPTION THREE!
NO!
I SAID TWO CHOICES! TWO! THAT'S NOT ONE OF THEM!

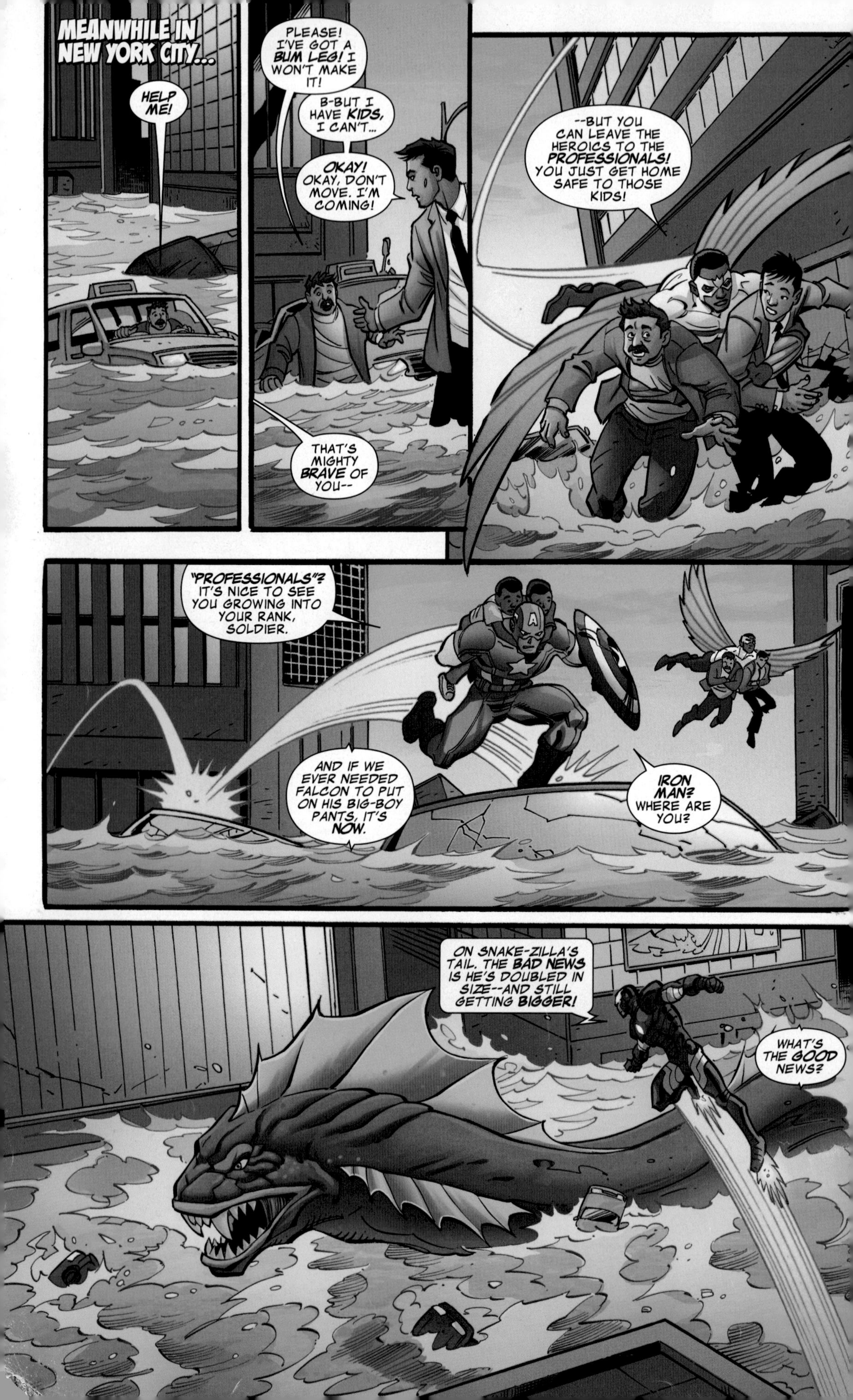
MEANWHILE IN NEW YORK CITY...
HELP ME!
PLEASE! I'VE GOT A BUM LEG! I WON'T MAKE IT!
B-BUT I HAVE KIDS, I CAN'T...
OKAY! OKAY, DON'T MOVE. I'M COMING!
THAT'S MIGHTY BRAVE OF YOU--
--BUT YOU CAN LEAVE THE HEROICS TO THE PROFESSIONALS! YOU JUST GET HOME SAFE TO THOSE KIDS!
"PROFESSIONALS"? IT'S NICE TO SEE YOU GROWING INTO YOUR RANK, SOLDIER.
AND IF WE EVER NEEDED FALCON TO PUT ON HIS BIG-BOY PANTS, IT'S NOW.
IRON MAN? WHERE ARE YOU?
ON SNAKE-ZILLA'S TAIL. THE BAD NEWS IS HE'S DOUBLED IN SIZE--AND STILL GETTING BIGGER!
WHAT'S THE GOOD NEWS?

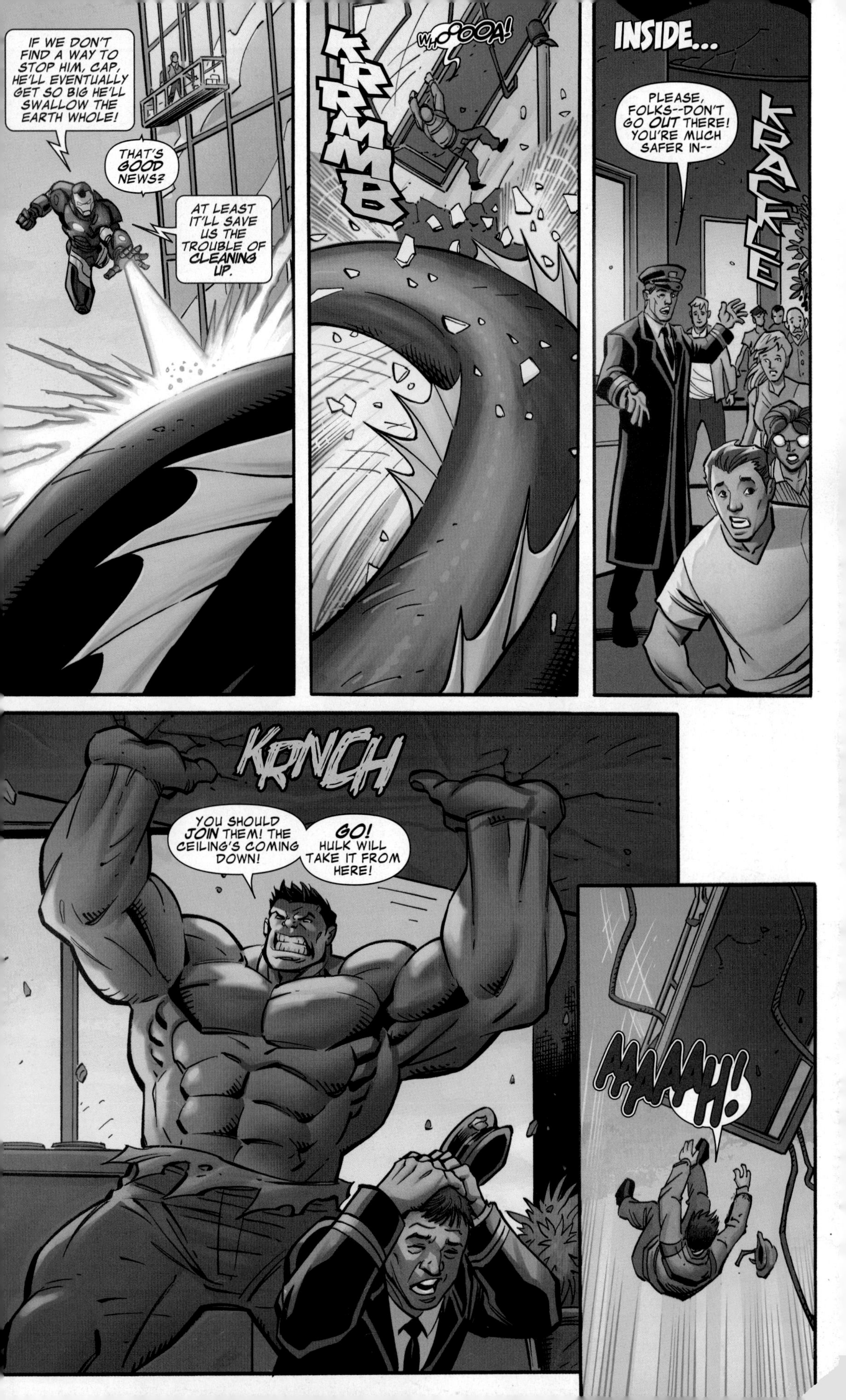
IF WE DON'T FIND A WAY TO STOP HIM, CAP, HE'LL EVENTUALLY GET SO BIG HE'LL SWALLOW THE EARTH WHOLE!
THAT'S GOOD NEWS?
AT LEAST IT'LL SAVE US THE TROUBLE OF CLEANING UP.
KRRMMB
WHOOOOA!
INSIDE...
PLEASE, FOLKS--DON'T GO OUT THERE! YOU'RE MUCH SAFER IN--
KRACKLE
KRONCH
YOU SHOULD JOIN THEM! THE CEILING'S COMING DOWN!
GO! HULK WILL TAKE IT FROM HERE!
AAAAH!

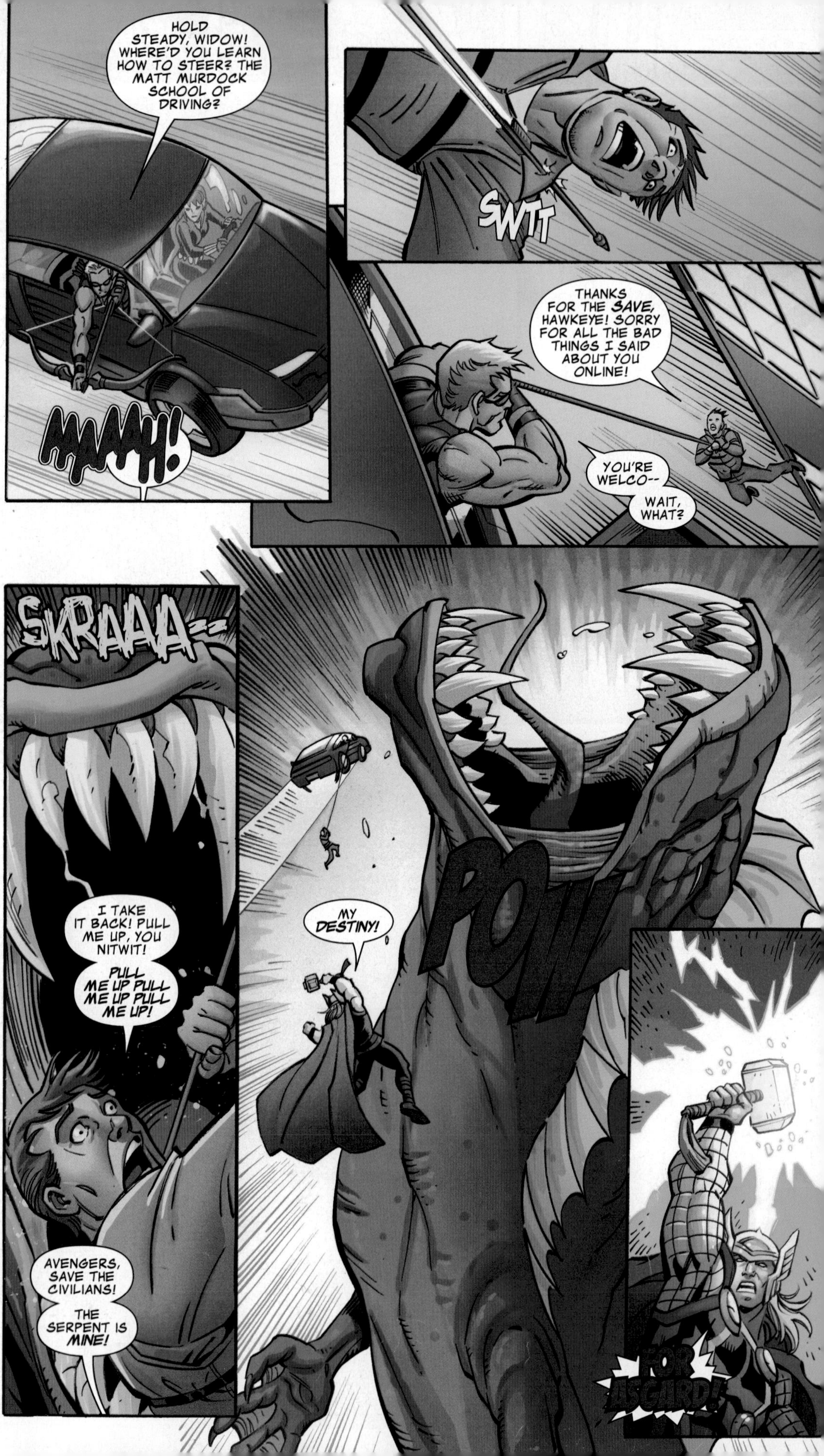
HOLD STEADY, WIDOW! WHERE'D YOU LEARN HOW TO STEER? THE MATT MURDOCK SCHOOL OF DRIVING?
AAAAAH!
SNTT
THANKS FOR THE SAVE, HAWKEYE! SORRY FOR ALL THE BAD THINGS I SAID ABOUT YOU ONLINE!
YOU'RE WELCO--
WAIT, WHAT?
SKRAAAA
I TAKE IT BACK! PULL ME UP, YOU NITWIT!
PULL ME UP PULL ME UP PULL ME UP!
AVENGERS, SAVE THE CIVILIANS!
THE SERPENT IS MINE!
MY DESTINY!
POW
FOR ASGARD!

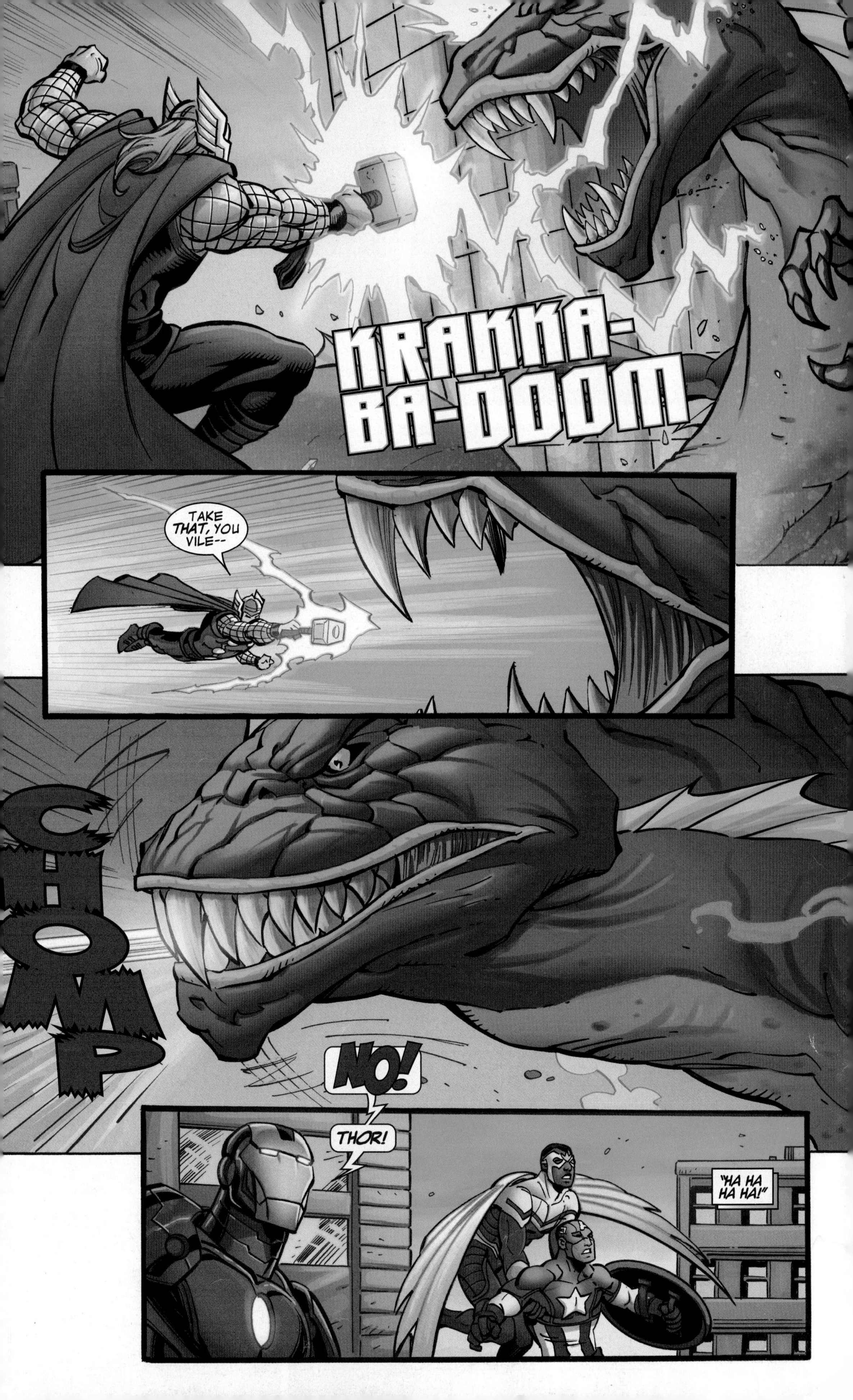
KRAKKA-BA-DOOM
TAKE THAT, YOU VILE--
CHOMP
NO!
THOR!
"HA HA HA HA!"

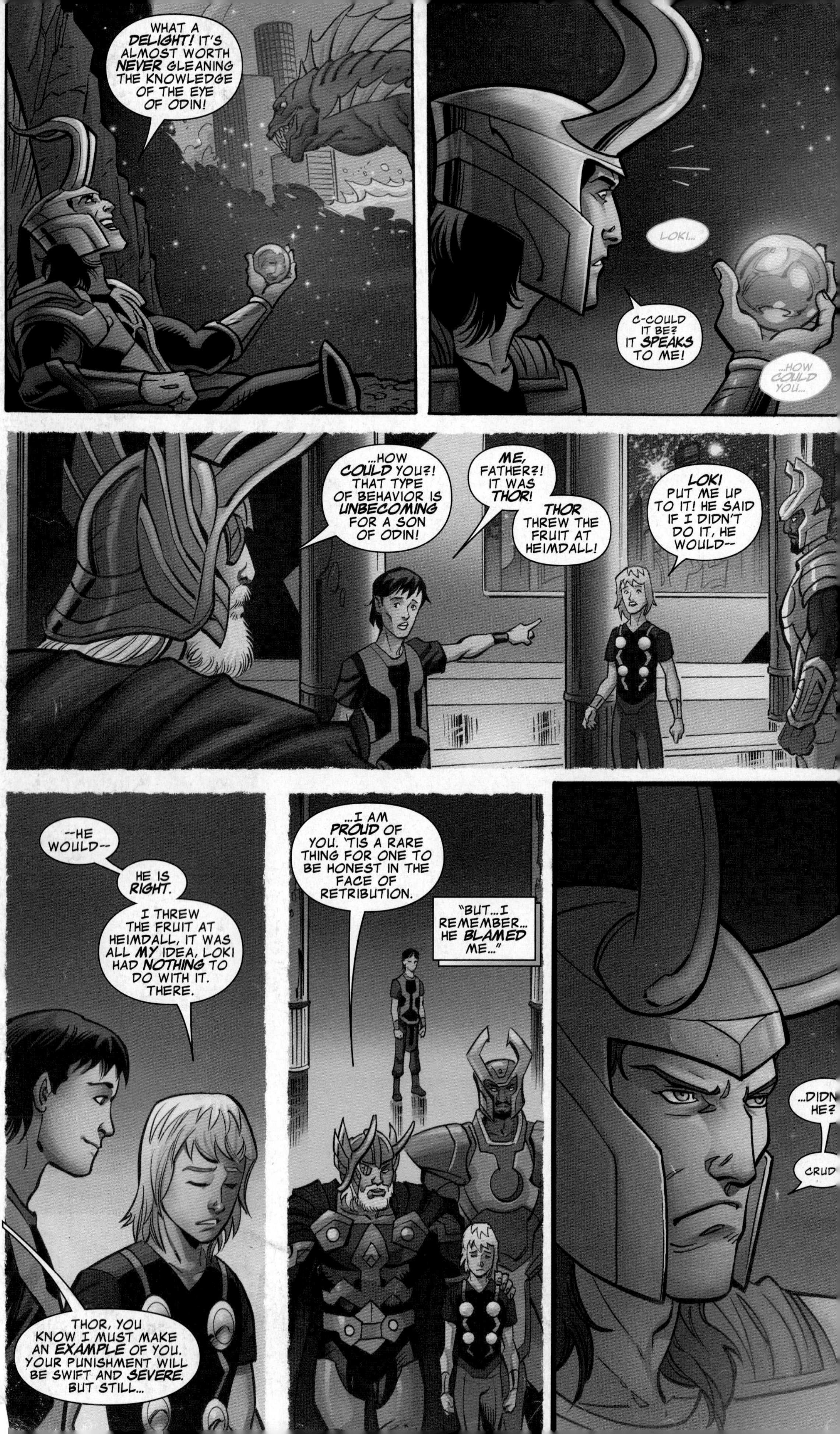
WHAT A DELIGHT! IT'S ALMOST WORTH NEVER GLEANING THE KNOWLEDGE OF THE EYE OF ODIN!
LOKI...
C-COULD IT BE? IT SPEAKS TO ME!
...HOW COULD YOU...
...HOW COULD YOU?! THAT TYPE OF BEHAVIOR IS UNBECOMING FOR A SON OF ODIN!
ME, FATHER?! IT WAS THOR!
THOR THREW THE FRUIT AT HEIMDALL!
LOKI PUT ME UP TO IT! HE SAID IF I DIDN'T DO IT, HE WOULD--
--HE WOULD--
HE IS RIGHT.
I THREW THE FRUIT AT HEIMDALL, IT WAS ALL MY IDEA, LOKI HAD NOTHING TO DO WITH IT. THERE.
THOR, YOU KNOW I MUST MAKE AN EXAMPLE OF YOU. YOUR PUNISHMENT WILL BE SWIFT AND SEVERE. BUT STILL...
...I AM PROUD OF YOU. 'TIS A RARE THING FOR ONE TO BE HONEST IN THE FACE OF RETRIBUTION.
"BUT...I REMEMBER... HE BLAMED ME..."
...DIDN HE?
CRUD

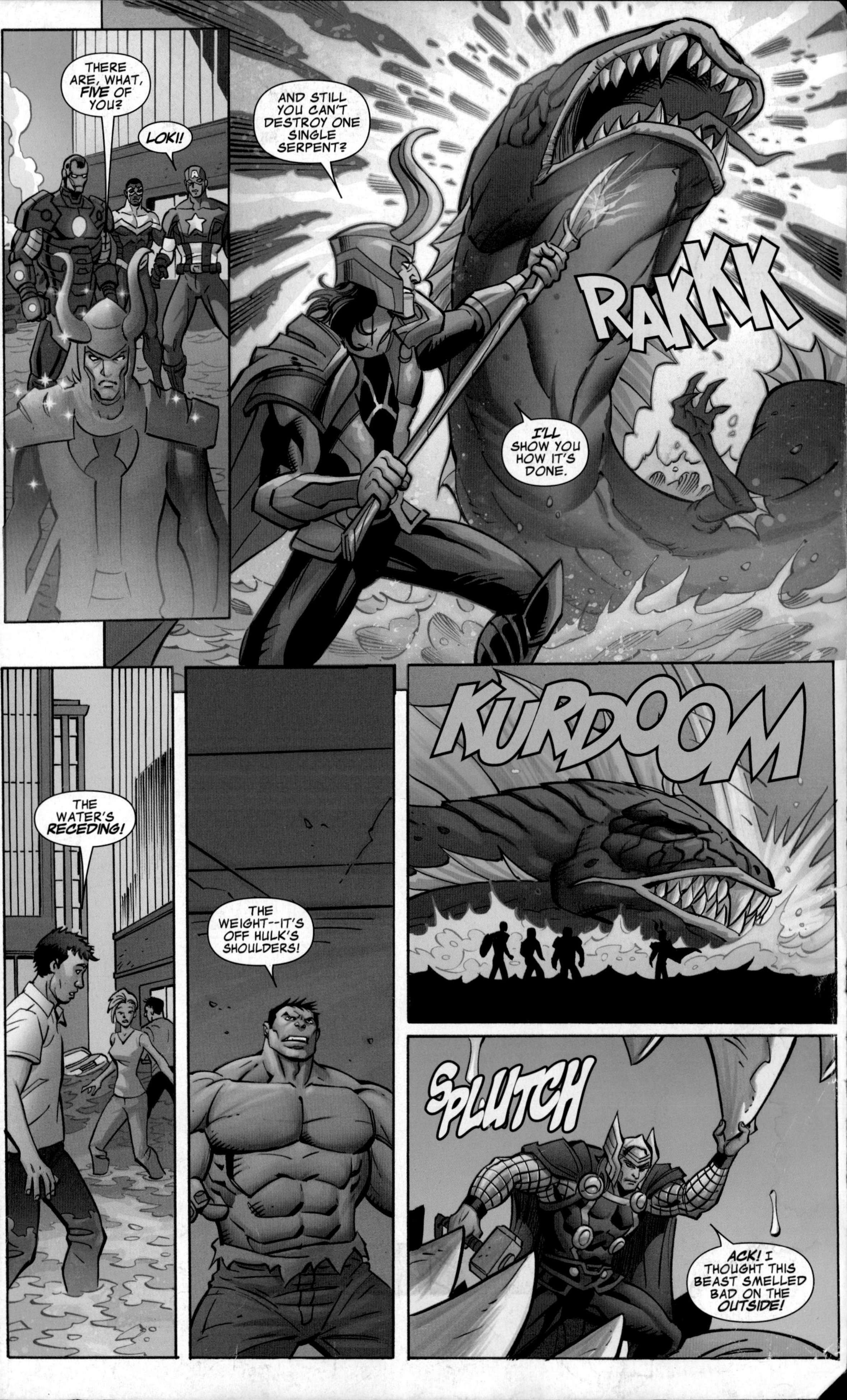
THERE ARE, WHAT, FIVE OF YOU?
LOKI!
AND STILL YOU CAN'T DESTROY ONE SINGLE SERPENT?
RAKKK
I'LL SHOW YOU HOW IT'S DONE.
THE WATER'S RECEDING!
THE WEIGHT--IT'S OFF HULK'S SHOULDERS!
KURDOOM
SPLUTCH
ACK! I THOUGHT THIS BEAST SMELLED BAD ON THE OUTSIDE!

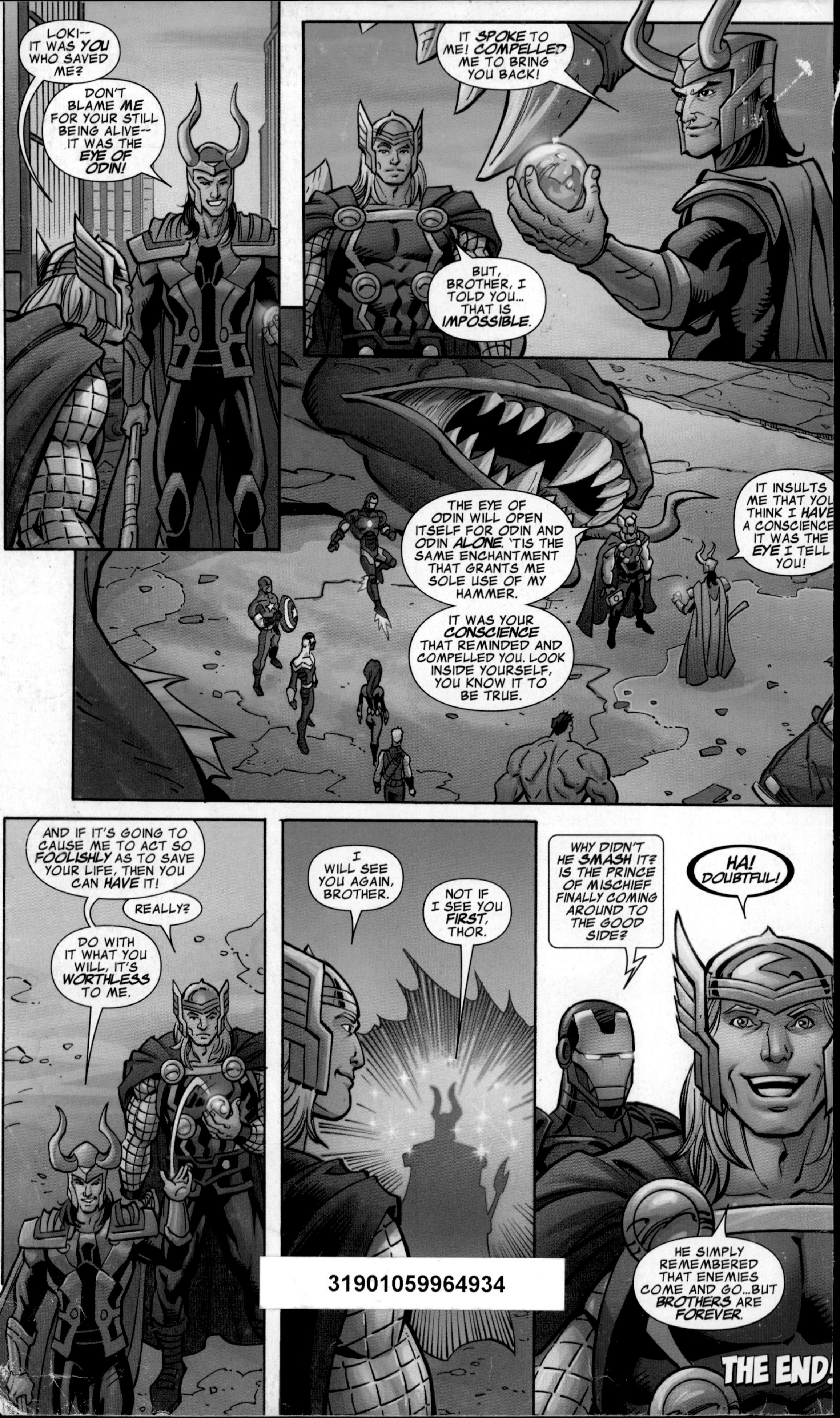
LOKI-- IT WAS YOU WHO SAVED ME?
DON'T BLAME ME FOR YOUR STILL BEING ALIVE-- IT WAS THE EYE OF ODIN!
IT SPOKE TO ME! COMPELLED ME TO BRING YOU BACK!
BUT, BROTHER, I TOLD YOU... THAT IS IMPOSSIBLE.
THE EYE OF ODIN WILL OPEN ITSELF FOR ODIN AND ODIN ALONE. 'TIS THE SAME ENCHANTMENT THAT GRANTS ME SOLE USE OF MY HAMMER.
IT WAS YOUR CONSCIENCE THAT REMINDED AND COMPELLED YOU. LOOK INSIDE YOURSELF, YOU KNOW IT TO BE TRUE.
IT INSULTS ME THAT YOU THINK I HAVE A CONSCIENCE IT WAS THE EYE I TELL YOU!
AND IF IT'S GOING TO CAUSE ME TO ACT SO FOOLISHLY AS TO SAVE YOUR LIFE, THEN YOU CAN HAVE IT!
REALLY?
DO WITH IT WHAT YOU WILL, IT'S WORTHLESS TO ME.
I WILL SEE YOU AGAIN, BROTHER.
NOT IF I SEE YOU FIRST, THOR.
WHY DIDN'T HE SMASH IT? IS THE PRINCE OF MISCHIEF FINALLY COMING AROUND TO THE GOOD SIDE?
HA! DOUBTFUL!
HE SIMPLY REMEMBERED THAT ENEMIES COME AND GO...BUT BROTHERS ARE FOREVER.
THE END!